Simon Scarrow is a *Sunday Times* No. 1 bestselling author. After a childhood spent travelling the world, he pursued his great love of history as a teacher before becoming a full-time writer. His Roman soldier heroes Cato and Macro made their debut in 2000 in UNDER THE EAGLE, and have subsequently appeared in all the books in the Eagles of the Empire series, including CENTURION and INVICTUS. Simon is the author of many more powerful novels, including HEARTS OF STONE, set in Greece during the Second World War, SWORD & SCIMITAR, about the 1565 Siege of Malta, and PLAYING WITH DEATH, a contemporary thriller written with Lee Francis.

For exciting news, extracts and exclusive content from Simon visit www.simonscarrow.co.uk, follow him on Twitter @SimonScarrow or like his author page on Facebook/OfficialSimonScarrow.

Praise for SIMON SCARROW's novels

'Ferocious and compelling' **** *Daily Express*

'I really don't need this kind of competition . . . It's a great read' Bernard Cornwell

'A new book in Simon Scarrow's long-running series about the Roman army is always a joy' Antonia Senior, *The Times*

'A satisfyingly bloodthirsty, bawdy romp . . . perfect for Bernard Cornwell addicts who will relish its historical detail and fast-paced action. Storming stuff!' *Good Book Guide*

'A fast-moving and exceptionally well-paced historical thriller' *BBC History Magazine*

'Scarrow's [novels] rank with the best' *Independent*

'Rollicking

'Scarrow's e

raph

By Simon Scarrow

The *Eagles of the Empire* Series
The Britannia Campaign
Under the Eagle (AD 42–43, Britannia)
The Eagle's Conquest (AD 43, Britannia)
When the Eagle Hunts (AD 44, Britannia)
The Eagle and the Wolves (AD 44, Britannia)
The Eagle's Prey (AD 44, Britannia)

Rome and the Eastern Provinces
The Eagle's Prophecy (AD 45, Rome)
The Eagle in the Sand (AD 46, Judaea)
Centurion (AD 46, Syria)

The Mediterranean
The Gladiator (AD 48–49, Crete)
The Legion (AD 49, Egypt)
Praetorian (AD 51, Rome)

The Return to Britannia
The Blood Crows (AD 51, Britannia)
Brothers in Blood (AD 51, Britannia)
Britannia (AD 52, Britannia)

Hispania
Invictus (AD 54, Hispania)

The Return to Rome
Day of the Caesars (AD 55, Rome)

The *Wellington and Napoleon* Quartet
Young Bloods
The Generals
Fire and Sword
The Fields of Death

Sword & Scimitar (Great Siege of Malta)

Hearts of Stone (Second World War)

The *Gladiator* Series
Gladiator: Fight for Freedom
Gladiator: Street Fighter
Gladiator: Son of Spartacus
Gladiator: Vengeance

Writing with T.J. Andrews
Arena (AD 41, Rome)
Invader (AD 44, Britannia)

Writing with Lee Francis
Playing With Death

SIMON SCARROW

EAGLES·OF·THE·EMPIRE

THE EAGLE
AND THE WOLVES

Llyfrgelloedd Caerdydd
www.caerdydd.gov.uk/llyfrgelloedd
Cardiff Libraries
www.cardiff.gov.uk/libraries

HEADLINE

Copyright © 2003 Simon Scarrow

The right of Simon Scarrow to be identified as the Author of
the Work has been asserted by him in accordance with the
Copyright, Designs and Patents Act 1988.

First published in Great Britain in 2003
by HEADLINE BOOK PUBLISHING

First published in paperback in Great Britain in 2004
by HEADLINE BOOK PUBLISHING

This paperback edition published in 2017
by HEADLINE PUBLISHING GROUP

1

Cataloguing in Publication Data is available from the British Library

ISBN 978 0 7553 4998 2

Offset in Bembo by Avon DataSet Ltd, Bidford-on-Avon, Warwickshire

Printed and bound in Great Britain by CPI Group (UK) Ltd, Croydon CR0 4YY

MIX
Paper from
responsible sources
FSC® C104740

Headline's policy is to use papers that are natural, renewable and recyclable
products and made from wood grown in well-managed forests and other
controlled sources. The logging and manufacturing processes are expected to
conform to the environmental regulations of the country of origin.

HEADLINE PUBLISHING GROUP
An Hachette UK Company
Carmelite House
50 Victoria Embankment
London EC4Y 0DZ

www.headline.co.uk
www.hachette.co.uk

This one is for my editor, Marion Donaldson,
and for the agent who convinced Marion to read
my first book, Wendy Suffield. It's been a great pleasure
to work with both of you.

Acknowledgements

The *Eagle* series of novels has been far more successful than I ever dreamed it would be. It's high time I got round to thanking some of the people behind the scenes. While completing this book I was lucky enough to be invited to a Headline sales conference and was struck by two things.

Firstly, by how many people are involved in making books and getting them on to the shelves in bookshops in Britain, and now the US, Spain, Germany, Finland, the Czech Republic and Portugal as well.

Secondly, by how positive everyone was about the series, especially the sales team, who really believed in the *Eagle* series and managed to convince book-buyers to share their enthusiasm. Thereafter, the success of the books has been down to word of mouth, and that really delights me.

So then, hats off to Merric Davidson, my agent – a gent in every sense, Sherise Hobbs – Marion Donaldson's assistant, always cheerful on the phone and frighteningly efficient off it, Kim Hardie, who fights a tireless battle for space in review columns, and Sarah Thomson, who has won some impressive foreign rights sales for the series.

Then there's Kerr MacRae and his team, who have managed to spread the word far and wide. In no particular order we have: Sabine Stiebritz (who organises some pretty mean social events), James Horobin, Katherine Ball, Barbara Ronan, Peter Newsom, Seb Hunter, Sophie Hopkin, Paul Erdpresser (who looks uncannily like a certain movie star), Jo Taranowski, Diane Griffith, Selina Chu and Jenny Gray. Out on the road there's Ruth Shern, Heidi Murphy and Breda Purdue in Ireland, Damon Richards, Nikki Rose, Alex MacLean, Clare Economides, Steve Hill, George Gamble and Nigel Baines in the UK. Last, and by no means least, there's Tony McGrath, with whom it is always a pleasure to meet up and swap stories about raising young children over a strong coffee at Starbucks in Norwich.

My thanks and gratitude to you all,
Simon

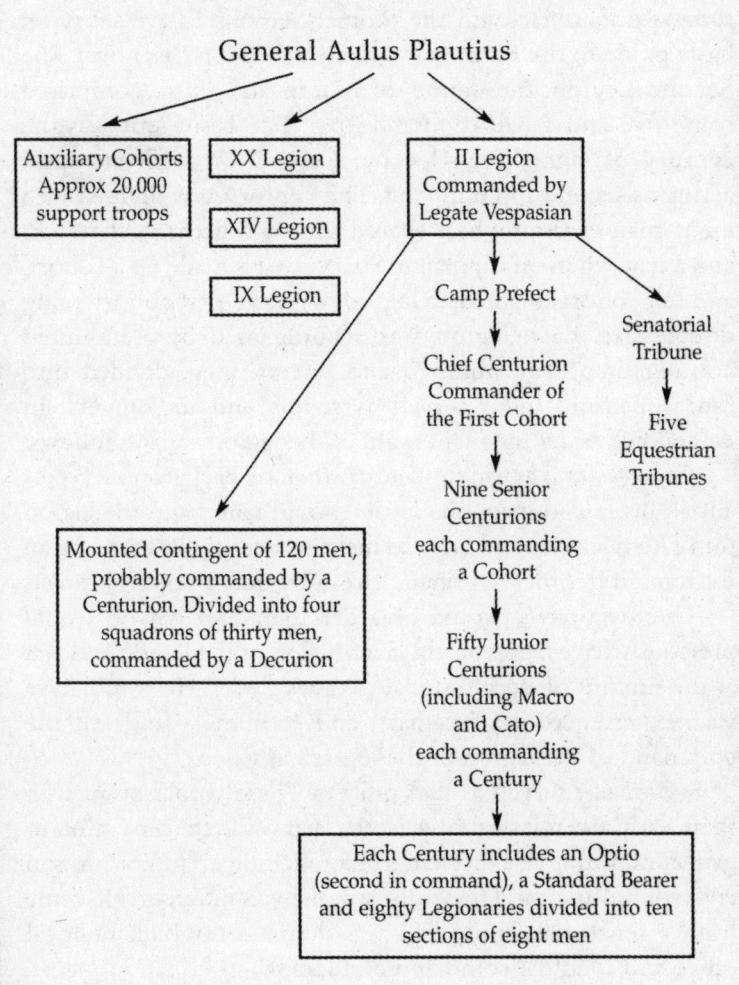

THE ROMAN ARMY CHAIN OF COMMAND IN BRITAIN IN 44 AD

General Aulus Plautius

Auxiliary Cohorts
Approx 20,000
support troops

XX Legion

XIV Legion

IX Legion

II Legion
Commanded by
Legate Vespasian

Camp Prefect

Chief Centurion
Commander of
the First Cohort

Nine Senior
Centurions
each commanding
a Cohort

Fifty Junior
Centurions
(including Macro
and Cato)
each commanding
a Century

Senatorial
Tribune

Five
Equestrian
Tribunes

Mounted contingent of 120 men,
probably commanded by a
Centurion. Divided into four
squadrons of thirty men,
commanded by a Decurion

Each Century includes an Optio
(second in command), a Standard Bearer
and eighty Legionaries divided into ten
sections of eight men

The Organisation of a Roman Legion

Centurions Macro and Cato are the main protagonists of *The Eagle and the Wolves*. In order to clarify the rank structure for readers unfamiliar with the Roman legions I have set out a basic guide to the ranks you will encounter in this novel. The Second Legion, the 'home' of Macro and Cato, comprised some five and a half thousand men. The basic unit was the century of eighty men led by a centurion with an optio acting as second in command. The century was divided into eight-man sections which shared a room together in barracks and a tent when on campaign. Six centuries made up a cohort, and ten cohorts made up a legion, with the first cohort being double-size. Each legion was accompanied by a mounted contingent of one hundred and twenty men, divided into four squadrons, who served as scouts and messengers. In descending order the main ranks of the legion were as follows:

The *legate* was a man from an aristocratic background. Typically in his mid-thirties, the legate would command the legion for up to five years and hope to make something of a reputation for himself in order to enhance his subsequent political career.

The *camp prefect* would be a grizzled veteran who would previously have been the chief centurion of the legion and was at the summit of a professional soldier's career. He would have vast experience and integrity, and to him would fall the command of the legion in the legate's absence.

Six *tribunes* served as staff officers. These would be men in their early twenties serving in the army for the first time to gain administrative experience before taking up junior posts in civil administration. The senior tribune was different. He came from a senatorial family and was destined for high political office and eventual command of a legion.

Sixty *centurions* provided the disciplinary and training backbone of the legion. They were hand-picked for their command qualities and a willingness to fight to the death. Accordingly their casualty rate far exceeded other ranks. The centurions were ranked by seniority based upon the date of their promotion. The most senior centurion commanded the First Century of the First Cohort and was a highly decorated and respected soldier.

The four *decurions* of the legion commanded the cavalry squadrons and hoped for promotion to the command of auxiliary cavalry units.

Each *centurion* was assisted by an *optio* who would act as an orderly, with minor command duties. Optios would be waiting for a vacancy in the centurionate.

The *legionaries* were men who had signed on for twenty-five years. In theory, a volunteer had to be a Roman citizen to qualify for enlistment, but recruits were increasingly drawn from provincial populations and given Roman citizenship on joining the legions.

Lower in status than the legionaries were the men of the *auxiliary cohorts*. They were recruited from the provinces and provided the Roman Empire with its cavalry, light infantry and other specialist arms. Roman citizenship was awarded on completion of twenty-five years of service, or as a reward for outstanding achievement in battle.

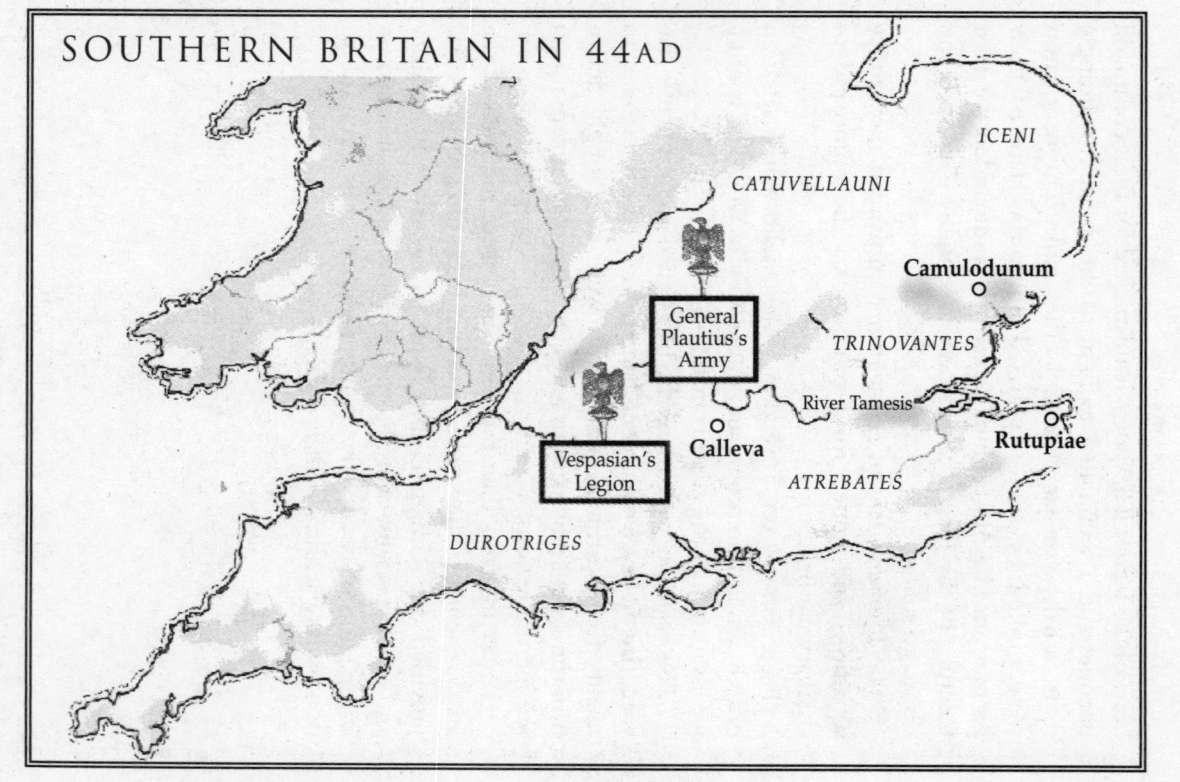

SOUTHERN BRITAIN IN 44AD

ICENI

CATUVELLAUNI

Camulodunum ○

General
Plautius's
Army

TRINOVANTES

Vespasian's
Legion

River Tamesis

○ **Calleva**

Rutupiae ○

ATREBATES

DUROTRIGES

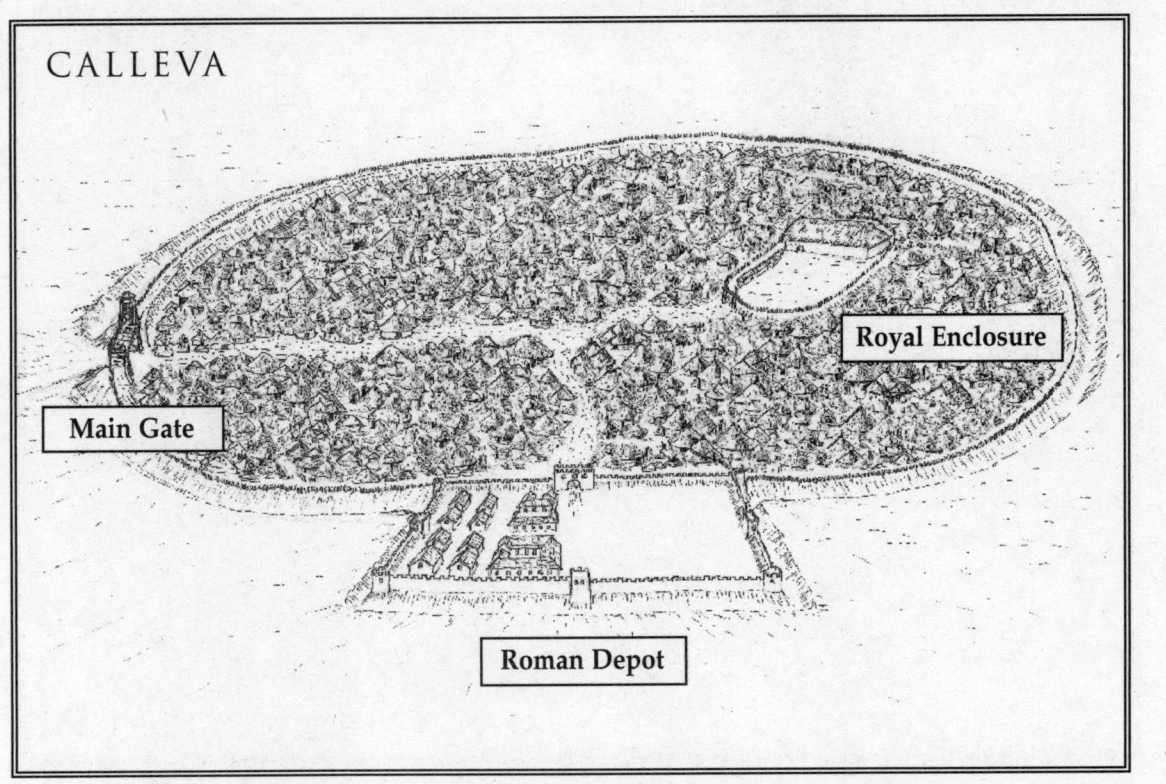

CALLEVA

Main Gate

Royal Enclosure

Roman Depot

Chapter One

'Halt!' the legate shouted, thrusting his arm up.

The mounted escort reined in behind him, and Vespasian strained his ears to catch the sound he had heard a moment before. No longer drowned out by the heavy clumping of hoofs on the rough native track came the faint braying of British war horns from the direction of Calleva, a few miles distant. The sprawling town was the capital of the Atrebatans, one of the few tribes allied to Rome, and for a moment the legate wondered if the enemy commander, Caratacus, had made a bold strike deep into the rear of the Roman forces. If Calleva was under attack . . .

'Come on!'

Kicking his boot heel into the flank of his horse, Vespasian bent low and urged his mount up the slope. The escort, a dozen of his scouts from the Second Legion, pounded along after him. It was their sacred duty to protect their commander.

The track inclined diagonally up the side of a long steep ridge, beyond which it sloped down towards Calleva. The town was being used as the forward supply depot of the Second Legion. Detached from the army, commanded by General Aulus Plautius, the Second had been ordered to defeat the Durotrigans, the last of the southern tribes still fighting for Caratacus. Only when the Durotrigans had been destroyed would the Roman supply lines be secure enough for the legions to advance further north and west. Without adequate supplies there would be no victory for General Plautius, and the Emperor's premature celebration of the conquest of Britain would be exposed for a hollow sham to the public in Rome. The fate of General Plautius and his legions – indeed the fate of the Emperor himself – depended on the overstretched and slender arteries that fed the legions, and which could be severed at a stroke.

Regular columns of heavy wagons trundled from the vast base camp on the estuary of the Tamesis – the river that snaked through the heart of Britain – where provisions and equipment from Gaul were landed. For the last ten days the Second Legion had been without supplies from Calleva. Vespasian had left his forces laying siege to one of the larger hillforts of the Durotrigans while he hurried back to Calleva to investigate the matter. The Second Legion was already on reduced rations, and small groups of the enemy lay in wait in the surrounding forests, ready to attack any foraging parties that dared to range too far from the main body of the legion. Unless Vespasian managed to secure food for his men soon the Second Legion would have to fall back on the depot at Calleva.

Vespasian could well imagine the anger with which General Plautius would greet news of such a setback. Aulus Plautius had been appointed by Emperor Claudius to command the Roman army whose task was to add Britain and its tribes to the Empire. Despite Plautius' victories over the barbarous tribes the previous summer, Caratacus had raised a new army and still defied Rome. He had learned much from last year's campaigning and refused to take the field against the Roman legions. Instead, he detached columns of men to attack the supply lines of the ponderous Roman war machine. With every mile General Plautius and his legions advanced, those vital supply lines became more vulnerable.

So the outcome of this year's campaign depended on whose strategy triumphed. If General Plautius succeeded in forcing the Britons to face him on the field of battle then the legions would win. If the Britons could avoid battle and starve the legions, they might weaken them enough to force the general into a perilous retreat all the way back to the coast.

As Vespasian and his escort galloped up to the crest of the ridge the blasts on the war horns became more strident. Now the soldiers could hear men shouting, the sharp clang of weapon striking weapon, and the dull thud of blows landing on shields. The long grass was silhouetted against the clear sky, and then Vespasian beheld the scene on the far side of the ridge. To the left lay Calleva, a huge sprawl of thatched roofs of mainly squalid little dwellings, ringed by an earth rampart and palisade. A thin haze of wood-smoke hung over the town. A dark gash of churned soil marked the track leading from the tall wooden tower of the gatehouse towards the Tamesis. On the track, half a mile from Calleva, only a handful of wagons remained of a supply convoy, protected by a thin screen of auxiliary troops. Around them swirled the enemy: small clusters of heavily armed warriors and lighter troops armed with slings, bows and throwing spears. They kept up a steady rain of missiles on the supply convoy and its escort. Blood flowed from the flanks of injured oxen, and the path of the convoy was dotted with bodies.

Vespasian and his men reined in as the legate briefly considered what to do. Even as he watched, a group of Durotrigans rushed the rear of the convoy and threw themselves on the auxiliaries. The commander of the convoy, clearly visible in his scarlet cloak as he stood atop the driver's bench of the first wagon, cupped his hands to bellow an order and the convoy slowly halted. The auxiliaries beat off the attackers easily enough, but their comrades at the front of the column provided a static target for the enemy and by the time the wagons were on the move again several more of the convoy's escorts lay sprawled on the ground.

'Where's the bloody garrison?' grumbled one of the scouts. 'They must have seen the convoy by now.'

Vespasian looked towards the neatly ordered lines of the fortified supply depot built on to the side of Calleva's ramparts. Tiny dark figures were scurrying between the barrack blocks, but there were no massing ranks visible. Vespasian made a mental note to give the garrison's commander a harsh bollocking the moment he reached the camp.

If he reached the camp, he reflected, for the skirmish was between his party and the gates of Calleva.

Unless the garrison made a sortie soon the convoy would be whittled down until the enemy could wipe it out in one final charge. Sensing that the decisive moment was near, the Durotrigans were edging closer to the wagons, screaming their war cries and striking their weapons against the edges of their shields to stoke up their battle frenzy.

Vespasian tore his cloak from his shoulders. Grasping the reins tightly in one hand, he drew his sword in the other and turned to his scouts.

'Form line!'

The men looked at him in surprise. Their legate intended to charge the enemy, but that was tantamount to suicide.

'Form line, damn you!' Vespasian shouted, and this time his men responded at once, fanning out on either side of the legate, making ready their long spears. As soon as the line was ready Vespasian swept his sword down.

'Let's go!'

There was no parade-ground precision in the manoeuvre. The small party of horsemen just jabbed in their heels and urged their mounts to swoop down on the enemy pell-mell. Even as blood pounded in his ears Vespasian found himself questioning the sanity of this wild charge. It would have been easy enough to bear witness to the convoy's destruction and wait until the triumphant enemy marched away from its wreckage before making for Calleva. But that would have been cowardly, and, in any case, those supplies were desperately needed. So he gritted his teeth and clenched the sword in his right hand as he made for the wagons.

Down the slope, the sound of approaching horses caused faces to turn towards them and the barrage of missiles on the convoy slackened.

'There! Over there!' Vespasian bellowed, pointing towards a loose line of slingers and archers. 'Follow me!'

The scouts swung into line with their legate and charged obliquely across the incline towards the lightly armed Durotrigans. Ahead of the horsemen the Britons were already scattering, their roars of triumph dead on their lips. Vespasian saw that the commander of the convoy had made good use of the diversion and the wagons were once more rumbling towards the safety of Calleva's ramparts. But the leader of the Durotrigans was no fool either, and a quick glance revealed to Vespasian that the heavy infantry and chariots were already moving towards the convoy to strike before their prey reached the gates. A short distance to his front, woad-stained bodies weaved madly, desperately trying to avoid the Roman horse-men. Vespasian fixed his sight on a large slinger wearing a wolfskin around his shoulders, and lowered the point of his sword. At the last moment, the Briton sensed the horse bearing down on him, looked round sharply, eyes wide with terror. Vespasian aimed his blow a short distance down from the man's neck and braced his arm for the impact, but at the last moment the slinger threw himself flat and the blade missed.

'Shit!' Vespasian hissed through clenched teeth. These bloody infantry swords were no good on horseback, and he cursed himself for not carrying a long cavalry sword as his scouts did.

Then another enemy warrior was in front of him. He just had time to register the thin, frail physique and white spiked hair before he slashed his blade into the man's neck with a wet crunching sound. The man grunted and tumbled forward, and was gone as Vespasian galloped on towards the convoy. He snatched a glimpse at his scouts, and saw that most had reined in and were busy thrusting their spears at any Briton they could find cringing on the ground. It was the perfect moment for any cavalryman: the killing frenzy that followed the breaking of the enemy line. But they were heedless of the danger of the chariots that were even now trundling across the slope towards the small party of Roman horsemen.

'Leave them!' Vespasian roared. 'Leave them! Make for the wagons! Go!'

The scouts' senses returned to them and they closed ranks, and galloped after Vespasian as he made for the rearmost wagon, no more than a hundred paces away. The auxiliaries in the rearguard raised a ragged cheer and waved them on with their javelins. The horsemen had almost reached their comrades when Vespasian heard a faint whirr, and the dark streak of an arrow shot by his head. Then he and his men were in amongst the wagons, halting their blown horses.

'Close up! Close up at the rear of the convoy!'

While his men eased their horses into formation behind the last wagon, Vespasian trotted forward to the convoy's commander, still standing astride the driver's bench of his vehicle. As soon as he saw the legate's ribbon fastened around Vespasian's breastplate the man saluted.

'Thank you, sir.'

'You are?' Vespasian snapped.

'Centurion Gius Aurelias, Fourteenth Gallic Auxiliary Cohort, sir.'

'Aurelias, keep your wagons moving. Don't stop for anything. *Anything*, you understand? I'll take charge of your men. You look after the wagons.'

'Yes, sir.'

Vespasian wheeled his horse round and trotted back towards his men, taking a deep breath before shouting out his orders.

'Fourteenth Gallic! Form line on me!'

Vespasian swept his sword out to the side and the survivors of the convoy escort hurried to take up position.

Beyond the cavalry scouts the Durotrigans had recovered from the shock of the charge, and now that they could see how pitifully few men had panicked them they burned with shame and thirsted for revenge. They advanced in a dense mass of mixed light and heavy infantry, and rumbling round to the side of the convoy came the chariots in an effort to head off the wagons before they could reach the gates and trap the Romans between them and their infantry, like a vice. Vespasian realised there was nothing he could do about the chariots. If they did manage to cut the convoy off from the gates then Aurelias would simply have to try to force his wagons through, trusting to the lumpen momentum of his oxen to push aside the lighter Durotrigan ponies and their chariots.

All that Vespasian could do now was hold off the enemy infantry as long as possible. If they should reach the wagons then all was lost. Vespasian took one last glance along his slender line of men, and the grimly determined expression on the faces of the tribesmen advancing on them, and knew at once that he and his troops stood no chance. He had to stop himself from laughing bitterly. To have survived all the bloody battles against Caratacus and his armies over the last year, only to die here in this squalid little skirmish – it was too ignominious. And there was still so much he wanted to achieve. He cursed the fates, and then the commander of the garrison at Calleva. If only the bastard had led his men out to support the convoy at once, they might have stood a chance.

Chapter Two

'Not in here you don't!' Centurion Macro shouted. 'Officers only.'

'Sorry, sir,' replied the orderly at the nearest end of the stretcher. 'Chief surgeon's orders.'

Macro glowered for a moment and then eased himself back down on to his bed, careful to ensure that he kept the injured side of his head away from the bolster. It had been two months since a druid had nearly scalped him with a sword blow, and while the wound itself had healed, it was still painful, and the blinding headaches were only just beginning to abate. The orderlies came into the small cell and carefully lowered the stretcher, grunting with the effort.

'What's his story?'

'Cavalryman, sir,' replied the orderly when he had straightened up. 'Their patrol was ambushed this morning. The survivors started coming in a short while ago.'

Macro had heard the garrison's assembly call earlier. He sat up again. 'Why weren't we told?'

The orderly shrugged. 'Why should you be? You're just patients here, sir. No reason for us to disturb you.'

'Hey, Cato!' Macro turned towards the other bed in the cell. 'Cato! You hear that? The man thinks that sorry little centurions like ourselves don't need to be told about latest developments . . . Cato? . . . CATO!'

Macro swore softly, looked quickly around, reached for his vine staff, leaning against the wall by the bed, and then gave the still form in the other bed a firm poke with the end of the staff. 'Come on, boy! Wake up!'

There was a groan from under the blanket, then the rough woollen folds were eased back and Cato's dark curls emerged from the warm fug beneath. Macro's companion had only recently been promoted to the rank of centurion. Before then he had served as Macro's optio. At eighteen Cato was one of the youngest centurions in the legions. He had won the attention of his superiors for his courage in battle and his resourceful handling of a sensitive rescue mission deep into enemy territory earlier that summer. That was when he and Macro had been severely wounded by their druid foes. The leader of the druids had hacked into Cato's ribs with a heavy ceremonial sickle, laying open his side. Cato had nearly died from the wound, but now, many weeks later, he was recovering well, and regarded the dull red scar tissue that curved round his chest with a measure of pride, even though it hurt like hell when he put any strain on the muscles down that side of his body.

Cato's eyes flickered open, he blinked and then turned to look at Centurion Macro. 'What's up?'

'We've got company.' Macro jabbed his thumb at the man on the stretcher. 'Seems that Caratacus' lads are making themselves busy once again.'

'They'll be after a supply column,' said Cato. 'Must have bumped into the patrol.'

'That's the third attack this month, I think.' Macro looked towards the orderly. 'Ain't that right?'

'Yes, sir. The third time. Hospital's getting filled up, and we're being worked to the bone.' The last few words were given heavy emphasis and both orderlies edged a step closer to the door. 'Mind if we get back to our duties, sir?'

'Not so fast. What's the full story on the convoy?'

'I don't know, sir. I just deal with the casualties. I heard someone say that what was left of the escort was still on the road, a short way off, trying to save the last few wagons. Stupid, if you ask me. Should have left them to the Britons and saved their own skins. Now, sir, do you mind . . .?'

'What? Oh, yes. Go on, bugger off.'

'Thank you, sir.' The orderly made a small smile and, shoving his partner ahead of him, he left the cell and closed the door behind him.

The instant the door was shut Macro swung his legs over the side of the bed and reached for his boots.

'Where are you going, sir?' Cato asked drowsily.

'To the gate, to see what's happening. Get up. You're coming too.'

'I am?'

'Of course you are. Don't you want to see what's going on? Or haven't you had enough of being shut up in this bloody hospital for the best part of two months? Besides,' Macro added, as he began to tie his straps, 'you've been asleep most of the day. Fresh air'll do you good.'

Cato frowned. The reason he slept most of the day was because his room-mate snored so loudly that sleep was almost impossible at night. In truth, he was heartily sick of the hospital and was looking forward to being returned to active duty. But it would be some time before that happened, Cato reflected bitterly. He had only just regained enough strength to get back on his feet. His companion, despite an appalling head wound, was blessed with a tougher constitution and, barring the occasional shattering headache, was almost fit enough for duty.

As Macro looked down at his boot straps Cato gazed at the livid red scar stretching across the top of Macro's head. The wound had left knotty lumps of skin and no hair grew around it. The surgeon had promised that some of the hair would return eventually, enough of it to hide most of the scars.

'With my luck,' Macro had added sourly, 'that'll be just in time for me to start going bald.'

Cato smiled at the memory. Then a fresh line of argument that might justify staying in bed occurred to him.

'Are you sure you should go out, what with you fainting the last time we sat in the hospital yard. Do you really think it's wise, sir?'

Macro looked up irritably, fingers automatically tying his straps as they had almost every morning for the best part of sixteen years. He shook his head. 'I keep telling you, it's not necessary to call me "sir" all the time – only in front of the men, and in formal situations. From now on, it's "Macro" to you. Got it?'

'Yes, sir,' Cato responded immediately, winced and smacked his forehead. 'Sorry. It's all a bit hard to adjust to. I still haven't got used to the idea of being a centurion. Must be the youngest one in the army.'

'In the whole bloody Empire, I should think.'

For a moment Macro regretted the remark, and recognised in himself a trace of bitterness. Much as he had been genuinely delighted when Cato had won his promotion, the older man had soon got over his enthusiasm and every so often let slip some remark about a centurion's need for experience. Or he would offer a few words of advice about how a centurion should conduct himself. It was all a bit rich, Macro chided himself, given that he had been promoted to the centurionate barely a year and a half before Cato himself. Granted he had already served sixteen years with the Eagles, and was a well-respected veteran with a generally good conduct record, but he was almost as new to the rank as his young friend.

As he watched Macro tie his boots Cato was uneasy about his promotion. He could not help believing it had come too soon for him, and felt shamed when he compared himself to Macro, a consummate soldier, if ever there was one. Cato already dreaded the moment when he would have recovered enough to be appointed to the command of his own century. It took very little imagination to anticipate how men far older and more experienced than he would respond to having an eighteen-year-old placed in command of them. Sure, they would see the medals on his harness and know that their centurion was a man of some valour, and that he had won the eye of Vespasian. They might note the scars he bore on his left arm, further proof of Cato's courage in battle, but none of that changed the fact that he had only just reached manhood, and was younger than some of the sons of the men serving in his century. That would rankle, and Cato knew they would watch him closely, and be utterly unforgiving of any mistakes that he made. Not for the first time he wondered if there was any way he could quietly request being returned to his previous rank, and slip back into the comfortable role of being Macro's optio.

Macro finished fastening his boot straps, stood up and reached for his scarlet military cloak.

'Come on, Cato! On your feet. Let's go.'

Outside the cell, the corridors of the hospital were filled with orderlies and casualties as the wounded continued to arrive. Surgeons pushed through the throng, making quick assessment of the injuries and directing the fatal cases to the small ward on the rear wall where they would be made as comfortable as possible before death claimed them. The rest were crammed in wherever space could be found. With

Vespasian continuing his campaign against the hillforts of the Durotrigans, the hospital in Calleva was filled to capacity already, and the construction of a new block was not yet complete. The constant raids on the supply lines of General Plautius' army were adding yet more patients to the over-stretched facilities of the hospital and men were already being accommodated on rough mats along the sides of the main corridors. Fortunately, it was summer and they would not suffer too much discomfort at night.

Macro and Cato made for the main entrance. Wearing only their standard-issue tunics and cloaks, they carried their vine staffs to indicate their rank, and other men respectfully gave way before them. Macro was also wearing his felt helmet liner, partly to conceal his wound – he was tired of the looks of disgust he was getting from the local children – but mostly because exposure to fresh air made his scar ache. Cato carried his vine staff in his right hand and raised his left elbow to protect his injured side from any knocks.

The entrance of the hospital opened on to the main thorough-fare of the fortified depot that Vespasian had constructed to the side of Calleva. Several light carts stood outside the entrance, and the wounded were still being unloaded from the last one to arrive. The beds of the empty carts were a jumble of discarded equipment and dark smears of blood.

'The other side are getting pretty ambitious,' said Macro. 'This isn't the work of some small group of raiders. Looks like they're hitting us with a large column. They're getting bolder all the time. If this carries on, the legions are going to have a real problem keeping up the advance.'

Cato nodded. The situation was serious. General Plautius had already been forced to leave a string of forts to protect the columns of slow-moving supply wagons. With the establish-ment of every new garrison, his strike force was shrinking and in its enfeebled condition must eventually prove an irresistible target for Caratacus.

The two centurions walked quickly down the track towards the depot gate where the fort's small garrison was hurriedly forming up. Men fiddled with straps and belts while Centurion Veranius, commander of the garrison, screamed abuse into the entrances of the barracks, swiping at the tardy few stumbling towards their comrades as they struggled with their equipment. Macro exchanged a knowing look with Cato. The garrison had been made up from the dregs of the Second Legion, the sort of men Vespasian could not afford to take with him on his lightning campaign into the heartlands of the Durotrigans. The soldiers' poor quality was readily apparent to an experienced eye, and mortally offended Macro's professionalism.

'Fuck knows what the locals make of this mess. One word of this gets out of Calleva, and Caratacus will realise he can walk in here any time he wants to, and kick Verica out on his arse.'

Verica, the aged king of the Atrebatans, had been allied to the Romans since the legions had landed in Britain a year earlier. Not that he had any choice in the matter. He had agreed to an alliance in return for being restored to power over the Atrebatans even before the legions had advanced on Caratacus' capital at Camulodunum. Once the campaign had extended to the hostile tribes of the south-west Verica had eagerly offered Calleva to General Plautius as a base of operations. So the depot had been constructed. Besides winning the goodwill of Rome, Verica had provided himself with a readily accessible bolt hole should the Atrebatans succumb to the appeals from the tribes still resisting the invaders, to change sides and turn on the Roman invaders.

The two centurions made their way down to the gateway leading through the rampart and into Calleva. Although

Vespasian had left a mere two centuries of legionaries, under one officer, to defend the depot, the area enclosed by its ramparts was large enough to hold several cohorts. Beyond the parade ground was the hospital and headquarters buildings. To one side of them stood a few rows of timber barracks. Beyond that stretched the granaries and other stores, which the Second Legion needed to draw on as they marched west. The Britons' leader, Caratacus, had laid waste to the land before the advance of Plautius' legions, hence the Roman columns' dependence on long lines of communication leading all the way to the vast supply base at Rutupiae, where the legions had first set foot in Britain.

The contrast between the ordered interior of the depot and the disorganised jumble of huts, barns, cattle byres and narrow, muddy thoroughfares of Calleva struck Cato once again. The tribal capital was home to nearly six thousand people in normal times, but with the enemy raiding supply convoys and farms across the kingdom, the population of Calleva had swelled to nearly twice the size. Packed into the crude hovels inside Calleva's walls, the people grew more hungry and desperate by the day.

Despite its ideal location on top of a gently sloping hill, there had been no attempt to create an adequate drainage system, and the deeply rutted streets, if they could be dignified by such a word, were covered with dung. Foul-smelling puddles formed wherever the ground was so saturated that nothing drained away, and Cato felt a wave of disgust at the sight of two children making 'mud' pies at the side of a waterlogged wagon rut.

By the time the two centurions reached Calleva's main gateway a mixed crowd of natives and Romans was packed on to the turf ramparts to watch the desperate drama on the slope below. Aside from the men from the garrison, the Empire was represented by the first wave of merchants, slave traders and land agents out to make a quick killing before the new province became settled enough for the natives to get wise to their profiteering ways.

Now they jostled with the Atrebatans for the best view as the remnants of the supply column struggled towards the safety of Calleva. Cato caught the eye of the optio in command of the legionaries manning the gatehouse, and raised his vine cane to indicate his rank. The optio immediately ordered a handful of his men to clear a path for the two centurions and they went about the task with the usual insensitivity of soldiers. Shield bosses slammed into native bodies without regard for their age or sex, and howls of anger quickly swelled above any cries of surprise and pain.

'Easy there!' Cato shouted above the din, cracking his vine cane down on the nearest legionary's shield. 'Go easy, I said! These people are the allies of Rome! They're not bloody animals. Understand?'

The legionary snapped to attention in front of his superior, and glared at a fixed point over Cato's shoulder. 'Yes, sir!'

'If I catch you, or any others laying into the locals again, I'll have you on latrine cleaning duties for the rest of the year.' Cato leaned closer to the legionary, and continued softly, 'Then you'll really be in the shit, won't you?'

The man tried not to smile and Cato nodded. 'Carry on.'

'Yes, sir.'

As the legionary led the way through the crowd the protests of the natives died away, now that the soldiers' heavy-handedness had been seen to be punished.

Macro nudged Cato. 'What was that all about? The boy was only doing his job.'

'It'll take him a few moments to get over his wounded pride. It takes a lot longer to build good relations between us and the Atrebatans. And almost no time to break them.'

'Maybe,' Macro said grudgingly, then recalled the legionary's smirk at Cato's final remark to him. The touch of humour had eased the man's resentment considerably. 'Anyway, it was neatly done.'

Cato shrugged.

They entered the shaded interior of the gatehouse and climbed the ladder to the deck above the thick timbers of the town gates. Emerging from the narrow hatchway Cato saw Verica and a handful of his bodyguards standing to one side. Cato saluted the king as he crossed the boarded floor towards the palisade and looked down the track that wound its way north, towards the river Tamesis. Half a mile away six large wagons, each drawn by teams of four oxen, crawled along the track. Around them marched a thin screen of auxiliary troops, with a small group of the legion's mounted scouts forming a rearguard. Sunlight glinted off a breastplate and Cato squinted at a figure on horseback, halfway along the column.

'Isn't that the legate?'

'How should I know?' Macro replied. 'Your eyes are better than mine. You tell me.'

Cato stared a little longer. 'Yes! It's him all right.'

'What the hell's he doing here?' Macro was genuinely surprised. 'He's supposed to be with the legion, kicking the stuffing out of those bloody hillforts.'

'I expect,' Cato reflected, 'he's come to find out where his supplies have got to. Must have fallen in with the wagons.'

'That's our bloody Vespasian all right!' Macro laughed. 'Can't help getting himself into a fight.'

Shadowing the column were several knots of enemy troops, accompanied by a number of the fast-moving chariots still favoured by many British tribes. A steady barrage of arrows, slingshot and spears was maintained on the Roman column. As Cato watched, one of the auxiliaries was struck in the leg by a spear and sprawled to the ground, his shield falling to one side. The man behind him, stepped round his wounded comrade, and continued forward, hunched behind his oval shield, without a backward glance.

'That's tough,' said Macro.

'Yes . . .'

Both men were frustrated by their inability to help their comrades. While they were under medical care, they were mere supernumeraries in the depot. Besides, the centurion in command of the garrison would take a dim view if they interfered with his command in any way.

Before the column had completely passed by the injured man, one of the animal handlers broke away from his pair of oxen and ran over to the auxiliary struggling to free himself of the spear. As the crowd on Calleva's gatehouse watched, the handler grasped the spear and wrenched it free. Then with the handler supporting his wounded comrade the pair staggered towards the rear of the last wagon.

'They won't make it,' said Cato.

The wagons trundled forward towards the safety of the town's ramparts, driven on by desperate lashes from the drivers' whips, and the gap between the rearmost vehicle and the two men steadily widened until they disappeared amid the ranks of the mounted rearguard. Cato strained his eyes for any further sign of them.

'Should have left him,' Macro commented sourly. 'Stupid sod's only wasted another life.'

'There they are!'

Macro looked beyond the legion's scouts and saw the pair still struggling after the supply column. Then he saw the nearest group of Britons racing in towards them for an easy kill. The handler looked over his shoulder and abruptly stopped. Pausing only for a moment, he pulled himself free of the wounded man and sprinted for safety. The auxiliary slumped to his knees and stretched a hand out towards the handler as the enemy closed in on him. He disappeared beneath a wave of woad-painted bodies with white limed hair. Some of the Britons sprinted on, intent on running down the handler. Younger, fitter and faster, they closed the distance rapidly and he was brought down with a spear thrust into the small of his back. Then he too disappeared under the savage blows of the British warriors.

'Too bad.' Macro shook his head.

'Looks like the rest of them are going to make a move.' Cato was watching the largest group of chariots where the tall figure in the lead was waving his spear above his head to attract attention. Then, with a swift stabbing motion he pointed the tip towards the remains of the supply column and the Britons roared their war cry and charged home. The auxiliaries closed ranks, forming a pitifully thin line between the Durotrigans and the wagons. The legate had rejoined his mounted scouts, and they quickly fanned out, screening the rear of the supply column and preparing to charge.

'What the hell does he think he's doing?' asked Cato, astonished. 'They'll be cut to pieces.'

'They might buy just enough time for the rest.' Macro turned and looked back towards the ramparts of the depot. 'Where's the garrison?'

The distant thrum of hoofbeats and a thin defiant cry of 'Augusta!' announced the charge of the mounted scouts. Cato and Macro watched with sickening dread as the handful of horsemen swept over the sunlit grassland towards the screaming wave of Britons. For a moment the two sides were distinct forces, Roman against Briton, and then there was just a swirling chaos of men and horses, their war cries and screams of pain carrying clearly to those watching helplessly from the ramparts of Calleva. A handful of the mounted men broke free of the enemy and pelted back towards the wagons.

'Is the legate with 'em?' asked Macro.

'Yes.'

The sacrifice of the scouts only delayed their enemy for a short while, by which time the wagons and their escorting infantry were only two hundred paces from the gateway. Those on the wall shouted encouragement and wildly beckoned to them.

On came the Durotrigans, a seething mass of men and chariots, closing with their prey. The auxiliaries prepared to receive the charge. The dark slivers of the remaining javelins curved through the air and lanced down into the enemy. Cato saw one strike the head of a chariot horse and the animal reared up and spun to one side, dragging the chariot over and crushing its driver and spearman. The Britons swept past, unheeding, and threw themselves on the shields and swords of the auxiliaries, pushing them back on the retreating wagons.

Cato heard the steady tramp of marching boots from behind and turned to see the head of the garrison emerge from the heart of Calleva and march up to the gate. Below the wooden flooring of the gatehouse tower Cato heard the graunch of the heavy timbers of the gates as they were heaved open ahead of the legionaries.

'About bloody time!' Macro grumbled.

'You think they'll make a difference?'

Macro watched the desperate fighting engulfing the rear of the supply column and shrugged. The sight of the legionaries might just make the Britons pause in their onslaught. Over the last two years the natives had come to fear the men behind the crimson shields, and with good reason. However, these were the oldest of the veterans, lame men no longer able to keep up with their comrades, and those malingerers who could no longer be trusted to stand their ground in pitched battle. The instant the enemy realised the true calibre of the men they were facing all would be lost.

The first ranks of the garrison emerged from beneath the gatehouse. The centurion barked an order and the column changed formation, men spilling out on either side of the track to create a line four deep. As soon as the manoeuvre was complete the line moved forward towards the embattled supply column. The rearmost ranks of the Britons turned to face the new danger and slingers and archers loosed their missiles against the Romans. The barrage rattled harmlessly off the shields and then the noise ceased as the enemy infantry stepped forward to meet the legionaries. There was no wild charge from either side: the two lines simply came together in a rising clatter of ringing blades and dull thuds of shields. The legionaries pushed towards the first wagon, remorselessly carving a path through the Durotrigans.

The century continued to fight its way forward, but it was evident to those on the gatehouse that the pace was slackening. Even so, they reached the oxen of the first wagon and forced enough of a gap through the swirling ranks of the enemy to permit the wagon to drive through, rumbling free of the mêlée towards the open gates. The second and third wagons followed, and the surviving auxiliaries struggled to form up with their legionary companions. Vespasian dismounted and threw himself into the fight alongside his men. For a moment Cato felt a pang of anxiety as he lost sight of his legate; then the distinctive red crest atop Vespasian's helmet appeared amid the wild, shimmering mass of gleaming helmets and bloodied weapons.

Cato leaned over the palisade to watch the wagons pass beneath the gatehouse, each one laden with stacks of amphorae packed in straw. A small quantity of grain and oil would be saved, then. But that was all. As he looked up he saw that the last two wagons had fallen into British hands, their drivers and handlers lying slaughtered beside them. Only one last wagon was contested, and as Cato watched, the Britons began to drive the Romans back from it.

'Look there!' said Macro, pointing away from the mêlée. The British chieftain had gathered most of his chariots about him and was leading them wide round the fighting, clearly aiming to crash into the rear of the Roman line. 'If that lot catches them before they can reach the gate, the lads will break.'

'Break?' Cato snorted. 'They'll be cut to pieces . . . If only they see the danger in time.'

The Roman line was giving ground steadily under the weight of the Britons' attack. The men in the front rank thrust and blocked, wholly concerned with killing the enemy immediately to their front, while their comrades behind them were glancing nervously over their shoulders and edging back towards the safety of the gate. With a wild shout of triumph the charioteers suddenly whipped their ponies on, charging towards the narrow gap between the legionaries and the gatehouse. Even where he stood Cato could feel the walkway tremble beneath his feet as the ponies' hoofs and the chariot wheels shook the ground.

The centurion commanding the garrison glanced towards the chariots and bellowed a warning. At once the legionaries and auxiliaries broke away from their enemy and ran for the gateway, Vespasian amongst them. On the gatehouse Verica cupped his hands and shouted an order to the men lining the palisade. Throwing spears were snatched up and arrows notched to prepare a covering barrage for the fleeing Romans. Already they were streaming in through the gates, but some were not going to make it. The oldest soldiers, struggling pitifully with their heavy equipment, were falling behind. Most had cast their shields and swords aside and threw themselves on, glancing to their right as the chariots closed in, the manes of the ponies whipping out as their nostrils flared and their mouths foamed; above them the savage expressions of the drivers and the spearmen, exulting in the imminent destruction of the Romans.

Centurion Veranius, true to his kind, still carried his shield and sword, and trotted along with the last of his men, shouting at them to keep moving. When the chariots were no more than twenty paces from him he realised he was a dead man. Veranius stopped, turned towards the chariots and raised his shield, holding his sword level at his waist. As Cato watched, feeling sick in his guts, the centurion glanced up at the gatehouse and smiled grimly. He nodded a salute at the line of faces witnessing his final stand, and turned his face towards the enemy.

There was a scream, abruptly cut off as the chariots rode down the first of the stragglers, and Cato watched as the chain-mailed bodies of the legionaries were crushed to a pulp by hoofs and wheels. Veranius charged forward, stabbing his sword into the chest of a lead pony, then he was knocked down and disappeared under the confusion of harnessed horse-flesh and the wicker superstructures of the chariots.

With a grinding thud the gates were heaved back together and the locking bar crashed back into its receiving sockets. The chariots slewed to a halt in front of the gate and then the air was filled with shouts and shrill agonised whinnies as the javelins and arrows of Verica's men on the palisade rained on to the dense mass below. The Britons answered with their own missiles and a slingshot cracked against the palisade just below Cato. He grabbed Macro by the shoulder and drew him back towards the ladder leading down to the inside of the ramparts.

'There's nothing we can do here. We're just in the way.'

Macro nodded, and followed him down the ladder.

As they emerged into the rutted open area just inside the gate they saw the confused tangle of wagons, oxen and the survivors of the escort and garrison. Men sat slumped on the ground, chests heaving. Those on foot supported themselves on their spears or bent double, gasping for breath. Many were heedless of their wounds, and blood dripped on to the ground around them. Vespasian stood to one side, leaning forward with his hands resting on his knees, gasping for breath. Macro shook his head slowly.

'What a complete fucking shambles . . .'

Chapter Three

The sounds of battle quickly died away as the Durotrigans fell back from the ramparts of Calleva. Even though they had just given the Romans and their despised Atrebatan allies a bloody nose, they realised that any attempt to scale the ramparts would be a waste of lives. With loud taunting cheers they ran back beyond slingshot range and continued their triumphant tirade of insults until dusk. As darkness thickened about them, the Durotrigans melted away; only the faint rumbling of chariot wheels lingered for a while, and then Calleva was surrounded by silent shadows.

The natives manning the gatehouse and the ramparts either side stood down and slumped wearily on the walkway. Only a few sentries remained standing, eyes and ears straining for any sign that the Durotrigans were merely playing a trick, and would slip back under cover of night. As Verica emerged from the gatehouse he looked tired, and his thin frame moved uncertainly. He rested a hand on the shoulder of one his bodyguards. In the flickering glare of a single torch the small party slowly made its way down the main thoroughfare towards the high thatched roofs of the royal enclosure. Along the route small groups of townspeople fell silent as their king passed by; sullen resentment filled every face illuminated by the wavering orange glow of the torch. While Verica and his nobles were well fed, his people were growing hungry. Most of their grain pits were empty and only a few pigs and sheep were left within the ramparts. Outside Calleva many farms lay abandoned, or in blackened ruin; their inhabitants either dead or sheltering within the town.

The alliance with Rome had brought none of the benefits that Verica had promised them. Far from being protected by the legions the Atrebatans had, it seemed, drawn upon themselves the wrath of every tribe loyal to Caratacus. Small columns of raiders from the lands of the Durotrigans, the Dubonnians, the Catuvellaunians and even the wild Silurans swept between the advancing legions and raided deep behind their lines. Not only were the Atrebatans deprived of their own supplies of food, they were being denied the grain promised to them by Rome as the convoys were hunted down and destroyed by Caratacus' warriors. What little survived the journey from Rutupiae was added to the stockpile in the Second Legion's supply depot, and the people of Calleva whispered rumours of the legionaries growing fat as their Atrebatan allies were forced to eat ever shrinking rations of barley gruel.

The resentment was not lost on Cato and Macro as they sat on a crude log bench just outside the depot gates. A wine trader from Narbonensis had set up a stall as close to his legionary customers as possible and had erected a bench each side of his leather tent with its trestle counter. Macro had bought cups of cheap mulsum, and the two centurions cradled the leather vessels on their laps as they watched the king of the Atrebatans and his bodyguard pass by. The guards on the gate stood to attention, but Verica only flashed them a cold glance and stumbled on towards his enclosure.

'Not the most grateful of allies,' Macro grumbled.

'Can you blame him? His own people seem to hate him even more than the enemy. He was forced on them by Rome, and now he's brought the Atrebatans nothing but suffering, and there's not much we can do to help him. No wonder he's bitter towards us.'

'Still reckon the bastard should show a little more gratitude. Goes running to the Emperor, whining that the Catuvellaunians have kicked him off his throne. Claudius ups and invades Britain and the first thing he does is return Verica's kingdom to him. Can't ask for more than that.'

Cato looked down into his cup for a moment before responding. As usual Macro was seeing things in the most simplistic light. While it was true that Verica had benefited from his appeal to Rome it was equally certain that the old king's plight was just the opportunity that Emperor Claudius and the imperial staff were looking for in their search for a handy military adventure. The new Emperor needed a triumph, and the legions needed a diversion from their dangerous appetite for politics. The conquest of Britain had preyed on the mind of every policy maker in Rome ever since Caesar had first attempted to extend the limits of Rome's glory across the sea and into the misty islands. Here was Claudius' chance to make a name for himself, to be worthy of the great deeds of his predecessors. Forget the fact that Britain was no longer quite the mysterious land that Caesar, with his eye forever on any chance to enhance his posterity, had vividly written about in his commentaries. Even in Augustus' reign the length and breadth of Britain had been traversed by merchants and travellers from across the Empire. It was only a matter of time before this last bastion of the Celts and the druids would be conquered and added to the provincial inventory of the Caesars.

Verica had unwittingly brought about the end of this island's proud and defiant tradition of independence from Rome. Cato found himself feeling sorry for Verica and, more importantly, for all his people. They were caught between the irresistible force of the legions advancing beneath their golden eagles, and the grim desperation of Caratacus and his loose confederation of British tribes, prepared to go to any lengths to dislodge the men of Rome from these shores.

'That Vespasian's a mad one!' Macro chuckled as he gently shook his head. 'It's a wonder he's still alive. Did you see him? Going at 'em like he was a bloody gladiator. The man's mad.'

'Yes, not quite the approved form of behaviour for senatorial types,' Cato mused.

'Then what's he up to?'

'I imagine he feels he's got something to prove. He and his brother are the first of their family to make it into the senatorial class – quite different from the usual run of aristocrats who serve their time as legates.' Cato looked around at Macro. 'That must come as quite a refreshing change.'

'You said it. Most of the senators I've served under think that fighting barbarian hordes is beneath them.'

'But not our legate.'

'Not him,' agreed Macro, and emptied his cup. 'Not that it's going to do him much good. Without supplies the Second Legion's campaign is going to be finished for the year. And you know what happens to legates who can't cut it. Poor sod'll end up as governor of some flea-bitten backwater in Africa. That's the way it goes.'

'Maybe. But I dare say there'll be other legates sharing the same fate unless something's done about these raids on our supply lines.'

Both men fell silent for a moment, pondering the implications of the enemy's switch in strategy. For Macro it meant the inconvenience of reduced rations and the frustration of losing ground, as the legions would have to retreat and construct more thorough defences of their communication lines before taking the offensive once more. Worse still, General Plautius' legions would have to set about the ruthless destruction of the tribes one at a time. The conquest would therefore proceed at snail's pace; he and Cato would have died of old age before the multifarious tribes of this benighted island were finally subdued.

Cato's thoughts skated over similar ground to his comrade's, but swiftly moved on to a more strategic level. This particular extension to the Empire might well have been ill-judged. Of course there were short-term benefits for the Emperor in that it had shored up his uncertain popularity back in Rome. But despite Caratacus' capital, Camulodunum, falling into Roman hands, the enemy had shown no great hurry to negotiate, let alone surrender. Indeed, their resolve seemed to have stiffened: under the single-minded leadership of Caratacus every effort was bent towards frustrating the advance of the Eagles. The whole enterprise was proving to be far costlier than the imperial general staff could ever have anticipated. It was clear to Cato that the logical thing to do was to exact a tribute and a promise of alliance from the British tribes and quit the island.

But that would not happen, not while the Emperor's credibility was at stake. The legions, and their auxiliary cohorts would never be permitted to withdraw. At the same time reinforcements would be drip-fed into the campaign – just enough to keep up a marginal momentum over the natives. As ever, politics overrode all other imperatives. Cato sighed.

'Heads up,' Macro hissed, nodding towards the depot gateway.

In the flickering glow of the braziers each side of the track a small body of men marched out into the street. First came four legionaries, then Vespasian, and then another four legionaries. The small party turned in the direction of Verica's enclosure and tramped off into the darkness, watched by the two centurions.

'Wonder what that's all about,' muttered Cato.

'Courtesy call?'

'I doubt the legate will get a warm reception.'

Macro shrugged with an evident lack of concern about the cordiality of Rome's relations with one of the very few tribes prepared to ally themselves to Claudius. He concentrated on a far more pressing issue.

'Another drink? My treat.'

Cato shook his head. 'Better not. I'm tired. Best get back to the hospital, before some bloody orderly decides to reallocate our beds.'

Chapter Four

Despite the thrill of having survived the desperate skirmish outside the gates of Calleva, Vespasian was in a foul mood as he marched up the stinking thoroughfare towards Verica's enclosure. And not just because he resented the curt summons he had received from the king of the Atrebatans. As soon as he had recovered his breath after entering Calleva Vespasian marched the survivors of the convoy, and the last of his scouts, to the depot. Every spare man had been placed on the walls in case the Durotrigans decided to chance a more ambitious assault on their enemy. At the depot the legate had to deal with a stream of junior officers jostling for his attention. Taking over the small office of the late Centurion Veranius, Vespasian dealt with them one at a time. The hospital was filled with casualties, and the legion's chief surgeon was demanding more men to set up a new ward. The centurion in command of the convoy requested a cohort of the Second Legion be placed at his disposal to guard his wagons on the journey back to the base on the Tamesis.

'I can't be answerable for any supplies until I can get adequate protection, sir,' he said warily.

Vespasian eyed the officer with cold contempt. 'You are answerable for supplies under any circumstances, and you know it.'

'Yes, sir. But those bloody Spanish auxiliaries I was given are useless.'

'Seemed to be doing well enough just now.'

'Yes, sir,' the centurion conceded. 'But it ain't the same as being protected by legionaries. Our heavy infantry put the shits up the natives.'

'Maybe, but I can't spare you any of my men.'

'Sir—'

'None. But I'll send a request to the general for some Batavian cavalry tomorrow. Meanwhile I want a full inventory of the supplies in the depot, and then get as many wagons ready to move as you can.'

The supplies centurion paused a moment, waiting for further explanation, but Vespasian curtly nodded towards the door and beckoned the next man. His priority was getting rations to his men as soon as possible. Already one of his scouts was riding back to the Second Legion with orders to send two cohorts to Calleva. It might be a disproportionate response but Vespasian needed to be sure that he could transfer as much as possible from the depot to the legion. With the enemy raiding in force there was no chance of guaranteeing a steady flow of supplies.

Caratacus had presented him with a neat paradox: if he continued to advance, his supplies would be cut off; yet if he concentrated on safeguarding his supply lines, the advance would be stalled. Further north General Plautius' forces were already stretched perilously thin, and almost none was available for strengthening the convoy escorts, or garrisoning the way stations and this vital depot at Calleva. The miserable show put on by the garrison that afternoon was indicative of the calibre of the men who could be spared for such duties. What Vespasian needed now, more than anything else, was manpower. Fit and well-trained. But, he realised with teeth-clenching bitterness, he might as well wish for the moon.

There was a further problem. The commander of the garrison was dead. Veranius had been an adequate enough officer – adequate enough to be spared for this command – but the Second Legion could ill afford to send another centurion from the campaign being waged against the hillforts. As always, the casualty rate amongst centurions was disproportionately high, given their duty to lead from the front. There were already a number of centuries being commanded by optios, hardly a satisfactory state of affairs . . .

It was at that point that a messenger had arrived from Verica requesting Vespasian's presence at the earliest convenience.

All of this weighed heavily on his mind as the legate made his way along the dark streets of Calleva, taking care not to slip on the mud and ordure beneath his boots. Here and there orange pools of light spilled across the rutted streets from the open doorways of native huts. Inside, Vespasian could see families clustered about their hearth-fires, but few seemed to be eating.

A tall gateway loomed ahead of the legate and his escort, and two Atrebatan warriors with spears stepped out of the shadows at the sound of approaching footsteps. They lowered the broad leaf-shaped tips of their spears until they could recognise the legate in the gloom. Then they stepped aside and one of the sentries pointed towards the large rectangular building on the far side of the enclosure. As the Romans crossed the open space Vespasian looked round keenly and noted the stables, small thatched storage sheds and a couple of long, low timber-framed buildings within which the loud, raucous voices of men could be heard. This was how Atrebatan royalty lived then – a far cry from the palaces of kings in the distant eastern lands of the Empire. Another standard of civilisation altogether, Vespasian reflected, and one which Rome might just as well not have bothered with. It would take a very long time to raise these Britons up to the level where they could comfortably take their place alongside the more developed of the Empire's subjects.

On either side of the entrance to Verica's great hall, torches wavered gently in the darkness. By their light Vespasian was surprised to see that the building had been completed since his last visit to Calleva. Clearly the king of the Atrebatans had aspirations towards a higher standard of living. Not surprising, Vespasian considered, given that so many of the island's nobles had enjoyed years of exile in the comfortable accommodation afforded by Rome.

A figure stepped out of the imposing entrance hall, a youth in his early twenties, Vespasian guessed. He had light brown hair tied back and was broad-shouldered and tall – taller than Vespasian by a few inches. He wore a short tunic over his check-weave leggings and soft leather boots, a compromise of native and Roman attire.

The man grasped Vespasian's arm with an easy familiar smile.

'Greetings, Legate.' He spoke in faintly accented Latin.

'Do I know you? I don't recall . . .'

'We haven't met formally, sir. My name's Tincommius. I was with my uncle's entourage when he rode out to greet you . . . when your legion arrived here at the beginning of spring?'

'I see,' Vespasian nodded, not recalling the man at all. 'Your uncle?'

'Verica,' Tincommius smiled modestly. 'Our king.'

Vespasian looked at him again, giving the man a more serious appraisal. 'Your Latin's pretty fluent.'

'I spent much of my youth in Gaul, sir. I fell out with my father when he swore allegiance to the Catuvellaunians. So I went and joined my uncle in exile . . . Anyway, if you would care to leave your bodyguards here, I can take you through to see the king.'

Vespasian ordered his men to wait for him, and followed

Tincommius through the tall oak doors. Inside there was an imposing open space, with a high vaulted thatch roof held up by huge timber beams. Tincommius noted that Vespasian was impressed.

'The king remembers his time in exile with a degree of fondness for Roman architecture. This was completed only a month ago.'

'It's certainly fit accommodation for a king,' Vespasian replied politely as he followed Tincommius into the hall. Tincommius had turned right and bowed respectfully, and Vespasian followed his lead. Verica was sitting alone on a dais. To one side stood a small table covered with dishes bearing a variety of luxury foods. To the other side, on the floor, rested an elegant iron brazier, from which a small bundle of logs hissed and cracked on red-hot embers. Verica beckoned to them, and with the sharp echoing footsteps of his nailed boots Vespasian approached the king of the Atrebatans. Though Verica was nearly seventy, underneath the wrinkled skin and long grey hair his eyes sparkled brightly. He was tall and lean, and still had the air of command that must have made him an imposing figure at the height of his powers, Vespasian realised.

Verica slowly finished the small pastry he had in his hand and then brushed the crumbs on to the floor. He coughed to clear his throat.

'I summoned you to discuss this afternoon's events, Legate.'

'I imagined that was the reason, sir.'

'You must stop these enemy raids into Atrebatan lands. They can't be allowed to continue a moment longer. It's not just your convoys that are being attacked; my people have been driven from their farms.'

'I understand that, sir.'

'Empathy does not fill stomachs, Legate. Why can't we have some of the reserves in your depot? You have plenty there, yet your Centurion Veranius refused to release any supplies to us.'

'He was acting on my orders. My legion may require everything that's in the depot.'

'Everything? There must be far more there than you could ever need. My people are starving now.'

'I've no doubt it'll be a long campaign, sir,' Vespasian countered. 'And I've no doubt we will lose yet more supplies to the Durotrigans before the season is over. Then, of course, I'll need to stockpile food at an advance base for next winter.'

'And what of my people?' Verica's hand moved over towards a dish of honeyed dates. 'They can't be allowed to go hungry.'

'Once we've defeated the Durotrigans your people can return to their farms. But we can't beat the enemy while my troops have no food in their stomachs.'

It was an impasse, and both men knew it. Tincommius eventually broke the silence.

'Legate, have you considered what might happen if you don't feed our people. What if the Atrebatans rose up against Verica?'

Vespasian had indeed considered the prospect, and the consequences of such a rising were deeply disturbing. If the Atrebatans deposed Verica and threw in their lot with the other tribes fighting for Caratacus then General Plautius and his legions would be cut off from the supply base at Rutupiae. With enemies before, behind and between the Roman columns, Plautius would have to retreat to the safety of Camulodunum. And if the Trinovantans there, cowed as they were, took heart from the revolt of the Atrebatans, then only a miracle could save Plautius and his legions from succumbing to a fate similar to that of General Varus and his three legions in the depths of Germania nearly forty years ago.

Vespasian controlled his anxiety and fixed Tincommius with a steady look. 'Do you think it is likely that your people will rise up against the king?'

'Not the king. Rome,' replied Tincommius. Then he smiled. 'They're only grumbling right now. But who knows what men might do if they're hungry enough?'

Vespasian kept his expression fixed while Tincommius continued, 'Hunger is not the only danger. There are some nobles who are less than enthusiastic about our alliance with Rome. Hundreds of our best warriors are fighting alongside Caratacus even now. Rome should not take the loyalty of the Atrebatans for granted.'

'I see,' Vespasian smiled faintly. 'You're threatening me.'

'No, my dear Legate!' Verica interrupted. 'Not at all. You must pardon the boy. Youngsters are prone to overstatement, are they not? Tincommius was merely stating the possibility in the most extreme terms, unlikely as it might seem.'

'Fair enough.'

'Be that as it may, you should know that there is a very real threat to my position, one that might be exploited if you continue to let my people go hungry.'

There was a palpable tension between the three men now and Vespasian's anger at the naked attempt to blackmail him threatened to erupt in a most undiplomatic flow of invective. He forced himself to suppress his feelings and reconsider the situation. It was bad enough that the Atrebatans were in two minds about their alliance with Rome; there was no point in making matters worse by fostering bad relations with those Atrebatans who still cherished the link.

'What would you have me do?'

'Hand over your food supplies,' Tincommius answered.

'Impossible.'

'Then give us enough men to hunt down and destroy these raiders.'

'That's impossible too. I can't spare a single man.'

Tincommius shrugged. 'Then we can't guarantee the loyalty of our people.'

The argument was going round in circles and Vespasian's frustration was turning to anger once more. There had to be a way through this. Then an idea did occur to him.

'Why can't you go after these raiders yourself?'

'With what?' snapped Verica. 'Your general permits me fifty armed men. That's barely enough to protect the royal enclosure, let alone the ramparts of Calleva. What could fifty men do against the force that attacked your convoy today?'

'Then raise more men. I'll petition General Plautius to suspend the limit on your forces.'

'That's all very well,' Tincommius said calmly, 'but we have very few warriors left. Many chose to join Caratacus rather than lay down their arms. Some – though not many – stayed loyal to Verica.'

'Start with them then. There must be many more who'd want revenge on the Durotrigans – all those whose farms have been destroyed by enemy raiders.'

'They're farmers,' Tincommius said dismissively. 'They know almost nothing about fighting. They don't even have proper weapons. They'd be slaughtered.'

'So train them! I can provide the weapons from the depot here – the moment we get permission from the general – enough for, say, a thousand men. That's more than sufficient to take on those raiders . . . Unless the Atrebatans are too afraid.'

Tincommius gave a bitter smile. 'You Romans, so brave behind your armour, your huge shields and all those cheap battlefield traps. What do you know of courage?'

Verica coughed. 'If I might make a suggestion . . .'

The other two turned towards the old man on the throne. Vespasian dipped his head in assent. 'Please do.'

'It crossed my mind that you might lend us some of your

officers to train our men in the ways of the Roman army. After all, it will be your equipment they will be fighting with. Surely you can spare that many men – if it helps solve both our problems?'

Vespasian considered the idea. It made good sense. Calleva would be able to take care of itself, and such a force might indeed take the strain off the legion's lines of communication. Well worth seconding a few officers for. He looked at Verica and nodded. The king smiled.

'Of course, such a force would need to be adequately provisioned in order to be effective . . . You said it yourself, Legate. Soldiers are only any good if they have full bellies.'

'Yes, my lord,' Tincommius nodded, and continued with a cynical edge to his voice, 'I dare say that the prospect of a decent meal will lead to no shortage of recruits. And a full belly has a wonderful way of dispersing rebellious instincts.'

'Now wait a moment.' Vespasian raised a hand, anxious not to commit himself to more than he could deliver. He was angry with the old man for manoeuvring him into this position, but accepted the cogency of his argument. The scheme might even work, provided, of course, that General Plautius agreed to the arming of the Atrebatans. 'It's an interesting proposition. I need to think about it.'

Verica nodded. 'By all means, Legate. But not for too long, eh? It takes time to train men, and we have very little time if it's to make a difference. Give me your response tomorrow. You may go.'

'Yes, sir.'

Vespasian smartly turned and marched out of the hall, under the silent gaze of the two Britons. He was anxious to be free of them and be somewhere quiet where his tired mind could think the plan through, without having to worry about being manipulated by the shrewd king of the Atrebatans.

Chapter Five

'Lift this please, Centurion.' The surgeon handed Cato a sword. He took it in his right hand and slowly raised it to his front. The early morning sunlight glinted along the blade.

'That's good. Push it out as far as you can, then hold.'

Cato looked down the length of his arm and grimaced at the effort of keeping the blade up; he could not stop the tip of the sword from wavering, and soon his arm began to tremble.

'To the side now, sir.'

Cato swept his arm round and the surgeon ducked beneath its arc. Macro winked at Cato as the surgeon straightened himself, well away from the blade.

'Well, no problem with the muscles there! Now then, how does your other side feel?'

'Tight,' Cato replied through gritted teeth. 'Feels like something's stretching badly.'

'Painful?'

'Very.'

'You can lower the sword now, sir.' The surgeon waited until the blade had been returned to its scabbard and then returned to the corner of the room. Cato stood before him, bare-chested and the surgeon ran his finger along the thick red line that curved round the left side of Cato's chest and a third of the way across his back. 'The muscles are quite tight under the scar tissue. You need to loosen them up. It's going to take plenty of exercise. It'll be painful, sir.'

'I don't care,' replied Cato. 'All I want to know is how soon I can get back to the legion.'

'Ah . . .' The surgeon made a face. 'That may take some time, and, well, frankly, you'd better not build your hopes up too much.'

'What do you mean?' Cato said with a quiet intensity. 'I *am* going to recover.'

'Of course you are, Centurion. Of course you are. It's just that you might have difficulty bearing the weight of a shield on your left arm, and the added strain of wielding a sword might well cause the muscles down the left side to tear. You'd be in agony.'

'I've endured pain before.'

'Yes, sir. But this would be quite incapacitating. There's no easy way to say this, sir, but your army career might well be over.'

'Over?' Cato replied softly. 'But I'm only eighteen . . . It can't be over.'

'I didn't say that it *was*, sir. Just that there is a chance that it *might* be. With thorough exercise and favouring of that side, there's a chance you could return to active service.'

'I see . . .' Cato felt sick. 'Thank you.'

The surgeon smiled sympathetically. 'Well, then, I'll be off.'

'Yes . . .'

Once the door was closed Cato pulled on his tunic and slumped down on his bed. He ran a hand through his dark curls. It was unbelievable. He had not even completed two years of service with the Eagles, and had only recently been promoted, and the surgeon was telling him it was as good as over.

'He can get stuffed,' said Macro, in an awkward attempt to cheer his friend up. 'You just need to get some exercise, get yourself back in shape. We'll work on it together, and I'll have you in front of your own century before you know it.'

'Thank you.'

Macro was only trying to be kind, and Cato, despite his inner agony, was grateful to the man. He straightened up and forced a smile on to his face. 'Better get started on the exercise as soon as possible then.'

'That's the spirit!' Macro beamed, and was about to offer some more encouragement when there was a sharp rap on the door.

'Come!' yelled Macro.

The door opened and a cavalry scout stepped smartly into the hospital room.

'Centurions Lucius Cornelius Macro and Quintus Licinius Cato?'

'That's us.'

'Legate requests your presence.'

'Now?' Macro frowned as he looked up through the open shutters. The sun was well above the horizon, by some hours. He looked at Cato with raised eyebrows. 'Tell him we'll be there directly.'

'Yes, sir.'

When the scout had closed the door behind him Macro quickly reached for his boots, and gave Cato a gentle nudge. 'Come on, lad.'

Vespasian waved his hand at a bench in front of the low table where he was eating his breakfast. There was a platter of small loaves, a bowl of olive oil and a jar of fish sauce. Macro met Cato's gaze and gave a disappointed shrug. If this was how legates ate, you could keep it.

'Now then,' Vespasian began, as he spread the dark fish sauce over a hunk of bread, 'how far have you two recovered from your wounds? Are you fit enough for light duties?'

Macro exchanged a quick look with Cato as their legate tore off a chunk of bread and popped it into his mouth. 'We're pretty much up for it, sir. Are we getting sent back to the legion?' Macro asked hopefully.

'No. Not yet, at least.' Vespasian couldn't help smiling at the centurion's eagerness to get back in the fight. 'I need two good men for something else. Something very important to the success of our campaign.'

Cato frowned. The last special task to which he and Macro had been assigned had nearly got them both killed. The legate read his expression accurately.

'Oh, it's nothing like last time. Nothing dangerous. Or at least, not likely to be dangerous.' Vespasian bit off another chunk of bread and started chewing. 'You shouldn't even have to leave Calleva.'

Cato and Macro relaxed.

'So then, sir,' Macro continued, 'what do you need us for?'

'You're aware that Centurion Veranius was killed yester-day?'

'Yes, sir. We were watching from the gatehouse.' Macro was momentarily tempted to add some phrase to register the sadness he imagined he was supposed to feel. But he refused to cheapen himself, especially since he had never particularly rated Veranius.

'He was the only officer I could spare to command this garrison.'

There was an implied judgement in that sentence and Macro was mildly surprised that the legate shared his view of the dead centurion.

'And now I need a new garrison commander. The duty should not be too onerous for you while you recuperate.'

'Me, sir? In command of the depot?' Now Macro's surprise was more pronounced. Then the prospect of his first independent command filled him with a warm glow of pride. 'Thank you, sir. Yes, I'd be happy – honoured – to do the job.'

'It's an order, Macro,' Vespasian replied drily, 'not an invitation.'

'Oh, right.'

'There's more.' The legate paused a moment. 'I need you and Centurion Cato to train a small force for the king here in Calleva. A couple of cohorts is what I have in mind.'

'Two cohorts?' Cato's eyebrows rose in surprise. 'That's over nine hundred men. Where are we going to find them, sir? I doubt there's enough men of the quality we need here in Calleva.'

'Then have Verica spread the word. I doubt you'll be short of volunteers in the current situation. Once they come forward, you pick them, train them in our way of waging war, and then you will serve as their commanders, personally responsible to Verica.'

Macro chewed his lip.

'Do you think that's wise, sir? Arming the Atrebatans? In any case, I thought the general's policy was to disarm the tribes. Even those allied to us.'

'It is his policy,' Vespasian admitted, 'but the situation's changed. I can't afford to spare any more men to protect Calleva, or to deal with these raids on our supply columns. I've no choice but to use the Atrebatans. So you start training them as soon as possible. I have to return to the legion today. I've sent word of my plans to General Plautius and asked him for permission to equip Verica's men from our stores here in the depot. Train them, and feed them, but don't arm them until you get word from the general. Understand?'

'Yes, sir,' said Macro.

'Do you think you can do it?'

Macro raised his eyebrows and gently rocked his head from

side to side. 'I should think we can make something of them, sir. Can't promise to supply you with front-line troops.'

'So long as they make Verica and his people feel safe, and make those damn Durotrigans think twice before they attack our convoys. Above all, make sure that no harm comes to Verica. If he is deposed, or dies, the Atrebatans might turn against us. If that happens . . . we may have to abandon the conquest of this island. You can imagine how well that will go down in Rome. The Emperor will not be pleased with us.' Vespasian stared at the two centurions to underline the significance of his warning. If Britain was lost, then there would be no mercy shown to the officers most directly accountable: the legate of the Second Legion and the two centurions he had entrusted with defending Calleva and protecting the Atrebatan king. 'So keep Verica alive, gentlemen. That's all I ask of you. Do a decent job and then you two can get back to the legion the moment you're fit enough.'

'Yes, sir.'

'Now then,' Vespasian pushed his platter to one side and rose from his stool, 'I've got a few things left to do before heading back to the legion. I want you to move into these quarters and take command of the garrison right away. As for the other matter, you'll need to go to the royal enclosure and see one of Verica's advisors. Tincommius is his name. Tell him what you need and he'll make the appropriate arrangements. He seems reliable enough. Right then, I'll see you two when I can. Good luck.'

Once Vespasian had left the room Macro and Cato sat down at the table.

'I don't like it,' said Cato. 'Legate's taking a risk arming these natives. How loyal to Verica will they be? How far can we trust them? You've seen what they're like in the streets. There's no love lost for Rome there.'

'True. But even less lost for the Durotrigans. Cato, think about it. We've got a chance to create and command our own army!'

'It'll be Verica's army, not ours.'

'His in name only, by the time I've finished with them.'

Cato saw the excited gleam in his friend's eyes, and knew it was pointless to try to contradict him for the present. He could foresee that training native levies was going to be more of a challenge than training recruits to the legions. There were so many factors to consider, language not the least of them. He had picked up a basic grasp of Celtic during the months spent in Calleva, but Cato knew he would have to improve on that as quickly as possible if he were to make himself understood to native levies. In one thing Macro was right: it was an exciting opportunity. They could quit the hospital and take the first tentative steps back towards proper soldiering.

Chapter Six

The sun had not yet reached the top of the depot palisade when Centurion Macro emerged from the headquarters building. He was in full uniform, from nail-studded boots, silvered greaves, chain-mail vest with its harness of medallions, right up to the transverse crested helmet, gleaming dully in the shadow of the ramparts. In his hand was a vine cane, symbol of the right conferred upon him by the Emperor, Senate and People of Rome to beat the otherwise sacrosanct body of a Roman citizen. He twirled the cane between the fingers of his right hand as he marched up to the silent mass of natives gathered together on the depot's training ground. Since news of the formation of the native cohorts had spread from the Atrebatan capital, thousands of men from the surrounding lands joined those from Calleva in coming forward to be selected.

After nearly two months in hospital recovering from his head wound, Macro felt good to be getting back to the familiar routines of a centurion's life. No, he corrected himself, barring the odd skull-splitting headache, life didn't just feel good, it felt bloody marvellous. He puffed out his chest, whistling contentedly to himself as he approached his new recruits.

Centurion Cato was standing to one side of the crowd, talking with Tincommius. It was the first time that Cato had worn the uniform and equipment of a centurion and Macro thought it suited him no better than that of an optio. Cato was tall and thin, and the chain mail seemed to hang on the youngster rather than fit him. The vine stick was held awkwardly and it was difficult to imagine Cato wielding that across the back of some recalcitrant legionary, or even one of these natives. Cato's recovery in hospital had been unkind to his already skinny body and the muscle wastage to his legs was evident in the way that the back of his greaves actually overlapped slightly.

Tincommius, by contrast, was evidently in rude health, and though even taller than Cato, he was broad in proportion and looked like he might be quick on his feet as well as strong. The young Atrebatan nobleman had been tasked by his king to serve as translator and advisor, and was keen to learn the ways of the Roman legions. Tincommius could only have been a year or two older than Cato, and Macro was pleased to see them laughing together as he strode over to join them. Let Cato befriend the man then; it would save Macro having to. The older centurion had an instinctive distrust of most foreigners, and all barbarians.

'Gentlemen,' he called, 'we're not here to crack jokes. There's a job to be done.'

Cato turned to face his superior and stiffened to attention. Even though both men held the same rank, seniority counted for everything, and Cato would always be outranked by Macro, unless – by some perverse whim of providence – Cato was given command of an auxiliary cohort, or promoted to the First Cohort of the Second Legion, neither of which was remotely likely for many years to come.

'Ready, lad?' Macro winked at Cato.

'Yes, sir.'

'Right then!' Macro tucked his cane under one arm and rubbed his broad hands together. 'Let's get 'em in formation.

Tincommius, how many of this batch have any military experience?'

Tincommius turned to the crowd and nodded. To one side, haughty and aloof, stood a small band of men, perhaps twenty or thirty, all in the prime of life.

'They're from our warrior caste. All weapon-trained from childhood. They can ride too.'

'Good. That's a start then. Tincommius?'

'Yes?'

Macro leaned close to him. 'Just a word about protocol. From now on, you're to call me "sir".'

The Atrebatan nobleman's eyebrows shot up in astonishment. To Macro's intense irritation Tincommius glanced questioningly over towards Cato.

'You look at me when I'm talking to you! Got that?'

'Yes.'

'Yes, what?' Macro said with a menacing edge to his voice. 'Yes, what?'

'Yes, sir.'

'That's better! Now don't forget.'

'Yes . . . sir.'

'Now, then. The rest of them – what experience have they got?'

'None, sir. Nearly all of them are farmers. Should be fit enough, but the nearest they've ever come to a fight is keeping foxes out of their chicken coops.'

'Well, let's see how fit they really are. We can only afford to take the best so we'd better start weeding out the rubbish. We'll use your warriors to form the rest of them up. Get 'em over here. Cato, you got the pegs?'

'Yes, sir.' Cato nudged a small sack with his boot.

'Then why aren't they already set out?'

'Sorry, sir. I'll see to it straight away.'

Macro nodded curtly and Cato snatched up the bag and strode off a short distance from the native volunteers. He stopped and rummaged inside before drawing out a numbered peg, which he thrust into the ground. Then Cato took ten paces and planted the next peg, and so on, until there were two lines of ten pegs each; enough for the first batch of two hundred men. Over the next few days the two centurions would recruit twelve centuries of eighty men, nine hundred and sixty in all, from the far greater number that had responded to Verica's call for volunteers. The mere promise of good rations had been enough to attract men from all over the kingdom.

'Tincommius!'

'Yes, sir.'

'Position one of your warriors by each of those pegs. Tell them they're going to be my section leaders. Once that's done, take nine out of the rest and line 'em up beside the first man. Understood?'

'Yes, sir.'

'Very good. Carry on.'

Macro stood patiently as Tincommius led the volunteers over to the pegs and Cato then pushed and shoved his charges into position. The sun had long since cleared the ramparts by the time everyone was in place, and Macro's highly polished helmet gleamed as he faced the Atrebatans to address them. To his right stood Tincommius, ready to relay the centurion's words. To Macro's left Cato stood stiffly to attention.

'First thing!' Macro bellowed, then paused to allow Tincommius to translate. 'Whenever I give the order "Form up", I want you all to go to exactly the same place you are standing now. Memorise it! . . . Second, right now you're a fucking mess. We need to dress these lines.'

Tincommius paused before translating. 'You want me to translate all of that, sir?'

'Of course I bloody do! Get on with it!'

'Right.' Evidently the linguistic education of Tincommius had been more refined than vernacular. He shouted out in Celtic and there was a roar of laughter from the volunteers.

'SHUT UP!' roared Macro. The volunteers fell silent without the need for translation. 'Now, then, each man raise his right arm horizontally, like me. Your hand should rest on the next man's shoulder. If it doesn't, then move yourself until it does.'

The natives started to shuffle around the moment Tincommius had finished translating and a soft babbling of Celtic broke out.

'IN SILENCE!'

With stilled tongues they continued positioning themselves, all save one poor soul, who caught Macro's eye almost at once.

'You there! You trying to make a fool of me? Right arm, I said, NOT YOUR BLOODY LEFT! Cato! Sort him out!'

The junior centurion trotted over to the object of Macro's rage. The native was short and thickset, with a dull bovine expression of incomprehension. Cato resisted the temptation to give him a friendly smile by way of greeting, and pushed the man's left arm down to his side. He tapped him on the right shoulder. 'This one!' Cato said in Celtic.

'Right arm . . . right arm. Got it? Right arm up!' Cato raised his hand to demonstrate and the native nodded like an idiot. Cato smiled and took a step back before trying again. 'Dress ranks! . . . No, the right arm, I said! Like everyone else!'

'What are you doing, Centurion Cato?' shouted Macro as he stormed over. 'Here! Get out of my way. There's only one way to teach dumb bastards like him.'

Macro stood in front of the tribesman, who was still grinning, more nervously now.

'What you smiling at? Think I'm funny, do you?' Macro

grinned. 'Is that it? Well, let's see how fucking funny you think I am then!'

He brought up his vine cane and slashed it against the man's left arm.

'LEFT ARM!'

The man yelped in agony, but before he could do anything else Macro whacked the cane against the man's other side.

'RIGHT ARM! . . . Now, let's see if we've learned anything . . . Left arm!'

The native quickly shot his left arm into the air.

'Right arm!'

Down came one arm, up shot the other.

'Bravo, mate! We'll make a soldier of you yet. Carry on, Centurion Cato.'

'Yes, sir.'

Once the volunteers could form up to Macro's satisfaction then came the time to assess their fitness. Section by section the Atrebatans led off into a steady run around the perimeter of the depot. Cato and Macro were posted diagonally opposite each other and urged each section on as it rounded the angle and started down the next length. In a short space of time the sections had merged into a stream of men, puffing and panting their way round the depot. As Macro had expected, the warriors clustered to the front, along with the fittest of the others and quickly began to move ahead of the rest.

'It's not a race!' Macro roared, cupping a hand to his mouth, 'Cato! Tell 'em I want to see how long they can keep it up. Slow 'em down.'

All morning he drove them on. After a while the first men began to drop out: the weakest and those too old to keep up. They were immediately escorted to the depot gates and shown out. Most took their rejection in good enough spirits. Some were evidently ashamed and snapped surly comments over their shoulders as they disappeared through the depot gates. The rest forced themselves to keep going, round and round, many with grim expressions of determination.

At midday Macro sauntered across the depot to join Cato at the parade ground.

'I think that's enough. We'll give this lot some food and rest and have a look at the next batch. Let me know how many we've got left as soon as you can.'

As the volunteers reached him, Cato waved them down and ticked the numbers off on a slate before directing them over to the headquarters building where some of the garrison were handing out flatbread and cups of watered wine. As the last man staggered away Cato made his report.

'Eighty-four remaining.'

'Any of Tincommius' warriors fall out?'

'Not one.'

'Impressive. Wonder how they'll do in full equipment? Let's have a look at the next lot.'

And so the process went on for the next three days, until Macro had his two cohorts. At dusk on the third day, a cohort of the Second Legion arrived to escort the supply convoy back to the legion. Every wagon that Macro could lay his hands on had been made ready and fully loaded with supplies. Vespasian would be able to maintain his army in the field for a few more weeks, but the men in the depot now depended upon the safe arrival of the next convoy from Rutupiae, due in less than twenty days. Only a small escort could be spared to protect it when it set out on the last leg of its journey from the fortress on the Tamesis. Unless a covering force from Calleva could meet it on the way, there was a good chance that it would be detected by the scouts of the Durotrigans and ambushed. With a thousand extra mouths to feed from the supplies in the depot the two cohorts were going to have to earn their keep.

'We're not going to be ready in time,' said Cato that night, as he sat at the table in Macro's quarters, eating cold chicken.

Macro and Tincommius looked up from their platters. Macro finished his mouthful and used the back of his hand to wipe the grease from his lips. 'Not unless we get the all clear to issue weapons we won't. Can't send men out armed with sticks and scythes – that'd be plain murder.'

'So what do we do?' asked Tincommius.

'We start drilling them. We've got some marching yokes on the inventory. I'll get the carpenters to cut them into lengths. At least we can begin basic sword practice.'

Tincommius nodded, and wiped his platter clean with his last hunk of bread. He pushed the platter away from him. 'Now, if you don't mind, sir, I've got to get back to the royal enclosure for the night.'

'What for?'

'The king's gathered some of his nobles together for a drinking session.'

'Drinking?'

'Well, there'll be dog-fighting, some wrestling and a few tall stories. But mostly drinking.'

'Make sure you're back here at dawn. We'll start training as soon as it's light.'

'I'll be there, sir.'

'You'd better be.' Macro nodded his head meaningfully towards his vine cane in the corner of the room.

'Are you serious?' asked Tincommius. 'You'd really strike a member of the royal household?'

'You'd better believe it, old son. The discipline of the legions applies to all men, or no men. That's how it is – how it must be – if we're going to sort out those bloody Durotrigans.'

Tincommius stared down at the centurion for the moment, and then nodded slowly. 'I'll be back before dawn.'

When the two Romans were alone Macro eased himself back from the table and patted his stomach. A burp rumbled in his throat, causing Cato to look up with a frown.

'What?'

'It's nothing, sir. Sorry.'

Macro sighed. 'There's that "sir" thing again. I thought you'd got over that.'

'Creature of habit.' Cato smiled weakly. 'But I'll work on it.'

'You'd better.'

'Meaning?'

'Meaning you've been a bit drippy these last few days. If you're going to help me train these Atrebatans so they can take on the enemy, you're going to have to buck up your technique.'

'I'll try.'

'Trying's not good enough, lad. Training men for war's a serious business. You have to be hard on them from day one. You have to punish them hard for every single mistake they make. Be as cruel and nasty as you can, because if you don't, then you place them at a disadvantage when they face the enemy for real.' Macro stared at him to make sure the point had got through. Then he smiled. 'Besides, you don't want them calling you a pansy wanker behind your back, do you?'

'Probably not.'

'That's the spirit. Decisive as ever. Now then, weapons drill starts tomorrow. You're in charge. I've got to catch up on some paperwork. Being a bloody garrison commander's a right pain in the arse. I've got to sort out accommodation and provisioning for Verica's boys. I'll have them issued with tents. They can set them up along the inside of the rampart. Then I have to make sure the inventory is bang up to date before we start issuing tunics and boots to the natives. Otherwise some bloody clerk on the imperial general staff's going to bill me for any discrepancies. Bloody auditors.'

Cato's eyes lit up as the obvious thought occurred to him. 'Would you prefer me to deal with the inventory? You can do the sword drill.'

'No! Damn it, Cato, you're a centurion now, so act like one. Besides, you know some of the lingo. Tomorrow, you're going to go out there and stick it to 'em. You can pick some men to help you, but you're on your own now, lad . . . Right, I'm off. You'd best get some rest yourself.'

'Yes. Soon as I've finished.'

Alone at the table Cato stared at his food, appetite completely gone. Tomorrow he would go out in front of a thousand men and tell them how to fight with the short sword of the legions. A thousand men; some far older, some with far more experience of fighting and none of them likely to take kindly to being given their orders by a centurion of two months' standing, who had only recently reached the legal age of manhood. He would feel like a fake, he knew it, and dreaded that most of the men on the parade ground would see through him in an instant.

Then there was the fact that the last three days had left him feeling drained. Two months of convalescence had weakened him dreadfully. His side ached abominably and Cato was beginning to doubt that any amount of exercise was going to make it comfortable.

Chapter Seven

Cato cleared his throat and turned towards the volunteers. One hundred of the Atrebatans stood silently in front of him, formed up, as they had been taught, along one side of the parade ground. In front of them stood the ten men from the garrison, selected for their skill at arms and chosen by Cato for training duties. Once this hundred had finished training for the morning they would split up and pass their learning on to the rest of the Atrebatan recruits. With only Tincommius to help with translation there was no other practical way to teach weapons skills. Cato turned to Tincommius.

'Ready?'

Tincommius nodded, and prepared to translate.

'Today, you will be introduced to the gladius, the short sword of the legions. There are some who claim this is our secret weapon. But a weapon is just a tool like any other. What distinguishes a tool from a weapon is the person wielding it. The short sword, in itself, is no more or less deadly than any other sword. Indeed, unless it is used properly it is no match for a cavalry sword, or the long swords you Celts choose to bear. In single combat it lacks reach, but in the press of battle there is no finer weapon for a man to carry.'

Cato went for his own sword, and remembered just in time that he no longer wore it on the right, as he had done as an optio. With a smile he grasped the ivory handle and drew it out of its scabbard, raising it for all to see.

'The weapon's most obvious feature is the tapered point. It's designed for delivering one type of blow in particular – the thrust. From this moment on there is one rule you must take to your hearts: a few inches of point is far more deadly than any length of edge. I'm happy to tell you this from personal experience. A few months ago someone was foolish enough to use an edged weapon on me. He's dead and I'm still here.'

Cato paused to let the moral of the story sink in, and as he listened to Tincommius' translation he remembered the druid's attack in vivid detail, and the terrible pain as the scythe sliced into his ribs. Cato felt more of a fraud than ever. If only these fools knew how terrified he had been. He gritted his teeth at the precise recollection and tried to banish the thought. After all, the druid had gone to meet his dark gods, and Cato was alive. If the druid had thought to use a pointed weapon instead, things might have been different.

Tincommius had finished, and was waiting for Cato to continue.

'It may not look very glamorous, but when you're in tight formation, with your shield pressed into the body of your enemy, and his face inches away from your own, then you'll know the true value of this weapon. Listen closely to your instructors, learn how to use the short sword as we do, and soon those bastards, the Durotrigans, will just be a nasty memory!'

A burst of cheering greeted the translation of the last remark, and Cato was wise enough to indulge it a while before raising his hands for silence.

'Now, I know how keen you are to get started, but before you can be permitted to wield the real thing you must be trained in the basic movements, as we legionaries have been. In battle you must be confident of your ability to use your weapons with ease, and without tiring quickly. To that end you will begin your training with these . . .'

Cato stepped over to a cart and threw back its leather cover. Inside were bundles of staves, cut to the approximate length of a short sword, but thicker and heavier. Deliberately so. As with all training equipment used in the legions the aim was to develop strength as well as technique. If and when these men were equipped with the real thing they would delight in the comfort of its use at once. Cato picked up one of the short staves and raised it for the volunteers to get a clear view. A ragged groan of disappointment rippled through the ranks, as Cato had anticipated, and he smiled. He had once shared this sentiment.

'It's not much to look at, but I can assure you it still hurts to be on the wrong end of it! Now, stand still!' He turned towards a small group of legionaries leaning against the corner of the nearest barrack block. 'Figulus! Get your instructors over here!'

The legionaries trotted over and drew their training weapons, enough for five pairs of combatants each. Figulus, a huge man from Narbonensis, had been chosen by Cato to act as his optio.

'Keep it basic for today,' Cato reminded them. 'Block, parry, thrust and advance for now.'

The legionaries set off for their assigned sections and distributed the weapons. As Figulus and other instructors introduced their trainees to the correct postures, Tincommius accompanied Cato as the centurion moved round each group and helped with translation where needed. The trainees were pushed into line and mimicked the actions of the legionaries as faithfully as they could. As with all training, the morning was punctuated with cries of anger and frustration from the instructors as they cajoled and kicked their charges. Cato, mindful of Macro's advice of the previous night, forced himself not to intervene, but hoped that his presence might at least cause his instructors not to be gratuitously rough.

A sudden shriek of pain drew Cato and Tincommius over to one group. The legionary instructor was standing over a figure on the ground, and whacked him on the back even as the centurion thrust his way through the line of Atrebatans for a closer look.

'What the fuck is the matter with you?' roared the instructor. 'How much more bloody simple can I make it for you, you stupid prick! It's block, parry, thrust and advance! Don't make it up as you go along!'

'What's going on here?'

The instructor snapped to attention. 'This twat's trying to take the piss, sir. Making out he can't remember four simple bloody steps.'

'I see,' Cato nodded, looking down at the figure crouched on the ground. The man slowly turned his head and grinned up at the centurion.

'Oh, no! Not you again. What's your name?' Cato asked in Celtic.

'Bedriacus.'

'Bedriacus, eh? You call me "sir".'

The man grinned again, displaying a jagged set of teeth. He nodded and pointed a finger at himself. 'Bedriacus, sir! Bedriacus, sir!'

'Yes, thank you. I think we've established that,' Cato smiled back, before turning to Tincommius. 'Know anything about him?'

'Oh yes. He's a hunter. Lost his family in a Durotrigan raid. He was injured, half dead when he was discovered.'

'Half-witted more like,' muttered the instructor.

'That's enough!' Cato snapped. He nudged Tincommius. 'I'm not sure he's up to it.'

'He's good. Especially with a blade. Saw him turn over a couple of our warriors yesterday.'

'Strength isn't everything.'

'No, no, it's not. But this man wants vengeance. Deserves it.'

Cato nodded with understanding. The desire for revenge was as powerful a motive as anything else in life, and the centurion had seen enough of the bloody work of the Durotrigans and their druids to be sympathetic to their victims.

'Fair enough. We'll take him, if he can be trained. Instructor!'

'Sir!'

'You can carry on, Marius.'

Cato was suddenly aware of a commotion over by the main gates of the depot and turned round for a better look. A group of horsemen had been admitted and were trotting over towards the parade ground. They were tribesmen, but Cato recognised only one face.

'Verica. What's he doing here?'

'Come to see how the training's getting on,' replied Tincommius.

Cato gave him a cold look. 'Well, thanks for the warning.'

'Sorry. He mentioned something about it last night. Just remembered.'

'Right . . .' Cato punched Tincommius on the shoulder. 'Come on.'

They left the instruction groups and walked over to meet the king of the Atrebatans and his retinue. Verica reined in and slowly dismounted before he waved a greeting to his kinsman and Cato. Tincommius looked at his uncle with apparent concern.

'It's all right, boy. Just feeling a bit stiff. Happens at my age,' the king smiled. 'Now then, Centurion Cato, how is my army coming along? . . . What on earth are they doing with all of those sticks? Where are their weapons?'

Cato had anticipated this moment and had his answer ready. 'They're in training, my lord. They'll be issued with the real thing as soon as they're ready for it.'

'Oh?' The old man's disappointment was clear. 'And when will that be?'

'Soon enough, my lord. Your subjects learn very quickly.'

'May we watch them for a while?'

'Of course, my lord. We'd be honoured. If you'd care to follow me . . .?'

Verica beckoned to his retinue and they obediently dismounted and walked slowly behind their king.

Cato leaned towards Tincommius and whispered, 'Whatever you do, steer him clear of that group with Bedriacus in it.'

'Right.'

Verica slowly made his way round the parade ground, watching the drill movements with apparent interest, occasionally stopping to comment on some detail or to ask Cato a question. As they returned to the first group, one of Verica's followers, a dark-haired man with a bare chest under his riding cloak, seized a training sword from the hands of one of the men. The instructor was about to protest when he caught sight of Cato gently shaking his head. The dark-haired man looked over the stave with a contemptuous expression and laughed.

'Who's that?' Cato whispered to Tincommius.

'Artax. Another one of the king's nephews.'

'Big family then?'

'If you only knew,' sighed Tincommius as Artax rounded on Cato.

'Why are our warriors being made to play with toys when they should be training to kill our enemies?'

Artax walked over to Cato, and threw the stave down at the centurion's feet with a sneer. Cato kept his face expressionless as Artax looked him up and down, and spoke in words that dripped contempt.

'It's no wonder that Romans give toys to their men when their officers are little more than boys themselves.'

Cato felt his pulse quicken and he couldn't help smiling. 'Then I'd like to see how well you can handle that toy, if you think you're man enough.'

Artax laughed and leaned forward to pat Cato on the shoulder. But Cato was too quick for him and, stepping back, he unfastened the clasp and handed his scarlet cloak to Tincommius. Then he stooped down, picked up the training sword and hefted it in the palm of his sword hand. Artax's expression turned into a sneer once again and then he too slipped off his cloak, and snatched another stave from the nearest recruit. Those around them backed away to give the two men sufficient space and Cato crouched lower, ready to fight.

Artax immediately hurled himself forward with a wild cry and rained a succession of blows at Cato's head. At once, the Atrebatans gave full throat to their cheers of support for Artax as he steadily drove Cato back, step by step. Cato coolly blocked every blow, gritting his teeth as the shock of the impacts travelled down his arm. Then, having roughly gauged the speed of his opponent's reactions Cato waited for Artax to raise his arm for the next flurry of blows. This time Cato feinted towards the man's throat. Artax jerked his head back and his midriff came forward to compensate. The centurion dropped the tip of his stave and thrust it hard into Artax's stomach. There was solid muscle behind the hairy gut, but even so, the Briton gasped at the pain of the blow, staggering back from Cato.

The centurion lowered his sword arm, his point made. Or so he thought. With a howl of rage Artax threw himself back at Cato, swinging his weapon ferociously. This time Cato knew the man intended him serious harm. And everyone else knew it too. The Atrebatans roared their support for Artax, and Cato heard his instructors shouting encouragement. To one side Verica and Tincommius watched in silence.

The sharp crack of wood on wood filled Cato's ears, and then suddenly there was burning pain in his chest as Artax slashed a blow past Cato's guard and struck the Roman on his injured side. Cato gasped, drawing back and only just managing to fend off the next attack. Artax broke away and half turned to his fellow tribesmen to revel in their applause. Cato's breathing came in shallow gasps; the agony in his side was too dreadful for any deeper breathing. His eyes glanced round at the cheering Atrebatans and he realised what a fool he had been. He had allowed his pride to jeopardise these men's training. If he gave way now, then they would never have faith in the Roman way of war again. Without that training they would not stand a chance against the Durotrigans. The pain in his side was getting worse. He must take a risk and end the fight as quickly as possible, one way or another.

'Artax!'

The nobleman turned back to Cato, mildy surprised as Cato beckoned to him. He shrugged and came on once more. This time it was Cato who attacked, going in low and fast, and taking Artax by surprise. The Briton skipped back, desperately swiping at Cato's weapon as he tried to block a succession of thrusts. Then Cato double-feinted, throwing Artax's rhythm. The first strike caught the Briton in the stomach again. The next high in the ribs, before the last one flattened his nose. Blood gushed out as Artax clenched his eyes shut against the shattering agony. Cato's last strike was rammed home into his opponent's groin and Artax crumpled to the ground with a deep groan.

The Atrebatans fell silent, aghast at the sudden reversal. Cato stood erect, and backed away from his beaten foe. He gazed round at the natives, and raised his stave.

'Remember what I said earlier: a few inches of point is far more deadly than any length of edge. There's your proof.' He pointed to Artax, slowly writhing on the ground.

There was an uncomfortable moment of silence, then one of the Atrebatan warriors raised his stave and saluted Cato. Someone else cheered, and soon all of the trainee swordsmen were cheering him. Cato stared back, defiant at first, and then smiled. The lesson was learned. He let it continue a short while and then waved his hands to quieten them.

'Instructors! Get 'em back to work!'

As the Atrebatans broke up and returned to sword drill, two of the king's followers picked Artax up, hoisted him on to his horse and held him steady while they waited for Verica to remount. The king eased his horse over to Cato and smiled down at him.

'My thanks, Centurion. That was most . . . educational. I'm sure my men are in good hands. Let me know if there's anything I can do to help.'

Cato bowed his head. 'Thank you, my lord.'

Chapter Eight

Over the next few days the rest of the recruits were trained in the basics of swordplay every morning. Cato had given orders for a series of thick wooden stakes to be set up on one side of the parade ground and the recruits practised landing their blows against these targets with a monotonous rapping that echoed round the depot. The more advanced recruits were being paired against each other and walked through the correct sequences of attack and defence in the event of a loose mêlée.

Cato, with Tincommius at his side, did the rounds of each instruction group to monitor progress and get to know his men. With the help of the Atrebatan nobleman, he was beginning to pick up the local dialect, and was delighted to discover that it was not so different from the smattering of Iceni Celtic that he had learned earlier that year. For their part the recruits, with the exception of Bedriacus, were beginning to respond quickly to Latin words of command. Macro had insisted on that; there would be no chance for translation when the men first faced the enemy.

The more Cato saw of Bedriacus, the more he despaired of the man. Unless he could grasp the fundamentals of military life Bedriacus would be more of a liability to his comrades than an asset. Yet Tincommius was adamant that the hunter would yet prove his worth.

'You haven't seen him at work, Cato. The man can track anything that moves on the ground. And he's lethal with a knife.'

'Maybe, but unless he can learn how to keep in formation and strike in sequence, we can't use him. We're fighting men, not beasts.'

Tincommius shrugged. 'Some say that the Durotrigans are worse than beasts. You've seen how they treat our people.'

'Yes,' Cato replied quietly. 'Yes, I have . . . Has it always been this way?'

'Only since they fell under the influence of the Dark Moon Druids. After that, they slowly cut themselves off from other tribes. The only reason that they fight alongside Caratacus is that they hate Rome above all else. If the legions quit Britain, they'll be at their neighbours' throats before the last of your sails crosses the horizon.'

'If we quit Britain?' Cato was amused by the thought. 'You think there's a chance of that?'

'The future is written in the dust, Cato. The faintest breeze can alter it.'

'Very poetic,' smiled Cato. 'But Rome carves its future in stone.'

Tincommius laughed at the riposte for a moment, then continued more seriously. 'You really do think you're a destined race, don't you?'

'That's what we're taught, right from the cradle, and history has yet to refute it.'

'Some might call that arrogance.'

'They might, but only once.'

Tincommius looked at Cato searchingly. 'And do you believe it?'

Cato shrugged. 'I'm not certain about destiny. Never have been. All that happens in the world is down to the actions of men. Wise men make their own destiny, as far as they are able to. Everything else is down to chance.'

'That's a strange view.' Tincommius frowned. 'For us there are spirits and gods that govern every aspect of our lives. You Romans have many gods as well. You must believe in them?'

'Gods?' Cato raised his eyebrows. 'Rome seems to invent a new one almost every day. Seems we're never satisfied unless we've got something new to believe in.'

'You're a strange one—'

'Just a moment,' Cato interrupted. He was watching a particularly huge Atrebatan warrior, covered in tattoos, screaming his war cry as he shattered his practice sword against the side of a target post. 'You there! You! Stand still!'

The warrior stood, breathing heavily as Cato took a spare training sword and approached the post.

'You're supposed to thrust with it. It's not a bloody hatchet.'

He demonstrated the prescribed blows, and tossed the sword to the warrior, who shook his head and spoke angrily. 'This is not a dignified way to fight!'

'Not dignified?' Cato fought down an impulse to laugh. 'What's dignified about fighting? I don't care how you look, I just want you to kill people.'

'I fight on horseback, not on foot!' the warrior spat. 'I wasn't raised to fight alongside farmers and peasants.'

'Oh, really?' Cato turned to Tincommius. 'What's so special about him?'

'He's one of the warrior caste, raised to be a cavalryman. They're quite touchy about it.'

'I see,' Cato reflected, well aware of the high regard for Celtic cavalry in the legions. 'Any more like him training with us?'

'Yes. Perhaps a few dozen.'

'All right, I'll think about it. Might be as well to have some mounted scouts with us when we start hunting Durotrigans.'

'Sa!' the warrior replied, and drew a finger across his throat with a grim smile.

Just then Cato noticed another man in the group, and froze. Glowering at him from amongst the ranks of the recruits was Artax. His face was covered in black and purple bruising and his broken nose was swollen.

'Tincommius, what's he doing here?'

'Artax? Training with the rest. Joined us this morning. The man's dead keen to learn the Roman way of fighting. Seems you made quite an impact on him.'

'Very funny.'

Cato looked at the man for a while, and Artax stared back, lips fixed in a thin line. The centurion was not sure that he cared to have a man he had so publicly humiliated serve alongside him. There was bound to be resentment simmering in the proud and arrogant Briton's breast. For now, however, it would be good politics to permit Verica's kinsman to remain in the cohort. In any case, if he had been moved to volunteer then maybe there was another side to him. Perhaps he nursed a desire to redeem himself and win back his pride. Maybe, Cato reflected. But it was best to be wary of him, for a while at least.

In the afternoons Macro took over the training and taught the recruits the fundamentals of mass manoeuvre. As ever, it was a slow business getting unaccustomed feet to march in step, but even the Britons could march, halt, wheel and change facing with minimal confusion within a week.

The training day ended with a quick march round and round the outside of Calleva, until dusk. Then the men were led back into the depot and, by sections, issued their rations to take away to cook. The hardest part of the strict routine for the natives to bear was the early end to their evening. As the trumpet sounded the second watch, the instructors strode up and down the lines of tents, screaming at the men to get inside and get to sleep, upsetting cooking pots over any fires that were not extinguished quickly enough. There was none of the drinking and raucous telling of tall tales and crude anecdotes that was so much a part of the Celtic way of life. Men undergoing a harsh training regime needed rest, and Macro refused to give way when Tincommius represented the views of a number of his warriors who had complained bitterly to him.

'No!' Macro said firmly. 'We go soft on them now and discipline goes down the shithole. It's hard, but no harder than is necessary. If they're complaining about being sent to sleep early then they're obviously not tired enough. Tomorrow I'll end the training with a run round Calleva instead of a march. That should do the trick.'

It did, but there was still an underlying resentment evident in the men's faces as Cato did his rounds each morning. Something was lacking. There was a vague sense of looseness, of incohesion, in the two cohorts. He raised the matter with Macro and Tincommius as they met in Macro's quarters one night after the first week of training.

'We're not doing this quite right.'

'What do you mean?' grumbled Macro. 'We're doing fine.'

'We were told to train two cohorts, and we've done it as best as we can. But they need something else.'

'What then?'

'You've seen how the men are. They're keen enough to learn how to use our weapons and manoeuvre as we do. But they don't have any sense of themselves as a discrete body of soldiers. We've got our legions, our eagle standards, our sense of tradition. They've got nothing.'

'What are you suggesting?' Macro smirked. 'We give them an eagle to follow?'

'Yes. Something like that. A standard. One for each cohort. It'll help give them a sense of identity.'

'Maybe,' Macro conceded. 'But not an eagle. Those are reserved for the legions. Has to be something else.'

'All right, then.' Cato nodded and turned to Tincommius. 'What do you suggest? Are there any animals that are sacred to your tribe?'

'Plenty.' Tincommius started counting them off on his fingers. 'Owl, wolf, fox, boar, pike, stoat.'

'Stoat?' Macro laughed. 'What the fuck is sacred about the stoat?'

'Stoat – swift and sleek, king of stream and creek,' Tincommius intoned.

'Oh, great. I can see it now: First Cohort of Atrebatan Stoats. The enemy will piss themselves laughing.'

Tincommius coloured.

'All right, so perhaps we don't use the stoat idea,' Cato interrupted before Macro caused too much damage to Atrebatan sensitivities. 'I like the idea of wolf and boar. Nice sense of wildness and danger. What do you think, Tincommius?'

'The Wolves and the Boars . . . sounds good.'

'What about you, Macro?'

'Fine.'

'All right then, I'll have some standards made up tonight. With your permission?'

Macro nodded. 'Agreed.'

Footsteps sounded down the corridor outside, and there was a rap on the door.

'Enter!'

A clerk stepped into the glow of the oil lamps. He held out a sealed scroll.

'What is it?'

'Message from the general, sir. Courier's just arrived.'

'Here!' Macro reached for the scroll, broke open the seal and ran his eyes over the message while his companions sat in silence. While Macro could read well enough, it was still something of an effort, and it took a moment to digest the contents of General Plautius' dispatch, as framed in the needlessly ornate language of staff officers with more time on their hands than they know what to do with.

'Well,' he drawled at length, 'apart from a few reservations about our scope of operations, and caveats about the amount of men we place under arms, it seems that the general has given us permission to arm the, uh, Wolves and the Boars.'

Chapter Nine

Some thirty miles to the west of Calleva, Vespasian gazed at the smoke billowing around the crest of a hill. The hillfort, scarcely two hundred paces across, was the smallest the Second Legion had razed so far. Yet the people who had built it had chosen the site well: a steep hill tucked into the bend of a fast-flowing river. The exposed flanks of the hill had been heavily fortified with earthworks, thick palisades and an inventive range of anti-personnel obstacles, some of which had clearly been copied, albeit crudely, from Roman originals. Crude copies they may have been, but they had inflicted some crippling injuries on the more unwary of the legionaries who had assaulted the ramparts at noon.

A steady stream of casualties passed the legate on their way to the dressing station just inside the Second Legion's marching camp: men with mangled and bloody feet where the barbed points of caltrops had driven through the soles of their boots; others with deep penetration wounds from being pushed on to the points of abatis by their unwitting comrades behind. Then there were men injured by the missiles that had rained down from the warriors fiercely defending the hillfort's gateway, men struck by everything from spears and arrows, to stones, old cooking pots, animal bones and shards of pottery. Finally, those who had been wounded when the legionaries had at last got to grips with the enemy. These men bore the usual stab, slash and crush injuries delivered by spear, sword and club.

It had been only two days since the legion had pitched camp a short distance from the outer defensive ditch, and already there were over eighty casualties – the equivalent of one century. The full butcher's bill, Vespasian knew, would be waiting for him on the campaign desk in his tent. That was why he was reluctant to turn away from the spectacle of the burning hillfort. If the Durotrigans continued to bleed his forces away at this rate, then before long the legion would be too weak to continue campaigning independently of the main body of General Plautius' army. That would be a bitter blow for Vespasian, who had counted on this opportunity to make something of a name for himself before his tenure of the legion came to an end. If his political career was to advance when he returned to Rome, then he would need a good military record to trade on. His family was too recently promoted to the senatorial class for him to depend on any help from the old boy network of those with an established aristocratic lineage. It constantly infuriated Vespasian that men less able than he were given greater responsibilities far earlier in their careers. Not only was this not fair, he spurred himself on, it was so obviously inefficient and prone to disaster. For the good of Rome, and her divinely sanctioned destiny, the system had to change . . .

The hillfort was the seventh settlement his legion had seized and sacked. This had taken only two days to achieve, yet there were certain aspects of the operation that Vespasian was certain could be improved. A handful of the enemy had managed to slip through his picket lines the first night the legion had camped in front of the hillfort. That was quite deplorable, and the optio in charge of the sentries had been broken back to the ranks. Next time, the legate firmly resolved, he would erect a palisade across any likely rat runs.

Then there had been only a limited supply of ammunition for his artillery engines to lay down a demoralising and destructive barrage upon the defenders. Although they had managed to damage the defences around the main gate, and take down a number of the enemy warriors, the catapults and bolt-throwers had failed to make a large enough breach. When the First Cohort had been thrown into the assault they met a far more determined resistance than they had anticipated. Next time the legion would wait until its artillery was able to lay down the kind of barrage that breaks the enemy's will to resist, Vespasian decided.

He felt guilty about rushing the assault, and was honest enough to admit the reason behind the order to attack was based on his ambition to have a high tally of victories to his name. Men had paid for his ambition with their blood. The legate quickly tried to repress the self-criticism by moving his thoughts on to a related problem. The Durotrigans were as fanatical in the final fight as they had been in the preparation of their defences. As a result there had been no survivors when the enraged legionaries had burst through the gateway and swarmed into the hillfort's interior. Every man, woman and child had been put to the sword.

That was a terrible waste, Vespasian reflected. Next time he would insist on taking as many of the enemy alive as possible. A good healthy Celt attracted a premium price in Rome at the moment with the latest fad for barbarian chic raging amongst those with more money than taste. Vespasian's share of the spoils would earn him a small fortune. Just as it would his men, if they could just manage to restrain their bloodlust long enough to realise that the pleasures of rape and pillage were transitory, whereas the profits from slave dealing could provide a nice supplement to their retirement funds. Orders must be given to the centurions to restrain their men when the legion took the next hillfort, Vespasian resolved. There would be no further waste of valuable lives, Roman or Briton.

Only the sheep, cattle and a few pigs had lived through the Roman assault. These livestock were being driven down the sides of the hill towards the camp. The animals would not survive very much longer than their erstwhile owners, and the delighted legionaries would be consuming fresh roast meat once again. Vespasian was pleased to have thus supplemented his supplies. However, the legion would soon be tackling a chain of much larger forts, and once again Vespasian would be reliant on a steady flow of supplies from the depot at Calleva.

Therein lay his most pressing difficulty. With Caratacus sending fast-moving columns to raid the legion's supply lines, Vespasian's men might be forced to live off the land. Worse, there would be no equipment to replace material lost in battle and losses due to wear and tear. It all depended on King Verica and the Atrebatans keeping to the terms of their alliance with Rome, and guaranteeing the safe passage of supply convoys through their territory. The formation of the two cohorts at Calleva might help ease the burden, and lift some of the weight of anxiety from Vespasian's shoulders. The legate was sure he could trust Centurion Macro with the task – and Centurion Cato, for that matter.

Vespasian smiled at the recollection of the moment he had informed the youngster of his promotion a few months earlier. Cato had been laying on a bed in the hospital at the Calleva depot. He had barely been able to blink back the tears of pride. Cato had great promise, and had justified the legate's estimation of his worth time and again. It would be interesting to see how the young man was coping with the responsibilities of his new rank, Vespasian mused. He was not quite in his twentieth year, and once Cato rejoined the Second Legion he faced one of the most daunting experiences a man could ever have in taking charge of the eighty legionaries of his first command.

Vespasian could clearly recall the painful self-consciousness with which he addressed the small patrol he had led when appointed a tribune nearly fourteen years ago. The grim veterans had listened to his introduction without comment but made no secret of their disdain for his lack of experience. At least Cato had that to bolster up his self-confidence. In the short time he had served with the Eagles Cato had already seen more combat than many legionaries did in a lifetime. And the youngster had been fortunate enough to be broken into his army life by Centurion Macro. Macro was as tough and reliable as Cato was intelligent and resourceful; the two complemented each other well.

The legate was sure that they would do a fine job of training Verica's men. Yet he longed to have them back with the Second Legion. When the two officers had fully recovered from their injuries, and the supply lines were safe, he would send for them straight away. A legion was only ever as good as the centurions who led it into battle. Vespasian wanted the Second to be good – to be a crack unit – and that meant making the most of men of Macro and Cato's calibre.

A trickle of sweat traced its way down his side under his linen tunic.

'Shit, it's hot!' he muttered.

One of the staff tribunes raised his head and looked towards the legate, but Vespasian dismissed him with a wave of a hand, as if swatting some annoying fly or gnat. 'It's nothing . . . Might have a swim later.'

Both men gazed longingly across the slope of the hill towards the river, a quarter of a mile away. The white forms of naked men lay stretched out on the grassy banks, while others waded and swam in the glistening water. Here and there the surface of the river burst into glittering spray where the more exuberant men were indulging in horseplay.

'I'd kill for a swim, sir,' the tribune said quietly as he wiped the sweat from his brow on the back of one hand.

'Some of them already have. Let them have their fun. But there's work to be done.' Vespasian nodded up at the remains of the hillfort. 'Keep 'em at it. I want nothing left by nightfall. Nothing that can be easily fortified.'

'Yes, sir.'

Even though it was late afternoon, the sun was blazing down on the legionaries toiling on the hill. The few native buildings that had escaped the incendiary bolts of the Second Legion's artillery battery had been set alight. Now the centurions were organising teams of men to tear up the palisade and hurl the timber down into the defence ditch. Soon the hillfort would be no more than a few black smouldering wooden frames and rings of ruined earthworks scarring the natural landscape. And after that, merely a fading memory in the minds of the legionaries who had destroyed the settlement and those natives who had ever passed this way.

Vespasian nodded his satisfaction at the progress in dismantling what fortifications remained, then turned away, striding back into the camp towards his headquarters. There were few men around, since most of those who were off duty were sheltering from the blazing sunshine in the shade of the leather tents that stretched out in neat rows on either side of the main thoroughfare. Even with both flaps open Vespasian knew that the interiors of the goatskin section tents would be stifling. That was why he had given permission for the cohorts that were stood down to swim in the river – they might as well be comfortable. Certainly they would be cleaner. To one who was raised in the Roman custom of frequent baths, the acrid stench of dirty sweating men was quite abhorrent. So the chance for the men to wash their clothes, and at the same time themselves, was to be seized with relish. Besides, the legion's chief surgeon was constantly urging his legate to force the men to adopt more hygienic practices. The men should wash as often as possible. Aesclepus claimed that it reduced the sick list. But then he would, being a follower of the more fancy eastern medical practices. Not that Vespasian lacked faith in Eastern medicine, it was just that he, like most Romans, believed that the East was a corrupt stew of soft, self-indulgent effeminacy.

The men of the headquarters guard stood rigidly at their posts in full armour. Vespasian wondered how they could stand the heat, and saw the glistening trickles of sweat running down their faces as he strode by them into his tent. Inside, the shade offered no respite from the hot, still air; indeed, it was actually far hotter inside the tent than outside. Vespasian beckoned to his steward.

'I want water. From the river. Make sure it's drawn upstream from the camp. I want a light tunic, my silk one. Then have someone take my desk outside and have an awning rigged over it. As fast as you can.'

'Yes, sir.'

When the man was gone, Vespasian stood still as his body slave unfastened the buckles of his armour and then lifted the breastplate away. Beneath, the thick military tunic was drenched with perspiration and clung awkwardly to his body as Vespasian impatiently lifted the hem and pulled it over his head. Outside the tent he could hear the commotion as men struggled to set up his campaign desk and the awning. There was too much to do and he shook his head when the body slave asked if he required a wash.

'Just get me the tunic.'

'Yes, master.'

The silk felt good against his skin – soft and smooth, and scented with dabs of the citron oil his wife had sent him from Rome. After he had briskly rubbed his matted hair in a linen cloth Vespasian made his way out of the tent and sat down at the desk. A clerk sat at one end, ready to take notes, and a neat pile of scrolls and wax tablets was waiting for the legate at the other end, beside the plain Samian jug and goblet. Vespasian poured himself some water and downed it in one go, relishing the cool and refreshing sensation. He poured another goblet and, with a deep breath, began to tackle the day's paperwork.

First he dealt with the casualty lists and unit strength returns. The numbers on the sick list for the Third Cohort looked excessive and he made a note on a wax tablet to call the cohort's commander in for a little chat. It was unlikely that Centurion Hortensius would sanction such a large number of men unfit for duty out of leniency. Vespasian well knew the man's reputation for driving his men on savagely, and while the legate approved of firm discipline, he would not countenance unnecessary harshness and cruelty. He sighed. It would not be an easy meeting. Most legates only served for a few years and it might seem presumptuous for Vespasian to lecture the vastly more experienced centurion on matters of discipline. Yet he could not afford to let the centurion abuse the men under his command, if that was what was causing the inflated sick list. If not that, then what? Either way, Vespasian had to know, and then deal with the problem.

Vespasian cast a quick glance over the latest set of supply and equipment inventories, approved them with a quick scratch of the stylus and thrust them towards his clerk.

'File them. We're low on javelin heads – add that to our next supply requisition.'

'Yes, sir.'

Next, Vespasian read the latest dispatch from Calleva. Centurion Macro reported that he had raised enough good men to fill out the ranks of two cohorts. Training had begun and, despite the language difficulties, the Roman instructors were making pleasing progress in training King Verica's men. Vespasian had received a copy of a message sent to Calleva, authorising Centurion Macro to arm his native cohorts, and was still surprised that the general had agreed to this quite so readily. While Plautius might be desperate for reinforcements to safeguard the supply lines south of the Tamesis, it was not accepted practice to raise units to serve in the province of their origin. There had been occasions in the past when loyal tribal allies had treacherously turned on their Roman friends. Despite Verica's obvious affection, and affectation, for all things Roman, he had not quite shaken off the taint of barbarian ways. Vespasian quickly drafted a reply to Macro, commending him for his efforts and requiring that the centurion report to him at once on any sign of disloyalty amongst the Atrebatans.

'Copy for our files and then get that off to Calleva at first light.'

'Yes, sir.'

Finally, the legate moved on to the intelligence reports. The small complement of mounted men that accompanied the legion served as scouts as well as messengers and last-ditch cavalry reserve. They had been patrolling the countryside around the hillfort, and the squadron commanders' reports provided detailed information about the surrounding geography, which was carefully added to the maps being prepared by Vespasian's clerks. The scouts also reported the presence of native settlements they encountered. The locals were then bribed or beaten into supplying information on any enemy troop movements they had observed.

Vespasian leaned over the desk to read the latest reports most carefully. He returned to an earlier report that seemed to confirm his growing suspicions. There was little doubt about it. The enemy was massing forces to the north, just this side of the Tamesis. Worse still, some natives claimed to have seen Caratacus himself amongst the enemy columns arriving in the area. Yet the latest dispatch from the general informed Vespasian that the main body of the enemy forces lay before Plautius and his three legions.

Vespasian stroked his chin and frowned. What was the wily Caratacus up to now?

Chapter Ten

The depot was filled with excited chatter as the Atrebatans examined their equipment. All morning Macro and Cato had sat with the quartermaster at his desk in the headquarters building, carefully noting the identification stamps on the equipment leaving stores to be issued to the natives. Silva had achieved his rank by virtue of an orderly mind, and by documenting everything; in another life he would have been an equally competent lawyer. Each of the Atrebatans was provided with sword, scabbard, belt, boots, tunic, helmet and shield from the vast stores of equipment in the depot. There was no spare armour, and the shields were the oval auxiliary issue, not the rectangular variant used by the legions. They would have been given javelins, but some bungling clerk at Rutupiae had not sent the fixing pins along with the iron heads and the wooden shafts.

'Wait till I find the twat responsible for this!' Macro growled. 'I swear I'll nail his balls to the floor the moment I find those pins.'

Cato winced in empathy.

'Nothing to do with me.' Silva shrugged with all the confidence of one who knew he could prove it. 'Must be a clerical error at army headquarters. The pins are probably in the depot somewhere, shipped under the wrong label. I'll have some of my lot hunt them down.'

Macro nodded his satisfaction. 'Still, I suppose we can cut the javelin training out for the moment, concentrate on the basics. Are those standards ready?'

Cato nodded.

'What did you use?'

'Tincommius got hold of some wood carvings, from gable ends.'

'Gable ends? Whose?'

'He said Verica wouldn't miss them.'

'Oh, great.'

'Anyway, we've got the head of a wolf and head of a boar. Well, pig actually. I fixed a couple of tent pegs in for tusks, and had the heads gilded. They look fine. I mounted them on a couple of spare vexillation standards and painted I and II Atrebatans on the leather drops.'

Macro eyed him coldly. 'You used vexillation standards?'

'I was in a hurry.'

'But they've been touched by the Emperor's own hand.' Macro was scandalised. 'Shit! If word of this gets back . . .'

'I won't tell if you won't.'

Macro struggled to control his temper. 'Cato, I swear, if you weren't still recovering from that bloody wound, I'd kick your fucking head in . . . Come on,' he continued in a resigned tone, 'let's go and see them.'

Cato locked the paperwork away in a chest and followed his superior outside on to the parade ground. The scene was chaotic, with the instructors hurrying round their charges to tighten straps, show which was the correct side to wear the sword and generally ignoring those who were trying to complain about their boots.

Macro gave them a brief moment to complete the arming, and then drew in a deep breath.

'FORM UP!'

The tribesmen were well used to the routine by now; the coloured pegs were no longer needed. They hurried into position and took their station from each section leader, automatically dressing their lines to ensure correct spacing between each man. Each century was made up of ten sections, and commanded by a legionary chosen by Macro. Six centuries made up each cohort.

'Who are those clowns?' Macro pointed to small groups of warriors on either wing of the parade ground.

'Cavalry scouts, sir.'

'Cavalry scouts . . . Aren't they, er, missing something?'

Tincommius stepped up to Macro's side. 'Verica's promised me some horses. Be here tomorrow.'

'Fair enough.'

'And I had a word with him about those standards. Thought it might be good for the men's spirits to have them presented by the king. I've sent word that we're ready for the ceremony. He'll be along directly.'

'That would be terribly nice of him,' Macro agreed sarcastically. 'Any thoughts on candidates for the posts of standard bearer?'

'One name comes to mind,' said Cato. 'Bedriacus.'

Tincommius laughed, incredulous. 'Bedriacus?'

'Why not? You said yourself he's strong and doesn't yield ground easily.'

'Yes, but—'

'And it keeps him from screwing up the formation.'

That was the clinching argument and Tincommius nodded his assent.

'Right then,' Macro continued. 'That's one. He's in your cohort then, Cato. Who else?'

'What about Tincommius for your cohort?'

'Me?' The Atrebatan prince looked unhappy. 'Why me, sir?'

'Macro could use a translator, isn't that right?'

'Rub it in, why don't you?' Macro grumbled.

'I'm honoured,' Tincommius managed to say.

'That's settled then, and by virtue of being the ranking officer, I'll have the first cohort of Atrebatans, with the boar as its standard.'

Cato touched his arm. 'Here's the king, sir.'

Verica was approaching on foot from the main gateway. Behind him was a small crowd of Atrebatan nobles in their finery. True to the ways of Celtic flamboyance, bright colours, startling patterns and burnished gold predominated. Macro's eyes instantly strayed towards the jewellery, automatically conducting a series of quick valuations.

'Hey, Cato,' he said softly, 'do you suppose the Durotrigans share the same dress code?'

Cato smiled indulgently and nudged Tincommius. 'He's only joking. Get the standards. They're just inside the door to my office.'

While Verica walked slowly by the massed ranks of his men, clearly impressed by the uniformed turn out, Tincommius ran off towards the headquarters building. He returned, at a more dignified pace, holding one standard in each hand, slanted against his shoulders. Verica finished his inspection and walked over to Macro and Cato.

'My congratulations, Centurion Macro! They look formidable.' He lowered his voice. 'But can they fight as well as they parade? In your professional estimation.'

'They're as good as any men I've trained. But I've never had to train men for battle so quickly. Most of them have never been near a fight.' Macro shrugged discreetly. 'I can't truly say. We'll have to wait and see, my lord.'

'Let's hope you won't have to wait long,' Verica smiled. 'Now, then. Let's get on with the ceremonies.'

Verica turned round to face his two cohorts and, drawing a deep breath, he began to speak. Cato was surprised at the rich timbre of the king's voice, and although he did not understand every word the delivery sounded wonderful. Verica, in his prime, must have cut a very impressive figure amongst the natives of this island. But there was something familiar about the delivery, something that Cato couldn't quite place, and he searched his memory for an echo of the feeling he was experiencing. Then it dawned on him; this was no natural gift, but the application of Greek rhetoric to a different cultural context, and he looked at the king of the Atrebatans with new respect. A man of many talents, and considerable learning.

Verica completed his peroration and wound up his address to his troops in a voice resonating with emotion. Cato was aware that Tincommius, at his side, was just staring at the ground without any expression on his face. Macro had noticed as well, caught Cato's eye and raised an eyebrow. But Cato had few doubts about the young Atrebatan nobleman; he had been just as nervous before his first battle. Cometh the battle, cometh the man. He was confident that Tincommius would do fine.

As soon as Verica had finished his speech the troops spontaneously roared their approval, drawing their swords and thrusting them up to the sky so that Cato looked upon a thicket of blades shimmering above the two cohorts.

'And now the standards, if you please,' Verica called over his shoulder.

'Give them here!' Macro snapped, realising how foolish it would look for Tincommius to hand him the standards only for one of them to be handed straight back to him. Tincommius did as he was told and moved to one side as Macro handed the stout shaft with boar's head to the Atrebatan king with as much formality as he could. Verica grasped the shaft and thrust it into the air, prompting his men to cheer even louder than before. As the cheering subsided Tincommius stepped forward and bowed his head to his uncle, before stretching out his hand. The cheering died away and the men watched expectantly. Then their king solemnly passed the standard to his nephew and, grasping Tincommius by the shoulders, kissed him fondly on each cheek. Holding the standard tightly in both hands Tincommius turned and marched over to take his place in front of the Boar Cohort.

Macro handed the wolf's head standard to the king as Cato barked out, 'Bedriacus! To the front!'

There was a moment's stillness before the man behind Bedriacus gave the hunter a gentle prod. Bedriacus started forward, marching as stiffly as he could as he approached his king. Even so, the moment the standard passed into his care, his face split into a wide smile and the craggy teeth glinted in the sunlight. He turned back to the Wolf Cohort, and impulsively raised the standard high over his head, thrusting it up and down. The air was split with a fresh wave of cheering as Bedriacus capered over to his comrades.

'Sure he was a wise choice?' Macro grumbled.

'As I said, keeps him out of the way. And now he's got that thing I think someone's going to have to kill the man before they get it off him.'

'Fair enough.'

Cato was suddenly aware of a mud-spattered warrior pushing his way through the nobles towards the king. When he reached Verica, he leaned forward to be heard above the cheering. Verica listened intently, and as soon as the man had finished speaking he waved him away. He turned to the two centurions, his eyes sparkling with excitement.

'Seems you'll discover the mettle of my men sooner than we thought.'

Macro had guessed the nature of the message and couldn't conceal his excitement. 'The Durotrigans are out!'

Verica nodded. 'That scout saw a column a day's ride to the south. They're almost certainly after the next convoy.'

'You can bet on it.' The prospect of action instantly erased any sense of decorum. 'How many?'

'He says no more than five hundred. Mostly infantry, with horse and a few chariots.'

'Marvellous!' Macro smacked his hands together. 'Bloody marvellous!'

Chapter Eleven

'Don't think I've ever seen a better spot for an ambush,' said Macro, hands on hips, as he surveyed the terrain around the ford. 'And there's just enough of the day left to make a clean sweep of it.'

'Thought you'd approve, sir,' smiled Cato.

They were standing with Tincommius on the edge of a small forested hill. Below them the ground sloped down to the track along which the Durotrigans would advance to ambush the convoy. Beyond the track the ground became soft as it fell away into a loop in the river. Half a mile to their right the river came close to the track before gently curving away, creating a natural bottleneck. To their left was the ford, and on the far side the track rose up towards a small ridge. The last century of Cato's cohort was just cresting the ridge and was soon out of sight. Cato had ordered them to cross a short distance down-river so that they would leave no trace of their passage on the far side of the ford. Macro's cohort was hidden along the treeline, with the scouts and their horses tucked down behind the forest, ready to charge round the base of the hill and close the trap. The mounted scouts had been given the pick of Verica's stables and would be able to run down any survivors with ease.

'The only way those bastards are going to get out of this is by swimming away,' Macro grinned, and turned to Cato. 'Of course, please don't feel obliged to attempt a pursuit down-river.'

Cato coloured. 'I just haven't had the time to learn properly. You know I haven't.'

'I'm just wondering if you'll ever find the time. I've seen cats with more affection for being dunked in water.'

'One day, Macro, I swear it.'

'You can't swim?' Tincommius was surprised. 'I thought all you legionaries could.'

Cato gave him a thin smile. 'Meet the exception that proves the rule.'

'Heads up!' Macro craned his neck to the right. A mounted scout had emerged round the corner of the hill and was galloping along the track, bent low over the flying mane of his horse. As he approached, Macro and the others trotted down the slope to intercept him. The man reined in, slewing his horse to a stop. He spoke very quickly, snatching for breath as the Celtic words tumbled from his lips. When he had finished, Tincommius asked him a brief question and then directed him to the cover of the forest. The scout dismounted and led his horse up the slope and out of sight.

'Well?' asked Macro.

'They're two miles down the track, marching in one column with a couple of riders a few hundred paces ahead of the main body. As we were told, about five hundred men.'

'Cato, you're going to have to bag those riders before they can raise the alarm.'

'That'll be tricky.'

'Let me deal with them.' Tincommius patted the handle of his dagger.

'You?' Cato asked. 'Why?'

'I want to strike the first blow for my people.'

'No.' Macro shook his head. 'You're not trained for it. You'd probably just give the game away. Besides, I need you close to me, to translate.'

Tincommius looked down and shrugged. 'As you wish, sir.'

'Right then, Cato,' Macro slapped him on the shoulder, 'back to your men. You know what to do. Just make sure we catch them both sides of the ford. See you later.'

Cato smiled, and then turned to jog down the track towards the ford, while the others climbed back up to their hiding place. Since he had begun to exercise again the pain in his side had become ever more pronounced, and the quick cross-country march of the last two days to intercept the Durotrigans had made it even worse.

Cato splashed down into the shallows at the edge of the ford and waded across the river. He emerged, dripping, on the far bank and ran up the track towards the brow of the low hill that followed the line of the river on each side. In the long grass on the reverse slope the centuries were already formed up in a line parallel to the river, in accordance with his orders.

'Lie down!' he shouted in Celtic, and the Atrebatans dropped out of sight into the grass.

'Bedriacus! On me!'

The wolf's head standard rose up from the ground, followed moments later by the grinning features of the hunter. He trotted over to the centurion and Cato indicated that they crouch down, before scurrying back up towards the crest of the ridge. As he reached the top, he moved to the side of the track and dropped on to his stomach. Bedriacus got down beside him, carefully laying the standard in the grass. Cato unstrapped his crested helmet and put it to one side as he propped himself up on his elbows and fixed his eyes on the track on the other side of the ford. For a moment his eyes wandered along the treeline where Macro's cohort was concealed but Cato saw no sign of movement. Everything was set, and the scene looked peaceful enough to allay the suspicions of the Durotrigans when they appeared.

The sun was low in the sky, and already the grass was tinged with a faint orange hue as a light breeze stirred the slender blades of green. There would be plenty of daylight for a few hours yet, and the Durotrigans would be wiped out long before they could escape under cover of darkness.

Half an hour must have passed before the advance scouts of the enemy column appeared half a mile from the ford. In all that time Bedriacus had kept absolutely still. Only his eyes moved, restlessly scanning the landscape, and Cato began to have more confidence in the hunter. Cato felt the faintest touch of a hand on his arm and looked round at Bedriacus. He nodded gently towards the track and Cato's eyes searched for a moment before they fixed on the distant figures. Two men on horseback, side by side, slowly approached round the curve of the hill. They came on cautiously enough, glancing around them as they approached the ford.

'Bedriacus . . .' Cato said softly.

'*Sa?*'

Cato pointed to the scouts and drew his finger across his throat, and then indicated the track just down from the crest. Bedriacus smiled his gap-toothed smile and nodded, shuffling away from Cato and easing his way behind a large tuft of spiky grass right at the edge of the track. Then he lay perfectly still again.

Peering carefully through the grass, Cato watched the scouts walk their horses up to the far side of the ford, no more than a hundred paces away. They stopped and exchanged some words, gesturing back in the direction of the main force of the Durotrigans. Then, both men slid from the backs of their mounts and led them into the pebble-bottomed shallows of the river. While the horses lowered their muzzles into the lazily sparkling current, one of the scouts waded a few steps downstream, untied his waist cords and unleashed a long golden arc of piss with a grunt of satisfaction that carried up the slope to Cato. When he had finished, the man just stood staring down-river for a moment and then hitched up his breeches and retied the waist cord. Making his way back to the riverbank, he sat beside his companion and gazed across the ford. Cato forced himself to keep still. With the sun low in the sky behind the scouts the crest of the hillock would be well lit, making any sudden movement easily detectable. But, as time crawled by, the scouts gave no sign that they were at all suspicious.

Something glittered in the distance and Cato shifted his gaze beyond the two scouts. A column of chariots came bumping along the track and the low sunlight was reflecting brilliantly off the highly polished bronze helmets of warriors riding on the small platforms above the axles. Fourteen chariots had come into sight before the first of the infantry appeared. With the sun almost at their backs Cato had to squint to make out any details of their equipment. His heart lifted as he saw that the vast majority were lightly armed and only a few sported helmets. Their shields were slung across their backs, and they carried a mixture of weapons, mostly swords and spears, together with large haversacks for their marching rations. At the rear of the loose column was a small band of more heavily armed warriors, and behind them a score of mounted men. Nothing that the Atrebatans could not handle, provided they stuck to their training and kept formation.

As soon as the scouts were aware of the approach of the column, they quickly stood up, mounted their horses, and crossed the ford. Cato ducked his head, turned towards Bedriacus and hissed. The hunter quickly met the centurion's eyes and nodded. Cato pulled his helmet on and clumsily fastened the ties with excited fingers before pressing himself down into the grass. He heard the voices of the scouts, chatting in cheerful tones in their lilting Celtic dialect, quite unsuspecting. Beneath the pitch of the voices was the distinct steady clumping of hoofs, and the breathy snorting of one of the mounts. As they came closer Cato felt his heart pounding against his ribs, and was momentarily surprised that the pain had gone from his side. He eased his sword from the scabbard and tightened his grip on his shield handle. The scouts sounded so near now that he was sure they must be only feet away. Yet time seemed to extend endlessly, and he watched a bee drone over his head, haloed by the orange glow of the sinking sun.

Then there were shadows darkening the longest blades of grass as the two Durotrigans started to cross the crest of the hillock. Surely they must see Cato now. Or if not Cato, then Bedriacus, or some sign of the hundreds of men lying further down the slope. But then Cato realised that his cohort was in the shadows. It would take a moment before the scouts' eyes adjusted to the gloom after the bright burnishing glow of the slope rising from the ford. He heard the scouts pass by him. They must be almost upon Bedriacus. Cato's mind raced. Why the hell didn't the hunter strike? What—

There was a gasp from the track, a horse whinnied, a man drew breath to shout and then there was the sound of a body thudding to the ground. By the time Cato had risen to his knees it was all over. Twenty feet away Bedriacus was easing one of the scouts from the back of his horse. The man was already dead: the handle of a knife protruding from under his chin, the blade punched up into his brain. His companion rustled in the grass for a moment, blood pumping from his slashed throat and spraying crimson droplets over the surrounding tussocks. Then he was still.

Bedriacus yanked his blade free of the scout's skull and wiped it clean on the man's long hair as he looked up at his centurion. Cato nodded his approval and pointed at the horses, nervous and a bit flighty at the shock of the hunter's sudden appearance. Moving slowly towards them Bedriacus whispered softly and gently ran his fingers across their silken flanks until his grip tightened on the reins.

'To the rear,' Cato whispered in Celtic.

The hunter nodded, clicked his tongue and led the animals down the track between the hidden centuries, and set them loose. Whatever magic he had worked on the beasts continued to have its effect and they calmly tore at the lush growth of grass beside the track. Bedriacus padded back to Cato to retrieve the wolf standard and took position beside his commander.

The rumble of chariot wheels on the other side of the ford was clearly audible now, and the moment Cato heard the first splashes he turned down the slope and, cupping his hands, called as loudly as he dared, 'Cohort! Stand up!'

Nearly five hundred men appeared from the long grass, silently rising to their feet, oval auxiliary shields tightly gripped. The splashing noises from the ford grew in volume as the infantry started across the river. They could no longer hear the noise of the chariots. They must have stopped, as Cato had guessed they would. The ford would make a perfect spot for the Durotrigans to camp for the night; largely hidden by the surrounding landscape, on dry ground with a river to water the horses and men.

'Draw swords! Make ready to advance!'

Cato turned back to Bedriacus. 'Stay here.'

The hunter nodded and Cato crept up the track, stretching his neck to catch sight of the situation at the ford. Half of the Durotrigan column was across. The chariot drivers were already unhitching their horses, while their warriors stood together at the edge of the river, clustered around a short, bull-like man with blond pigtails, who was evidently giving them their orders for the evening. As he looked round at his men, he suddenly froze, staring straight up the track in Cato's direction. He had seen the scarlet crest on the centurion's helmet, brilliantly illuminated by the rays of the setting sun.

'Shit!' Cato angrily slapped his sword against his thigh. He rose to his feet, plainly visible to the men down by the ford now. A ripple of alarmed shouts passed through the ranks of the Durotrigans. The men still in the ford stumbled to a halt at the sight of the figure on the crest of the ridge, sunlight glittering off his silvered armour.

'Cohort!' Cato roared out the order. 'Advance!'

The six centuries of Atrebatans marched up the slope, trampling down the long grass in their path. As they reached the crest they moved out of the shadows and formed a brilliant line of scarlet along the top of the hillock, with the gilded wolf's head sparkling on top of its standard, as if it were on fire. Down by the ford the leader of the Durotrigans had quickly recovered from his shock and was bellowing orders. Already the chariot drivers were desperately trying to replace the harnesses and traces on their horses. The infantry column stumbled forward again, spilling out along the far bank of the ford as they anxiously watched the approaching line of shields.

Beyond the ford Cato saw movement along the treeline of the forest, and then Macro and his cohort spilled down the slope and started forming up across the track, sealing the Durotrigans in the trap. At first the Durotrigans did not notice the new threat, so rapt were they by the vision of the red lines of Cato's men sweeping down the slope towards them. Then there were shouts, arms pointed and more and more heads turned to look back across the ford. A groan of despair and terror rose up from the disorganised mass of men with their horses and chariots.

Cato slowed his pace until he fell into a gap in the front line of his cohort, with Bedriacus directly behind him. The Durotrigans were no more than twenty paces away now, a mass of dark shapes silhouetted against the glittering sweep of the river. Straightening his shield in front of him, Cato raised his sword into the thrusting position.

'Wolves! Charge!'

With a roar, the Atrebatan line broke into a run down the last stretch of the slope and slammed into the confused enemy mass with a clattering, crunching thud. Immediately the air was rent by screams of agony and the sharp ring of edged weapons striking each other. The centurion thrust his shield in the press of bodies, jabbing his short sword through the gap between his shield and that of the Atrebatan warrior to his right. The blade connected with something, began to twist, and Cato rammed it home. He heard the man grunt as the breath was driven from his body, and then the Roman wrenched the sword back, blood spraying past the handle and on to his arm. To his right the Atrebatan warrior was screaming his war cry as he smashed his shield boss into an enemy's face and finished the man with a thrust to the throat. For an instant Cato felt a surge of pride that all the intensive training of recent days was paying off and these Celts were fighting like Romans.

Cato stabbed again, felt his blade being parried, and threw himself forward behind the shield, conscious that the Atrebatan line was steadily pushing forwards on either side. Even so, he must keep up the momentum of the initial charge. Keep going forward and the enemy would be shattered.

'Forward, Wolves!' Cato shouted, his voice shrill, almost hysterical. 'Forward! On! On!'

Men either side took up the cry and drowned out the Durotrigans' cries of panic and terror. Cato sensed a body at his feet, carefully lifted his foot and planted it on the other side as he prepared to strike his next blow.

'Roman!' Bedriacus cried out right behind him, and Cato felt the torso turn against the back of his calf. He just had time to glance down and saw the bared teeth of the Durotrigan warrior as he pushed himself up from the ground, and the arm drawing back a dagger. Then the man shuddered, grunted and collapsed as the spiked end of the wolf standard burst through his chest, just below the collarbone.

There was no time to thank the hunter, and Cato pushed on, driving the Durotrigans back towards the ford. Over their heads he caught sight of the other cohort as it piled into the rear of the Durotrigans' column, scattering the mounted warriors and cutting them down before they had the wit to try and escape.

Suddenly a huge shape burst out from among the Durotrigans in front of Cato: an older warrior, wearing chain mail over a light tunic. His sword arm was raised over his head and the long blade flashed in the sun as it reached the top of its arc. Then, as it slashed down, Cato threw himself into the man's body, punching his short sword into the chest. It caught on the chain mail, not penetrating, and the man gasped explosively as the blow drove the air from his lungs. His own blow faltered slightly, but because Cato had leaped inside its sweep the blade passed over his shoulder and instead the pommel caught the centurion a shattering blow on the side of his helmet, flattening the horsehair crest. Cato's jaw crashed shut on the end of his tongue as his vision exploded into a dazzling white for an instant and he fell back on the ground.

He heard a cry, he blinked and his vision cleared. The enemy warrior sprawled beside him, skull cleaved in two. Cato looked up and saw Artax standing over him. Their eyes met, and the Atrebatan noble's sword rose towards Cato's throat. For an instant Artax's eyes narrowed and with a cold chill of certainty

Cato knew that he would strike and have his revenge here in the heat of battle where Cato's death would be easily accepted. Just as Cato tensed himself to try to dive out of the path of Artax's blade, the Atrebatan smiled and wagged the point mockingly. Then he turned and was gone, lost in the press of men determined to crush the Durotrigans.

Cato shook his head, clambered back to his feet, and pushed forward. He was aware of the splash of water, and realised that the charge of the Wolf Cohort had carried them as far as the ford. One last effort and the fight was over. He could even hear Macro now, bellowing in triumph and battle-rage as he cut through the rear of the enemy column. Already Cato could see the red auxiliary shields and tunics of the other cohort through the shattered ranks of the Durotrigans before him. One of them suddenly looked at Cato, threw his sword into the river and kneeled down, pleading. Before the centurion could respond the Atrebatan warrior to his right thrust his sword into the man's chest. Cato looked round and saw that more and more of the enemy were foolishly lowering their weapons and trying to surrender. But the blood-crazed Atrebatans continued to strike them down where they stood.

'Stop!' Cato desperately shouted above the din. 'Wolf Cohort! Halt! STOP!'

When the warrior to his right made to strike down his next victim Cato whacked him on the arm with the flat of his sword, knocking the blade from the man's hand.

'Enough!'

Slowly sense returned to the Atrebatans as their Roman officers bellowed orders to end the carnage. The surviving Durotrigans were cowering on the ground or had retreated into deeper water, to escape the savage short swords, and waited for their fate, up to their chests in the bloodstained current.

'Cato! Cato, lad!' Here was Macro, beaming face spattered with blood. Beside him, holding the Boar standard was Tincommius, with a gash on his upper arm. 'We did it!'

But Cato was looking down-river, where a small band of the Durotrigans was escaping along the bank.

'Not yet, sir. Look there!'

Macro followed where Cato pointed. 'All right, get your men after them. I'll tidy up here.'

Cato turned away, splashing back to the edge of the ford, taking care not to stumble over the semi-submerged bodies. On the track he dragged Bedriacus clear of the mêlée and cupped a hand to his mouth.

'Wolves! Wolves! On me!'

The commanders of his centuries obediently came trotting over, but the Atrebatans had started mutilating the bodies of their enemies.

'Wolves!' Cato shouted again.

'What the hell are they up to?' muttered Figulus. 'Oh, no . . .'

Cato turned round and saw one of his men standing above a dead enemy, holding the hair in one hand as he hacked through the last few tendons of the neck with his short sword. Looking round, Cato realised they were all at it. He glanced back at the escaping Durotrigans.

'Centurion Cato!' Macro bellowed from the ford. 'What the hell are you waiting for? Get after them!'

Cato ran back down to his men, grabbed the nearest warrior by the arm and shoved him towards the Durotrigans. 'GO! MOVE!'

Some of the others looked up, saw what he was gesturing at and started after the enemy, tucking the severed heads under their arms.

'For fuck's sake!' Cato exploded. 'Leave the heads until later!'

They ignored him and started the pursuit along the river-bank. Cato stopped one man, and, with a grimace, pulled the head out of his hands. The Atrebatan warrior growled a warning and raised his sword threateningly.

'Tincommius!' Cato shouted, keeping an eye on the warrior. 'Get over here!'

The Atrebatan noble pushed his way through the men of the cohorts and approached Cato.

'Tell 'em to leave the heads alone.'

'But it's a tradition.'

'Fuck tradition!' Cato yelled. 'The Durotrigans are getting away. Tell our men to drop the heads and get moving.'

Tincommius shouted Cato's order to the cohort, but the only reaction was an angry muttering. By now the Durotrigans had a lead of nearly a quarter of a mile and were fading into the gathering dusk.

'All right,' Cato continued desperately, 'tell 'em they can keep the heads they're already carrying. We'll come back for the rest, I swear it.'

Contented by their commander's compromise, the Wolves left the mangled corpses, and few remaining prisoners, in the care of their comrades of the Boar Cohort. With heads jammed under arms, they began to chase after the Durotrigans, Cato leading the way and Bedriacus right at his heels.

The surviving Durotrigans were mainly from the chariots, and weighed down by their equipment. Despite their head start, slowly the distance closed as Cato sprinted after them, constantly looking back to make sure that his men were keeping up. Those unburdened by gory trophies stayed with him, anxious to win their share of the final glory of the skirmish. The rest struggled manfully with shield, sword and one or more heads.

There was no track on the riverbank and the Durotrigans

scrambled along, fleeing for their lives, their pigtailed leader among them. Some were injured and began to fall behind.

At last Cato had almost run down the rearmost man. His heart pounded as he pushed himself to move faster, and he prepared to sink his sword in between the man's shoulder blades. When no more than ten feet separated them the man glanced back and his eyes widened in fear. So he missed the small gap where part of the riverbank had crumbled, and tripped, sprawling on the ground at Cato's mercy. The centurion paused long enough to run him through and continued after the others.

Several more of the stragglers were dispatched, and the men of the Wolf Cohort remorselessly closed on the last group of Durotrigans as the light of the dying day cast long shadows of running men across the grass of the riverbank. In the end the enemy realised the game was up and their leader shouted an order to the surviving members of his band. They stopped running, turned to face their pursuers, and closed ranks, chests heaving for breath.

Cato and his men were in equally poor shape as they surrounded the score of warriors who stood in a tight semi-circle with their backs to the river. The enemy were clearly experienced fighting men, and even though they knew their end had come, they were preparing to take as many of the Atrebatans with them as possible.

But Cato still wanted to offer them a chance to live. He pointed to their leader and waved his hand down.

'Give in,' he panted in Celtic. 'Drop your weapons.'

'Fuck you!' The enemy leader spat on the ground before screaming something unintelligible to Cato. Whatever it was, it provided the Atrebatans with the excuse to attack and they rushed forward in a wave of scarlet. Cato went with them, Bedriacus shouting his war cry at his side. The stocky enemy leader wielded his sword two-handed in a fast whirling sweep, and the first of the Atrebatans keen to have the honour of killing him was almost cut in half as the heavy blade splintered his shield, severed his arm and tore through his midriff. More of the lightly armed Atrebatans fell at the feet of the small knot of Durotrigan warriors, but there was never any doubt about the outcome. One by one the Durotrigans fell, to be butchered on the ground. At last only their leader remained, blood-streaked and exhausted.

Cato pushed himself forward opposite the pigtailed man, raising his shield and readying his sword for the decisive thrust. His opponent sized up the skinny Roman and snarled his contempt. Just as Cato knew he would, he swung his great sword up to cut his Roman foe in two. The centurion threw himself forwards and down, rolling into the man's legs. The man fell headlong over Cato's back, right at the feet of Bedriacus. With a savage howl of triumph the hunter rammed his short sword into his enemy's skull with a dull crunch. The body trembled a moment, and was still.

As Cato climbed wearily to his feet Bedriacus hacked through the dead leader's stocky neck. It was hard going, and Cato turned away, looking towards the ford, nearly half a mile away. He was so tired that every breath was agony and he felt light-headed. When he looked back Bedriacus was trying to tie the head on to the standard's crosspiece using the pigtails.

'No!' Cato shouted angrily. 'Not on my bloody standard you don't!'

Chapter Twelve

Word of the victory swept through the muddy streets of Calleva as soon as the excited messenger, sent by Macro, brought the news to Verica. When the two cohorts approached the main gates they saw that a large crowd had gathered outside the ramparts. At the sight of the cohorts the crowd let out a roar of triumph and delight. The Durotrigans, who had been causing so much misery and grief over recent months, had at last been given a bloody nose. In truth, it had been no more than a brief skirmish, but desperate people are inclined to celebrate the smallest of victories. And so the wild cheering carried on as the column neared Calleva. A short distance behind the two cohorts trundled the wagons of the supply convoy the Durotrigans had hoped to intercept and destroy. They had linked up with the cohorts the morning after the ambush.

At the head of the Boar Cohort, Macro proudly marched along the track. Despite his reservations about the calibre of these natives, they had performed creditably enough. Most of them had been farmers a few weeks before, used to wielding nothing more deadly than a hoe. But now they had been blooded, their spirits were high, and they might yet win his grudging approval. The Durotrigan raiders had been completely crushed; only a handful had escaped by swimming down-river as night fell. Fifty prisoners had been taken, once the Roman officers had managed to restore control over their men and stop them competing for head trophies. The Atrebatans had been particularly merciless to the handful of former warriors of their own tribe discovered amongst the enemy, and few of these had been spared.

The Atrebatan renegades could not stomach what they saw as Verica's craven alliance with Rome. So they had deserted their tribe and fled to the ranks of Caratacus, fast swelling with all those who still kept faith with the past glories of the Celtic peoples. The surviving captives stumbled along between the cohorts in two lines, tethered together around their necks, with their arms bound behind their backs. While Macro hoped to sell them to the dealers waiting in Calleva, he was realistic enough to know that the Atrebatans would almost certainly want to make a bloody sport of them to slake their thirst for revenge. Such a waste, Macro sighed, when able-bodied slaves were fetching high prices in the markets of Gaul. Perhaps Verica might be persuaded to throw the injured and weak to the mob and save the best stock for a more profitable fate.

Macro turned back towards Tincommius. The young nobleman looked solemn as he held the gleaming boar standard as high as he could.

'Quite a reception.' Macro nodded towards the crowd at the gate.

'That lot would cheer anything . . .'

Macro could not help smiling at the youngster's cynicism. 'Go and ask Cato if he wants to join us. We might as well enjoy this together.'

Tincommius fell out of line and trotted back down the rippling column of red shields, ignoring the cheerful jibes and comments from the men as he passed. When he reached the junior centurion at the head of the Wolf Cohort Tincommius nodded a greeting to Bedriacus and fell in beside the Roman.

'Centurion Macro wonders if you'd like to join him when we reach the gates.'

'No.'

'No?' Tincommius raised his eyebrows.

'Thank him, but I think it'd look better if I marched in with my cohort.'

'He thinks you deserve the acclaim just as much as he does.'

'As do all these men.' Cato thought it only natural that Macro would want to relish his moment of triumph. Natural, but bad politics. 'My respects to Centurion Macro, but I'll march into Calleva at the head of my own men.'

Tincommius shrugged. 'Very well, sir. As you wish.'

As Tincommius returned to his unit. Cato shook his head. It was important that Verica and the Atrebatans saw this victory as their own. This was no time to indulge himself in some petty triumph, much as the prospect of being hailed as a hero appealed to some craven spirit within him.

Besides, the victory had been easily won. The enemy had been careless. No doubt they had grown used to freely scouring the lands of the Atrebatans for easy pickings. When they were fast enough to elude the legions and strong enough to overcome any pitiful attempts at resistance offered to them by the Atrebatans, it was small wonder that they had fallen so readily into the trap. A successful ambush was one thing, but how would these barely trained men cope when drawn up in front of an enemy prepared to fight a pitched battle? How quickly would their current high spirits fail them? Their proud boasting would soon die away. Their mouths would dry up. The icy grip of fear would tighten on their imaginations, squeezing out every dark dread that plagued men poised on the threshold of battle.

Now that he had been appointed to the rank of centurion the impulse to scrutinise himself was worse than ever. Despite the vibrant mood of celebration washing around him on all sides, Cato was consumed by a bitter melancholy and had to force himself to smile as he turned and met the inane grin of Bedriacus the hunter as the latter raised the Wolf standard high over his head and waved it from side to side.

Ahead the excited crowd was spilling forwards along the sides of the two cohorts, and Verica's bodyguards struggled to protect their king from being jostled. The cheers of the people of Calleva were ringing in Cato's ears as their ruddy features beamed into his face and rough hands clapped him on the shoulders. All attempt at preserving any sense of marching discipline collapsed and the men of the two cohorts merged with the rest of their folk. Here and there proud warriors were holding up the heads of their enemies for family and friends to admire. Cato felt a little sickened by the display, much as he had come to like and, in some small way, admire these men. Once the island had been pacified, the Atrebatans might be induced to adopt more civilised ways, but for now he must tolerate the quaint traditions of the Celtic way of war.

There was a sudden scream in the crowd, sliding into a high-pitched wail of grief and those nearby turned to look for its source. A woman stood with her hand to her mouth, teeth clenched into the flesh above her thumb as she gazed wide-eyed at a head being held up to the crowd by one of Cato's men. She wailed again, then lurched forward, snatching at the lank locks of hair, matted with dry blood. The warrior raised the head higher, out of her reach, and laughed. The woman shrieked, tearing at his arms, until the warrior cuffed her to the ground with his spare hand. From there she lapsed into sobbing that welled up from the pit of her stomach, and she shuddered as she clasped the hem of the warrior's tunic and begged.

'What's that all about?' asked Cato.

Like everyone else, Tincommius had been watching the confrontation. 'Seems that the head belongs to her son. She wants it for burial.'

'And its new owner wants it for a trophy?' Cato shook his head sadly. 'That's tough.'

'No,' muttered Tincommius. 'It's dishonourable. Here, take this.'

He thrust the Wolf standard at Cato and pushed himself between the woman and the warrior still holding the severed head aloft. Dragging the man's arm down, Tincommius spoke angrily, indicating the woman as he did so. The warrior shifted the head behind his back and responded with equal anger and indignity. At his words the people crowded around and shouted their support, although, Cato noted, a handful kept silent, implicitly on the side of Tincommius. The Atrebatan prince was in no mood to brook any disrespect to his rank, and suddenly smashed his fist into the warrior's face. The people around them shrank away as the warrior staggered back. Tincommius instantly kicked him hard in the stomach to wind him and keep him down. As the man snatched for breath, open-mouthed and staring wildly at his attacker, Tincommius calmly eased his fingers from the stiff hair of the severed head and gently offered it to the woman. For a moment she was still, then with a pained grimace she reached out for all that was left to her of her son. Oblivious to her grief, most of the crowd howled in protest and angrily pressed forward round Tincommius.

'STOP!' Cato cried out, drawing his sword and raising the Wolf standard above his head to command attention. 'SILENCE!'

The protests died away, and everyone looked towards Cato with hostile expressions, resentful of his intervention, yet nervous enough of the men of Rome to be wary of his wrath. Cato's eyes swept over the crowd, daring them to defy him, then came to rest on the woman sitting on the ground, cradling the head in her lap as she stroked its cold cheek.

Cato felt a great pain inside his chest as he watched the woman for a moment, empathising with her heart-rending sorrow. Then he swallowed and steeled himself before he looked up again at the crowd. He had to please these people, give them what they wanted for the sake of the alliance between Rome and the Atrebatans, however much it revolted him.

'Tincommius!'

'Centurion?'

'Give the head back to this man.'

Tincommius frowned. 'What? What did you say?'

'Return the head to this man. It's his trophy.'

Tincommius stabbed a finger at the woman. 'It's *her* son.'

'Not any more. Now do it.'

'No.'

'I order it,' Cato said quietly as he stepped up to Tincommius so that their faces were no more than a foot apart. 'I order you to do it . . . right now.'

For a moment Cato read the determination to defy the Roman in those striking blue eyes. Then Tincommius breathed deeply and glanced away at the faces of the crowd. He nodded slowly.

'As you command, Centurion Cato.'

The Atrebatan prince turned towards the woman and spoke gently to her as he reached out a hand. She looked at him in terror, still stroking her son's cheek, then shook her head. 'Na!'

Tincommius squatted beside her, speaking softly and he nodded towards Cato as he eased her hands away from the head. She regarded the centurion with a look of icy, fanatic hatred, until she was aware that the head was being taken from her. With a scream she snatched at it, but Tincommius pushed her down with his spare hand as he thrust the grisly trophy back to the warrior with the other. The man could not disguise his surprise and joy at having the head returned to him and instantly raised it up high; the crowd roared in triumph at the gesture.

The woman reached forlornly towards the head one last time, but Tincommius held her down, and she suddenly turned on him and spat into his face. The Atrebatan prince recoiled in surprise and with a last snarl the woman curled into a ball on the ground and wept bitterly. Cato pulled Tincommius away from the scene.

'It had to be done. There was no other way. You saw how the crowd reacted.'

Tincommius slowly wiped the spittle from his brow before replying.

'But it was her son. She had a right to do him honour.'

'Even after he'd betrayed his people? Betrayed her?'

Tincommius was still for a moment. Then he nodded slowly. 'I suppose so. I suppose it was necessary. I just felt . . .'

'I know how you felt.'

'Do you?' Tincommius looked startled for an instant, before his expression recomposed and he nodded. 'I suppose even a Roman understands grief.'

'You can count on it.' Cato gave him a faint smile. 'Now take the standard, and get yourself back to Centurion Macro.'

Fortunately there were no more such scenes as Cato and Bedriacus pushed themselves through the throng towards the entrance to Calleva. To one side of the gate Verica stood on a wagon, surrounded by his nobles and the royal bodyguard. Cato caught sight of the Boar standard unsteadily making its way over towards Verica and turned round to pull Bedriacus within earshot. The centurion pointed towards the Atrebatan king.

'Come with me!'

The hunter nodded, and before Cato could stop him, Bedriacus ploughed into the throng, roughly shoving his people aside to make way for his centurion. For a moment Cato feared that the mood might turn nasty, but the Atrebatans were in too good a humour to take offence. A huge quantity of the local beer had already been consumed during Calleva's celebration, and the returning soldiers were doing their best to make up for lost time as unstoppered jugs were passed around. Despite the hunter's best efforts it still took a long time before Cato finally joined Macro and Tincommius. After the tight, heaving mass of the excited tribe Cato was relieved when he finally managed to squeeze through the shields of the bodyguards into King Verica's presence.

'Centurion Cato!' Verica smiled, raising a hand in greeting. 'My heartiest congratulations on your victory.'

'The victory is yours, my lord. Yours, and your people's. They deserved it.'

'High praise indeed, from an officer of the legions.'

'Yes, my lord. And I'm sure the men will continue to justify your pride in them.'

'Of course. But for now we must let them celebrate.' Verica turned to Macro. 'I'd like to hear the whole tale after you've rested. Please be my guests tonight in my great hall.'

Macro bowed his head. 'We'd be honoured, my lord.'

'Very well, until then.'

Verica was helped down from the wagon. He turned towards the gate and his bodyguard quickly formed round him and opened a path through the crowd.

'Come on,' said Macro, after he had passed the word for the cohorts to reassemble in the depot the following morning. 'We've got to get that convoy inside the depot before the locals recover their wits enough to ransack it.'

* * *

Once Macro and Cato had escorted the supply wagons through the gatehouse into Calleva, it quickly became clear that many of the Atrebatans were not in a celebratory mood. Small groups of men squatted outside some of the huts, staring silently at the wagons as they trundled along the rutted street towards the depot. Only the children seemed oblivious to the tense division of sympathies in Calleva, and ran happily alongside the wagons, laughing and teasing the drivers. A rumour had carried through the town that some of the supplies would be distributed to the townspeople, and even the children were excited by the prospect of filling their bellies.

At the sight of Macro and Cato the children ran over to the two centurions who had defeated the Durotrigans and crowded round them, babbling away in their singsong Celtic.

'All right! All right!' Macro grinned as he raised his hands. 'See? I've got nothing for you. Nothing!'

Cato's grim expression had deterred all but the most thick-skinned of the children and he glared at the others who finally got the point and turned their attention to Macro.

'Why so glum? Hey, Cato!'

Cato looked round. 'Glum?'

'You look like someone who just lost a bloody fight, not won it! Come on, lad. Join the celebrations.'

'I will, later.'

'Later? What's wrong with now?'

'Sir.' Cato nodded down at the children.

One of the urchins, more daring than the others, was fiddling with the fastening of one of the silver medallions on Macro's harness.

'Why, you little bastard!' Macro cuffed the boy heavily on the ear. 'What the bloody hell do you think you're up to, sunshine? All of you! You've had your fun, now piss off!'

He swept them away with broad strokes of his arm, sending several sprawling on the street with a shrill chorus of shrieks and screams. The others kept out of the centurion's reach and giggled as he made a wild face at them. 'Grrrrr! Get out of here before the big bad Roman eats you all for his supper.'

When the children continued to dog his footsteps Macro's tiredness soon won out over his good spirits, and he turned and drew his sword. At the sight of the glinting blade the Atrebatan children fled screaming into the narrow alleys between the huts.

'That's better.' Macro nodded with satisfaction. 'Though they don't give up easily, that lot.'

'Blame it on the parents,' Cato smiled humourlessly. 'The speed the general's campaign is going, I shouldn't be surprised if those children are old enough to fight the Durotrigans before we're through. Or fight us.'

Macro stopped and looked at his junior centurion. 'You really are in a shitty mood, aren't you?'

Cato shrugged. 'Only thinking. That's all. Just ignore me.'

'Thinking?' Macro raised his eyebrows, then shook his head sadly. 'Like all things, there's a time and a place for that, my boy. We should be celebrating, like our lads. You, particularly.'

Cato raised his eyebrows. 'Me?'

'You've proved the quacks wrong. A few weeks ago they were all for giving you a medical discharge. If only they could have seen you in action! So let's celebrate. In fact, the moment we've seen these wagons safely inside the depot, you and me are going to have a drink. My treat.'

Cato tried not to show his alarm at the prospect of one of Macro's drinking binges. Unlike his friend, who enjoyed a cast-iron constitution, and quickly recovered from any amount of drink, wine and beer went straight to Cato's head, and he suffered the appalling consequences for days. Much as he was relieved to prove the surgeon wrong, there were other matters that required his attention.

'Sir, we must make a report to the legate, and the general, at once. Then we have to join Verica tonight.'

'Screw Verica. Let's get drunk.'

'We can't do that,' Cato continued patiently. 'We dare not cause any offence. Vespasian's orders were very firm about that.'

'Bloody orders.'

Cato nodded sympathetically, and then tried to change the subject. 'And we need to think about how the men performed at the river crossing.'

'What's there to think about? We kicked the stuffing out of the Durotrigans.'

'This time, maybe. When we next face them we might not have the advantage of surprise.'

'The lads did well enough,' protested Macro. 'Got stuck into the enemy like pros. Well, maybe not professionals – they'll never match up to the legions.'

'Quite. That's what worries me. They're overconfident. That can be a very dangerous thing. They need more training.'

'Of course they do!' Macro slapped him on the shoulder. 'And we're just the men to give them it. Why, we'll drill 'em into the ground, make them curse the day they were born. In the end they'll be as good as any auxiliaries serving with the Eagles. Mark my words!'

'I hope so.' Cato forced himself to smile.

'That's the spirit! Now let's get back to the depot and see if we can find a jar or two of wine.'

Chapter Thirteen

As soon as he left the celebrating crowd King Verica returned to the royal enclosure and summoned his council of advisors and the most trusted members of his family. He waited until the last of the kitchen slaves had left the chamber before he spoke. His audience was seated at a long table, watching their king with keen expectation. Each man had a drinking goblet, and several pitchers of wine had been left for them to share. Although Verica wanted sober heads to consider the situation, this was balanced with a need for each to speak his mind as honestly as possible, and wine, consumed in quantity, was generally a sound way to loosen tongues.

Besides his wise council, made up of the most ancient and respected of the Atrebatan nobles, the younger blades of nobility were represented by Tincommius, Artax and the captain of the royal bodyguard, Cadminius. Verica needed to sound out the broadest range of opinion in those upon whose loyalty his rule of the Atrebatans depended. The youngsters were looking excited and not a little awed to have been consulted in this manner.

After the latch on the door clanked down there was a moment of silence before Verica began. He knew the value of silence as a means of focusing attention. He cleared his throat and began.

'Before we get to the substance of this meeting I want you to swear an oath that whatever is said here this afternoon goes no further than these walls. Swear it now!'

His guests slid their hands down to their dagger hilts and made the vow in a collective low mumble. One or two looked slightly offended by the instruction.

'Very well, let's begin. By now you all know about the Atrebatan prisoners taken by our men at the ambush. Most of you were there to welcome the cohorts home. You may have witnessed the unfortunate scene when that woman discovered her son's head amongst the war trophies.'

Cadminius grinned at the memory, and a cruel sense of mirth at the woman's grim discovery caused some of the others to chuckle. Verica's face remained expressionless, except the eyes, which involuntarily widened with mild shock and a little anger at the laughter. When the laughter had died away he leaned forward slightly.

'Gentlemen, there's nothing in the situation that should amuse you. When our own people are killing each other there's no room for rejoicing.'

'But, sire,' protested an old warrior, 'the man betrayed us. All those men betrayed us. They deserved their fate, and that woman should never have shamed herself grieving for a son who turned on his own people, turned against his own king.'

There was a mumble of approval for these words, but Verica quickly raised his hand to quiet them.

'I agree, Mendacus. But what of the people out there? The people of Calleva, and our lands beyond the walls of the town? How many of them agree with us? Surely not all. How could that be when so many of them are now fighting with Caratacus? Fighting against us, as well as our Roman allies. Answer me that!'

'Such men are fools, sire,' Mendacus replied. 'Hot heads. The kind of impressionable young men who are easily talked into anything . . .'

'Fools?' Verica shook his head sadly. 'Not fools. Not that, at least. It's no easy thing to turn your back on your people. I should know.'

The king raised his eyes and scanned the faces around the table. His shame was mirrored in their expressions. He had fled for his life when Caratacus had marched on Calleva several years earlier. Fled in the night like a coward, and run to the Romans to throw himself on their mercy. They had seen that the old man might yet have a part to play in the Empire's designs and had given him shelter and looked after him well. But such hospitality is not without its price. When the time came, the favour was called in and the Emperor's chief secretary, Narcissus, made it quite clear to him that the price demanded by Rome for returning him to his throne was eternal obedience. Nothing short of that would do. And Verica had readily agreed, as he and Narcissus had both known he would. So when the legions landed in Britain, Verica marched with them. His kingdom had been returned to him at the point of a Roman sword and the many who had clung to their Catuvellaunian overlords ran into exile, or resisted and died.

Most of the men sitting round the table had been quick to see the futility of resisting the advance of the iron might of the legions. They had turned out to welcome Verica when four cohorts of legionaries escorted the former king through the gates of Calleva, up its winding streets, and into the royal enclosure. Only a year before they had been denouncing Verica as the weak and cowardly puppet of Rome. Now they had swallowed their pride and principles and were puppets themselves. And they knew it.

Verica leaned back in his chair and continued, 'Those men we call traitors are acting out of personal conviction. They have an ideal – something, I might add, that is in short supply around this table tonight . . .' Verica dared any of them to look him in the eye and deny it. Artax alone met the challenging glint in his king's eyes. Verica nodded his approval and continued. 'Such men believe in a bond that unites the Celts across tribal boundaries. They believe in a greater loyalty than mere blind obedience to their king.'

Cadminius shook his head. 'What greater loyalty could there be than that?'

'Loyalty to one's race, to one's culture, to the bloodline from which we spring. Isn't that a loyalty worth fighting for? Worth dying for?' Verica concluded quietly. 'Well . . .?'

There was a power to the old king's rhetoric that touched the souls of some of the men round the table. A few were even bold enough to nod their agreement. But Tincommius was staring at his uncle with a calculating expression.

'What are you suggesting then, sire?'

'What do you think I am suggesting? If indeed I am suggesting anything at all. I merely wished to try to explain to you why some of our tribe should choose to turn their backs on us, abandon their families and go and fight for Caratacus. We must try to understand what drives them to this if we are to resist such forces acting on the minds of others.'

'Must we also reconsider our alliance with Rome?' Tincommius asked quietly.

There was a stunned intake of breath as the other nobles wondered at the brash candour of Tincommius' question. King Verica stared at him, and slowly a smile formed on his lips.

'Why?' Verica asked his kinsman. 'Why would I want to reconsider?'

'I'm not saying you would want to, I'm merely suggesting that we need to consider all the choices before us. That's all . . .' Tincommius' voice tailed off as he became aware that all the other men were watching him closely.

'For the sake of argument,' Verica spoke in an even tone, 'what choices do we think we have? I'd appreciate it if everyone here spoke his mind. We must have a thorough airing of all the possible positions, even if we decide against them at the end of the evening. So, Tincommius, what choices are there, in your . . . humble opinion?'

The young man knew he had been set up, and tried not to sound resentful when he spoke after a short pause to arrange his thoughts.

'Sire, it's obvious that the fundamental choice is between Caratacus and Rome. Neutrality is impossible.'

'Why?'

'Caratacus might respect our neutrality, because it would cost him nothing and it could only serve to frustrate Roman operations. Rome would never countenance our neutrality, since our lands sit astride the main lines of supply for the legions. So we must choose a side, sire.'

Verica nodded. 'And so we have. The question is, my lords, have we chosen the right side? Will Rome win this war?'

The nobles reflected a moment, then Mendacus leaned forward on his elbows and cleared his throat. 'Sire, you know that I've seen the legions fight. I was there at the Mead Way last summer, when they crushed Caratacus. No one can beat them.'

Verica smiled. Mendacus had been there, all right – fighting alongside Caratacus, as had some of the others in this room. Verica had been there as well, albeit on the other side of the river, with Tincommius. But that was all in the past. After his restoration, Verica, under orders from Narcissus, had exercised clemency and welcomed the rebel nobles back into his court.

He had questioned the wisdom of this, but Narcissus had been adamant. The imperial secretary intended to set a wider example of Roman magnanimity. So Verica had returned their lands to the nobles and pardoned them. He glanced round the table, then back to Mendacus.

'Unbeatable, you say?'

'No one is unbeatable!' Artax snorted his contempt. 'Not even your Romans.'

' "Your Romans"?' Mendacus repeated, and raised an eyebrow. 'After *your* recent service under our two Roman centurions I'd have thought you'd have a greater sense of belonging?'

'What are you saying, old man? What are you accusing me of? I serve King Verica and no other man. I dare you to say different.'

'I merely wondered how successful your training had been?' Mendacus continued smoothly. 'How far you had been . . . Romanised.'

Artax smashed his fist down on the table, sending some the goblets flying. 'Outside! Outside now, you old bastard! You and me! We'll soon settle this.'

'Peace! Gentlemen, please . . . please,' Verica intervened wearily. The divisions between the Atrebatan nobles had been hopelessly complicated by the events of the last few years and now there was just too much political dirt that could be flung back and forth. Clarity of understanding and purpose were needed now more than ever. Verica glared at Artax until the latter subsided, and slumped back on to his bench with a sullen expression. Only then did Verica continue.

'The whole point of this meeting is to find a way that our people can be left in peace, or as much peace as is possible. Now, I know there are differences of opinion amongst us. Put them aside. Clear your minds of past injustices and grievances. Focus on the present situation. If I can summarise . . .

'For now we serve Rome, and Rome appears to be winning the fight. But, as Artax has pointed out, this does not mean that Rome must win in the end. They've been defeated in the past, and doubtless they'll be defeated again. If Caratacus can beat them, then what will be the consequences for us? I doubt we could expect much mercy from the Catuvellaunians. If the Romans look like being defeated, or are forced to retreat, we could abandon our alliance with them and join Caratacus. We would be perfectly positioned to deal the Romans a lethal blow from the rear. That would serve us well in the subsequent division of spoils amongst the tribes. Of course, there is the chance that we switch sides and then the Romans still win the war. In that case our nation would be finished. Rome would show us no pity, I am certain of that.' Verica lowered his voice to emphasise his final words. 'Everyone here would be hunted down and executed. All our families would have their land seized and they would be enslaved. Think on that . . . Now, what should we do?'

'You gave your word to Rome,' said Artax. 'You swore a treaty with them. Surely that's what matters, sire?'

Tincommius shook his head. 'No. What matters is the result of the struggle between Rome and Caratacus. That's all that matters.'

'Wise words, my boy,' Verica nodded. 'So then, who will win?'

'Rome,' said Mendacus. 'I'd stake my life on it.'

'You already have,' Tincommius smiled. 'But I'd say the odds are slowly shifting.'

'Oh, would you?' Mendacus folded his arms, and smiled back. 'On what basis do you offer such a view? From what vast experience of military matters? Pray tell. I'm sure we're all ears.'

Tincommius refused to rise to the bait. 'We don't have to

look very far for the evidence. Why would Rome be prepared to train and arm our two cohorts if they weren't desperate for manpower? They're overstretched. Their supply lines are more vulnerable than ever and Caratacus can send raiding columns far behind the Roman legions, almost with impunity.'

'I thought you'd beaten one of them a few days ago?'

'We defeated one column. How many more are out there? How many more can Caratacus send out? The raids are getting more frequent. The legions, for all their might in battle, are only as strong as their lines of supply. Destroy those and General Plautius and his army will slowly be starved of food and weapons. They'll be forced to retreat to the coast, harassed every step of the way. They'll be bled to death, by and by.'

Mendacus laughed. 'If it's so obvious the Romans will be defeated then why fight for them?'

'They're our allies,' Tincommius explained simply. 'As Artax said, our king swore a treaty with them and we must honour that. Unless, or until, the king changes his mind . . .'

Everyone looked surreptiously at the king but Verica was gazing over their heads, at the dim framework of timbers in the rafters. He appeared not to have heard the last remark and there was a troubled lull, filled with quiet shuffling and one or two coughs as the nobles waited for him to respond. In the end Verica simply changed the subject.

'There is something else we have to consider. Whatever decision I make about our alliance with Rome, we must consider how the other nobles will respond, and our people.'

'Your people will do your will, sire,' said Mendacus. 'They are sworn to.'

An amused expression flickered across Verica's lined face. 'Your desire to do my will is rather short-lived, wouldn't you say?'

Mendacus coloured with embarrassment and barely checked

anger. 'I speak now as one of your most loyal servants. You have my word on it, sire.'

'Oh, that's reassuring,' muttered Artax.

'Quite.' Verica nodded. 'With all deference to your word, Mendacus, I know that many of our finest warriors take a dim view of our alliance with Rome, as do many of our subjects on the streets of Calleva. I'm old. I'm not stupid. I know what people are saying. I know that there are some nobles who are already plotting to overthrow me. It would be strange if there weren't, and I fear it's only a matter of time before they take the chance to put their plans into action. Who knows how many of our warriors would follow their lead? But if I join with Caratacus, would my own position be any more secure? I doubt it . . .'

Mendacus made to speak but Verica raised his hand to stop him. 'Don't. Don't say another word about the loyalty of my subjects.'

Mendacus opened his mouth, then good sense got the better of sycophancy and he closed it with as much dignity as he could, and heaved his shoulders in a quick shrug of resignation as the king continued.

'I think the course I must take has become clearer to me tonight, my lords. It would seem that maintaining our alliance with Rome best serves the needs of our people. For the present, then, we play as full a part as we can in aiding the Emperor, and his legions.'

'And what of those people who oppose the alliance, sire?' asked Tincommius.

'The time has come to show them the cost of defying my decisions.'

'Why do harm to them, sire? Surely they're a small minority. Small enough for us to ignore.'

'No opposition to a king is ever small enough to ignore!'

Verica snapped. 'I've learned that to my cost once already. No, I've made the decision, and we must brook no opposition. I offered my opponents peace on good terms last time. If I allowed opposition to thrive, to the smallest degree, I would look weak this time, not merciful. I need to show General Plautius that the Atrebatans are utterly loyal to Rome. I need to show my people what will become of them if they ever defy me.'

'How will you do that, sire?' asked Tincommius. 'How can you?'

'A little demonstration is called for tonight, at the end of the feast. I have an idea. Once it's done then I can assure you it will be a very brave man indeed who even thinks about defying me and my authority.'

Chapter Fourteen

'What do you think?'

'I'm not quite finished yet,' muttered Cato, his gaze flickering up from the draft report Macro had dictated. The clerk had obviously had a hard time of it, judging from the number of crossed-out phrases and other corrections. Cato wished that Macro had not had quite so much to drink before beginning work on the report that would be sent to Vespasian and copied to the general. Now that the sun was setting, and they were sitting in the thin gleam of oil lamps at the wooden table in Macro's office, the effects of the wine were receding a little. Enough, at least, for them to check through the reports. Macro had been brief to the point of terseness in his description of the ambush, but the salient facts were there clearly enough, and the two senior officers who would read the document should be pleased with the result, Cato decided. Only the final part concerned him.

'I'm not sure about this bit.'

'Which bit?'

'Here, where you describe the situation in Calleva.'

'What's wrong with it?'

'Well,' Cato paused a moment to consider. 'I think the situation's a bit more complicated than you make it sound.'

'Complicated?' Macro frowned. 'What's complicated about

it? We've got the population onside and Verica's bathing in the glory won by his troops under our command. Things couldn't be better. Our allies are happy, we've given the enemy a good kicking and it hasn't cost us one Roman life.'

Cato shook his head. 'I don't think that we can count on the happiness of a great many of the Atrebatans, judging from what I saw today.'

'A few sour grapes, and that shrieking old crone you told me about? Hardly amounts to a serious threat of insurrection, does it?'

'No,' Cato admitted, 'but we don't want Plautius getting the wrong impression.'

'And we don't want to worry the general about a few malcontents when he's got his mind fixed on pushing the legions forward against Caratacus. Cato, old lad, the way to get on in this man's army is always to err on the side of optimism.'

'I'd prefer to err on the side of realism,' Cato replied bluntly.

'That's up to you.' Macro shrugged. 'But don't count on any further promotions. Now, if there's nothing else you think I should change, let's get tarted up and join the celebrations.'

The royal enclosure was brightly illuminated by torches blazing around its perimeter. Every noble, every warrior held in any regard, and the most respectable of the foreign traders and merchants, had been summoned to Verica's feast. As Cato glanced round at the loose throng of people making their way across the compound to the great hall he felt more than a little shabby. He and Macro were wearing their best tunics and, neat as they were, the dull material could not compare with the exotic weaves of the local Celts, or the fine cloth adorning the merchants and their wives. The only concession to luxury permitted by the centurions' military wardrobe were the torcs

Macro wore on his wrist and around his neck. The latter was a fine example. So it should be, having once been the possession of Togodubnus, brother of Caratacus. Macro had killed him almost a year earlier, in single combat, and the torc was already drawing admiring glances from Verica's other guests. For his part, Cato possessed only a single set of medallions and he tried to console himself with the thought that the character of a man was worth more than anything he might buy to display his worth.

'Going to be quite a night,' said Macro. 'Seems like half the population of Calleva must be here.'

'Just the well-heeled half, I think.'

'And us.' Macro winked at him. 'Don't worry, lad, I've never yet met a centurion who hasn't done well out of a campaign. That's the main reason Rome goes to war – to keep the legions grabbing enough booty to stay happy.'

'And distracted from any political ambitions.'

'If you say so. But personally I don't give a shit about politics. That's the traditional hobby of your aristocrats, not the likes of us footsloggers. All I want is enough loot to retire to a nice little estate in Campania, and have plenty left over to spend my twilight years in a permanent drunken stupor.'

'Good luck, then.'

'Thanks. Just hope I can get a little practice in tonight.'

They were greeted at the entrance to the great hall by Tincommius. The Atrebatan prince had discarded his army-issue tunic and wore a finely patterned native tunic over his leggings and boots. He smiled a greeting and waved the Roman guests inside.

'You joining us for a drink?' asked Macro.

'Maybe later, sir. I'm on guard duty right now.'

'What? No night off with the rest of us to celebrate?'

'All right,' Tincommius laughed. 'Once everyone's here.

Until then, I'm afraid I'm going to have to search you for weapons.'

'Search us?'

'Everyone, sir. Sorry, but Cadminius was very firm about that.'

'Cadminius?' Cato raised an eyebrow. 'Who's he? I'm not familiar with the name.'

'He's the captain of the bodyguard. Verica appointed him while we were away.'

'What happened to the last one?'

'Died in an accident, apparently. Got drunk, fell off his horse and caved his skull in.'

'Tragic,' Cato muttered.

'Yes, I suppose so. Now, sir, if I may. . .?'

Tincommius quickly frisked them both and then stood aside respectfully as they passed into King Verica's great hall. The cool evening air outside instantly gave way to a warm, clammy atmosphere. A large brazier fire burned at each end, providing a wavering orange glow throughout the hall, throwing strange shadows against the walls that made it seem as if all the guests were taking part in some slow, sinuous dance. Long trestle tables had been set up on three sides, lined with benches. Only Verica was permitted any trappings of splendour, and sat on an ornately carved wooden throne at the head of the hall, close to one of the fires. To either side of him the bodyguard stood armed and watchful.

'Our boy Verica doesn't seem to be taking any risks.' Macro had to raise his voice above the noisy chatter and loud drunken laughter of the native guests.

'Can't blame him,' Cato answered. 'He's old and nervous and wants to die peacefully in his bed, I imagine.'

Macro, who was looking around for something to drink, was not listening. 'Oh shit!'

'What's the matter?'

'There's only that crap beer again. Bloody barbarians.'

Cato was suddenly aware of a looming presence at his shoulder and turned quickly. A huge warrior with flowing blond hair and a broad face regarded the two Romans curiously. He had narrow eyes that glinted in slits of reflected firelight.

'Can I help you?'

'You Romans?' The accent was thick, but comprehensible. 'Romans who lead the king's men?'

'That's us,' Macro beamed. 'Centurions Lucius Cornelius Macro and Quintus Licinius Cato, at your service.'

The Briton frowned. 'Lucelius . . .'

'Never mind, old son. Let's keep it simple – Macro and Cato will do for now.'

'Ah! Those are the names I need. Come.' Without waiting for any reply to the abrupt summons the Briton turned and strode off towards the throne at the end of the hall where his king was seated, drinking goblet in hand, surveying the scene as he chewed on a leg of roast lamb. At the sight of Cato and Macro he tossed it to one side and sat up smiling. A brace of huge hunting dogs pounced on the half-eaten leg and wrestled for its possession.

'There you are!' Verica called out to the approaching soldiers. 'My guests of honour.'

'My lord.' Cato bowed his head. 'You praise us too much.'

'Nonsense. I was afraid you would be too busy with your paperwork to join us. I know, from all my years in exile, that you Romans are sticklers for making reports,' Verica smiled. 'But now Cadminius has found you. You are most welcome. There are two seats for you at the high table when the food is served. If it's ever served.' He turned towards Cadminius and made some sharp remarks that clearly stung the captain of the bodyguard. At his master's bidding he trotted off towards a small door at the rear of the hall. Through the small opening Macro could glimpse bodies stripped to the waist, glistening as they laboured over suckling pigs slowly roasting over cooking fires. The prospect of some juicy roast pork after several days of field rations made Macro's mouth water.

'Tell me, Centurion Macro, what are your plans for my cohorts now?' asked Verica.

'Plans?' Macro frowned. 'I suppose we keep training them. They're, er, they're still a bit rough around the edges.'

'Rough?' Verica looked a little unhappy.

'Nothing that a bit of hard drilling won't improve,' Macro rushed on. 'Ain't that right, Cato?'

'Yes, sir. A man can never have enough drilling.'

Macro shot him a warning look; this was no time for irony. 'Lads can't ever have enough drilling. Keeps them honed and ready to fight the enemy at any moment. You'll see the benefit of it soon enough, my lord.'

'Centurion, I want soldiers – not martinets. I want soldiers for the sole reason of killing my enemies . . . wherever they may be found.' With the lightest wave of his slender hands Verica indicated the figures crowding his great hall.

Cato felt a chill tingle the length of his spine at the king's words. He glanced quickly at the nearest faces amongst the guests, wondering how many amongst them harboured treachery towards their leader. Verica had noticed the change in the young officer's expression and laughed softly.

'Relax, Centurion! I doubt I'm in much danger, for tonight at least, thanks to your victory over the Durotrigans and their allies. We must enjoy the interlude for as long as it lasts. I merely wished to discover what plans you two have for taking the campaign to the Durotrigans.'

'Campaign?' Macro was startled. 'There's no campaign, my lord. The ambush was a one-off – a lucky chance we seized and made the most of. That's all there is to it. The cohorts, your cohorts, were only raised to protect Calleva and the supply convoys, my lord.'

'And yet they've proved their worth in the field. Why not make the most of the opportunity? Why not lead them against the enemy directly? Why not?'

'My lord, it's not as simple as that.'

'Simple?' Verica's smile abruptly disappeared.

Cato swallowed nervously and interceded to save Macro any further discomfort.

'What Centurion Macro means to say is that the cohorts need to be trained to prepare for a more demanding role. This victory is only the first of many, and when the Wolves and the Boars next march to war you can be assured they will crush your foes and extend the limits of your glory.'

Macro looked at him open-mouthed, but Verica was smiling again, and seemed to be satisfied at the prospect the young centurion held up to him.

'Very well then, gentlemen! Later, perhaps, I'll propose a toast to the continuing success of the partnership between my people and Rome. But here's Cadminius coming back. The food must be ready – it had better be. Would you two be kind enough to take a place at the table there? I'll join you in a moment.'

The two centurions bowed their heads and made their way over to the head table.

'What the fuck was that all about?' Macro hissed. 'What are you thinking of? Those two cohorts are for garrison duty, and convoy protection. And that's bloody well it. They'll not win him an empire, let alone a proper battle.'

'Of course not,' replied Cato. 'What kind of a fool do you take me for?'

'But you said—'

'I said what he wanted to hear, that's all. He'll change his mind soon enough, the moment his people start grumbling again. That's when he'll want his cohorts as close to him as possible.'

Macro glanced at his young companion. 'I hope you're right. I hope you haven't planted any stupid ideas in his head.'

Cato smiled. 'Who in their right mind would listen to the advice of someone barely old enough to be considered a man?'

'Who indeed?' grumbled Macro.

Chapter Fifteen

The kitchen slaves eventually arrived with the food, straining under the weight of the glistening spitted pigs. Cadminius' shoulders slumped with relief now that his master had stopped tapping his foot and eagerly eyed the steaming hunk of meat and crackling being carved for him. Verica had quit his throne and lay on a couch, Roman style, overlooking the hall, and his most privileged guests were arranged round the remaining three sides. The head table was on a raised platform so that the king and his party would have the best view of the entertainments. Macro and Cato had been given the place of honour to Verica's right, and the remaining places were taken up by Atrebatan nobles, and a plump Greek merchant with heavily oiled and scented hair. Close to Cato sat Artax, with Cadminius at his side. Their eyes briefly met, and Cato saw the same sullen arrogance in them that Artax had displayed at their first encounter in the depot. Tincommius, relieved from his duties at the entrance, had joined them and sat with the two centurions.

Cato gently nudged him as they waited for Verica to start eating. 'Any idea what the entertainment will be after the banquet?'

'None. The old boy's been playing it close to his chest. I think Cadminius is in on it. That's why he's been so nervous all afternoon – wants to make sure the big surprise is a real treat for the audience.'

'Doubt I'll last until then if I have to wait for my food a moment longer . . .'

There was a palpable tension in the great hall as the king's guests waited silently for their host to take his first mouthful. Only then could they eat from the heaped plates in front of them. With theatrical grace the aged king lifted a sliver of pork to his lips and nibbled a corner. Behind him a bodyguard raised the royal standard, paused and let it slip back down so that it rapped sharply on the flagstone. At once the guests burst into renewed conversation and began to cram their mouths with food and beer. Cato lifted his drinking horn and peered into the brew: a dark honey colour with a light froth around the edges. Cato felt sick at the sweet malty smell that filled his nostrils. How could these people drink this stuff?

'Whatever you do,' said Macro, close to his ear, 'don't pinch your nose when you swallow. Take it like a man.'

Cato nodded and braced himself for the first sip. The bitterness came as a surprise, a pleasant surprise, he decided. Maybe there was a future for British beer after all. He lowered the cup and started chewing on a crudely cut hunk of steaming pork.

'Good!' He nodded to Macro.

'Good? 'S bloody wonderful!'

For a while, the guests at the top table ate in silence, grateful for the food after the lengthy delay. Verica, older and more gracious than his nobles, held his meat in a delicate manner and nibbled steadily at the pork with his remaining teeth. His appetite quickly deserted him and, wiping his greasy fingers in the long fur of one of his hunting dogs, he raised his drinking horn and looked over towards the two Romans.

'A toast to our Roman friends, their Emperor Claudius and the swift defeat of those foolish enough to resist the advance of Rome.'

Verica repeated the toast in Celtic and his words were taken up by the others seated around the table – although not all of them looked quite as enthusiastic as their king, Cato decided, as he glanced sidelong at Artax. Following the king's cue Cato raised the horn to his lips.

'You must drink it in one go,' whispered Tincommius.

Cato nodded, and as everyone began to down their ale he forced himself to begin, fighting off the impulse to gag at the heavily flavoured brew, and clamping his teeth shut to strain the clutter of sediment and other solids at the bottom of the horn. He wiped the flotsam clear of his lips with the back of his hand and set the nearly empty vessel back down on the table.

Verica nodded approvingly and signalled to one of his servants to refill the drinking horns before looking meaningfully at Macro, who was busy tearing off a piece of crackling with his teeth.

'Sir,' muttered Tincommius.

'What? What is it?'

'You're supposed to return the gesture.'

'What? Gesture?'

'Make a toast.'

'Oh!' Macro spat the crackling out and raised his drinking horn. Everyone was looking at him expectantly and suddenly Macro couldn't think of anything suitable to say. He glanced beseechingly towards Cato but his friend seemed to watching Artax closely and did not notice his appeal for help. Macro quickly licked his lips, coughed and then began with a stammer, 'R-right then. To King Verica . . . his noble cohorts and . . . his interesting tribe.'

As Tincommius translated, the native guests frowned at the strange and awkward choice of words. Macro flushed with embarrassment, little used to such social ceremonies. He tried to continue in a more appropriate vein.

'Long may the Atrebatans remain faithful allies of Rome. May they profit from the speedy defeat of the barbarian tribes of this island.'

Macro raised his cup and beamed at the other guests. With the exception of Verica, they looked uncomfortable. Artax pointedly sipped from his horn before setting it down and glaring at the meat on his Samian ware platter.

As the other guests looked away Cato whispered, 'That might have been phrased better.'

'Well then, you do it next time.'

The Greek merchant delicately placed his drinking horn to one side and started a quiet conversation with his neighbour, neatly drawing the man's attention away from the tense silence on the head table. Verica was eating some dainty pastries and waved a finger to attract Macro's attention.

'Interesting toast, Centurion.'

'My lord, I did not mean to offend. To be honest, I've never been called on to do this kind of thing before – at least not in front of a king. I just meant to celebrate our alliance, and look forward to the future . . . that's all.'

'Of course,' Verica replied smoothly. 'No offence was taken. At least not by me, although I can't speak for some of the hotter heads in my family.' He nodded towards Artax with a laugh. 'And young Tincommius there – his father was no friend of Rome while I was in exile. Took a while for Tincommius to see that his father was wrong. Now look at him.'

Cato saw a flush of embarrassment in the young prince's face, before Tincommius replied, in Latin, 'I was younger then, sire, and more easily led. Since I've learned more of Roman ways, and fought alongside them, I've come to respect them and value what they have to offer the Atrebatans.'

'And what do they have to offer the Atrebatans?' the Greek merchant interrupted. 'I'd be interested in your opinion. To hear it straight from the horse's mouth, as it were.'

'I should have thought a Greek would know.'

The merchant smiled at Tincommius. 'Forgive me, but we've lived under Roman rule too long to remember what it was like before. And since I'm investing quite a fortune in developing trading links with the new province I merely wish to understand the native view of the situation. If you wouldn't mind, young man?'

Tincommius looked round the table uncomfortably, meeting Macro's curious gaze only briefly.

'Tincommius, tell us,' Verica urged him gently.

'Sire, like you I've lived a while in Gaul and have seen what you saw: the great towns with all their marvels. And you've told me of the endless network of trade routes that bind the empire together, of the wealth that flows along them to the very fringes of their world. Above all, you told me there is order. An order that tolerates no conflict, that forces its subjects to live in peace with each other, or face terrible consequences. That's why Rome must prevail.'

Macro watched Tincommius closely. The man seemed sincere enough. But you could never really tell with these Britons, Macro reflected as he downed another horn of ale.

'As long as I can remember the Atrebatans have been fighting other tribes,' Tincommius continued. 'Always the Durotrigans, and lately the Catuvellaunians, who so cruelly threw you out, sire.'

Verica frowned at the tactless mention of his eviction from the throne by Caratacus and his tribe.

'I never knew any different. War was our way, the way of all the Celtic tribes of this island. It's why we live in these poor huts, why we can never have our own empire. We have no common purpose, so we must bind ourselves to one who has . . . the Emperor.'

'Although Caratacus hasn't been doing too badly on that score!' Macro chipped in, with a faint slur to his voice. Cato did a quick calculation and realised with alarm that Macro was already into his fourth horn of beer – on top of all the wine he had been drinking that afternoon. Macro nodded at Tincommius. 'I mean, look how many tribes he's managed to line up against us so far. If we don't kill the bastard quickly, who knows what trouble he's going to cause our general?'

'Quite!' The merchant gave an oily smile. 'But we wouldn't want to give any credence to the idea that the enemy has any realistic chance of defying the legions, would we, Centurion? What does the other Roman officer think, I wonder?'

Cato, who had been looking down in embarrassment while Macro spoke, raised his head to see that everyone was looking at him expectantly. He swallowed nervously, and made himself pause a moment to avoid blurting out anything that might make him look foolish. 'I speak with little authority on the matter. I've been serving with the Eagles for less than two years.'

The merchant's eyebrows rose. 'And already a centurion?'

'A good one!' Macro nodded, and might have continued to say more, but Cato quickly continued.

'In that time I've fought the Germans as well as the Catuvellaunians, the Trinovantans and the Durotrigans. They're all fine warriors, as are the Atrebatans. But none of them can hold their own against the legions. When a nation takes up arms against Rome there can only ever be one result. The outcome may be delayed by the odd setback, or by an enemy who resorts to the kind of hit-and-run tactics Caratacus seems to be employing against us now. But the legions will always be on the advance, grinding down every enemy strongpoint under their heels. In the end, even Caratacus will not be able to keep the field. There will be no one left to supply him with new men, new equipment and, above all, food and shelter.'

Cato paused to allow Tincommius to translate his words to those with little or no Latin. Artax snorted with contempt and shook his head.

'I mean no disrespect to the tribes of these lands,' Cato continued. 'In fact, I have come to admire them, in many ways.' A vision of the gory trophies his men had taken after the ambush flashed through his mind. 'There are many great warriors amongst them, and that's their weakness. An army comprised of a multitude of such men has little value unless it is moulded into a single entity with unity of purpose, unity of action and subordinate to one will. That's why the legions will beat Caratacus. That's why they will destroy everyone that opposes them until Caratacus submits. By now he should know that he cannot win. He should know that he can only prolong the suffering of the tribes by continuing to resist, and it makes me grieve.'

'Grieve?' interrupted Verica. 'You grieve for your enemy?'

Cato nodded. 'Yes, my lord. I desire peace above all else. A peace in which both Rome and the Celtic people can profit. Peace will come one way or another, but always on Rome's terms. The longer some other tribes persist in refusing what you and the Atrebatans have come to accept, the longer the suffering on all sides will continue. It's pointless to resist. No, it's worse than pointless. It's immoral to cause suffering to continue when you know you can't prevail.'

There was a short silence after Cato's words had been translated. Then Artax spoke quietly.

'I wonder if it's immoral for us to be to be forced into such a position in the first place. Why has Rome come to these shores? What need has she of our poor hovels, when she has great cities, and immeasurable wealth of her own. Why does Rome seek to take what little we have?' Artax glared at him.

'You may have little now, but join the Empire and you will have more in the future.' Cato replied.

Artax laughed bitterly. 'I doubt that Rome is here for *our* benefit.'

Cato smiled. 'You're right, for now. But in the end you might live to see this land a better place, thanks to Rome.'

Tincommius frowned. 'But I still don't understand why Rome would want to come here if there was no profit in it.'

'Politics!' said Macro. 'Bloody politics. Gives the nobs a chance to grab themselves a little glory. They get a nice write-up in the history books, while us rankers get ourselves killed. That's the way it is.'

'So it's all about making Emperor Claudius look good?'

'Of course.' Macro looked shocked at the naïvety of the British prince. 'Besides,' he continued, wagging his finger, 'what makes you think it's any different over here? That's what all war is about – making some bastard or other look good. Now, where's the bloody beer gone? Slave! Come here!'

While Macro waited for his horn to be filled up Cato quickly changed the subject.

'My lord, when do we get to see this mysterious entertainment you've arranged for us?'

'Patience, Centurion! First we must eat.' Verica nodded towards some of the noblemen's wives talking loudly at one of the nearest feasting tables. 'I doubt some of the more sensitive stomachs would care to continue eating when they see what I have in store for them.'

When the last platters had been taken away by the kitchen slaves, Cadminius called for the guests to rise while the long trestle tables were pushed to the sides of the hall by the kitchen slaves. Verica retired to his high throne with a commanding view down the length of the hall, and those at the head table joined the rest of the packed throng sitting and standing at the cleared tables. More jugs of beer emerged from the kitchen and were distributed amongst the crowd, already loudly drunk, and the smoky rafters echoed to their shouts. The Celts kept to themselves and the foreigners formed a small, conspicuous group close to Verica's throne. Only Tincommius remained with them. Artax and the other high nobles had joined their warrior friends and were competing amongst themselves to see who could drink the most ale in one go. A handful of those with weaker stomachs had already passed out, while others were puking against the stone walls of the hall.

'Your king certainly knows how to throw a party,' Macro smiled approvingly as he looked round the crowd. 'Can't bloody wait for the main event.'

'Won't have to,' Tincommius replied. 'Look there.'

The main doors were swung open and some of the body-guards manoeuvred a covered wagon into the centre of the hall. The noise from the crowd took on an excited tone as everyone strained to get a good view of the wagon. The wheels ground on the flagstones as something lurched under the cover and Cato heard a deep grunt above the hubbub of the guests. The bodyguards heaved the wagon into position just short of the dead centre of the hall. The covers were drawn back and the guests gave gasps of surprise and delight at the sight of two cages. In the larger was a huge boar, wild with fright and rage. In the smaller cage were three long-limbed hunting dogs, with deep chests and grey wiry hair, which rose stiffly along their backs as they growled at the boar.

'This should be good!' Macro beamed, and drained his cup. 'Haven't seen a decent animal fight since Camulodunum.'

Cato nodded.

While some of the guards levered the cages into position others began lighting torches from the fire at the far end of the hall. They then formed a loose circle around the end of the wagon, casting a bright pool of illumination over the makeshift arena. When all was ready Cadminius gave the signal for the cages to be opened. The boar was first, goaded out of the cage and off the end of the wagon with prods from the spears of the men assigned to control the beast. It lumbered forward and made for a gap between the torch carriers. They hurriedly closed ranks and waved the crackling brands before its snout until it retreated to the centre of the hall, grunting deep in its throat as its dark eyes rolled at the sight of the drunken raucous crowd. The dogs were led out of their cage on leashes, already straining to get at the boar, and requiring all the strength of their handlers to hold them back. The boar eyed them nervously, swaying as if dancing to some slow music. The dog handlers pulled in the leashes, unslipped the chains and then held on to the collars tightly.

On his throne Verica sharply rapped a goblet against the end of the wooden arm rest, the sound carrying over the general laughter and excited taking of bets. His guests dutifully fell silent, and then there were just the strangled whines of the dogs and the crackle of the fires and torches. Rising from his chair Verica's voice carried the length of the hall. Cato whispered a translation to Macro.

'He apologises for the hounds, but there were no wolves to be had in such a hurry. He means the fight to honour the Wolf and the Boar Cohorts, and their commanders. The winner of the fight will be given the chance to do one more deed to complete the evening's entertainment.'

'One more deed?' Macro turned towards Tincommius. 'What's that all about?'

Tincommius shrugged. 'No idea. Honestly.'

'As long as the old boy keeps the show going,' said Macro.

Verica raised his arm, held it up for a moment, then swept it down with a dramatic flourish. The dog handlers released their grips on the collars and scurried for safety behind the ring of torches. The crowd roared as the hunting dogs bounded towards the boar, still swaying on its feet, but now with its shoulders hunched and jaws open and ready to deal terrible injury to its attackers.

The first dog to reach its prey jumped for the boar's neck, jaws open, ready to clamp shut on the boar's throat and tear it out. But the boar struck first, swatting the hunting dog to one side with its snout as if it weighed no more than a sack of feathers. The dog crashed to the stone floor with a sickening thump and a pained yelp. The crowd cried out: a strangely dissonant chorus of groans from those who had backed the dogs, and cheers from those who had bet on the boar. The other dogs, true to the intelligence of their breed, swerved aside and took up positions either side of the boar, feinting with sudden darting movements and snaps of their great jaws. Slowly shifting round, the boar kept its tusks lowered, ready to deal slashing blows at any dog that came within reach.

'No two dogs alive are ever going to kill that beast,' Macro yelled above the roar of the crowd. Cato nodded his agreement; the first dog was still struggling to get back on to its feet.

'Don't be too sure, sir,' Tincommius shouted back. 'Have you ever seen this breed before?'

Macro shook his head.

'They come from across the sea.'

'Gaul?'

'No. The other way. I think you Romans call it Hibernia.'

'I've heard of it,' Macro bluffed.

'From what they say, it's so inhospitable that I doubt even a Roman would consider invading it. They breed good hunting dogs, though. Like those three. That boar's in for the fight of its life.'

'Care to take a wager?'

'What's the stake?'

'Wine. I'd kill for something to take away the taste of this beer.'

'You haven't had a problem with it so far.'

Macro slapped a friendly arm around the young Celt's shoulder as he grabbed the nearest jug of beer. 'Soldiers will drink anything to get shit-faced. Anything, old son. Even this crap. Cheers!'

'An amphora of wine on the dogs then, sir,' said Tincommius, as he casually shrugged off the centurion's arm.

'Done.' Macro raised the jug to his lips and guzzled a deep draught, brown drips spilling from each side of his mouth.

The first dog had finally regained its feet, and took position between the other two, warily waiting for a chance to dash in and snap at the boar. The latter now had to keep watch in three directions and its great dark head was constantly turning this way and that. Cato watched the spectacle with a curious mixture of sentiment. He had been to the games in Rome a few times and had witnessed the bloody contests between beasts before. They had always struck him as somehow distasteful, even as he had thrilled to the tense atmosphere, and the excitement of the fights themselves, but afterwards he was left feeling guilty, sordid. Now, this fight between the hunting dogs and the boar induced that same sense of compulsive interest and repulsive self-awareness.

There was a sharp yelp of agony as the injured dog feinted towards the boar's leg and retreated too slowly to avoid the tusks. Now it lay where it had fallen, belly and chest ripped open. Glistening intestines slipped out into a smeared pool of blood as the dog jerked its legs in a pathetic attempt to rise back to its feet.

Macro smacked his thigh. 'I can taste that wine already!'

The boar took advantage of the fallen adversary, padded over and slashed at the stricken dog. In doing so, it brought about its own destruction. In a blur of grey one of the other dogs leaped on to the boar's back and buried its teeth in the boar's bristling neck. The third dog flew in from the side and clamped its teeth round the boar's throat. Instantly the boar lowered its head, frantically trying to shake its attackers loose, but the powerful jaws held firm, crushing its windpipe. Slowly the beast weakened, the flailing of the trotters gradually fading. At last the boar swayed a moment before its legs gave out and it slumped to the ground, with the dogs' jaws still clamped below its head. A roar of delight erupted from the crowd, drowning out the groans of those who had backed the boar.

'Fuck!' Macro shouted. 'Where'd they get that boar from? Bloody fight was rigged!'

Tincommius laughed. 'Shall I collect my wine in the morning, Centurion?'

'Do what you like.'

Cato ignored them, and watched in sick fascination as the dogs tore out the boar's throat with all the vicious efficiency of many years of training for their role in the hunt. Once the boar was quite dead the handlers moved in and carefully replaced the leashes on their charges. The dead dog was heaved back into the wagon, then half a dozen bodyguards strained with the loose mass of the boar, struggling to lift it on top of the mangled form of its erstwhile foe. Then the wagon was trundled out of the hall again, and a fresh murmur of excitement rippled through the crowd as they waited for the final entertainment of the evening.

After a short pause the bodyguards returned to the hall. Between each pair of men was a prisoner, bound hand and foot, eight of them in all. The prisoners were dragged to one side of the hall, close to the guests sitting on the tables. Opposite them were the hunting dogs, blood dripping from their muzzles and flanks still heaving from the frenzied effort of their attack on the boar.

'What the hell's going on?' asked Macro, turning to Cato. 'They're our bloody prisoners!'

Cato looked at the prisoners. 'I know them. They're the Atrebatans we captured . . . Oh, no. He can't mean to . . .' The colour drained from Cato's face.

'What?' Macro asked. 'What's going on? Who are you talking about?'

Verica was back on his feet, and the guests needed no prompting for silence as their gaze flickered between the king of the Atrebatans and the bound prisoners, glancing anxiously at the dogs. Verica started to speak. This time there was no warmth in his voice, no hint of his earlier hospitality.

'The traitors are to die. If they had been Durotrigans they might be spared with a less terrible end. There can be no easy death for those who turn on the tribe that gave life to them and demands loyalty unto death in return. Therefore, they will die like dogs, and their bodies will be cast into Calleva's midden for the carrion to feed on.'

'He can't be serious,' Cato whispered to Tincommius. 'Surely?'

'Not with my bloody prisoners!' Macro added indignantly.

Before they could raise any protest, a figure leaped from the crowd and ran into the space between the hunting dogs and the huddle of bound prisoners. Artax pointed to the prisoners and addressed his king and the guests in a deep, commanding voice.

'What's he saying?' asked Macro.

Cato could understand some of the words, but Artax's passion had been inflamed. That, and far too much beer, made the torrent of words hard to follow. Cato grasped Tincommius' arm and nodded at Artax.

'He knows those men,' Tincommius explained. 'One is his half-brother. Another is his wife's cousin. He wants them spared. No member of our tribe should die like this.'

A grumble of assent accompanied Artax's words, but Verica pointed a trembling finger at the prisoners and replied in tones of indignant anger, 'They will die. They must serve as an example to all those who would side with the enemies of the Atrebatans and Rome. The lesson must be learned. All those who even think of betraying their king must learn of his terrible revenge.'

A loud chorus shouted in support of their king and an empty goblet sailed across the hall and struck one of the prisoners on the head. Artax was shaking his head as the king spoke, and then raised his voice in protest once again. Tincommius translated for the two Romans.

'He begs the king not to proceed with this, that such an atrocity will turn the people against him.'

Verica angrily shouted Artax down and gestured to Cadminius to remove the nobleman. Artax continued to shout his protests, even after the captain of the bodyguard had grasped his arm, wrenched Artax towards the entrance of the great hall and thrust him outside. Without any further delay Cadminius strode over to the huddle of prisoners, took the nearest man by the chain binding his wrists together, and dragged him into the centre of the hall. Left alone, the prisoner struggled desperately against his bonds and screamed for help. The dog handlers unleashed the hunting dogs and snapped their fingers to attract the animals' attention. The victim was pointed out, then there was a moment's awful silence, even from the prisoner, who watched the dogs, transfixed. Then the word of command was given and the dogs leaped on the helpless man. He screamed, shrill and terrified as the dogs mauled his face, struggling to reach his throat. Then the screams were muffled, and there was only a gurgling whimper. Then nothing. The man went limp. The dogs jerked the corpse around like a straw training dummy.

There were cheers from the crowd. But as Cato looked round it was clear that many of the guests were horrified by the spectacle, and they watched in silence.

'Shit . . .' muttered Macro. 'Shit . . . That's no way for a man to die.'

'Not even a traitor?' Tincommius said acidly.

The handlers pulled the dogs back from the body. It was no easy task now that their killer instincts had been roused. Two men dragged the body away as Cadminius selected his next victim and dragged the man out on to the blood-smeared flagstones where the first man had died. Cato looked towards Verica, hoping that the king might change his mind, even now. But the cold look of satisfaction on Verica's face was clear for all to see.

Cato nudged Macro as he stood up. 'I have to go. I can't watch this.'

Macro turned towards him and Cato was surprised to see that even this hardened veteran had seen more than he could stomach.

'Wait for me, lad.'

Macro heaved himself off the table, and struggled to find his legs under the influence of all the beer he had drunk that evening. 'Give me a hand here. Tincommius, we'll see you in the depot tomorrow.'

Without tearing his eyes away from the fate of the second man Tincommius nodded faintly.

Cato slipped Macro's arm over his shoulder and made his way towards the main entrance, keeping as far from the dogs as possible, while the beasts tore into another victim. Outside the hall Macro could take it no more. He wrenched himself free, staggered a few steps away from his friend and doubled over, vomiting. While Cato waited for Macro to finish, a steady stream of Atrebatan nobles left the great hall, struggling to hide their feelings of horror and disgust as, behind them, fresh screams split the night air.

Chapter Sixteen

'When did this arrive, exactly?' General Plautius tossed the report on to the desk of his chief clerk. The man turned the scrolled parchment the right way up, and by the light of an oil lamp he ran his finger across the top until he found the index notation.

'Just a moment, please, sir,' the clerk said, rising from his chair.

The general nodded, and turned away to stare out through the tent flaps. The sky was overcast and even though the sun had only just set it was already quite dark. Dark and hot. The humid air was oppressively uncomfortable, and threatened a break in the good weather of the last few days. Much as a storm might clear the prickly discomfort in the atmosphere, the general dreaded the effect it would have on his transport vehicles. Of all the places he had fought in his career, this ghastly island had to be one of the worst as far as the weather went. Even though this land never knew the long savage cold of a German winter or the seething heat of the plains of Syria, it had a peculiar discomfort all of its own.

The problem with Britain was that the island was always more or less damp, the general decided. A few hours of rainfall left the ground slick with mud, and any attempt to move even a small force of men and vehicles across it soon churned up a glutinous bog, which sucked the army down and caked everything in filth. And this was on the good ground. Plautius had seen enough of the British marshes to know how impenetrable they could be to his forces. The natives, however, had made good use of their local knowledge and had sited a number of their forward camps on whatever firm ground existed in the vast spread of wetlands west of the upper reaches of the Tamesis. From these bases Caratacus was launching his raiding columns through the thin Roman screen of fortlets. They struck at the legions' supply convoys, destroyed the farms and settlements of those tribes allied to Rome and, when ambition caused the warlike Celtic blood to rush to their heads, they even took on the odd Roman patrol or minor fortification.

The invaders were dying the death of a thousand cuts, and Plautius had used up all his political capital with the Emperor; there would be few reinforcements from now on. And those troops that were sent to Britain would be accompanied by the inevitable terse and sarcastic request from Narcissus for a speedy defeat of Caratacus. The last such message had left the general in an icy rage, with its politely worded sting: 'My dear Aulus Plautius, if you are not using your army for the next few months would you mind awfully if I might borrow it awhile?'

The general ground his teeth in frustration at the easy manner in which those in the lofty marbled offices on the Palatine sent out their orders with no regard for the actual conditions in which their far-flung soldiers fought to defend or extend the Empire. Plautius tensed his shoulders and smacked his fist into the palm of the other hand.

A handful of clerks were still busy at desks placed along the side of the tent, and looked up as he gave vent to his frustration. Plautius glared at them.

'Where the hell has that bloody clerk got to? You!'

'Sir?'

'Get off your arse and go and find him.'

'Yes, sir.'

As the man hurried off to the staff tents Plautius rubbed his shoulder. The damp had got at his joints terribly over the winter and a nagging ache in his shoulders and knees still made itself felt at times. Plautius longed for the dependable heat and sunshine of his villa at Stabiae. Endless hot summer days spent with his wife and children by the sea. He smiled at the way nostalgia had worked its way with him. The last time he had spent a summer with them was nearly four years ago – a few days snatched after a brief trip to Rome to report on the situation on the Danube. The children had spent the time bickering endlessly, tormenting each other, and every adult in earshot, with shouts and screams of rage and injured indignation as they snatched toys from each other. Only when the children had been trusted to the care of a nurse had their parents had time to pay uninterrupted attention to each other. Plautius' imminent return to his command lent a difficult poignancy to those few days and he had sworn to his wife that he would come home for good as soon as he was able.

Now he was still in the early stages of another campaign. Likely as not he'd die of old age before these Britons gave in. He would never see the children grow up, never grow old and grey with his wife.

The thought of his family filled him with an aching longing. At the start of the year his wife and children had attempted to join him on the campaign, but with such disastrous consequences that there was no possibility of them ever returning to Britain.

Plautius knew that he was close to the limit of his physical and mental endurance. A younger man was needed for this job, someone with enough energy to see the job through; to see Caratacus roundly defeated, the British army crushed and the tribes of this land cowed into submission to Rome. Someone like Legate Vespasian, the general reflected.

Although Vespasian had come to command a legion some years later than most of his peers, he had made up for the delay in his hard-driving style. That was why Plautius had singled Vespasian and the Second Legion out for detached duties across the southern sweep of Britain. So far the legate had proved more than worthy of his superior's trust, smashing his way through a succession of hillforts. The trouble was that Vespasian was being rather too successful. Racing ahead of his supply columns the legate had risked exposing his slender lines of communication to enemy raids in force. Plautius had reined him in for a while, ordering him to finish off the remaining hillforts on the Atrebatan borderlands before the Second Legion struck south to seize the large island off the south coast. When the time came for Vespasian to move, the gap between the two Roman forces would widen. Vespasian was equally aware of the danger, and had voiced his concerns in the most recent report that he had sent to his superior. Everything hinged on the continued loyalty of the Atrebatans.

A muffled rumble of thunder rolled across the landscape and General Plautius looked out over the undulating lines of tents towards the horizon where a dull flash of light heralded a break in the weather. A cool light breeze suddenly sprang up and filled the folds of the tent flap with a soft rustling. Plautius would have a good view of the approaching storm. His headquarters had been erected on a slight rise at the centre of the camp. The engineers had protested that the site was not suitable, being some distance from the intersection of the two main thoroughfares, but Plautius wanted to be able to see out over his legions and, beyond them, the palisade and, beyond that, the fall of the downs leading away to the west. In the distance a cluster of tiny sparks of light were visible at one end of a heavily wooded hill.

That was the camp of the enemy, under their commander, Caratacus. For days now the two armies had sat several miles apart, their scouts sparring every so often across the ground that separated the two forces. Plautius knew that if he attempted to move in on the enemy the shrewd Caratacus would simply retreat and draw the legions after him again. So it would go on, and all the time Caratacus would be falling back on his supply lines, just as Plautius was stretching his even further. Accordingly Plautius had halted his advance for the moment and was busy consolidating the chain of forts protecting his flanks and rear. When that was done he would push his legions forward and force the Britons to give more ground. Eventually they must run out of land and would have to turn and fight. Then the Romans would crush them utterly.

That had been the plan, at least, Plautius smiled bitterly. But the plan was always the first casualty in any military operation. A few days ago he had received a worrying report from Vespasian about the presence of another British army forming up to the south of the Tamesis. It was possible that Caratacus intended to join the two armies, in which case he might attempt to steal a march on Plautius and rush south and destroy Vespasian. Alternatively, the Briton might feel strong enough to take on the main Roman force. That, Plautius chided himself, was purely wishful thinking, and he must pay more respect to Caratacus, particularly in the light of the document he had thrown down on his chief clerk's desk: another report, this time from that centurion Vespasian had left in command of the tiny garrison at Calleva.

Centurion Macro detailed a recent skirmish he had won with one of the enemy raiding columns. That was fine, and the general had read through the account with some relish. Then he had reached the section where the centurion reported on the situation in Calleva. Despite Macro's attempt to sound reassuring, by the time Plautius had finished the report his anxiety was fully aroused.

'Sir!'

General Plautius turned round as the chief clerk entered through the entrance at the back of the tent.

'Well?'

'Five days ago, sir.'

'Five days?' Plautius said quietly. Behind him lightning flickered over the deserted farmland. Moments later the thunder cracked and the clerk flinched.

'Quintus, would you mind explaining why this took five days to come to my attention?'

'It seemed like a low-priority report, sir.'

'Did you read it?'

'Yes, sir.'

'All of it?'

The clerk was silent for a moment. 'I can't remember, sir.'

'I see. This isn't very satisfactory, is it, Quintus?'

'No, sir.'

The general stared at him a moment, until the clerk could no longer meet his eyes and looked down, shamed.

'Make sure that every report is read in its entirety from now on. I will not tolerate this kind of cock-up again.'

'Yes, sir.'

'Now fetch me Tribune Quintillus.'

'Tribune Quintillus, sir?'

'Caius Quintillus. Joined the Ninth a few days ago. You should find him in their mess. I'll speak to him in my private quarters at his earliest convenience. Go.'

The clerk turned and hurried out of the tent, keen to get away from his general as quickly as possible. As Plautius watched him disappear through the tent flaps he wondered at his leniency. A few years ago he'd have broken the man back to the ranks for that kind of error. He must be going soft. Further proof of his failings as a commander in the field.

The storm was right over the camp as Tribune Quintillus read through the report. Lightning flashed white at the gap in the curtains left open at the entrance to the general's tent. For the instant of each burst of brilliant light the raindrops outside were held still like weightless shards of twinkling glass in a lurid white-washed world. Then the lightning was gone. At once thunder cracked and boomed, rattling the goblets resting on the table between the two officers. Then there was just the drumming of the rain on the leather tent and the moan of the wind.

General Plautius studied the man sitting opposite, head bowed over the scroll as the tribune scrutinised the report. Quintillus came from one of the older families that still owned several vast estates south of Rome. The tribune was the latest in a long line of aristocrats with distinguished careers in the senate. His appointment to the Ninth Legion was in return for a large interest-free loan Quintillus' father had made to General Plautius some years earlier. But there was more to the appointment than the settling of an old debt. The tribune had connections to the Imperial Palace and the only reason why any aristocrat would cultivate such connections was because he was driven by ambition. Very well, Plautius reflected, an ambitious man was generally a ruthless man, and that would serve the general's current purpose well.

'Most interesting, I'm sure,' Quintillus said, placing the scroll down on the table and gracefully sweeping up his goblet in the same gesture. 'But might I ask what this has to do with me, sir?'

'Everything. I'm sending you to Calleva at first light.'

'Calleva?' For the briefest instant a look of surprise flashed across the tribune's fine features, and then the mask of supreme indifference dropped back in place. 'Well, why not? It would be nice to take in some of the local culture, before we eradicate it . . .'

'Quite,' Plautius smiled. 'But do try not to give the impression when you meet the natives that alliance with Rome is necessarily a euphemism for surrender. Tends not to go down very well.'

'I'll do my best . . .'

'. . . Or be killed in the attempt.' The general's smile had disappeared and there was no mistaking the serious tenor their conversation had taken on. Quintillus took a sip and lowered his cup, watching his superior intently.

'You have something of a reputation as a smooth operator, Quintillus. That is precisely the skill I need for this task. I hope your reputation has been fully earned.'

The tribune nodded modestly.

'Good. You only arrived a few days ago, I recall.'

'Ten days ago, sir.'

'Ten days. Not much time to familiarise yourself with our operations, then?'

'No, sir,' Quintillus admitted.

'Well, never mind. Narcissus speaks highly of you.'

'That's uncommonly generous of him.'

'Yes . . . very uncommon. That's why I've chosen you. I need a good pair of eyes and ears on the ground in Calleva. Centurion Macro is understandably reticent in expressing his concern about the firmness of King Verica's grip on his people. He's enjoying his independent command and doesn't want senior officers breathing down his neck. To be fair, he's doing an excellent job. He's raised a scratch force of Atrebatans, and they've already scored a victory over the Durotrigans. Quite an achievement.'

'Yes, sir. Sounds like it.' The tribune nodded at Macro's report. 'Must be a good officer, and the men he's trained sound formidable, as natives go.'

The general fixed him with a cold stare. 'Condescension is a dangerous luxury. That's a hard lesson I've had to learn from these Britons.'

'If you say so, sir.'

'I do. And you should profit from my experience.'

'But of course, sir.' Quintillus bowed his head.

'Very wise . . . Macro's success has put me in something of a difficult situation. You see, King Verica is an old man. I doubt he'll live through another winter. So far he's managed to carry his people with him in making a treaty with Rome. But there are some in his tribe who are not so well disposed towards us.'

'Ain't that always the way?'

'Sadly. The trouble is that these discontents are quite influential, and they might just put forward a candidate when the tribe's council of elders meets to choose a successor to Verica. If that man is successful . . .'

'Then we'd be in the ordure, sir.'

'Right up to our necks. Not only will we have a hostile tribe to our rear, but Centurion Macro will have provided them with the wherewithal to cause a lot of damage to our supply lines.'

'Did he exceed his orders in training and arming these cohorts, sir?'

'Not at all. He was acting on Legate Vespasian's orders.'

'Then the legate is responsible.'

'No, he sought and received my approval for the formation of the cohorts.'

'I see,' the tribune responded tactfully.

'The trouble is that Centurion Macro has not been very forthcoming about the divided loyalties of our Atrebatan friends.'

'You could order him to disband the cohorts, and confiscate their weapons.'

'That's not very practicable. You don't know these Britons like I do. About the most disrespectful thing you could do to a British warrior is take his weapons away from him. They treat them as a birthright. If we seize their weapons then there's every chance we'll have a revolt on our hands. We might even lose Verica's loyalty into the bargain.'

'It's quite a mess,' the tribune replied thoughtfully. 'One wonders why it was permitted to occur in the first place. Narcissus will want to know.'

Plautius leaned across the table. 'Then you tell your friend Narcissus to send me more troops. If I'd been given enough auxiliary units in the first place, we'd never have had to rely on Verica, or raise those two cohorts.'

'Sorry, sir,' Quintillus replied calmly. 'It was an observation, not a criticism. I apologise if I gave the wrong impression. It's a complicated situation.'

'To put it mildly. Now you can see why I need a clear picture of what is happening in Calleva. I need to know if we can risk keeping the cohorts in existence. If you judge that they might present a danger to us then we'll have to disband them, and take the chance that we can deal with the consequences. At the same time, I need to know if the Atrebatans will honour their treaty with us under a new king. If there's any question of the tribe going over to Caratacus then we will have to act at once.'

'That's quite a job for one man,' Quintillus mused.

'You won't be entirely alone. One of the local nobles is on our payroll. He's close to Verica and can provide you with whatever help you need. I'll give you the details later.'

'Fair enough, sir.' Tribune Quintillus looked closely at the general. 'What authority will you grant me for this mission?'

Plautius reached to the side of his chair and handed a scroll to the tribune. The scroll was wrapped around an ivory rod, touched by the hands of Emperor Claudius, and bore the seal of the general. 'In the first instance you are to observe, and then report to me. If you deem it necessary to act then you may invoke the powers of procurator. All Atrebatan lands will be ceded to Rome and administered as a province. You are empowered to order Vespasian's forces to annex and garrison Verica's kingdom.'

'That's quite a responsibility,' Quintillus mused. 'The legate won't be a happy man when he hears about this.'

'If we're lucky he won't ever have to.'

Chapter Seventeen

A strained atmosphere filled the depot for several days after the banquet. The training continued under the disciplined eyes of the legionary instructors, and even Cato was pleased with the improvement in the recruits' drill technique and weapons handling. But he was also aware of a general pall of distraction and tension that hung over the native levies like a black cloud. So Cato drove them on, keeping them as busy as possible in a bid to occupy their minds with something other than the terrible spectacle their king had provided for his guests at the banquet. To make matters worse, Verica had stuck his victims' heads on posts either side of the track leading up to the main gateway into Calleva. The mangled remains of the bodies had been dumped, unceremoniously, in the defensive ditch beyond the palisade, where they were worried by wild animals.

The reminder of the grim price paid by those who defied the king stilled any open debate about the Atrebatans' alliance with Rome. Instead, a few words were infrequently exchanged between those who still trusted each other, and men would fall silent at the approach of anyone else, watching them with mixed expressions of guilt and suspicion until they had passed by. As he walked through the muddy streets of Calleva, Cato came across this time after time, and where before there had only been a dim sense of resentment, now he read guarded hostility in many of the faces he encountered.

Nor was this confined to the townspeople. The men of the two cohorts were also divided between those who felt the traitors had deserved to be thrown to the dogs, and a sizeable minority who kept silent and thus made implicit their criticism of Verica. Not so implicit that it failed to draw the attention of some of their comrades. The drill instructors had already reported a number of fights that had broken out in the ranks. Mercifully most had occurred off duty and could be dismissed as minor disciplinary infractions. But one small fight had flared up during a weapons drill that had taken place under Macro. The five men involved had been punished before a special assembly in the depot.

The men of the Wolf and the Boar Cohorts were made to stand at attention on three sides of the parade ground to witness their comrades' beating. Cato, standing stiffly beside Macro, clamped his teeth together to stop himself flinching as a pair of instructors rained their blows down on the backs and limbs of each man in turn, while they lay curled on the ground in the open space between the assembled ranks. Macro counted off the blows for each man in an even voice and called a halt when twenty had been received. A pair of medical orderlies quickly carried each victim off to the hospital.

As the third man was led forward Tincommius leaned towards Macro.

'I don't get it, sir,' whispered Tincommius. 'First you beat them, now they're being given medical attention. So what's the point of the punishment?'

'The point?' Macro's eyebrows rose. 'They have to be punished. But the army can't afford to let that get in the way of their duty. Those men are still soldiers. We want them back in fighting condition as soon as possible.'

'Sir?' One of the legionaries nodded at the man curled up at his feet.

Macro stiffened his back and bellowed, 'Proceed with the punishment!'

The two legionaries began to lay into the man on the ground, the sharp whack of their vine staffs driving the air from his lungs so that he grunted and gasped through gritted teeth. The gnarled surface of the canes began to tear at his exposed flesh, leaving bloody welts of gouged flesh. Macro counted the blows in a voice loud enough to be heard by all the men looking on in silence.

'Twelve! . . . Thirteen! . . . Fourteen!'

Cato questioned how Macro could be so untroubled as the naked men grunted or cried out as they lay on the blood-flecked ground, arms wrapped over their heads. The young centurion had often wondered at the harshness of army discipline, with its emphasis on excessive pain and humiliation for almost any infraction that occurred within duty hours. There were few fines or fatigues, and many brutal punishments. Yet to Cato it seemed that men might respond more willingly to a system that treated them as more than mere beasts of burden, driven to war. Men could be reasoned with, after all, and could be encouraged to perform as much by a considerate form of leadership as by cruelty.

He had suggested as much to Macro once, over a jug of wine. The veteran had laughed at the idea. For Macro it was simple. Discipline was tough in order to make the men tough, to give them a fighting chance against the enemy. If the lads were treated kindly it would kill them in the end. If they were treated cruelly, it would keep them hard, and give them a decent chance of surviving their long years of service in the legions.

Macro's words came back to him vividly as Cato watched the third man being led away by the medics. The fourth man was hauled forward to take his place and Cato felt his blood chill as Bedriacus was flung down at the feet of the two legionaries and their bloodstained vine canes. The hunter raised his head and smiled as his eyes found those of his commander. For an instant the corners of Cato's mouth flickered. It was an automatic response, but thankfully for Cato he was quickly able to fix his face in a cold, austere expression. Bedriacus frowned for a moment before the first blow landed across his shoulders. Instantly his ugly weathered features twisted in agony as he let out a shrill cry. Cato flinched.

'Keep still,' Macro said quietly. 'You're a fucking officer. So act like one . . . Three! . . . Four!'

Cato clamped his arms to his sides and forced himself to watch as the blows continued to land on bare flesh in a steady rhythm. A knotty lump in one of the vine staffs split open the skin above a shoulder blade and the blood flowed from the mangled flesh. Cato felt his throat tighten as the desire to be sick welled up from deep down in his guts. On the tenth stroke Bedriacus was staring at Cato wide-eyed, his mouth hanging half open and uttering a horrible high-pitched whine. The noise was punctuated by a short gasp as each blow drove the air from his lungs. At last Macro counted twenty. Cato sensed a pain in his palms and, glancing down, he saw his hands balled into fists so tightly that the knuckles were white. He forced himself to relax and watched two medics bend over the prostrate Briton. Bedriacus had gone totally limp and they struggled awkwardly to raise him from the ground and start making their way over to the hospital block. His eyes remained wide open, staring like a wild animal as the awful strained whine continued from deep in his throat.

The last offender was led out from the ranks. Tincommius started, and quickly turned towards Macro.

'Not him. You can't have him beaten!'

'Shut up!'

'Sir, I beg you! He's a blood relation of the king.'

'Shut your mouth! Get back in position.'

'You can't—'

'Do it, or I swear you'll join him.'

Tincommius sensed the gravity of the centurion's threat and stood back a pace. In front of the officers Artax was unceremoniously dumped on the ground. He looked up, eyes gleaming in bitter defiance. Before Macro could order the punishment to start Artax spat in the direction of the two centurions. Macro calmly glanced down at the damp, dark stain in the dust.

'Thirty strokes for this one. Begin punishment!'

Unlike Bedriacus, Artax took his beating without a murmur. His lips were clamped shut and his eyes bulged with the effort of resisting the waves of pain. He never once shifted his gaze from Macro and breathed in sharp explosive snorts through his flared nostrils. At the end, he rose stiffly to his feet, angrily shaking off the helping hands of the two medics. He glared once at Cato, then back at Macro. The veteran returned his gaze with cold, expressionless eyes. Artax turned away and walked unsteadily towards the hospital block.

'Punishment is over!' Macro bellowed. 'Return to training duties!'

The two cohorts were dismissed by centuries and marched off by their Roman instructors, back to the endless regime of drilling and weapons training. Cato watched them closely, his keen senses aware of a subtle change in their mood; a kind of quiet automation of bearing where before there had been a contained flow of energy.

Macro regarded Artax's retreating back for a moment, then muttered quietly, 'He's tough, that one. Lad's got balls of solid bronze.'

'That's as maybe,' Cato replied evenly, 'but I'm not sure how far I can trust him. Especially after he's taken that beating.'

'Right!' Tincommius nodded.

The critical tone of the last words was not lost on Macro and he rounded on Cato and Tincommius with a thin smile. 'You two experts think I shouldn't have punished him?'

Cato shrugged. 'Experts?'

'Sorry. Thought for the moment that you lads must be experts in the art of discipline and the ways of soldiering. I mean, I've only been serving with the Eagles, for what, sixteen years? Course, that don't count for much beside your breadth of experience . . .'

Macro paused to let Cato make the most of his embarrassment. It would do the young centurion good to be cut down to size. Macro was honest enough to accept that Cato was a far more intelligent being than himself, destined for great things if he survived long enough. Nevertheless, there were times when experience carried more weight than any amount of education, and a wise man should know that much at least.

Macro smiled. 'Artax'll be fine, trust me. I know the type: strong enough that you can't break 'em, and proud enough that they'll want to prove you wrong.'

'He's not some type, sir,' protested Tincommius. 'Artax is a royal prince, not some common soldier.'

'While he serves under me he's a common soldier. He takes his strokes with the rest of the men.'

'And what if he decides to quit? You lose Artax, and you'll lose a quarter, maybe even half, of the men.'

Macro stopped smiling. 'If he runs, I'll treat him the same as any other deserter, and even you know the punishment for that one, Cato.'

'Stoning . . .'

Macro nodded. 'I wouldn't think twice about doing that to a Roman, let alone some Celt with grand ideas about himself.'

Tincommius looked appalled by the prospect of such a dishonourable death for his kinsman. 'You can't treat a royal prince like some petty criminal!'

'I told you, while Artax serves in my bloody army, he's a soldier. Nothing more.'

'Your army?' Tincommius raised an eyebrow. 'Funny, I thought the cohorts served Verica.'

'And Verica serves Rome!' Macro snapped back. 'Which makes you, and these people of yours, subject to my command, and you *will* call me "sir" when you address me from now on.'

Tincommius' jaw dropped at being talked to in this manner. Cato noticed the young nobleman's hand tighten round the handle of his dagger and quickly intervened.

'What the centurion means is that all allies of Rome find it best to work within the traditions of the Roman army. It keeps things simple, and makes for a more harmonious spirit of co-operation between the legions and their allied comrades.'

Tincommius and Macro were both staring at him now, frowning.

'I know what I meant to say,' Macro said coldly, 'but fuck knows what you're on about. What are *you* trying to say, Cato?'

'Just trying to reassure Tincommius that our interests are the same. And that we're proud to lead such fine warriors in the service of King Verica, and Rome. That's all.'

'That's not how it sounded to me . . . sir,' said Tincommius. 'Sounded more like we were your servants, slaves even.'

'Slaves!' Macro barked out a laugh of frustration. 'What have bloody slaves got to do with it? I'm talking about discipline, that's all. I'm not singling out your lads for a hard time. There's no difference between the way I treat 'em and the way I'd treat our own boys. Ain't that true, Cato?'

'Oh, that's true all right.'

'There! See?'

Tincommius shrugged. 'I don't like to see my people treated like animals, sir.'

'They only fight like animals,' laughed Macro. 'And they're bloody good at it!'

'You sound as if you were proud of us, Centurion.'

'Proud? Of course I'm fucking proud. They carved those Durotrigans up a treat. Lack a bit of finish, mind you. But once Cato and I have trained them up, you'll have the deadliest bunch of Celts in the land.'

Tincommius nodded his approval.

'Happy now?'

'Yes, sir. Sorry I questioned you, sir.'

'I'll let it pass, this time. Now you'd better join the instructors. Born fighters you Britons may be, but you're piss poor at languages. Now bugger off.'

Once Tincommius had left them Macro turned on Cato, stabbing a finger into his chest. 'Don't you ever contradict me in front of him again!'

'Yes, sir.'

'Don't call me sir.'

'Sorry.'

'And don't apologise all the bloody time!'

Cato opened his mouth, closed it again and nodded.

'Now then, Cato, what was that all about? That stuff you were spouting about comrades?'

'I just thought, given the current tensions in Calleva, that we should play up the fact that the Boars and the Wolves were raised to serve Verica.'

'That's what we tell them,' Macro agreed. 'But any idiot can see that they're really just another two auxiliary cohorts serving Rome.'

'Be careful who you say that to. I wouldn't repeat it in front of the likes of Artax.'

'Or that youngster Tincommius!' Macro snapped back. 'Although I can see he's taken you in . . . Look here, I'm not a complete fool, Cato. But at the end of the day, we trained them, armed them and fed them. That makes 'em ours.'

'I doubt that's how most of them see it.'

'Then they're fools. Now, stop worrying about it.'

'And if someone like Artax takes exception to being given his orders by a Roman?'

'Well, we'll deal with that when the time comes,' Macro concluded impatiently. 'Now, I've got a pile of records to audit, and you've got training duties.'

But Cato was looking over his shoulder towards the depot gates. A small party of horsemen had just ridden in from Calleva. They were led by a tall figure in a scarlet cloak riding a beautifully groomed black horse. Macro turned round to see what his subordinate was gazing at. One of the horsemen kicked his heels in and trotted his mount over towards the two centurions.

'Your eyes are better than mine. Who's that over at the gate?'

'No idea,' replied Cato. 'Never seen him before.'

'We'll know soon enough.' Macro nodded towards the horseman, who reined his beast in a short distance from the two officers and slid smoothly from its back. The man quickly glanced over the centurions and snapped a salute at Macro.

'Sir! Tribune Quintillus presents his compliments and desires the presence of the commanding officer of the depot at once.'

'Who exactly is this Tribune Quintillus?' Macro cocked his head towards the gateway.

'From headquarters, sir. On the general's orders. If you'd attend the tribune at your earliest convenience, sir . . .?'

'Yes,' Macro growled. 'Of course.'

The horseman saluted, slid back on to his mount and trotted back towards his superior.

Macro exchanged a quick glance with Cato and spat on to the ground. 'What the bloody hell is that tribune doing on my patch?'

Chapter Eighteen

'You've done a fine job,' Tribune Quintillus smiled. 'Both of you.'

Macro shuffled uncomfortably in his chair, while Cato smiled modestly. The tribune, encouraged by the younger centurion's response at least, continued pouring on the praise in his silky aristocratic accent.

'General Plautius is delighted with the report that you submitted.'

Macro felt he should have been basking in this approval from on high. Outside the window the sky was a perfect blue, and birds were singing, completely unfazed by the savage shouts of the drill instructors on the parade ground. He had been enjoying his independence, and had successfully raised and trained his own small army, and led it to a grand victory over the enemy. Everything should have felt right in the world. And it would have done, had it not been for the tribune sitting before him.

'So much so that he sent you down here to check it out . . . sir.'

The bitterness in Macro's voice was clear as the summer sky and the tribune's thin lips narrowed even further for an instant, before the smile returned and he shook his head. 'I haven't been sent here to spy on you, Centurion. And I have no orders to take control either. So rest easy. The depot, its garrison and the two native cohorts are still yours to command. The way you and your men have performed wouldn't justify any change, nor would the general tolerate it. He likes his heroes, and he knows that success needs to be encouraged if it is to breed success.'

Macro was not fully satisfied by this response, and nodded curtly. He had dealt with enough tribunes in the past to know that they were weaned on to politics from the teat. He had met one or two who had seemed to put soldiering first. Such men were the exception. The rest were all men on the make, desperate to prove themselves and thereby catch the eye of Narcissus, the senior official of the imperial general staff. Narcissus was ever on the look out for young aristocrats who managed to blend political capability with moral flexibility.

Accordingly Macro had a dim view of almost every tribune – and most of the legates, he decided, then relented. Vespasian was all right. Their legate had proved himself an honest man, a man of courage, who was not above sharing all the discomforts and dangers faced by his men. It was that quality that Macro always looked for in his commanders. It was a shame then, he concluded, that Vespasian was inevitably fated to a life of obscurity once his tenure of command over the Second Legion had expired. The legate's very integrity was his worst enemy.

Macro shook off this line of thought and concentrated on the tribune sitting opposite him. Macro decided that Quintillus was typical of his kind in most respects. Young. Not so young as Cato, but young enough to lack experience where it counted. Cato, despite his years, was tough, intelligent, and as deadly in battle as almost any soldier Macro had ever known. By contrast Quintillus looked soft. There was no fat on his tall elegant frame, but the skin had that well-scrubbed smoothness that spoke of a pampered upbringing. His dark hair was neatly cropped, with oiled ringlets along the fringe. The tribune's uniform was likewise adorned with expensive little touches that spoke of his family's rank and richness in a knowing but understated manner. Quintillus spoke with calm assurance, and emphasised his words with low-key theatrical flourishes of the hand that he had been trained to use by some fancy tutor of rhetoric. With such grace, good looks and a generous fortune behind him, no doubt Quintillus was very successful with women. Macro disliked him instinctively.

'There is, unfortunately, an aspect of the report that I would like to discuss further.' Quintillus smiled once again, drawing a scroll from a leather satchel at his feet.

Macro looked at his report with a sinking feeling. 'Oh?'

The tribune unrolled the report from the bottom and skim-read the conclusion.

'You mention, in passing, that elements amongst the Atrebatans are not quite as keen as their king on the tribe's alliance with Rome.'

'Yes, sir.' Macro tried to recall the exact phrasing he had used in his report. He hated being put on the spot like this, called to respond to words he had written several days previously, by a senior officer who had the advantage of having the entire report at his disposal. It was unfair, but there wasn't much that was fair in the legions.

'What do you mean, precisely?' Quintillus asked.

'There's nothing much to it, sir. A few malcontents grumbling about Rome's long-term plans for the Atrebatans, but nothing the king can't handle.'

Cato shot his friend a quick look of surprise, and quickly composed his expression as the tribune looked up from the report.

'Yes, that's pretty much what you say here. But I understand that the king's way of handling these, er, malcontents is perhaps a little more dogged – if you'll pardon the pun – than you imply. I mean to say, feeding one's critics to the hounds is a little extreme . . .'

'How'd you find out about that?'

The tribune shrugged. 'That's not important. Right now what is important is for you to tell me what the true situation is here in Calleva.'

'They weren't critics, sir. They were traitors and got what was coming to them. Bit harsh, perhaps, but these people are barbarians, after all. Verica's dealt with the problem.'

'True. But why not mention it in this report?'

'That was written before Verica had the traitors killed.'

'Very well,' Quintillus conceded. 'Can't fault you on that one.'

'No, sir.'

'So what has been the situation since then?'

'It's calm enough. A bit of tension on the streets, but that's it.'

'And it would be safe to say that King Verica is secure on his throne?'

'I'd say so.' Macro glanced at Cato. 'Wouldn't you?'

Cato gave the faintest of nods and Macro glared angrily at him.

'Centurion Cato would seem to have a slightly different view of matters,' Quintillus suggested quietly.

'Centurion Cato is not very experienced, sir.'

'I can see that.'

Cato blushed.

'Yet it would be useful to have a second opinion, just for clarity.' The tribune gestured towards Cato. 'Well?'

Cato felt a black wave of anxiety and depression engulf him. He must answer the tribune, yet his loyalty to Macro meant that he must not be seen to undermine his friend's version of events. He cursed his comrade's touchiness. Cato was no more enamoured of aristocratic hauteur than Macro, but having been raised in the imperial palace at least he was used to it and had found a way to cope with such arrogance. Much as Macro might want to enjoy his independent command far from the view of senior officers, Cato knew that it would be dangerous to underplay the political difficulties facing Verica. Moreover, being somewhat more speculative than Macro he could see the wider strategic implications faced by Rome. If the Atrebatans turned against Rome then not only would the current campaign be lost, but the conquest of Britain might well have to be abandoned. The shameful consequences of such an outcome would threaten the Emperor himself. Cato drew himself back from speculation to focus on the present. Much as Cato might be aware of the wider issues Macro was in trouble here and now, and needed his support.

'Centurion Macro is right, sir . . .'

Macro rested his hands on his knees and eased himself back into his chair, trying hard not to smile.

'He's right,' Cato repeated thoughtfully. 'But it would be wise if we considered the possibility of some kind of trouble brewing up. After all, the king is an old man. Old men have a predilection for mortality, unassisted or otherwise . . .'

The tribune chuckled. 'And are you aware of any potential assistants in the field – besides Caratacus and the Durotrigans?'

'The families of the men he executed would have motive enough, sir.'

'Anyone else?'

'Just the malcontents Macro was talking about.'

'How many of them would you say there were, Centurion?'

Cato desperately thought about his response. If he estimated too many then Macro would be seen as complacent at best and a liar at worst. If Cato underestimated their number then the tribune would report back to General Plautius that the Roman alliance with the Atrebatans was safe. If it turned out not to be safe . . .

'How many?'

'It's difficult to say, sir. With Verica taking a hard line on those who oppose him, they're hardly making themselves obvious.'

'Is there any cause for concern?' asked Quintillus, and then added a qualification. 'Is there anything else you think I need to tell the general?'

'In my judgement, it is as Centurion Macro has said, sir. We can contain the problem for now. But if the situation changes, if Verica dies, or we meet with any serious defeat and Verica is deposed, who knows? The man chosen to succeed him by the king's council might not stay loyal to Rome.'

'Is that likely?'

'It's possible.'

'I see.' Tribune Quintillus leaned back in his chair, gazing at the beaten earth floor between his feet. He rasped a thumb along the stubble under his chin as he considered the situation. At length, just as Macro began to shift in his seat, the tribune looked up.

'Gentlemen, I'll be honest with you. The situation is causing me more concern than I thought it would. The general's not going to be a happy man when he reads my report. Right now, the four legions are disposed along a wide front, trying to hold on to Caratacus until we can fix him, and close for the kill. Behind the legions we've got lines of communication stretching right back to Rutupiae. Most of them pass through Atrebatan land. We're already having a hard enough time keeping the enemy's raiding columns at bay. If the Atrebatans go over to Caratacus, then the show's over. General Plautius will be forced to retreat all the way back to the fortress on the Tamesis. It would take us years to recover the ground. In that time

Caratacus will be sure to make good use of our setback; the tribes would flock to his side. Given enough men, even though they're Celts, Caratacus might just defeat our legions.' Quintillus looked at Cato and Macro. 'You appreciate the seriousness of the position?'

'We're not idiots, sir,' Macro replied. 'Of course we know the score. Right, Cato?'

'Yes.'

Quintillus gave a faint nod as he seemed to make a decision. 'Then you'll understand the general's thinking when I tell you that he has granted me full procuratorial powers over this kingdom, and I'm to exercise them the moment I perceive any danger to the legions' supply lines.'

'You're not serious, sir?' Cato shook his head. 'Annexation? The Atrebatans would never stand for it.'

'Who said we'd give them any choice in the matter?' Quintillus said coldly. 'While they've the good sense to do our bidding then they can have their king. But the moment they pose any threat to our interests I will be forced to act. The Second Legion will be recalled to Calleva to enforce my orders. These natives, and their lands, will come under direct Roman rule; the kingdom of the Atrebatans will cease to be.'

'No,' muttered Macro. 'They'd die first.'

'Nonsense! Don't be so melodramatic, Centurion. They'll do whatever it takes to survive, like everyone who has no real power to change events. They must already have a pretty good idea of the cost of defying Rome.' The fire of ruthless ambition glinted in the tribune's eyes. 'For those who don't know, I'll teach them.'

'If it comes to that,' said Cato.

'Yes.' The tribune nodded. 'If it comes to that.'

Cato's mind was reeling from the boldness of the blow that the tribune was willing to strike. He could readily imagine how the proud and prickly Artax would react. Tincommius as well. Even the lowly Bedriacus might well resent the arbitrary imposition of direct Roman rule. Over the last few months Cato felt he had come to know something of these people. As he had picked up some of their language he had learned about their culture and had even come to respect them in many ways. These Britons had an integrity that was quite lacking in those races that had lived for many years in the shadow of the Eagles. In Gaul, Cato had seen the extent to which the land had been turned into a rough facsimile of the vast estates that covered Italy. Generations of natives had lost their ancestral territories and now worked the same fields in exchange for a pittance. Where the estates were worked by chain gangs, the descendants of the once-proud tribes who had nearly bested Caesar himself were now forced to find work in the small industries that had sprouted up around the new Roman cities stamped across Gaul.

Whatever the strategic exigencies of the current situation, Cato felt that the Atrebatans deserved better than this. Good men had shed their blood to defend the supply routes of the legions. He had seen them die. To be sure, they had also been defending themselves from their warlike neighbours, but what had truly impressed him was the mutual respect and, dare he admit it, affection that had forged a bond between the warriors of the Atrebatans and their instructors from the Second Legion. Particularly Figulus, who was familiar with their tongue and, once out of uniform, looked every inch a Celt.

The sounds of the men training across the parade ground were clearly audible through the open window of Macro's office, and Cato was struck by the suddenness with which so much good work was now threatened by coarse power play. The terrible tension following Verica's banquet could be assuaged eventually and the rift in the tribe would heal. But what Quintillus was proposing would unite all but a handful of men against Rome. It was madness, and he must make the tribune see that.

'Sir, we've raised two good cohorts of warriors here. They fight well and they fight alongside Rome because they believe we are friends, not oppressors. In time they might be allowed to serve as auxiliary units, and where they lead, other tribesmen will follow. All of that would be lost if you reduced their kingdom to a province. Worse, you would find them ranged against us . . . I doubt the general would approve.'

Quintillus frowned for a moment, before his expression relaxed and he smiled. 'You're right, of course. We must not squander this opportunity you two have created. While these cohorts of yours are still around we'd better tread carefully.'

Cato relaxed and nodded. Then the tribune gracefully rose from his chair. Macro and Cato shot up from their seats and stood to attention.

'Now, gentlemen, if you'd excuse me, I really must pay my respects to King Verica, before I cause our ally any further offence.'

After the tribune had gone Macro smiled. 'You got him in a nice twist! Bastard'll have to leave us be, for now at least.'

'I'm not so sure.'

'Come on, Cato! Why do you always have to be so bloody suspicious? You heard the man: he thinks you're right.'

'That's what he says . . .'

'And?'

'I'm not sure.' Cato looked down between his feet. 'I don't trust him.'

'You think he's dodgy?'

'No. Not deceitful, maybe. Just ambitious. It's not everyday the general hands out procuratorial powers.'

'Meaning?'

'Meaning our friend Quintillus might be awfully tempted to exercise those powers, come what may. Even if that means provoking the Atrebatans into open rebellion.'

Macro looked at him a moment, then shook his head. 'No. Nobody would be that foolish.'

'He isn't a nobody,' Cato said quietly. 'Quintillus is a patrician. His kind doesn't serve Rome. The way he sees it, Rome is there to serve him, any way he can make her. If the Atrebatans rise up, then he can use his powers to take command of all available troops to crush the tribesmen. A glorious victory has a funny way of erasing memories of the reasons why a victory was needed in the first place.'

When Cato had finished the older centurion let out a deep laugh. 'The gods help me if you ever decide to take to politics. You've got a bloody devious mind, young Cato.'

Cato blushed a little at the implied criticism, before he shrugged. 'I'll leave politics to those who are bred for it. I just want to survive. Right now, we're sitting on the top of a scorpions' nest. We've got two cohorts of native troops, dangerously cocksure that they can take on anything. We've got a town packed to the seams with a starving rabble, and an old king who's jumping at every shadow because he fears that his own nobles are plotting against him. Outside the walls there are enemy columns raiding Atrebatan lands and butchering our supply convoys. And now . . . now we have some jumped-up tribune on the make, just itching for an excuse to annex the natives.' He looked at Macro and shook his head. 'What's not to be worried about?'

'You've got a point.' Macro nodded. 'Let's get something to drink.'

Chapter Nineteen

Tribune Quintillus walked slowly through the soiled thorough-fares of Calleva. Behind him trudged the bodyguards he had brought with him from army headquarters: six men selected for their toughness; each as tall and broad-shouldered as the tribune. He knew what kind of impression he wanted to cast before these barbarians. As a representative of the general, and by extension the Emperor, he must be the very image of the all-conquering race, chosen by the gods themselves to subdue the backward peoples who blighted the world beyond the frontiers of the Empire.

Quintillus glanced curiously around as he made his way between the thatched huts towards the royal enclosure. Most of the townspeople were sitting around the entrances to their huts, a tableau of gaunt faces with desperation etched into their expressions. They had not quite reached the stage where starvation made them too listless and apathetic to act. Accordingly, the tribune calculated, they still constituted a danger. They might yet have the energy to respond to an appeal to rise up against Verica and Rome.

The quiet was eerie after the noise of training in the depot and Quintillus was relieved when he turned the final corner and caught sight of the wooden gates and raised palisade of the royal enclosure. To the tribune's surprise the gates were closed.

It would seem that those inside the enclosure were well aware of the simmering tensions wreathing the hot streets of Calleva. At the approach of the Romans one of the sentries on the walkway over the gates turned towards the king's great hall and bellowed notice of the new arrivals. But the gates remained closed as Quintillus strode towards them. He was just beginning to fear that he might face the huge indignity of being denied admission when a face appeared over the palisade above the solid timber gates. Quintillus looked up, squinting into the bright sunshine as he made out the form of a large warrior.

'Do you speak any Latin?' the tribune asked, with a smile.

The man nodded.

'Then please be so good as to tell your king that Tribune Quintillus desires an audience. I have been sent by Aulus Plautius.'

The Briton's eyes widened a little at the sound of the general's name. 'Wait, Roman.'

Then he was gone, and the gate was shut again. Quintillus glared at the shadowed timbers and slapped his hand against his thigh in frustration. The Romans waited in the bright sunshine, between the crude huts lining the rutted street. The stench from a nearby midden, heated to a sharp pungency, filled the still air and the tribune wrinkled his nose in disgust. Flies buzzed lazy looping paths around the tribune and his bodyguards, and a short distance away a dog barked endlessly. Quintillus affected an air of detachment and slowly paced up and down in front of the gate, hands loosely clasped behind his back. The entire town was crying out for demolition, the tribune decided. He began to visualise Calleva as the seat of government for this province: neat ranks of tiled houses arranged around a modest palace and basilica that would proclaim that Roman law and Roman order had triumphed once more.

At last there came a heavy rumble from behind the gates as the locking bar was removed. Moments later one of them slowly swung inwards. The Briton they had seen earlier beckoned them inside, and then the gate was swung back into place.

'This way.' The Briton waved a finger and turned towards the great hall. Quintillus bit back on his anger at the blunt lack of manners exhibited by the man and nodded at his bodyguards to follow him.

The enclosure was almost as quiet as the town beyond the gate. A handful of guards walked slowly along the palisade, keenly watching over the spread of thatched roofs. Other men sat, or slept, in patches of shade, and Quintillus was aware of several pairs of eyes watching him closely as he marched past. At the entrance to the great hall stood four warriors, squatting in the shadows. They rose to their feet as the small party approached. At the doorway the Briton turned towards Quintillus.

'Your men will wait here.'

'They're my bodyguards.'

'They wait here,' the Briton said firmly. 'You come with me.'

After the slightest hesitation, to indicate that he was making a concession to his hosts, Quintillus followed the man inside. The contrast with the bright sunlight outside was striking and Quintillus wondered at the echoing darkness as he followed the dim form of the Briton across the roughly paved floor. A small opening in the apex of the roof allowed a shaft of light to fall between the beams, and tiny motes of dust glided through the soft golden hue. Quintillus noted that the air was pleasantly cool, but smelled of beer and cooking. At the far end of the hall was a small doorway with a leather curtain hanging across the inside. A guard stood to one side of the entrance, his sword drawn with the point resting on the ground between his feet. The tribune's companion nodded to the guard, who stepped aside, and then rapped on the wooden doorframe. A voice answered and then the Briton pushed the leather curtain to one side, stepped through the door and beckoned the tribune to follow him into the chamber.

The king's private quarters were crudely appointed by Roman standards and Quintillus had immediately to suppress an undiplomatic betrayal of his distaste and condescension. The daubed walls were hung with animal skins and lined with chests to store the king's possessions. Close by the entrance was a large table with several chairs arranged around it. At the far end of the chamber was a large bed covered with yet more skins. Verica stood beside the bed, pulling a long tunic over the sagging wrinkled flesh of his skinny body. A light shrill of laughter drew the tribune's attention more closely to the bed, and he saw the face of a young woman, not much more than a girl, above the covers. Verica said something to her and clicked his finger towards the door. At once the girl threw back the covers, jumped to her feet, grabbed a tatty cloak from the end of the bed and ran towards the new arrivals. Quintillus stepped aside to let her pass and cast an approving look over her lithe body.

'Would you like her?' asked Verica, walking stiffly towards him. 'After we've talked, I mean. She's good.'

'Most kind of you, but I fear I shall be too busy to enjoy her. Besides I prefer them slightly older – they have more experience.'

'Experience?' Verica frowned. 'I grow more sick of experience every day. At my age one craves the life one had before experience soiled it . . . Sorry,' Verica smiled and raised a hand. 'I've become a bit too preoccupied by questions of age lately. Please sit down, Tribune, here at the table. I've sent for some wine. I know how my Roman friends prefer wine to our beer.'

'Thank you, my lord.'

As the two men seated themselves at the table a slave boy arrived with a pair of Samian cups and a jug. He poured a dark red stream into each cup. As soon as the task was complete the boy scurried from the room. Verica nodded his head towards a chair at the far end of the table and the Briton who had escorted the tribune joined his king and the Roman.

'Cadminius is captain of the royal bodyguard,' explained Verica. 'I keep him close to me. Whatever you have to say to me can be trusted to him also.'

'I see.'

'Now then, Tribune Quintillus, to what do I owe the pleasure of your visit?'

Quintillus deplored the man's bluntness. But one had to make allowances for the Celt's lack of social grace and diplomatic finesse. After all, the man had been raised amid barbaric squalor and had only spent a few brief years as a guest of Rome. Even so, Quintillus forced himself to smile.

'I appreciate your directness, my lord.'

'I have little time for formalities, Tribune. I have too little time for anything these days.'

Except indulging his appetite for young flesh, Quintillus reflected, then made himself smile again. 'My general sends his warmest greetings to King Verica, most close of Rome's friends.'

Verica laughed. 'It's an odd world where a tribe as insignificant as the Atrebatans can assume any degree of importance in the eyes of a power as great as Rome.'

'Nevertheless, you and your people are important to the Emperor, and my general, as you must know.'

'Surely. Any man who stands with another at his back is

inclined to wonder if that man is a friend or enemy. That is the measure of our importance, is it not?'

Quintillus laughed. 'You describe both our situations in an admirably succinct way. And that brings us to the purpose of my visit.'

'Aulus Plautius wants to know how far he can depend on me.'

'Oh, no, my lord!' Quintillus protested. 'The general has no doubts at all about your loyalty to Rome. None at all.'

'How very reassuring.'

Verica raised his cup and drank, his Adam's apple bobbing backwards and forwards in his scrawny throat as the base of the cup rose higher and higher. Then, with red drops dribbling down the white hair of his beard, Verica drained the cup and set it down with a sharp tap on the table.

'Good stuff! Try it, Tribune.'

Quintillus raised his cup to his lips, found the scent to his liking and took a sip. The sweet liquid was resonant with flavour and had a pleasing warming sensation as it passed down his throat. This was no cheap wine. He could not place it exactly, but could guess at its cost.

'Very nice. A legacy of your days as Rome's guest?'

'Of course. And do you think for a moment I'd be mad enough to turn on Rome and give this up?'

They both laughed, then Verica shook his head.

'Seriously, Tribune, there's much to gain from our alliance with Rome. Even if that were not so, I'd rather take my chances with Rome than throw my hand in with that bastard Caratacus. I'd be dead in a matter of days, and some anti-Roman fanatic would be sitting here in my place.'

'And such a man would be easy to find from amongst the Atrebatans?' Quintillus probed.

Verica looked at him for a moment, all trace of amusement

gone from his expression. 'There are some who might think our tribe is on the wrong side, yes.'

'Some? Many?'

'Enough to cause me concern.'

'What concerns you concerns Rome, my lord.'

'Oh, I'm sure it does.'

'Do you know who these men are?'

'I know of some,' Verica admitted. 'I suspect many more. As for the rest, who knows?'

'Then why not take care of them, my lord?'

'Take care of them? What kind of a euphemism is that? Say what you mean, Tribune. We must be clear about what we say. Euphemisms are for cowards and only ever lead to later misunderstanding and recrimination. You want me to kill my people?'

Quintillus nodded. 'For you own safety, and as an example to others.'

'I assume the good Centurion Macro has told you that I've already tried that approach, and it's failed.'

'Perhaps you didn't remove enough of your enemies?'

'Perhaps I "removed" more than enough. Perhaps I should never have removed any of them. That's what Cadminius thinks, though he dare not say it.'

At the end of the table the captain of the king's bodyguard lowered his gaze. Quintillus ignored the man and leaned closer to King Verica.

'That would have looked like weakness, my lord. It would have encouraged others to speak out against you. In the end tolerance always leads to weakness. Weakness leads to defeat.'

'It's all so easy to you, isn't it, Roman?' Verica shook his head. 'All so black and white. One solution fits all situations. Rule with an iron fist.'

'It works for us, my lord.'

'Us? How old are you, Tribune?'

'Twenty-four, sire. Next month.'

'Twenty-four . . .' The Atrebatan looked him in the eyes for a moment, and shook his head. 'Calleva is not Rome, Quintillus. My situation is more finely balanced. I kill too many of my enemies and I provoke a rebellion from those who resent oppression. I kill too few and I provoke a rebellion from those who abuse my tolerance. You see my problem? Now, I ask you, how many should I kill to achieve the desired effect, without provoking a rebellion?'

Quintillus could not answer, and was angry for letting himself fall into such an obvious rhetorical trap. He had been trained by the most expensive tutors his father could afford, and felt ashamed. Damn King Verica. Damn this wizened old man. He had made a mess of things and now Rome must sort it out. Always Rome.

'My lord,' the tribune responded quietly. 'I appreciate that ruling a kingdom is not a precise science. But you have a problem. Your people are divided, and some are hostile to Rome. That makes it our problem too. You must find a solution, for the good of your people.'

'Or else?'

'Or else Rome will have to solve the problem.'

There was a silence, and the tribune was aware that Cadminius had straightened up in his chair and had bunched one hand into a fist. At the other end of the table Verica leaned back and pressed his hands together, resting his lips on the fingertips as he watched Quintillus through narrowed eyes.

'Are you threatening me?'

'No. Of course not. But let me describe the options for your people as I see it, if I may?'

'Go ahead, young man.'

'The Atrebatans must remain allies of Rome. We need to be sure that our supplies can pass safely through your lands. As long as you can guarantee that then you will find us a grateful and valuable friend. And, as long as whoever eventually succeeds you pursues the same policy, Rome shall be content to let the Atrebatans run their own affairs – as long as we do not perceive any developments that might endanger our interests.'

'And if you do?'

'Then we would have to help you administer your kingdom.'

'You mean annex us? Turn us into a province.'

'Of course I hope that it would never come to that.'

There was a tense pause before Verica continued speaking. 'I see. And if our "policy" changes?'

'Then we will be forced to crush any forces operating against Rome. All weapons will be confiscated. Your lands and those of your nobles who oppose us will be forfeit, and any prisoners we take will be sold into slavery. That is the fate of those who break faith with Rome.'

Verica stared at the tribune for a moment, then his eyes flicked over to the captain of his bodyguard. Cadminius was having difficulty containing his rage at the naked threat posed by the Roman envoy.

'You don't leave me and my people much choice for our future.'

'No, my lord. None.'

Chapter Twenty

Two days after the tribune's arrival King Verica announced that he was going to hold a hunt. One of the forests several miles from Calleva was a royal hunting ground and farmers living nearby were forbidden to hunt any animals within its leafy boundary.

The afternoon before the hunt was to take place the air was breathless. A brilliant sun blazed down on the quiet streets of Calleva as the townspeople sought out shade. Inside the royal enclosure servants and slaves scurried about making preparations. The romantic, spontaneous image of noble man pitting his wits against the cunning forces of nature was far removed from the logistical realities of the exercise. Hunting spears had to be carefully selected to make sure their shafts were still true after months in storage. Then they had to be cleaned and their edges honed to a lethal sharpness before being put into thick leather cases for transporting. Horses had to be checked for fitness and the weaker mounts returned to the stables for general duties. Riding tackle was greased and polished and carefully fitted to the animals that would be ridden by the royal hunting party. Sweating slaves struggled under the burden of bedding and furs as these were packed away into the wagons parked along one side of the enclosure. Anxious stewards directed kitchen servants as they heaved sacks of bread, haunches of meat and jars of beer and wine from the dark storerooms at the back of the king's hall and carried them across to the wagons. The captain of the king's bodyguard sat at a trestle table busy recruiting able-bodied beaters from the long line straggling towards the gate. With food in such short supply the people of Calleva were desperate to win a share of the meat that was to be divided up after the hunt.

'Anyone'd think this lot were about to launch an invasion,' muttered Macro as he and Cato made their way through the bustling mass. 'Thought we were just going for a nice simple hunt.'

Cato smiled. 'For the other half there's no such thing as a simple hunt.'

He spoke from experience, having been brought up behind the scenes at the imperial palace in Rome. Every time the Emperor had decided, often on a whim, that he wished to 'pop over to Ostia', or 'nip up into the hills' to escape the dead heat of a Roman summer, it was Cato's father who had been tasked with organising the myriad necessities and luxuries that accompanied such a trip.

Caligula had been the worst, Cato recalled. The mad Emperor's whims had exhaustively tested the boundaries of the possible and nearly driven Cato's placid father to despair. Like the time Caligula had decided he rather fancied a stroll across the bay at Misenum. There was no hope of reasoning with him. After all, the man was a god and when a god wished a thing done, it was done. And so thousands of engineers constructed a pontoon bridge between Baiae and Puteoli on the backs of commandeered shipping and fishing boats. While Caligula and his entourage paraded back and forth across the bridge thousands of starving fishermen and ruined merchants looked on, and were encouraged to cheer the Emperor, at the point of a Praetorian sword. Cato had seen all this, and now the practical implications of Verica's decision to go hunting did not surprise him.

Macro was still gazing around with a disapproving frown. 'I thought it'd just be a matter of picking up some spears and running down a few of the feral buggers in the forest. Not all this. Where's the bloody tribune got to?'

They had been summoned from the depot late in the afternoon and had dismissed the two cohorts from training before heading through the hot stinking streets to find Tribune Quintillus. Both centurions were uncomfortable in their thick tunics and Cato shivered as he felt sweat trickle down from his armpits under the prickly wool.

'Can you see him?' asked Macro, craning his neck round. Being several inches shorter than Cato, his field of vision was limited by the lofty Celts surrounding them. What Macro lacked in height he made up for in the solid muscle of his broad frame. Right now, Cato sensed, he was irritable enough to want to throw some of that bulk around.

'No.'

'Then ask someone, idiot.'

For an instant Cato glared back at his comrade, and only just managed to bite back on the desire to tell Macro that he should have made a greater effort to learn the native tongue.

'All right.' Cato looked round and caught the eye of a royal bodyguard, lounging against one of the wagon wheels, thumbs tucked into the cord that held checked breeches around his hairy stomach. Cato beckoned to the man, but the Briton merely flickered a smile back, and continued to stare languidly at the slaves toiling around him. With a low curse Cato pushed his way over to the bodyguard.

'Hey! You!'

The bodyguard looked round at the approaching Romans with an irritated expression.

'You seen the tribune?'

Cato knew that his accent was clear enough, but the man stared at him blankly.

'The tribune. The Roman who arrived four days ago. Is he here?'

'Sa!' The bodyguard nodded, once.

'Where?'

The Briton tipped his head towards the great hall.

'Inside?'

'Na! Training.'

Cato turned to Macro. 'He's here. Behind the hall.'

'Right.' Macro was staring hard at the bodyguard. 'Chatty type, aren't you?'

The Latin was incomprehensible to the bodyguard and he simply returned Macro's stare, silent and unyielding.

'Come on,' said Cato. 'Can't keep the tribune waiting. Save that one for later.'

With Cato leading the way, the two centurions pushed through the throng towards the entrance to the great hall. The two guards knew them well enough by now to wave them through. The interior was dark and cool, and it took a moment for Cato and Macro to adjust to the contrast. Then Cato could see a few of the nobles resting quietly along the benches lining each side of the hall. Discarded cups and the remains of a meal lay on wooden platters strewn along the wide wooden tables. Lying stretched out on the floor were the dim shapes of hunting dogs – all still, save one bitch who was licking one of the puppies nestling against her side. Overhead, a few stray beams of light pierced the thatch and shafted through the gloom.

'Not everyone is hard at work,' Macro sneered. Then they heard the sharp ring of swords clashing through the smaller doorway directly opposite. 'Sounds like one of 'em at least is working up a sweat.'

They walked towards the rear entrance of the hall and screwed up their eyes as they emerged into the bright sunshine that filled the timber doorframe. Behind the great hall was a wide bare space contained by the far palisade of the royal enclosure. Several racks of spears and swords stood to one side. A handful of the royal bodyguard sat in the shade against the side of the great hall, watching the display taking place in the centre of the training area. There, bathed in the bright sunshine, stood tribune Quintillus, poised on the balls of his feet, sword arm fully extended towards the British warrior ten feet in front of him. Cato caught his breath at the sight of the tribune. Quintillus looked superb. Stripped to the waist, his perfect physique would have graced a champion gladiator: the oiled skin glistened over perfectly contoured muscles and his chest swelled and subsided in an easy rhythm as he faced his opponent.

The Briton was armed with a longer, heavier sword than the tribune, but seemed to have come off worse so far in this bout. A livid red streak extended across one shoulder and blood oozed from the shallow cut. He was breathing heavily and could not keep his sword still. He suddenly gasped a deep breath and rushed the tribune with a roar. Quintillus feinted, ducked under the Briton's rising blade, then neatly tapped it to one side and smashed the pommel against the side of the man's head. The Briton grunted and crashed to the ground. There was a murmur of approval from the bodyguards sitting in the shade and one or two jeers for their fallen comrade. Quintillus casually flicked his sword into the ground and leaned over to help the man back on to his feet.

'There you are. No harm done. Thanks for the exercise.'

The Briton looked at the tribune uncomprehendingly and shook his dazed head.

'I'd sit down for a while if I were you. Catch your breath, and that sort of thing.'

As the two centurions emerged from the entrance to the hall, Quintillus looked up with a frown that was instantly replaced with a genial smile.

'Ah! Wondered where you'd got to!' He straightened up, letting go of the Briton, who sagged back on to the ground.

'Came as soon as we could, sir,' replied Macro, saluting.

'Yes, well, fair enough. But next time, put a little more effort into it, eh?'

'We'll do our best, sir.'

'Quite.' Quintillus flashed a quick smile. 'Now then, to business. I gather you've been invited to the hunt by King Verica.'

'Yes, sir.'

'Well, that raises an interesting question of protocol, doesn't it?'

'Does it, sir?'

'Oh, yes!' Quintillus' eyebrows rose in surprise at the centurion's ignorance. 'You see, I've been invited as well.'

'I wouldn't imagine that Verica would have left you out, sir.'

The tribune's look of surprise switched to one of annoyance. 'Of course not! The thing is, it really won't do for me to be mixing with the other ranks. It lacks a certain dignity wouldn't you agree? I am, after all, a procurator acting in the Emperor's name.'

'Yes, sir,' Macro replied patiently. 'I do recall.'

Quintillus nodded. 'Excellent! Then I imagine you'll be wanting to get off and make your apologies to King Verica.'

'Apologies?'

There was an embarrassed pause, until Quintillus laughed and slapped Macro on the shoulder. 'Come on, Centurion! Don't be so thick! Go and tell the old boy you can't go.'

'Can't go?'

'Just make up some excuse. Duties, or something. Isn't that what you centurions do all the time, duties?'

Cato sensed his friend stiffen with indignation and anger, and decided to intervene before Macro's prickly pride dropped him in any trouble.

'Sir, the thing is we've already accepted the invitation. If we back out now it'll look terribly rude. These Celts take a dim view of the slightest discourtesy, sir.'

'Nevertheless—'

'And we cannot afford to offend the Atrebatans. Not right now, sir.'

'Well . . .' Tribune Quintillus stroked his chin and pondered the situation. 'I suppose, for the sake of good diplomatic relations, we might overlook the usual arrangements on this occasion.'

'I think that would be wise, sir.'

'All right, then.' The reluctance in the tone was effortlessly conveyed to his social inferiors. Cato risked a quick glance at Macro and saw the firm line of his clamped lips. Trinbune Quintillus pulled a silk cloth from the hem of his breeches and dabbed at his brow. 'Have either of you hunted before? Socially, I mean.'

'Socially?' Macro frowned. 'I've been hunting, sir. The army trained me to go hunting. To get rations.'

'That's nice. But hunting for food is a little different from hunting for sport,' Quintillus explained. 'There's a certain question of form.'

'A question of form, is there?' Macro said quietly. 'I see.'

'Yes. Have you used a hunting spear?'

'I've used a javelin once or twice, sir.' Macro's voice was laced with irony.

'Right, that's a good start. Let's see you in action, then I can offer you a few pointers before we have a chance to make complete arses of ourselves on the hunt.'

Quintillus walked over to a rack of hunting spears, picked one out and tossed it to Macro. While Cato forced himself not to flinch Macro expertly fielded the weapon and then hefted it into a throwing grip. Fifty feet away stood some wicker targets shaped like men. Macro sighted along his free arm, drew back the hunting spear and hurled it towards the centre target. The spear shot across the training ground in a shallow arc and pierced the target at thigh level. Macro turned towards the tribune, trying not to smile.

'Not at all bad, Centurion. How about you, Cato? Here take this one!'

Cato caught the spear clumsily in both hands.

'Try not to look too cack-handed in front of the natives,' hissed Macro.

'Sorry.'

Cato readied the spear in his right hand, took his aim on the same target as Macro. With a last deep breath he drew his arm back to its fullest extent, then whipped it forward. The spear flew through the air, narrowly missing the chest of the target, and clattered on to the ground beyond. Tribune Quintillus tutted, the bodyguards laughed, and Cato's cheeks burned.

'Perhaps you'd care to show us the correct method, sir?' said Macro.

'Certainly!'

The tribune selected one of the spears, sighted the same target and hurled his weapon. With his powerful muscles the spear flew in an almost flat trajectory and struck the target in the region of the heart with a sharp thwack.

'Shot!' Cato exclaimed in admiration.

A ragged murmur of approval rippled along the bodyguards.

'There! You see?' Quintillus turned to Macro. 'Just takes a little practice.'

'Quite a lot of practice, I should imagine, sir.'

'Not really.' The tribune pursed his lips. 'No more so than any other weapon.'

'Is that so?' Macro replied quietly.

'Of course.'

'There's a difference between throwing a spear and using a sword. And there's a difference between using it against a wicker target and a real man, sir. Quite a big difference.'

'Nonsense! It's all about technique, Centurion.'

'No, sir. It's about experience.'

'I see.' Tribune Quintillus crossed his arms and carefully looked Macro over. 'Care to put that to the test, Centurion?'

Macro smiled. 'You want to fight me, sir?'

'Fight? No, just a little fencing practice. Chance for you to prove your point about experience.'

'Excuse me, sir,' Cato intervened quietly, 'but I doubt it would do Roman prestige much good if we had a fight in front of the natives.'

'Like I said, it's not a fight. Just a little practice. Well, Centurion Macro?'

For a moment Macro glared back, and Cato noticed a little tightening of his friend's jawline. Cato felt a dead weight settle on his heart as he knew Macro would not be able to refuse the tribune's challenge. Then, to the younger centurion's surprise Macro shook his head.

'I don't think so, sir.'

'Oh? Don't fancy your chances, then?'

'No, I don't. It's clear to me that you've spent years training for this. I haven't had that luxury, sir. My swordplay is fairly basic, just the moves necessary for battle, and the rest is gut instinct. Right now, I doubt I could hold a lamp to you. But if we met in battle, I should think the odds would be a little more even.'

'You think so?'

'I know so . . . sir.'

'I'm still not convinced. Fight me, Centurion.'

'Is that an order, sir?'

Quintillus opened his mouth to reply before he thought it through, and then shook his head instead. 'Perhaps not. That would hardly be fair.'

'No. Is there anything else, sir?'

'Just make sure you don't let the side down tomorrow. Both of you. And keep a respectful distance from me at all times. Understood?'

'Yes, sir,' replied Macro and Cato.

'Dismissed.'

As the two centurions passed back through the hall Cato turned to Macro. 'For a moment there I thought you were going to take him up on that offer.'

'I was. But a sensible man picks his fights, he doesn't let others pick them for him. That twat would have thrashed me. He knew it and I knew it. So what reason was there to fight?'

'Put like that, none at all.' Cato was pleased. It was one of those rare moments in all the time he had known Macro that the veteran centurion had allowed logic to triumph over bullish pride. Better still, in some neatly discreet way Macro had got one over the preening artistocrat, as the ruffled haughtiness of the tribune's parting words clearly revealed. 'That was nicely done.'

'Course it was. I eat cunts like that for breakfast.'

'Must be something in the porridge.'

Macro glanced at him, and roared with laughter. At the sound, one of the hunting dogs snapped upright, ears pricked up and nose pointing at the two centurions. His owner raised his head, scowled at the Romans and gave his hound a kick.

Macro slapped Cato on the back. 'You're all right, lad! You're all right.'

Back in the royal enclosure the business of preparing for the hunt continued in the boiling heat, and the two centurions were pushing their way through the heavily laden servants when Cato heard someone call his name. Looking through the crowd, he saw Tincommius. The Atrebatan prince frantically waved a hand and pushed towards the centurions, his expression wrought with anxiety.

Cato pulled on his friend's arm. 'There's Tincommius. Something's wrong.'

'Eh?' Macro tried to peer over the shoulders of the men around him. Then Tincommius was before them, breathless and desperate.

'Sir! Please, come with me at once!'

'What's happened?' Macro snapped. 'Make your report!'

'It's Bedriacus, sir. He's been stabbed.'

Chapter Twenty-One

'What happened exactly?'

'Come now, sir!' Tincommius pleaded.

'Tell me what happened?' Macro replied harshly.

'I don't know. I found him inside the headquarters building. He was lying on the floor in the corridor. There was blood everywhere.'

'Is he still alive?'

'Yes, sir. Just.'

'Who's looking after him?'

'Artax. He was in the corridor just after I found Bedriacus.'

Cato grabbed Tincommius' arm. 'You left him with Artax? Alone?'

Tincommius nodded. 'I sent a man for the surgeon before I came to find you.'

'Why the hurry?' asked Macro.

Tincommius glanced round before he leaned closer. 'He was losing consciousness. He called out Cato's name and said something about Verica being in danger.'

'Verica?' Macro said loudly. 'What kind of danger?'

'Keep it down!' Cato warned, as one of the stewards looked in their direction. 'Want everyone to hear?'

For a moment Macro was startled by the vehemence of

Cato's tone. Cato turned back to Tincommius and spoke quietly. 'What exactly did Bedriacus say?'

'He had to see you. Had something important to say; he'd overheard someone talking about the king. About killing him . . . That's all I got out of him before Artax found us.'

'Artax heard him say all that?'

Tincommius nodded. 'Then he sent me to find you.'

Cato exchanged a look with Macro. 'We'd better get back to the depot quick as we can.'

'Right.'

'Has he said anything?' Tincommius gasped as they burst into Cato's quarters, breathless. The surgeon was crouched over the body. Opposite him Artax was kneeling on the floor and looked round.

'Na . . .'

A pool of blood glistened in the light from the high window in Cato's office. More blood was splashed about the beaten earth floor, and was smeared on the whitewashed lathe walls either side of the wooden doorframe.

Cato took a sharp breath at the sight of Bedriacus. The hunter's face looked whiter than snow, with a waxy pallor. His eyes flickered open and shut as his mouth hung loose, the tongue feebly moving over his trembling lips. Bedriacus' red tunic had been removed and lay to one side, dark and wet. Only the loincloth remained on the hunter, and the drained white skin smeared with his blood made him look to Cato like a creature that had been caught and skinned.

'How is he?'

'How is he?' Macro looked up from the surgeon. 'Use your bloody eyes. He's had it. Don't need to be a quack to work that one out.'

'Quiet, please, sir,' the surgeon requested. 'It's best for him.'

204

Cato slowly crossed the room and kneeled to one side of the huddle of men. 'Artax? He say anything to you?'

Artax raised his shaggy head and looked levelly at Cato, his expression clear of any feeling of any kind.

'Did he say anything to you while you were waiting with him?'

Artax was still for a moment, and then gently shook his head.

'Nothing? Nothing at all?'

'Nothing that made any sense, Roman.'

Cato and Artax stared at each other, then Cato continued softly, 'I find that difficult to believe.'

Artax shrugged, but said nothing. Before Cato could question him more closely Bedriacus let out a long gasping groan. His eyes opened wide, stared wildly round at the faces of the men leaning over him, and then fixed on Cato.

'Sir . . .'

'Bedriacus, who did this? Did you see who did this?'

'Here . . . closer . . .'

Cato leaned forward, until his face was no more than a foot from Bedriacus' staring eyes. The hunter's left hand shot out and clenched Cato's tunic by the collar. The centurion instinctively tried to pull back but there was an insane power in the dying man's grasp and he pulled Cato closer. Cato could smell the stale odour of the hunter's breath and the sweeter, thicker stench of his blood.

'The king . . . in great danger.'

'I know . . . Now, just—'

'Listen! I came to tell you . . . Heard some men talking. Nobles . . .' Bedriacus' face contorted, and a violent spasm shot through his body.

'Hold him down!' the surgeon ordered, pulling Cato's cloak off a peg on the nearby wall. He threw the thick woollen folds over Bedriacus' body. The spasm quickly passed and the hunter's grip on Cato's tunic relaxed. His breathing now came in shallow gasps, his eyes fixed desperately on Cato. The centurion grasped the hunter's face between his hands.

'What the hell are you doing?' shouted the surgeon.

'Quiet!' Cato snapped. 'Bedriacus! Bedriacus! Who did this? Tell me! Tell me, while you can!'

Bedriacus tried to answer, but the fight had almost died in him. His eyes flickered towards Tincommius, then back to Cato and he managed to whisper. 'My eyes . . . grow dim . . .'

Tincommius gently pushed Cato away and rested a hand on Bedriacus' brow. 'Sleep, Bedriacus the hunter. Sleep.'

'Stop that!' Cato snapped. 'You bloody fool! We have to know.'

Tincommius looked up with a dark and angry expression. 'The man's dying.'

'I can't stop that. No one can. We have to know. You heard him: someone's after Verica. Now, get out of my way!'

'Too late,' murmured Artax. 'Look. He's gone.'

Cato turned away from Tincommius, and looked down at Bedriacus. The hunter was quite still, eyes staring up at the ceiling, mouth slack and without breath. The surgeon leaned closer to inspect Bedriacus for any sign of life. He turned his head, and placed an ear on the Briton's breast. A few moments later he sat up, and released the bloodstained wad of cloth that he had been holding to the hunter's stab wound. As the material came away, Cato saw the dark puncture, like a glistening mouth. Then the macabre illusion was broken as blood welled up and trickled down the skin and on to the floor.

'He's dead,' the surgeon said officially.

'Right then, better get it in a report,' said Macro, rising to his feet. 'You want the body taken anywhere?'

The surgeon nodded towards the two Britons still sitting

beside Bedriacus. 'Ask them, sir. I don't know the local customs.'

'Goodbye, Bedriacus,' Artax said quietly. Cato looked up and saw a faint smile playing at the corners of Artax's lips as the nobleman continued, 'Safe journey to the next world.'

Cato quickly went to the door and shouted an order for the headquarters guard. As distant footsteps pounded across the courtyard he turned back to the two Britons, still squatting over the body. Macro came over to him.

'What's up? Why call the guard? We can get someone else to take the body away.' The older centurion's gaze flickered over the blood smeared across the floor. 'Better get 'em to clean up your office as well.'

'We can deal with that later,' Cato replied. 'Right now I want Artax taken and held somewhere safe. Somewhere nice and quiet, where we can ask him a few questions.'

'What the bloody hell is going on?' Tribune Quintillus exploded as he marched into Cato's office. 'Why was I called away from my training?' Then he noticed the body on the floor. Cato had arranged his cloak so that it covered Bedriacus' face. Only his bare feet stuck out from the heavy material. 'Who is that joker?'

'Joker, sir?' Cato followed the direction of the tribune's glance. 'That's one of my men. My standard bearer, Bedriacus.'

'Dead?'

Macro nodded. 'Well spotted, sir. Glad to see the army is still pursuing its policy of recruiting the brightest and the best.'

Quintillus ignored the comment, and turned to Cato. 'How?'

'Stabbed, sir.'

'Accident?'

'No.'

'Ah, I see,' Quintillus nodded thoughtfully, and then decided what must have happened. 'Some kind of local grudge thing no doubt. Give the Celts long enough and they'd all kill each other. Save us the job. Do we have the culprit?'

'No, sir,' replied Macro.

'Why not?'

Macro gave Cato a look of exasperation as Quintillus continued without pausing for any kind of response, 'If you haven't caught the killer, then why send for me? Why waste my time? I can't do your job for you, you know. Well?'

'We haven't positively identified the killer yet,' Cato said apologetically. 'But the matter is more complicated, sir.'

'Complicated?' Quintillus smiled. 'What could possibly be complicated about some native brawl?'

'It's not a brawl, sir. Or at least it doesn't seem like one. Tincommius found him in the corridor.'

'Tincommius?' The tribune frowned, before he placed the name, and his face brightened. 'One of those clowns that hang around King Verica? What on earth was he doing in here?'

'He's serving with the two cohorts we raised,' Cato explained. 'So are a great many of the nobles, as it happens.'

'They've done us proud, sir,' Macro added. 'They're good men.'

'Yes, well, quite.' Quintillus turned on Cato. 'What's Tincommius got to do with this killing?'

'As I said, sir, he found Bedriacus on his way to find me.'

'Who was on his way to find you?'

'Bedriacus!' Macro snapped.

Cato shot him a warning look. 'Yes, sir, Bedriacus. He was trying to tell me about something he'd overheard. Something about a plot against King Verica.'

'A plot?' Quintillus laughed. 'What is this? Some cheap matinée performance at Pompey's theatre?'

Cato fought to control his exasperation as he replied. 'Never having had the opportunity to attend Pompey's theatre I wouldn't know about that, sir.'

'You haven't missed anything. But it sounds like someone is trying to make up for your lack of education. Or pulling your leg.'

'Pulling his leg!' Macro shot a finger at the body. 'That's a dead man there, sir. Pretty harsh practical joke, wouldn't you say?'

'Centurion, if you only knew the kinds of things the young blades get up to back in Rome . . . Still, in this instance, maybe there's something more to it. Please continue, Centurion Cato. About this plot?'

'Yes, sir. That's all we got out of Bedriacus before he died.'

'He didn't happen to let you know who stabbed him?'

'No, sir,' Cato admitted.

'Oh, come on! This is ridiculous. There must be more to it than that!'

'Maybe, sir. Tincommius was joined by another man before he set off to find us.'

'And who is this man? Let me guess – another one of Verica's little friends?'

'As it happens, yes, sir. But one who might have less cause to be fond of Rome than some of his comrades.'

'Imagine that.'

Cato shrugged. 'I find it difficult to believe that he just happened to be nearby when Tincommius found this man dying, right outside my quarters. Especially when Bedriacus had something vital he had to tell me. Too much of a coincidence, wouldn't you agree, sir?'

'It might be. Then again, it might just be coincidence that Artax was there. Have you any other proof?'

A puzzled expression passed fleetingly across Cato's face, but he was interrupted by Macro before he could answer the tribune.

'Artax is a fishy one, all right. Arrogant sod has been giving us the evil eye ever since we showed up in Calleva.'

'And yet he still serves with your cohorts,' Quintillus pointed out.

'Well, yes . . . But what better way to keep an eye on us?' The tribune shook his head. 'No. I doubt he's plotting anything. Plotters don't tend to try to stand out, let alone act suspiciously.'

'Speaking from experience, sir?'

'Only from common sense, Centurion . . .'

Some people just couldn't help being confrontational, Cato decided as he watched the two men. But this was not helping things. Artax was being held in a cell on the far side of the headquarters block, and Cato was sure the Briton knew something about the stabbing, if not the plot that Bedriacus had mentioned. He had to be questioned, and soon.

'Sir, we must interrogate Artax. He's keeping something from us. I'm sure of it.'

'You're sure of it?' the tribune said scathingly. 'On what grounds? Gut feeling?'

There was nothing Cato could say to that without looking foolish. It was true that there was no hard evidence on Artax, just Cato's observations of the man over recent days, the weight of coincidence and, if he was honest with himself, gut instinct.

'So, I'm right then?' Quintillus gave a small smile of triumph. 'Well, Centurion?'

Cato nodded.

'So then, this Artax. Just how close is he to the king?'

'Very. Blood relation, and part of his entourage before he joined the cohorts.'

'Sounds like a model ally, and well enough placed for you to treat him with respect, wouldn't you say?'

'Yes, sir.'

'Then I suggest you release him as soon as possible, before he reconsiders his view of Rome. Given the sensitivity of the situation I don't think we should risk any unnecessary offence.'

'Sir, if we could just question him first—'

'No! You've caused enough trouble already, Centurion. I'm ordering you to release him immediately. Now see to it. I've got training to get back to.' Quintillus strode to the doorway, and paused in the wooden frame, almost filling it with his well-honed physique. He looked at Macro and Cato as he spoke. 'If I hear that you've delayed acting on my order I'll break you both and send you back to the ranks. Understand me?'

'Yes, sir.'

'I want to see this Artax in the king's party when we leave on the hunt tomorrow. If there's so much as a scratch on him, I'll have your balls for paperweights.'

As the tribune's footsteps faded down the corridor Macro clenched his fist and pounded the palm of his other hand.

'Bastard! Utter bastard! Coming in here and telling us how to bloody proceed. Who the fuck does he think he is? Bloody Julius Caesar? Cato? I said who does he think he is? . . . What the hell's up with you? Cato!'

Cato started. 'Sorry. Just thinking.'

Macro rolled his eyes. 'Thinking are we? Tribune's ordered the release of our only likely suspect, and you sit there daydreaming. Pull yourself together, lad. We need to act, not think.'

Cato nodded absently. 'Didn't you think it was a bit odd?'

'Odd? No, not really. Typical twat behaviour for a tribune, sticking his oar in when it's not needed.'

'No. Not that.' Cato frowned.

'What then?'

'The fact that he knew Artax was involved before we even mentioned his name . . .'

Chapter Twenty-Two

Only a few hundred of the people of Calleva turned out to watch the royal hunting party set off for the forest. And even these failed to lend the event the customary festival atmosphere. As Cato and Macro rode out of the gate they saw the pinched faces of the starving on both sides of the track leading away from the town. But hungry as they were, the children still capered alongside the procession of carts, horses and the small column of servants from the royal household. Cato turned his gaze away from the people of Calleva. It was not as if he hadn't seen starvation before. Even Rome, for all its exotic food markets and the corn dole, had a multitude of beggars and drifters starving on its streets.

At the insistence of tribune Quintillus, the two centurions were riding just ahead of King Verica's household slaves and the wagons bearing all the supplies and luxuries for the hunt. In front of them were the lesser nobles of the tribe, dressed in loose tunics and brightly coloured leggings. Even though it was early morning, the men had already dipped their drinking horns and were talking and laughing loudly, quite oblivious to the eyes staring at them from thin hungry faces each side of the track. At the head of the hunting party rode King Verica, his closest friends and advisors, and a small band of his body-guards; armed and ready to deal with any threat. They watched the people lining the track closely, sword hands resting near the top of their scabbards. But there was no move towards the king. Some of the crowd cheered weakly. Most watched in silence until the supply carts rumbled past them, some filled with haunches of cured meat, stoppered jugs of wine and beer, baskets filled with bread and fruit.

A low moan of despair slowly rose into a collective keening whine. Then a voice was raised in anger. Cato turned back to look, and saw a man holding up a grubby infant, eyes bulging from its skeletal head. The man was shouting, but the raw emotion straining his voice made it difficult for Cato to understand the words. Not that he had to. The dull lethargic look in the baby's eyes and the man's terrible anguish were clear enough. Others took up the angry cry and the crowd slowly shuffled towards the food wagons.

The stewards who were driving the vehicles rose from their benches, shouting and waving the townspeople back. But their warnings were ignored as every eye hungrily focused on the contents of the wagons. Before the first hand could reach inside there was the loud crack of a whip and a scream of pain. Cato saw a man clutching his face, and blood streamed through his fingers. The crowd paused, silent for an instant, as if they were all having a sharp intake of breath. Then they closed on the wagons, and the stewards laid about them with their whips, shouting curses at the starving crowd.

'Stop them!' Cato heard Quintillus shout.

The tribune was galloping back past the party of nobles, sword drawn. Behind him thundered the king's bodyguard, scattering people away from the track.

'Macro!' Cato called out. 'Help me!'

The younger centurion wheeled his horse and urged it towards the nearest wagon as he shouted in Celtic. 'Back, you fools! Get back!'

Faces turned towards him, filled with anger and then fear as they tried to push themselves away from the flaring nostrils and gleaming bulk of Cato's horse. Cato drove his mount on, forcing it between the crowd and the wagon. 'Get back! Back, I said! Now!'

Then he was aware of Macro, on the far side of the wagon, following Cato's lead as he drove a gap between it and the shrieking mob. The townspeople fell back from the two horses, just long enough for them to be aware of the tribune and the bodyguard charging down on them, drawn weapons glinting. Then in a stumbling tide the crowd swept back from the wagons, desperately seeking escape from the hoofs and blades of Verica's warriors.

'After them!' Quintillus shouted, waving his sword at the retreating townspeople.

'Hold still!' Cato shouted in Celtic at the bodyguards. They paused. For a moment he feared that they would ignore him and ride the people down. Cato thrust his arm up. 'Hold still, I said! Leave them alone. The wagons are safe.'

The bodyguards checked their mounts and lowered their weapons. Quintillus looked at them with a shocked, then enraged expression.

'What do you think you're doing? Get after them! Kill them!'

The warriors looked at him blankly and the tribune turned to Cato. 'You speak this bloody barbaric language. Tell them to get after that mob! Before it's too late.'

'Too late for what, sir?'

'What?' The tribune glared at him. 'Tell them! What are you waiting for, Centurion?'

Cato saw the crowd breaking into a loose mass, rushing back towards the gateway.

'There's no point now, sir.'

'Just do it! Tell them!' Quintillus screamed at him. 'I command it!'

'Yes, sir. At once.' Cato saluted, turned to face the bodyguard and frowned. 'Soon as I can remember the right words.'

The tribune's face drained of blood as his mouth clenched in a tight line. Macro had to look away before he laughed, and he busied himself with an adjustment to his sword belt. He heard Cato click his fingers.

'That's it! I remember now! . . . Hey! Where'd they go?'

Tribune Quintillus glared at Centurion Cato for a long time, and Macro began to worry that his young friend had over-stepped the mark. Then, as Verica's bodyguard lowered their weapons and began to trot back towards the head of the small column, the tribune rammed his sword into its sheath and nodded slowly at Cato.

'Very well, Centurion. So be it. This time you've had your way, but I'm warning you, if I detect one shred of disrespect or disobedience from you again, I'll see to it that you're finished with the Eagles. At the very best I'll have you broken back to the ranks, on latrine duty, shovelling shit for the rest of your life.'

'Shovelling shit. Yes, sir.'

Tribune Quintillus clenched his teeth angrily, then wheeled his mount, savagely dug his heels in and galloped it on towards the king and his entourage. The two centurions watched him go. Macro scratched the bristles on his chin and shook his head slowly.

'You know, Cato, old son, I really wouldn't make a habit of pissing off tribunes. Likely as not he'll make legate one day, and what if he happens to be in command of any legion you might be serving with? What then, eh?'

Cato shrugged. 'I'll deal with that when the time comes. But if pricks like that are ever trusted with command of a legion then we might as well hand the Empire over to the barbarians right now.'

Macro laughed. 'Don't take it to heart! He just sees you as something in the way of him grabbing the glory that's his due. It's nothing personal.'

'Oh?' Cato muttered. 'Well, it's personal now. Personal to me.'

'Bollocks!' Macro reached over and slapped Cato on the shoulder. 'Forget it. He's out of your reach. You can't afford to have him as an enemy. Pick on someone that fits your purse. Better still, just forget the whole thing.'

Cato glanced at him. 'That's rich, coming from you.'

The royal hunting party left Calleva and its troubled population behind them. The capital of the Atrebatans soon disappeared behind a hill as the column of riders, wagons and servants on foot followed the rutted track through the rolling landscape, with its scattered farms interspersed with small clumps of unfelled woods and slender coppices. Despite the fears over the raids that Caratacus and his Durotrigan allies were conducting deep into Atrebatan lands, some of the farms were still being worked. Occasional fields of barley and wheat rippled yellow and gold in the light breeze that wafted fluffy white clouds across a deep blue sky.

Cato's sullen mood was gradually assuaged once Calleva was far behind them. Tribune Quintillus was lost amid the cluster of men crowding about the king, and Cato soon forgot him as he let his eyes dwell on the fertile British landscape. True, it wasn't as dramatic, or cultured and cultivated as the countryside around Rome, but it had a gentle unspoiled beauty of its own and he savoured the sweet scents it offered up to him.

'It'll be a nice spot to retire in,' mused Macro, correctly

reading his companion's expression. 'Once we've given the enemy a good kicking.'

'How long have you got to serve?' Cato asked, with a tinge of anxiety as he anticipated life in the Second Legion without Macro at his side.

'Eleven years, assuming the Emperor honours the end-of-service rituals.'

'You think he won't?'

'I don't know. After the Varus disaster they kept some time-served veterans on until they could barely walk, or eat. Some of those boys had to put Germanicus' hand on their bare gums before he realised they'd had enough of the army.'

'Really?'

'Oh yes! There were still some of 'em around when I joined up. Poor sods. If the Germans had known the Rhine legions were made up of old men barely strong enough to lift a sword, they'd have swept through Gaul like crap through a goose.'

'Colourful.'

'No. Just truthful. It'd have been us soldiers buried up to our necks in shit, while those bloody politicians in Rome tried to pin the blame on each other. Bastards.'

'Still, it's different now,' countered Cato. 'Those who have served their time seem to be getting the discharge, with a full gratuity. The Emperor seems to be honouring that well enough.'

'Sure. Old Claudius seems to be an honest type, but he ain't going to last for ever.' Macro shook his head sadly. 'The better ones never do. Bound to get some little shit like Caligula, or worse, like Vitellius next, knowing our luck.'

Cato shook his head with a wry smile. 'Vitellius? Oh, come on! Even scum like him get found out in the end. Vitellius becoming Emperor? No. It isn't possible.'

'You don't think so?' Macro looked serious. 'I'd bet good money on it.'

'Then you'd lose it.'

'I know his type: no ambition is ever too high.' Macro pointed towards the front of the column. 'Like our friend Quintillus there.'

Cato's eyes followed the direction Macro was indicating, and saw that the king's companions were riding in a loose column, in twos and threes. Amongst them, Cato could just make out the scarlet cloak of the tribune. A man was riding close by the side of Quintillus; a broad-shouldered man with dark hair braided into pigtails, and Cato wondered what Artax was doing in such deep conversation with the tribune.

Chapter Twenty-Three

At dusk they camped beside a small pebbly stream that chuckled along the edge of the forest where the next day's hunting would take place. The sun hung low in the sky, massive against the western horizon as it washed the underside of the few thin clouds in orange and red. Long dark shadows stretched across the grass growing along the stream, which was short, eaten down by sheep from a nearby farm that had evaded the attentions of the Durotrigans. The farm, a low huddle of thatched round huts surrounded by a flimsy stockade, stood half a mile away on the other side of the stream. A small fire glinted from within the opening of the largest hut and a thin trail of smoke gradually dispersed above the thatched roofs.

The king, spying the fattened sheep, had decided that he wanted to dine on roast mutton. The best specimen had been slaughtered by his kitchen steward, and the body had been opened up and spitted, ready for roasting over the fire being prepared by some of the household slaves. When the flames died down the kitchen slaves raked the embers over and began to roast the carcass. Fat oozed from the meat and dripped down on to the glowing heart of the fire where it exploded in short-lived flares of smoky orange flame.

Macro's nose twitched. 'Smell that! You ever smelled anything so good?'

'It's just your stomach speaking,' said Cato.

'Sure it is, but go on, take a sniff.'

Cato had never particularly liked the smell of roasting meat. The resulting meal was fine, but the smell reminded him of funeral pyres.

'Mmmm,' Macro continued his reverie with half-closed eyes. 'I can almost taste it.'

There was so much smoke now that their eyes began to water. Without saying a word the two of them got up and moved away to a spot by the stream. The water looked clear and Cato cupped a handful to his lips and guzzled it down, cool and refreshing after the hot day's ride. A day in which he had had plenty of time to think.

'Macro, what are we going to do about Bedriacus' murder?'

'What can we do? Bloody tribune's gone and released the only suspect. Bet that Artax is laughing at us.'

Macro looked over his shoulder at the nobles, sleeping off their ride before the evening meal. Only a few were awake, Artax and Tincommius amongst them, talking in quiet tones as they sipped beer from gilded drinking horns. Verica, on the cusp of dotage, needed a nap and was propped up against a lamb's hide bolster, mouth hanging open as he snored. Around him squatted his bodyguards, very much awake and with their weapons within reach.

Macro shifted his gaze back to Artax as Cato continued quietly, 'Question is, why did he let Bedriacus die the way he did?'

'A good stab in the chest is generally a sensible way to proceed.' Macro yawned. 'He could have tried your method, of course, and talked poor Bedriacus to death.'

Cato ignored the bait. 'Talking is very much the issue.'

Macro sighed. 'Somehow I knew you'd come up with something like that. Go on then, tell me what talking has got to do with it.'

'It's just this. Bedriacus wanted to warn us about something. He was stabbed by someone who wanted to prevent him passing on the warning. And the most likely suspect is Artax.'

'Yes. So?'

'So why didn't Artax finish him off when Tincommius went to find us?'

'I don't know.' Macro shrugged. 'Maybe the surgeon turned up too quickly.'

'How long would it have taken to add another, lethal wound? Or smother him? He must have had time. He had to take the risk and kill Bedriacus. He couldn't afford to let him speak to us.'

'Maybe. But if that's the case, then why didn't he finish Bedriacus off while he had the chance?'

'I don't know . . .' Cato shook his head. 'I don't know.'

'It might be that he was just passing by, as Tincommius said.'

Cato turned and looked straight into Macro's eyes. 'Do you really believe that?'

'No. He did it, all right. Just look at the shifty sod. Would you trust him with your sister?'

Artax was still talking with Tincommius, hunched forward as they conversed in tones so low that they were inaudible from where the centurions were sitting.

Before Cato could reply, a horn sounded across the small campsite, calling everyone to the evening meal. The two centurions rose up from the side of the stream and strolled across the grass to where the Atrebatan nobles were slowly waking from their slumbers. To one side lay Tribune Quintillus, on his back, one foot crossed over the other as he stared towards the setting sun. At the second sounding of the horn the tribune sat up and saw Macro and Cato approaching. With a discreet nod of his head he directed them away from where he was sitting and they altered course towards the area where the lesser nobles squatted.

'Hobnobbing with the rich and powerful, as usual,' Macro complained quietly. 'Don't know why he bothers. I doubt they have much in common.'

'Some of them speak Latin – not brilliantly, but enough to get by. They can translate for the rest.'

'That's only half the problem!' Macro laughed. 'What the hell are they going to speak about? The latest fashion in Rome? Or what well-bred Trinovantian matrons are wearing this season? I don't think so.'

'I don't think he'll have much of a problem,' said Cato. 'Social class is a pretty universal language. The sons of the aristocracy are a clubbable bunch, they'll have no problem communicating.'

Nor did they. As darkness thickened and the king's party fell to feasting, the tribune and his newfound Atrebatan friends got roaring drunk, singing and talking in loud slurred voices and splitting their sides at the slightest joke or mishap. Carved chunks of roast mutton were eagerly devoured and washed down with yet more drink as the night wore on. All the while the king sat quietly by, indulging the raucousness of his youthful companions. He ate little and drank nothing but a little watered wine. A brilliant moon rose, outshining all but the brightest stars and casting a thin blue mantle of light across the sleeping landscape. At last, drowsiness overcame most of the royal companions and one by one they crawled off to their sleeping lines and dropped into the warm skins their servants had made ready for them. Just as Cato and Macro drained the last of their beer, the king's chief steward approached from the shadows and bent down over them.

'The king desires you to join him by his fire.' The steward

spoke softly in his tongue and, without waiting for a reply, turned and made his way back to his master.

'What was that?' asked Macro sleepily.

'Verica wants to speak with us.'

'Now?'

'Apparently.'

'What about?'

'The servant didn't say.'

'Shit! Just when I was ready to drop off. Hope the old boy doesn't keep us long.'

'I think he might,' said Cato. 'Has to be something important. Why else wait until almost everyone is asleep? Come on.'

Macro swore softly and then rose unsteadily to his feet and followed Cato past the snoring forms of sleeping men towards the dying fire, set slightly aside from the rest of the camp site. King Verica sat on an oak stool, flanked by the still forms of two of his bodyguards. A wan orange glow played over his wrinkled face and wispy beard, and his hand slowly turned a gold goblet resting on his lap. He looked up as the two centurions approached and a smile flickered across his face as he gestured them to take a place beside the glowing embers. A few others were already seated: Tincommius, Tribune Quintillus and Artax. Cato paused in mid-stride as he made out the last face, and then sat himself on the warm ground, on the opposite side of the fire to the tribune. Macro slumped heavily beside him. Cato suddenly felt very awake, and wary. Why had these three been summoned to sit with them before the king? What was it that Verica had to say, so late in the night, and so secret?

The king waved his steward over and handed him the empty goblet. The steward muttered something and Verica shook his head.

'No. No more. See that we are not disturbed. No one is to come near enough to hear our words.'

'Yes, my lord.'

When the steward had left them the king silently raised his head towards the gleaming moon for a moment before he addressed his guests. When he began there was a great weariness in his voice.

'I'll speak mostly in my tongue, since what I have to say affects my kinsman Artax more than anyone else. Centurions Macro and Cato are here because they have earned my gratitude and, more importantly, my trust. The tribune is present because he represents General Plautius. Centurion Cato, do you have enough of our tongue to translate for your Roman companions?'

'I think so, my lord.'

Verica frowned. 'Be sure that you do. I want no misunderstanding over what I am about to say. You will all bear witness to my wishes this night, and I task you all to honour them in the coming months. Understand me, Centurion?'

'Yes, my lord. If there's any doubt, then Tincommius can help me with the translation.'

'So be it. Now explain this to the others.'

After Cato finished translating this exchange to Macro the latter leaned close to whisper. 'What's going on, lad?'

'I've no idea.'

Verica lowered his head and gazed into his lap. 'I've had a strange feeling these last few days. I sense that my death is imminent. I've even had a dream: Lud came to claim my spirit . . . during tomorrow's hunt.'

He looked up at his listeners, as if seeking a response, but none came. What could a man say to a king who voiced intimations of his own mortality? For Cato, more used to the ready assumption of divine status by the three emperors he had lived under, there was something very touching about Verica's admission. Perhaps he feared death as much as other men. It would be unconscionably crass to offer any reassurance that the king need not fear death. That was the sort of remark best left to the most obsequious of men; the sort of remark that almost any senator in Rome could be relied upon to make loudly and publicly should anyone voice any doubts that the current Caesar would be with them for ever.

'Sometimes a dream is merely a dream, my lord,' said Quintillus in a comforting tone. 'I'm sure the gods are determined to bless the Atrebatans with many more years of your rule.'

'Whose gods, Tribune? Yours or ours? I'm sure that I've done quite enough to appease the great Jupiter in recent months, but at what cost to the gods of my people?'

'As long as Jupiter is content, then you need fear no other god, my lord.'

'Really, Tribune?'

'Of course. I'd stake my life on it.'

Verica smiled. 'Let's hope you, and your two centurions, don't have to do anything quite so dangerous in the coming days.'

Quintillus looked offended. For a man who appeared to have drunk quite freely earlier that evening, he was surprisingly serious, thought Cato. Then he realised that the tribune had been putting on an act for the benefit of the Atrebatan nobles. No, Cato smiled, it was for the benefit of the tribune himself: wine and easy company loosened some tongues far more effectively than any amount of intrigue or torture.

'Are we in danger, my lord, from your people?' asked Cato. 'Are you in danger?'

'No!' Tincommius protested. 'Your people revere you, my lord.'

Verica smiled fondly at his nephew. 'You may still hold some affection for me, as might Artax there, but you are in no position to speak for the rest of my people.'

'They feel as I do, my lord.'

'Maybe, but I hope they don't think as little as you do.'

Tincommius' mouth opened in shock at the rebuke, then he looked down with an ashamed expression.

Verica shook his head sadly. 'Tincommius . . . Tincommius . . . don't feel angry with me. Truly, I value such loyalty. But you mustn't be blinded by it. You must look up and see the world as it really is. And plan accordingly. I know that there are some nobles who question my alliance with Rome. I know that they say I should never have been permitted to regain my kingdom. I know that they would dearly love to throw their lot in with Caratacus and go to war against Rome. I know all this, as does any man with the sense to see and hear what goes on in Calleva. But this is foolishness of the worst order.' Verica raised his eyes to the heavens again before continuing, 'We are a little people caught between two great forces. You remember how I was thrown out of my kingdom?'

'I was young, my lord, but I remember. When the Catuvellaunians crossed the Tamesis?'

'Aye. They are truly a greedy nation. First the Trinovantans, then the Cantiians, and then they demanded our unconditional loyalty, or our lands. So I had to quit Calleva and leave the kingdom in the hands of Caratacus' place man. There was no choice. I had to bear the indignity and shame of exile to spare my people far worse at the hands of Caratacus. You see, that's the true burden of being a king. You must rule for your people, not for yourself, whatever the cost. Do you understand me?'

'Yes, my lord.'

'Good. Then you will know how that shame was redoubled when the legions landed and returned my kingdom to me at the point of their swords. Whether it is me, or any other, who rules in Calleva, we do so at the whim of greater powers than the Atrebatans. All we can do is survive as best we can. And that means throwing ourselves at the mercy of the strongest force.'

'But, my lord,' Cato protested, 'you are an ally of Rome, not some vassal.'

'Really? And what might the difference be in the long run? Ask your tribune. Ask him what will happen to us when Rome eventually crushes Caratacus.'

Cato translated, and silently prayed that the tribune would phrase his response carefully.

Quintillus replied with no trace of his usual cordiality. 'King Verica, I'd have thought you'd be a bit more grateful to the Emperor. Why, if it wasn't for us you'd still be stuck in some backroom suite at the Governor's palace in Lutetia. You've done well by Rome, and as long as you stay a loyal ally you will continue to do well.'

'And you will leave us be?' Verica replied in Latin. 'Leave us to rule ourselves?'

'Of course! As long as it's expedient.' Quintillus drew himself up stiffly. 'You have my word.'

'Your word?' Verica tipped his head to one side with an amused expression, as he turned towards Tincommius. 'You see, Tincommius? That's the choice before us. The certainty of being conquered if Caratacus wins against the probability of being turned into a province if Rome wins.'

'It might not ever happen,' said Cato.

'It is happening already, Centurion. I know the full scope of the tribune's powers, as I'm sure do you and Centurion Macro. It's time that his orders are revealed.'

Cato forced himself not to glance at Artax, and flashed a warning glance at Macro, but he needn't have bothered. The older centurion was fighting back a yawn and his eyelids were heavy with the desire for sleep.

'Tribune,' Verica continued, 'why not tell us the real purpose of your visit to Calleva? What were your instructions? The ones you discussed with me two days ago?'

'Sir, that was in strictest confidence.'

'It won't be. Not in a few more weeks. I may not be alive then. My closest kinsmen, Tincommius and Artax, need to know the full truth. Tell us now.'

Tribune Quintillus pressed his lips together as he considered the best response to make. In the end he took the least honourable way out.

'I can't. My orders were specific – I should tell only you. A soldier never disobeys orders.'

'Very brave of you,' Verica replied scathingly. 'Well then, I'll have to break the news. Your General Plautius fears that our people will not honour the treaty I made with Rome. Accordingly, he has . . . what was the word? . . . requested! He has requested me to be ready to disband the two cohorts as soon as he gives the word.'

As Cato translated, Macro sat up abruptly, wide-eyed and angry. Tincommius and Artax were similarly shocked.

'There's worse news, far worse,' Verica continued. 'As well as the disbanding, he requires that every single Atrebatan warrior is disarmed, and the weapons are to be . . . placed beyond use. I believe that was the expression.'

'No!' Artax growled. 'No! My lord, it can't be. It's not true. Say it's not true!'

After his silence thus far, the awful anguish and outrage in Artax's voice stilled the tongues of the others as the Atrebatan noble jumped to his feet. Verica reached out a hand, open-palmed, to calm his relative.

'Artax, please . . .'

'No! I will not surrender my arms! None of us will! We'd rather die.'

Cato translated the man's outburst.

'I'm sure the tribune's happy to arrange that,' Macro whispered to Cato as Artax continued to rant in Celtic. 'And the bastard's going to kill our cohorts.'

'Quiet, please, sir.' Cato tapped his friend's arm.

Verica had risen from his stool and walked over to Artax, gently grasping him by the shoulders. 'Think what you're saying, Artax! Think! It is the Roman general's order. If we resist it, then we are finished. They'll crush us like an egg. We must disarm our people. We must disband the cohorts. Whatever the dishonour. Dishonour is better than death.'

'Not for warriors!' Artax spat back.

'This isn't about warriors. This is about all of our people. Do you think for a moment that the legions will stop to discriminate between the people they butcher? Do you?' Verica shook him. 'Well?'

'No . . .' Artax admitted.

'Then we have no choice . . . You have no choice.'

'Me?' Artax looked at his king closely. 'What do you mean, sire?'

'If I die, for whatever reason, in the near future, it is my wish that you will become king. I call these others to bear witness to my wish . . . Now do you see why you must carry out General Plautius' order?'

Every face turned towards the king in astonishment. Then Cato looked round the men gathered by the dying fire. Tincommius was shocked and clearly fighting back some kind of emotion. Tribune Quintillus was surprised and then smiled contentedly. Verica simply looked relieved to have unburdened himself of this decision. Macro looked angry.

'Me?' Artax shook his head in bewilderment. 'Why me?'

'Yes,' Tincommius said quietly. 'Why him, Uncle? Why not me? You have no son, and I am your brother's son. Why not me?'

'Tincommius, since you left your father you have been as a son to me. A much-loved son. But you are too young, too inexperienced, and I fear that there are some of our nobles who would twist your thoughts, and turn you against Rome. I would that you were older, and more resilient to such conniving spirits. Also, like me, you have only recently returned from exile, and are something of an unknown quantity to those men that matter in our kingdom. Artax is known and respected by all. Others look up to him, especially those who fear or hate Rome. He is a man of honour and I have no doubt about his loyalty. I'm sorry. I've made my decision and there's no more to be said.'

Tincommius' face twisted into an expression of pained bitterness as the king turned back to Artax. 'Of course, my choice will have to be agreed by the council, but I doubt there will be any opposition. When you become king, Artax, you will see things as clearly as I have come to see them. Then you will know what has to be done.'

Artax nodded slowly. There was a long silence around the fire. Then, as Cato watched him, a smile flickered at the corners of Artax's mouth. 'Of course, my lord. I am truly honoured by your decision, and I see now what must be done.'

Chapter Twenty-Four

The weather changed the next day. A slow drizzle began just before dawn and the king's kitchen slaves struggled to get a decent fire going to cook a light morning meal. Verica and his hunting party gathered round a fire that continually hissed from the raindrops spattering down. There was no hint of orange in the dawn, only a dirty pale yellow away to the east. As the pallid light strengthened the sky became an unbroken grey.

'Great day for it,' grumbled Macro as he tightened the straps on his leather leggings.

Cato squinted up into fine spray. 'Might clear up later.'

'Pigs might fly.'

'Let's hope not,' smiled Cato. 'I think I'm going to have enough of a problem with ground-based boar.'

Cato was already dressed for the hunt, and leaning on the shaft of a long hunting spear. Unlike the legionary javelin, this weapon was broad-bladed, with vicious barbs that could only be dislodged by tearing away huge chunks of flesh. Although the spear could be thrown, the heavy shaft meant that this could be done at only very short range. Too short for Cato's liking.

'Ever hunted boar before?' Macro asked with a sinking feeling.

'I got as close to a boar as I ever want to be the other night.'

Macro grunted.

'Mind you,' Cato continued. 'I've seen them hunted in the arena.'

'That's not quite the same thing,' Macro said gently.

'Ugly brutes.'

'Yes. Ugly and bloody dangerous. If you find yourself on the ground facing one, watch those tusks. I've seen 'em carve a man up really nicely. Didn't kill him straight off. His wounds got infected with some poison they carry on the tusks. Must have been agony. He died screaming a few days later...'

'Thanks for that. Feel so much happier now.'

'You'll be all right,' Macro laughed, slapping his companion on the shoulder. 'Just stick close to me and watch your back.'

'Someone else could use that advice,' Cato muttered, nodding at the king and his nobles gathered about the fire and toasting each other with beer. Artax was standing close by the side of his king. Cato noticed that he was not drinking like the others, but seemed distracted. As well he might, Cato reflected. Verica was old. In months, maybe even weeks, Artax would be ruler of the Atrebatans. That kind of prospect was likely to turn a man's mind from the here and now. It was vexing Cato almost as much. Would King Artax be every bit as fiercely proud and prickly as Artax the young nobleman? If so, what hope was there for good relations between the Atrebatans and Rome? But maybe Verica was right. The old king was shrewd enough to see that the Atrebatans needed a ruler who would offend the least number of people and in that respect Artax was indeed a wise choice. But would he be wise enough in turn to see where the only possible destiny of his people lay?

'Verica's safe enough,' said Macro, 'now that he's got Artax onside.'

'Yes. I suppose. But I still don't trust him. He's up to something.'

'You're jumping at shadows.'

'Shadows don't kill people.'

'No.' Macro raised his head to the sky and squinted round. 'Come on then. Doesn't look like it's going to get any warmer or drier.'

They just had time to grab a hunk of cold mutton and a small loaf of bread when Cadminius sounded his horn to summon everyone to the hunt. Mouths full, and chewing frantically Cato and Macro stuffed the remains of their barely started meal into their haversacks and hurried over to the horseline. The hunting party heaved themselves on to the backs of their ponies and made themselves comfortable before reaching for the spears their slaves held ready for them. Verica was helped on to his mount, and Artax roughly pushed aside a slave to make sure that it was he who helped his king into the saddle. Verica looked down and smiled warmly, before reaching over to pat Artax on the shoulder.

'Touching, isn't it?' Macro muttered. 'Nothing quite like having someone throw a kingdom your way to improve your manners.'

Tincommius urged his horse over towards the two centurions.

'Good morning!' Cato called out to him.

'Good? Is it good?' Tincommius replied sourly.

'Boy's got a pine cone up his arse,' Macro whispered before Tincommius came within earshot. The Briton pulled the reins and drew his horse up beside the two Romans. Macro smiled at him.

'Cheer up, old son. Just as long as it doesn't really piss down we should be in for a good hunt. That forest is teeming with boar, if Artax is to be believed.'

'Artax . . . Oh, I'm sure he's right.'

Macro and Cato exchanged looks, before Macro continued

in a hearty tone, 'I take it you aren't best pleased with Verica's choice of successor?'

Tincommius turned towards them, cold resentment on his face. 'No. Are you?'

'Provided he does good by Rome, he'll do well enough for me.'

'And you, Cato – what do you think?'

'I don't know. I just hope Verica lives for a while yet. Just to keep things settled.'

'Settled?' Tincommius laughed softly. 'Is that what you call it? Nothing's settled. Not while we're waiting for the old man to die. Everyone's thinking about what happens next. Do you really think Artax can hold the kingdom together?'

Cato watched him closely as he replied. 'Do you think someone else could do a better job?'

'Maybe.'

'You for instance?'

'Me?' Tincommius looked startled.

'Why not? You're closely related to Verica. You have some influence with the court. You might persuade the king's council to choose you instead of Artax.'

'Cato,' Macro growled, 'best keep our noses out of it. All right?'

'Just thinking.'

'No. Thinking's what you say to yourself up here.' Macro tapped his head. 'What you're doing is shit-stirring. We keep out of tribal politics.'

'We might not be able to for much longer. We have to think ahead. Tincommius has to think ahead. For all our sakes.'

Tincommius nodded slowly, but Macro shook his head.

'Leave it out. We're soldiers, not diplomats. Our job is to protect Calleva and prepare the Wolves and the Boars for battle. That's it, Cato. We leave the other stuff to cunts like Quintillus.'

Cato raised his hand in surrender. Just then the horn sounded again and there was a jostling of horses as the hunting party formed a loose column behind King Verica. Macro's horse was squeezed forward and for a brief moment Cato found himself pressed close alongside Tincommius. Their eyes met.

'Think about what I said,' Cato said softly.

Tincommius nodded and turned his gaze away, fixing his eye on the stooped figure at the front of the column. Then he clicked his tongue and urged his mount forward.

'What the hell are you playing at?' Macro whispered. 'You trying to plant ideas in his head?'

'I don't trust Artax,' said Cato.

'I don't trust anyone,' Macro replied in a furious undertone. 'Not Artax. Not Tincommius and certainly not that oily shit of a tribune. You start messing with the likes of them and you'll get us both killed.'

When the hunting party reached the edge of the forest the horsemen spread out along the tree line. Cadminius found Macro and Cato and told them to take up position close to the king, along with Artax, Tincommius and Cadminius himself.

'Why?' asked Macro.

'He needs men around him he can trust,' Cadminius replied quietly.

'What about them?' Macro nodded towards the king's bodyguards, who hung back behind the hunting party and formed a screen a short distance from the tree line.

'They'll make far too much noise if they stick close to the king. Scare all the boars away.'

'Doesn't he think that's a bit risky?' asked Cato.

Cadminius shook his head wearily. 'You've seen how he is these last few months. He's growing old and he knows it. He wants to get as much out of what's left of his life as he can. You can't blame him.'

'I might not, but his people might.'

Cadminius shrugged as he turned his horse away. 'We're his people, Centurion. He can do as he likes.'

Once the hunting party was settled in position they waited for the first sounds of the beaters. The horses lowered their heads and grazed on the wet grass while their riders sat quietly on their backs, spears resting across their thighs. The rain continued to patter a gentle drizzle on the leaves of the trees and soaked through the clothes of the hunting party. Cato's hair was soon plastered across his scalp and irritating rivulets began to trickle down his nose. With a muttered curse he pulled the cold mutton from his haversack, placed the bag on his head and sat there miserably chewing on the stringy meat waiting for the hunt to begin. As he sat, he wondered about the wisdom of having Artax so close to the king. Chosen successor he might be, but given the man's impatient and impetuous nature would Artax be willing to wait for his benefactor to die a natural death? It was as well that Macro, himself, Cadminius and Tincommius were close at hand, and Cato resolved to stay near to the king in the coming hunt.

'Cato!' Macro called out from twenty paces away. Macro pointed towards the trees. 'Listen!'

Cato cocked his head towards the forest. At first all he could make out was the steady rhythm of rain falling on leaves. Then he heard it: the long-drawn-out note of a horn, faintly in the distance. Other men looked up at the sound, grasped the shafts of their spears and made ready to move. King Verica turned his head and nodded towards the captain of his bodyguard. Raising his own horn, Cadminius drew a deep breath and blew a single powerful note. The line of horsemen walked forwards into the trees, out of view of the king's bodyguard and the handful of slaves who had accompanied the hunting party with cases of fresh spears.

Inside the forest the dimness of the day was accentuated by the thick leaf canopy, and Cato found that he had to squint to see clearly. Through the tall ferns and saplings to his left rode Macro. To his right was Tincommius. Beyond him the king was already out of sight and beyond the king rode Artax. In a short space of time the dense patches of undergrowth separated the huntsmen. Cato could hear them well enough: a constant cracking of branches and the occasional curse from some rider struggling through a tangled thicket.

To Cato's front the horns of the beaters were much clearer now, and he could hear faint shouts passing up and down the line. Somewhere between himself and the beaters lay the prey they had come to hunt. Besides boar there might be deer or even wolves, wild and terrified by the unaccustomed sound of the beaters. But it was the boars that caused Cato most anxiety. Besides the captured beast at Verica's feast, he had seen the animals at the games in Rome. Imported from Sardinia, these great brutes had had brown bristling hair and long snouts from which wicked tusks curved. Nor were the tusks their only weapon. Mouths filled with razor-sharp teeth had made short work of the condemned prisoners in the arena that day. Cato had seen one boar close its jaws on a woman's arm, and shake its huge head from side to side until it had ripped the limb away. The vivid memory made him shudder, and Cato prayed to the goddess Diana that the British boars were wholly unlike their terrifying Sardinian cousins.

The sound of something rustling through a bed of ferns ahead made Cato rein in his horse. He lowered the tip of his hunting spear and guided the point towards the sound. An instant later a ripple of moving fronds revealed the passage of some beast and Cato gritted his teeth and tightened his grip on the spear shaft. A fox burst out of the ferns on to the bare forest floor and stopped the instant it saw the horse. Crouching low, and quite still, it stared at Cato for a moment. Then it was gone, before Cato could even decide if it was worth a prod. He laughed at the release of tension and tapped his heels into the side of his pony. Further down the line, away to his left, there was an excited shout as one of the hunters came upon his prey and there was a brief mad confusion of cries, a piercing whinny then the long grating squeal of an injured boar.

'Cato!' Macro called out. 'You hear that?'

'Yes! Sounds like someone's had some luck.'

His head was turned towards Macro when the beast broke cover. So he heard it before he saw it and instinctively tightened his grip on the horse's reins. The horse, spooked by the sudden appearance of the animal, and responding to the sharp tug on the reins, reared up. Cato threw himself forward, against its neck, to avoid falling off and the boar charged beneath the belly of the horse and crashed into its groin. A shriek of agony burst from the horse's foaming muzzle as it tumbled back and to the side. Cato saw the ground rushing up towards him and just had time to throw himself clear. He landed heavily and the breath was driven from his lungs with an explosive grunt of pain. He was aware of the horse thrashing on the ground nearby, and there was an enraged squeal from the boar as it turned on the horse once again, its short powerful legs kicking up dead leaves as it charged. Cato forced himself to his feet, gasping for air and frantically scrabbling through the bed of ferns for his spear.

'Cato!'

Cato raised his head and opened his mouth to cry for help, but he was too winded to sum up more than a terrified wheeze. Then he saw the spear tip, glistening close to his feet. He reached for the shaft and snatched the spear up, spinning back towards his horse. It lay on its side, front hoofs thrashing at the ground, rear legs strangely limp, and Cato realised its back must be broken. There was a sickening thud as the boar charged home again and Cato, circled round the rear of the horse, crouching low, the blade of the spear poised for a thrust.

'Cato!' Macro's voice sounded anxious now. 'What's happening?'

As the other side of his mount came into view Cato saw the boar toss back its head, its tusks goring their way deep into the belly of the horse. With a savage wrench the long snout came clear, glistening with blood as a length of intestine was torn away on the tip of one tusk. The boar's wild red eyes widened as it caught sight of Cato and at once it turned and charged.

'Oh shit!' Cato grunted, diving back round the rear of the horse. The boar swept through the space he had been an instant before and then swerved and charged after him. With a terrified glance over his shoulder Cato ran, spear in hand, away to the right where the forest floor was clear. The boar came after him, like a battering ram, screeching for his blood. Any moment now his legs would be swept from under him and his back would be torn open by those tusks.

Ahead there was a thick tree trunk, an ancient oak that had fallen many years earlier and was now covered with a verdant moss, glistening in the rain. Bracing his legs, Cato leaped over it and sprawled on the far side. There was no chance of escape now. He rolled on to his back, and with the butt of the spear braced against the earth he raised the point towards the tree trunk. There was a scuffle as the boar prepared itself for the leap on the far side and then there it was, huge, bloody-faced and horrifying, sharp teeth gleaming in its open maw. It threw itself forward at Cato and its chest slammed into the broad point of the hunting spear. The boar's flesh swallowed up the point of the spear as it plunged deep into the animal's vital organs. The impact wrenched the shaft from Cato's grip and the length of the spear carried the huge beast clear over Cato before the shaft snapped with a sharp splintering crack.

The boar crashed to the ground with a grunt, squealing in agony as it struggled to regain its feet. The spear had broken near to the blade and the splintered shaft protruded from a bloody wound just below the boar's neck. Blood was gushing out and spattered the surrounding moss and the ferns as the beast tried to shake the spear tip free. Cato snatched up the broken shaft and drove the splintered end into the animal's side, thrusting his full weight behind the length of wood. The squealing intensified and Cato felt his legs battered by the scrabbling trotters of the boar. He ignored the pain and pressed the spear shaft home, wrenching it from side to side as he leaned his weight on it. Slowly the creature's efforts became weaker, and then ever more feeble, and Cato thrust harder with gritted teeth, hissing at the beast, 'Just die, you bastard! Die!'

The trotters were no longer lashing at his leg, but hung limp and still. For a moment longer the boar's breath came in short, snatched gasps. At last, with a final sighing wheeze, it was dead.

Cato slowly relaxed his white-knuckled grip on the spear shaft and slumped to his knees, shaking with relief and excitement. He'd done it, he'd made his kill and he was alive and uninjured. His heart pounded as he looked over the boar. Now that it was dead it seemed smaller, somehow. Not much, but smaller all the same. Looking down at the head Cato saw the jaws hanging slightly open, with a blood-flecked tongue protruding between the sharp teeth. He shivered and rose to his feet.

'Cato!' Macro called from nearby, from the direction of the mortally wounded horse. There was no mistaking the anxiety in Macro's voice.

'Over here!'

'Hold on, lad! I'm coming.'

As Cato rose to his feet there was a shout from close by, from the direction of the king. As he held his breath and strained his ears the voice cried out again.

'Help! Help! Murder!'

Cato recognised Verica's voice now, and turned to shout over his shoulder, 'Macro! This way! Quick!'

Then he was running towards the shouts, crashing through beds of ferns and being lashed by branches as he sprinted in the direction of the king's voice. Behind him he heard Macro calling out his name.

'This way!' he shouted back over his shoulder as he ran. His feet struck an object and he went flying forwards, arms instinctively raised to protect his face as he landed. He hit the ground hard, and rolled over before scrambling back to his feet. There was Tincommius, lying on the ground clutching his head. Blood oozed from between his fingers and his eyes flickered in a daze. His spear lay across his chest.

'Tincommius! Where's the king?'

'What?' The Briton shook his head, dazed.

'The king?'

Tincommius' eyes cleared and he rolled on to his side, his arm raised as he pointed down a narrow track. 'That way. Quick! Artax is after him.'

'Artax?'

'I tried to stop him. Go! Get some help! I'll follow Artax!'

Cato ignored him, and ran along the track. Looking down, he saw bright crimson drops on the ground and smeared on the ferns that he passed. The path suddenly opened out into a small glade. Twenty feet away was the thick trunk of an oak tree. At its base Verica lay crumpled on the ground. His white hair was matted with blood from a deep gash on the top of his head.

Standing over him was Artax, a thick length of wood in one hand. As Cato crashed out of the undergrowth lining the path Artax looked up and bared his teeth in a grim smile.

'Cato! Good! Come here, boy!'

'Drop the club,' said Cato. 'Drop it!'

'I've had enough of your orders,' Artax sneered, and took a step towards Cato. Then he paused and glanced round anxiously. 'Where's Tincommius?'

Cato launched himself at the man and both fell clear of the still form of Verica. Cato was on his feet first and swung his boot into Artax's face. There was a crunch as the iron studs connected with the bridge of the other man's nose and Artax cried out in surprise and pain. Then he too rolled to his feet and swung his club at the centurion. Cato ducked the blow and crouched low, preparing to spring forward again. Where the hell was Tincommius? And Macro?

Artax's teeth clenched in a snarl. 'You'll pay for that, Roman! I warn you, get back!'

Cato jumped forward. This time Artax was prepared and stepped to one side as he swung the club down across Cato's shoulders. The centurion crashed to the ground, utterly winded by the blow. He saw Artax nod his satisfaction and waited for the killer blow to land that would dash his brains out. Instead, Artax turned and walked back towards the king. But he never reached him. There was a dull thud and Artax grunted under the impact of Tincommius' hunting spear. The blow toppled him sideways and he fell to the earth, the dark shaft of the spear angling up towards the sky. Tincommius staggered over to the body, grasped the shaft and placed his foot close to the wound. With a great wrench he tore the barbed point out of Artax's chest and blood gushed from the gaping wound. Artax's body shuddered for a moment and he seemed to be trying to rise up. Tincommius kicked him to the ground and just before he died Artax reached a hand out to his king and clenched a fold of Verica's tunic.

'My lord! . . . Verica . . .'

Then he was still.

Cato was still too winded to rise. The blow had left his arms and shoulders numb and they refused to move. So he could only watch as Tincommius kneeled down beside his king, bloody spear in hand, checking for signs of life.

With a great snapping of branches Macro rode into the clearing, spear raised, ready to thrust it into the first enemy he came across. He looked round in confusion and reined in his horse before sliding off its back. He ran to Cato and turned him over.

'You all right?'

'Will be, in a moment.'

Macro nodded, then looked to where Artax lay dead, his hand still clutching his king's tunic. Tincommius turned and met his gaze coldly.

'What the fuck's been going on here?'

'Artax,' Cato mumbled. 'He tried to kill Verica.'

'The king,' Macro called across to Tincommius, 'is he alive?'

Tincommius nodded. 'Just.'

'Oh great!' Macro muttered. 'Now what?'

Chapter Twenty-Five

'How's the old man?' asked Macro. 'Any improvement?'

Cato shook his head as he sat down on the bench beside Macro. He had just returned from the royal bedchamber where the depot's surgeon was attending the king, under the watchful eye of Cadminius. Macro was drinking some of the local beer and slowly drying out beside the glowing embers of a brazier. It had been a long, uncomfortable day. The rain had closed in around the hunting party as they hurried back to Calleva with their wounded king. They reached Calleva at dusk, drenched and shivering, Tribune Quintillus had ordered Cato and Verica's bodyguards to accompany the king back to the royal enclosure while Macro rode to the depot to fetch the surgeon. Quintillus roused the Wolf Cohort from its quarters and had them mount guard on the depot and the looping ellipse of the ramparts of Calleva, in case any of Verica's enemies tried to take advantage of the attack on the king. While the men took up their stations under the flare of hastily lit torches, and waited for further news, Macro made his way up to join Cato in the royal enclosure.

The great hall was filled with men clustered in small groups around the trestle tables. Several of the king's bodyguard barred the way into Verica's private quarters, swords drawn and alert to any danger. Whispers and carefully moderated voices filled the air, and all eyes frequently flickered towards the doorway leading into Verica's bedchamber. Word of Verica's injury had started to spread beyond the royal enclosure, through the muddy byways of Calleva, and Atrebatans of every rank anxiously waited for further news.

Earlier Cato had watched the surgeon carefully clean the blood and mud away from the old man's torn scalp. The surgeon sucked in a deep breath before he gently probed the discoloured skin beneath the thinning hair. Then he sat back and nodded at Cato.

'He'll live, for now.'

'What are his chances?'

'Can't say. With this kind of injury he might be fine in a few days, or dead.'

'I see,' Cato muttered. 'Do what you can.'

The king lay on his bed, his face deathly pale where it showed beneath the dressing the Roman surgeon had applied to the wound. The old man's breathing was shallow. But for the faint rise and fall of his chest he looked as good as dead.

'Let me know the moment there's any change,' Cato told the surgeon.

'Yes, sir.'

Cato stepped away from the bed and headed towards the door leading into the hall. He paused before leaving the chamber. On the opposite wall was another door leading to the king's private audience chamber, through which Cato could hear the muffled sounds of a heated debate. Then Quintillus called loudly for silence. It was tempting to go to the door and listen more closely, but Cato would not demean himself in such a way in front of the surgeon. Outside in the great hall Cato caught sight of Macro taking a seat at the nearest bench and hurried over to his friend to report on the king's condition.

'No improvement? What did the surgeon say?'

'Not much,' Cato replied, conscious that many eyes were on him as he had emerged from Verica's bedchamber. 'Artax must have hit him pretty hard. Verica's lost a lot of blood, but the skull's intact. He might live.'

'He'd better.' Macro glanced round the hall. 'I get the impression that there's quite a few of the locals who might welcome a change of regime. Not much love lost for us here.'

'Maybe,' Cato shrugged wearily, 'but I think they're just scared.'

'Scared?' Macro's voice rose in surprise and a score of faces, dimly lit by the glow of the hall's torches, turned towards the two centurions. Macro tilted his head closer to Cato. 'A bunch of scared Celts? There's something I thought I'd never live to see.'

'You can hardly blame them. If the king dies they've lost him and his chosen successor in one go. Anything could happen. There's no one named to succeed him. The king's council will have to choose a new ruler. Just hope Quintillus can persuade them to pick someone who'll keep the Atrebatans on our side.'

'And where is our fine tribune?'

'He's with them now, in Verica's audience chamber.'

'Hope he's turning on the charm.'

'Charm doesn't come into it,' muttered Cato. 'I imagine he'll be quite blunt about the consequences of any change in the tribe's relations with Rome. Just hope he can scare them enough to be sensible, for all our sakes.'

Macro was silent for a moment before he continued softly. 'Do you think the tribune'll succeed?'

'Who knows?'

'Any idea who they might choose?'

Cato thought briefly. 'Tincommius is the obvious candidate. Him or Cadminius. If they want peace with Rome.'

'That's what I thought.' Macro nodded. 'Cadminius would be best.'

'Cadminius? I'm not sure that we know him well enough.'

'And you think you really know Tincommius?' Macro looked at his friend earnestly. 'Enough to trust him with your life? We'd be fools to trust any of this lot.'

'I suppose.' Cato ran a soiled hand through his lank hair and frowned. 'But I think if we can trust anyone it would be Tincommius.'

'No. I disagree.'

'Why?'

Macro shrugged. 'I don't know exactly. Something doesn't quite feel right about what happened with Artax.'

'Artax?' Cato sniffed. 'Always thought he was plotting something, especially after I showed him up on the training ground. Wouldn't trust Artax as far as I could spit him. And I was right.'

'Yes . . .'

'I don't know what Verica could have been thinking when he named him for the succession. That was as good as signing his own death warrant.'

'You're wrong, Cato.' Macro shook his head. 'What Artax did doesn't make much sense. Verica's an old man. He couldn't be expected to live much longer. Why didn't Artax just wait?'

'You know what they're like.' Cato nodded surreptitiously towards the natives clustered around the great hall. 'Impatient and hot-headed. My betting is that Artax came across the king alone during the hunt and thought he'd take a short cut to the throne. Lucky for us that Tincommius was there.'

'So you say.'

'The last thing we need is someone like Artax running things here in Calleva. We've got enough to worry about with

Caratacus still on the loose, without having to watch our backs in case the Atrebatans decide to have a change of heart. We'd be caught out nicely. Lucky escape for us . . . On the other hand . . .'

'Yes?'

'I can't help feeling that something worse is about to happen. It's not over yet.'

'Oh, for fuck's sake!' Macro cuffed Cato on the shoulder. 'When will you stop seeing the worst in everything? Ever since I've known you, it's always been the same. "Something worse is going to happen." Get a grip on yourself, boy. Better still, get a grip on this cup. Here, I'll pour. Nothing quite like the sight of the bottom of a cup to cheer a man up.'

For a moment Cato took umbrage at being referred to as a boy. That might have been all right some months before, when he was Macro's optio, but not now he had been appointed centurion. Cato bit back on his resentment; it would serve no purpose for the two officers to be seen to be at odds in front of this crowd of anxious natives. So he forced himself to drain the cup that Macro had filled for him, gritting his teeth to sieve the sediment that clouded the local beer like mud. He held his cup out for a refill.

'That's more like it!' Macro smiled. 'Might as well make the most of this while we wait for the tribune.'

They sat at the table and let the heat from the glowing brazier warm them through, and small wisps of steam curled up from the folds of their damp tunics as they drank more beer. Cato, far more responsive to the effects of drink than his companion, became drowsy, slowly slumping back against the wall behind him. His eyes fluttered a moment and then closed. Moments later, chin drooping on to his chest, the young centurion was asleep.

Macro watched him with an amused expression, but did

nothing to disturb his friend. He took a perverse satisfaction in this moment of weakness. While he had celebrated Cato's promotion with a full heart, there were times when it pleased Macro to feel that, after all, his experience counted for more than Cato's undoubted ability. Despite every battle the lad had fought his way through since joining the Eagles, despite all the courage and resourcefulness Cato had shown in the most desperate of circumstances, he was still not even twenty years of age.

In the orange glow of the gently wavering flames Cato's face was smooth and unblemished, not scarred and wrinkled like his own, and Macro indulged himself in a moment of fatherly tenderness towards his companion before he took another swig of beer and looked round the great hall. The anxiety of the Atrebatan noblemen was palpable, and already they were forming distinct factions, gathered in close groups in the gloomy depths of the hall. Perhaps the lad was right, Macro reflected. Perhaps there was worse to come.

'Wake up! Come on, Centurion! Wake up!'

'What! What's up?' Cato mumbled anxiously as a hand shook his shoulder roughly. His eyes flickered open and he jerked upright. Tribune Quintillus was leaning over him. Macro stood to one side, bleary-eyed but erect. Beyond them the hall was almost still. The braziers had burned down, and the dim red embers revealed only the dark forms of men sleeping on the rush-covered floor.

'You with us, Cato?' asked Quintillus.

'Yes, sir . . . Yes.' Cato rubbed his eyes. 'How long have I been asleep?'

'It's almost dawn.'

'Dawn?' Cato was immediately wide awake and furious with himself. Macro saw his friend's brow crease into a frown and couldn't help smiling. Quintillus eased himself back and wearily rubbed the stubble on his chin.

'We have to talk. Follow me.'

The tribune turned abruptly and strode towards the door to the king's bedchamber as Macro and Cato scrambled to their feet, hurrying after him. The royal bodyguards edged away from the entrance to the chamber to let them through, closing ranks the moment the door shut behind Cato. Once inside, the small group instinctively looked over to the bed where Verica lay. There was no movement, only the rhythmic thin rasp of breathing.

'Any change?' asked Quintillus.

The surgeon, seated on a stool beside the bed, shook his head. 'He hasn't regained consciousness at all, sir.'

'Let us know the moment there's any change, for the better, or worse. Understand?'

'Yes, sir.'

Quintillus gave a curt wave for the others to follow him and led the way through to the king's private audience chamber. Apart from the large table, the benches and Verica's ornate wooden throne, the chamber was empty.

'Sit,' ordered Quintillus, as he made his way over to the throne and sat himself down without the slightest sign of hesitation. Macro exchanged a quick look with Cato and raised his eyebrows. Quintillus leaned forward on his elbows and pressed the tips of his fingers together.

'It seems that I have persuaded the council to name Tincommius as Verica's new heir.'

'Of course, we all hope that Verica lives,' said Macro. Reservations about Tincommius still filled his thoughts.

'Goes without saying,' the tribune nodded. 'He's the best guarantee of peace between Rome and the Atrebatans.'

'We'll do all right by Tincommius, sir,' said Cato.

'I hope so.' Quintillus pressed his palms together. 'But, if the worst should happen and Verica dies, then we'll need to move fast. Anyone who opposes the new regime must be rounded up and held in the depot until Tincommius has a firm grip on his people.'

'You don't think Artax was acting alone then, sir?' said Cato.

'I'm not sure. I had never suspected him of being a traitor.'

'Really?' Cato was surprised. 'Why not, sir?'

'Because he was supposed to be one of General Plautius' agents. I doubt the general is going to be too pleased when he finds out that Artax was such a poor investment.'

'Artax, a spy!' Macro was surprised. 'He was a prickly sod, but I thought he was straight enough.'

'Apparently not, Centurion. Anyway, he wasn't a spy. He was a double agent,' Quintillus corrected him. 'Or at least that's what he became, it seems . . . It might be that being made Verica's heir simply went to his head, and he was acting alone.'

'Maybe, sir.' Cato shrugged. 'Either way, I never trusted him. But I think he's not the last of the locals we have to worry about. Now that Verica's off the scene I think we can expect some trouble, particularly with Tincommius lined up to succeed him. There are bound to be those who think he's too young and inexperienced for the job. And others who want to be king themselves.'

'Some of them may resist the council's choice,' Quintillus conceded. 'Some of them might even take up arms against their new king, if Verica dies. They will be dealt with by your cohorts.' A smile flickered across the tribune's lips. 'Your, er, Wolves and Boars.'

Cato ignored the jibe, too concerned with the implications of the tribune's orders. A chilling sense of foreboding traced its way up the scalp from the back of his neck.

'That might not go down too well with some of the men, sir. You saw how it was out there in the hall: the tribe is already beginning to break apart. We can't afford to make the situation worse.'

'Don't be so melodramatic, Centurion. Your men are under your orders. They'll do as you say. Or, is it that you fear you can't control your men? That's a real man's job, and you're not much more than a boy. I can understand that. How about you, Macro? Will your men obey orders?'

'They will, sir, if they know what's good for them.'

'That's the spirit!' The tribune nodded in satisfaction. 'Glad to know there's one officer I can rely on.'

Cato stared at the tribune, fighting back his anger and wondering if he was being cruelly baited, or tested. He resolved to remain calm – as calm under this attack on his integrity as he tried to be in front of his men in the face of the enemy.

'You can rely on me, and my cohort too, sir.'

The tribune stared at him for a moment. 'I hope so, Cato. I hope so . . . But for now the situation is hypothetical. Verica still lives, and while he lives we must all endeavour to make sure that relations between Rome and the Atrebatans continue as they were before.'

'Yes, sir.' Cato nodded. 'And we must do our best to make sure the Atrebatans keep the peace amongst themselves.'

Tribune Quintillus smiled. 'That goes without saying, Centurion.'

'Bastard!' Cato muttered as he and Macro walked back to the depot. The rising sun was still below the level of the roofs of the native huts lining the muddy track. The air was cool and damp, and by the thin light of this early hour Cato had seen how filthy he was and yearned for a good wash and a clean tunic. But the withering contempt of the tribune clung to him like a shadow and the young centurion knew that would be a lot harder to shift than a layer of dirt and grime.

'Don't carry on so!' Macro laughed. 'You're whining like a jilted bride.'

'You heard him. "That's a real man's job," ' Cato mimicked. 'Bastard. Arrogant patrician bastard. I could show him a thing or two.'

'Of course you could,' Macro said soothingly, and held his hands up as Cato shot him a withering look. 'Sorry. Wrong tone. Anyway, look on the bright side.'

'There is one?'

Macro ignored the bitter remark. 'Verica's still with us for the moment. And even if he drops off the twig we've got a man lined up to replace him. Tincommius wouldn't be my number one choice but at least he's not a traitor, like Artax. Things could be a lot worse.'

'Which means they will be . . .'

This was too much for Macro. Much as he liked Cato, the lad's constant pessimism could have a profoundly depressing and irritating effect on a generally cheerful soul like Macro, and he stepped in front of Cato, blocking the young centurion's path. 'Don't you ever stop being defeatist?' he snapped. 'It's really starting to get on my wick.'

Cato looked down into his superior's face. 'I'm so sorry, sir. Must be nerves.'

For an instant the older man tensed up, hands balling into fists at the end of his thick hairy forearms. Macro felt an overwhelming urge to knock some sense into Cato and get him to quit his grinding mood of depression. Then Macro relaxed his hands, slowly rested them on his hips and spoke very deliberately.

'You know, I wonder if the tribune wasn't right after all. If you get so riled by a few harsh words then maybe you've no place commanding grown-ups.'

Before Cato knew what he was doing his fist shot out and slammed into Macro's jaw. The older centurion's head snapped back and he staggered away from Cato. Macro recovered his balance and felt his jaw, raising his eyebrows as he saw blood on the palm of his hand from a split lip. He looked up at Cato, with a cold glint in his eyes.

'You'll pay for that.'

'I – I'm sorry, Macro. I don't know what I was thinking, what I was doing. I didn't mean to—'

'But it felt good, eh?' Macro smiled faintly.

'What?'

'You feel any better?'

'Better? No! I feel dreadful. Are you all right?'

'I'm fine. Hurts like hell, but I've had worse. But it took your mind of the bloody tribune for a moment there, didn't it?'

'Well, yes,' Cato admitted, still feeling embarrassed by his loss of control. 'Er, thank you.'

Macro waved his hand dismissively. 'Come on, let's get back to the depot. Forget the tribune, forget this bloody tribe of barbarians and let's get some decent food inside us.'

'Yes . . .' Cato was still standing where Macro had stopped him. He was staring over Macro's head, a faint look of concern in his expression.

'Relax,' Macro chuckled. 'I'll get you back sometime . . . What's the matter?'

'Look.' Cato pointed towards the eastern sky, painted pale gold by the rising sun. Macro turned to follow the direction of Cato's finger. Some miles distant several faint columns of smoke smudged the pale sky of the new day.

Chapter Twenty-Six

'Supply column?' Cato muttered.

'Looks like it.'

'I didn't know one was due.'

'Neither did I.' Macro grabbed his arm. 'Come on. Let's go.'

Macro led the way as they ran back to the depot. As soon as they were through the gate he sent one of the sentries to summon the tribune and Tincommius. As the man ran off down the lane towards the royal enclosure Macro turned to his subordinate.

'Get the Wolves formed up by the gate. I'll rouse the Boars and join you as soon as I can.'

'Yes, sir.'

Cato sprinted towards the headquarters building and burst through the door into the admin hall. Catching sight of one of the garrison's trumpeters, he shouted at the man to get his instrument and follow him to the main gate of Calleva. The man arrived on the walkway breathless from running under the weight of the curved brass horn, and having to climb the ladders to join his commander. Cato slapped his thigh impatiently as he waited for the man to catch his breath. At last he spat to clear his mouth, drew in a deep breath and blew into his mouthpiece. The strident notes of the assembly call rang out over the town and the men of the Wolf Cohort hurried towards the sound.

Over in the depot another signal rang out and, glancing round, Cato saw the men of the Boar Cohort tumbling out of their tents to assemble on the parade ground. The squat figure of Macro emerged from the headquarters building, helmet glinting in the first rays of the sun beneath the red flare of his transverse crest. He was fully armoured and ready for action. With a pang of self-contempt Cato realised that he had left his armour in his quarters, and he turned to the nearest man and sent him to fetch it.

Beneath the walkway the gates groaned as they were swung inwards. The first men appeared in the muddy street below and Cato leaned over the parapet to shout his orders down to Figulus.

'Form the cohort up on the road inside the gate!'

As the Roman instructors bustled the men into position and began to form the cohort into a marching column Cato looked over the wall towards the distant spires of smoke rising into the sky, perhaps four or five miles away. The air was quite still this morning and it was possible to distinguish several separate sources of the smoke: the individual supply wagons fired by the attackers, Cato reasoned. As the last men hurried into line the native he had sent to fetch his equipment arrived on the walkway, panting from his exertions. Cato frowned when he saw that the man had not brought him a fresh tunic, but there was no helping that now, and he pulled the shoulder padding over his head and reached for the heavy mass of his chain mail.

'Will there be a fight, Centurion?' the man asked as he fastened the buckle of Cato's sword belt.

'Depends if we catch them in time,' Cato replied in Celtic. 'Let's hope so.'

Cato noticed the warrior smile after his last remark, and realised that the man was spoiling for a fight. Cato shared the desire to lay into the enemy. Then, after a moment's reflection, it occurred to him that his reasons were more selfish and had everything to do with proving a point to the smug tribune whose remarks had cut him to the soul.

As soon as the last buckle of his harness had been fastened Cato snatched up his felt helmet liner, jammed it down over the top of his head and pulled on his centurion's helmet, hurriedly tying the leather thongs at the end of each cheek guard.

'Right! Down you go,' he ordered the warrior. 'Back to your century.'

Cato spared a quick look towards the depot and was gratified by the sight of the Boars, in column, marching towards the gate, Macro at their head. Then the young centurion clambered down the ladders to the foot of the gate and trotted to the front of the Wolf cohort.

'Figulus! Figulus! To me!'

The young Gaul came running down the column towards him, face flushed with excitement.

'Get 'em moving,' ordered Cato, staring towards the distant columns of smoke, already dissipating now that the fury of the blaze had passed its peak. 'I want them outside and ready to march. I'll catch you up as soon as I've spoken with Centurion Macro and the tribune.'

'Yes, sir!' Figulus saluted and ran towards the front of the small column. He called the men to attention, and gave the order to advance. The natives were well accustomed to the standard commands and at his word, broke into a rhythmic tramp, through the gate and down the track towards the distant columns of smoke. Cato watched them march by for a moment, then, once the rear rank of the last century had passed him, he made his way back to the open gate. There was a pounding of hoofs and then Quintillus and Tincommius galloped down the street leading from the royal enclosure. They were armed and ready to fight, and slewed their ponies to a halt as they caught sight of Cato.

'What's happening?' barked Quintillus. 'Report!'

'Smoke, sir!' Cato replied, indicating the direction. 'Looks like they've attacked another supply column.'

The tribune glanced down the track towards the Wolf Cohort. 'Where's Macro?'

'He's bringing up the other cohort from the depot, sir.'

'Good!' Quintillus rubbed his hands together. 'We might catch 'em loaded down. Let's get moving!'

'Sir, don't you think we might want to send scouts out first?'

'We're wasting time!' Tincommius said excitedly. 'We must attack at once.'

Quintillus nodded. 'It's clear enough what's happening, Centurion. And there's no time to waste.'

'But what about Calleva? We can't leave it unguarded, sir. Not under the present circumstances.'

'The men in the depot can handle the gate. Send for them. Now, we must move!'

Waving aside Cato's protests the tribune kicked his heels in and urged his pony out of the gate and down the track, closely followed by Tincommius. Cato ordered the nearest sentry to run to the depot and have every able-bodied man sent to guard the town's main gate, then he set off in pursuit of the tribune, running down the length of the column until he reached the wolf's head standard at the front of his cohort. Beyond, far down the track, galloped Quintillus and Tincommius, riding straight for the distant smoke. Cato fell into step with his men, and glanced sideways at the new standard bearer. Although a youngster, like himself, Cato reflected ruefully, the man was huge – none of the wiry strength of Bedriacus, just a mass of muscle.

'You're Mandrax, aren't you?'

'Yes, sir.'

'Well, Mandrax, keep the standard high and keep it safe, and you'll do fine.'

'Yes, sir.'

Cato looked round and saw, beyond the last century of the Wolves, the head of Macro's cohort emerging from the gateway. The Boars were stepping out at a fast pace to join their comrades and only slowed down when they caught up with Cato's men. Macro jogged forward to join Cato.

'Where's the tribune?'

'Gone ahead with Tincommius to see what's happening.'

'Hope the twat's careful,' Macro grumbled. 'Last thing we want is to give ourselves away.'

'Or lose another of Verica's heirs.'

'Quite.'

'Do you think this is wise, Macro?'

'What?'

'Taking both cohorts out of Calleva.'

'We did it before. Anyway, those were Vespasian's orders: to have a go at the enemy whenever possible and keep them away from our lines of communication.'

'Bit late for that now.' Cato nodded towards the columns of smoke.

'Granted. But if we get the buggers who did that then there'll be a few less of the enemy in the world. They won't be tucking into our supplies any more. That's a positive outcome in my book.'

Cato shrugged and decided to keep his concerns to himself.

The Wolves and the Boars continued down the track, heading towards the thinning smoke. They had covered just over three miles, according to Cato's estimate, when the tribune and Tincommius returned. Macro halted the column and moments later the two riders reined in their mounts and slid to the ground, breathless and excited.

'Round the next hill,' Quintillus panted. 'Small supply column. All dead, all the wagons burned. The raiders are still there, picking over the bodies. We've got them! Macro, send the scouts and two of your centuries round the back of the hill to cut them off. The rest will form a line at the base of the hill. Then we'll advance and catch them in a trap. Understood?'

'Yes, sir.'

'Now, Tincommius, rejoin your cohort, and try to stay out of trouble.'

'Of course, Tribune.' Tincommius grinned.

'I mean it. I went to a great deal of effort making sure you succeed Verica. Get yourself killed and you'll have me to answer to.'

Tincommius chuckled nervously. The tribune turned towards Cato and muttered. 'Keep an eye on him. He's to stay out of harm's way. I'll hold you personally responsible for his safety, Centurion.'

'I understand, sir.'

'Good.'

'Sir?' said Cato, as the tribune turned back towards his pony.

'What is it?'

'The enemy, sir. How many of them are there?'

Quintillus quickly estimated. 'Two hundred, two hundred and fifty. That's all. Why? Is that too many for you?'

'No, sir,' Cato replied tonelessly. 'I'm just surprised that they haven't made off yet. Particularly since there are so few of them. They must know we'd send a force out to investigate. Why take the risk?'

'Who knows, Centurion? Who cares? All that matters is that they're there and we've got the chance to put them in the bag. Now, you have your instructions. See to them.'

'Yes, sir.' Cato saluted.

Macro had already run off to issue his orders and the first two centuries of the Boars doubled away from the main body, moving obliquely in the direction of the near side of the hill that Quintillus had indicated. The tribune galloped to the nearest slope and headed up towards the crest. By the time that Cato had prepared his men the tribune had ground-tethered his pony and was creeping forwards, bent double and moving carefully through the long grass.

'At least he's doing that properly,' muttered Cato.

'You don't like him much, do you?' asked Tincommius.

'No. Not much. There's little his kind won't do to grab whatever glory is going.'

'And I thought the Celts were bad enough.'

Cato turned towards his Atrebatan companion. 'Tincommius, you don't know the half of it. Anyway, you heard the tribune – keep out of it today. No heroics. That's my order.'

'Don't worry,' Tincommius smiled. 'I know my duty.'

'Good.'

The century commanders were taking no chances, and passed down the lines of their men to give orders in unaccustomed low voices. The Wolves formed a line two deep to the left of the track, and Macro's remaining centuries formed up to the right. Ahead of them Cato could see that there was a steep slope beyond the hill that concealed the ravaged supply convoy and its attackers. With luck the enemy would be neatly caught, with no way out of the small vale, except by hacking a path through the Atrebatan lines. It looked like Quintillus would have his slice of glory after all.

As soon as the two cohorts were in position, Macro drew his sword and swept it forward. The Wolves and the Boars advanced through the long grass, still wet with the morning dew. The men rested the iron heads of the javelins on their shoulders as they rustled forward and began to sweep round the edge of the hill. Macro stayed in position on the extreme right of the line, its most vulnerable point, with the first century of his cohort –

handpicked men who could be trusted to fight hard and not yield.

Cato trotted to the left-hand flank, anxious to get the first possible sighting of the ground ahead of them in the vale. Far off, to the right, the two centuries dispatched to close the trap on the raiders were disappearing round the edge of the hill. With a little luck they would be able to get in position quickly enough to compel the enemy to surrender the moment they realised there was no way out for them. If the Atrebatans spared them, the best they could expect was a lifetime of slavery. From his recent experience of fighting the Durotrigans, Cato doubted whether they would surrender. The Durotrigans were being driven to resist the legions by druid fanatics, who promised their warriors that the very finest rewards the afterlife had to offer were reserved for the men who died fighting Rome.

As the line began to swing round the base of the hill Cato caught sight of the supply column. The charred remains of eight wagons came into view, flames still licking up from some of them. Bodies in red tunics were sprawled on the ground around the wagons. Close by were the raiders, a small party of men herding the supply column's draught animals together. One man leaned against the serpent banner of the Durotrigans, while a handful of others picked over the bodies lying on the ground. As yet none of them appeared to have spotted the Wolf Cohort marching steadily towards them, and for the first time Cato thought that the tribune's hasty plan might come off. Still, the raiders must be a dozy lot not to have detected the approaching danger. Cato found it hard to believe that they had not posted a lookout, at least.

The two cohorts had almost blocked the end of the vale before the alarm was raised. Cato saw the serpent standard bearer suddenly stand upright, then turn and shout a warning to his companions. Instantly the raiders sprang to their weapons and turned to face the Wolves and the Boars.

'Won't be much of a fight,' Figulus muttered beside Cato. 'We must outnumber them five or six to one. No contest.'

'No.'

But still the Durotrigans prepared themselves to meet the enemy. Clustering together in a shallow crescent, they raised their shields and shook their spears. A movement, away to the right, drew Cato's attention, and he saw Quintillus galloping his horse down the slope. He tore round the back of the advancing cohorts and took up a position just behind the centre of the line, drew his sword and shouted encouragement to the native troops.

'Wasting his bloody breath,' said Figulus. 'They don't understand much Latin.'

'No, but it might make him feel good.'

The distance between the two forces closed quickly, then the Durotrigans began to give ground, moving back past the burned wagons towards the far end of the vale, where the gap between the steep sides of both hills was narrow and offered better defence than the open floor where the Atrebatans would easily overrun them through sheer weight of numbers.

'That's not going to do them much good, not when Macro's lads come up on them.'

'Figulus?'

'Sir?'

'Just shut up for the moment. I don't need the running commentary.'

'Yes, sir.'

The two cohorts continued to pursue the enemy up the vale and began to pass by the burned-out supply column. Cato spared the charred wagons a quick look, and frowned. There was something about them that did not look right. The axles were far too thin and the light wheels and wicker-frame sides bore little resemblance to the heavy transport carts of the legions. As he stepped over one of the bodies Cato was aware of a faint putrid smell and he saw the blotchy skin on the corpse. The man must have died some days ago. The next body he came across was the same. All at once a dreadful doubt chilled his blood and he glanced anxiously at the trees that sprawled down the slopes of the hills on either side. Cato looked towards the tribune, but Quintillus had his gaze fixed on the small band of raiders directly ahead and was still shouting his encouragement. Cato drew a deep breath and threw up his arm.

'Cohort! Halt!'

The Wolves stumbled to a halt, some warriors not quite understanding the order, or not willing to obey it immediately. The result was a straggling line spread across the floor of the vale. After a moment's hesitation Macro echoed the order to halt and started running across towards Cato.

'Dress your lines!' Cato bellowed out to his men and the century commanders immediately started to shove and kick their men into order. A pounding of hoofbeats announced the arrival of the tribune.

'What the bloody hell are you doing, Centurion? Get your men forward!'

'Sir, there's something wrong about this.'

'Get your men forward! That's an order! You want that lot to escape?'

'Sir, the wagons. Look at them.'

'Wagons?' Quintillus glared at him. 'What about the bloody wagons?' He thrust the point of his sword towards Cato. 'Get forward, I say!'

'Those aren't wagons,' Cato insisted. 'Look at them. They're chariots.'

'Chariots? What bloody nonsense is this?'

'Chariots tied back to back, to look like wagons,' Cato

explained quickly, and stepped over to one of the bodies. 'And these men, dead long before the chariots were set alight.'

Macro came running up, breathless and angry. 'What's going on? Why'd you call a halt?'

Before Cato could reply, there came the distant roar of a war cry. The raiders at the end of the vale had seen their pursuers stop. Now they turned and were charging back towards the Atrebatans, screaming like madmen.

'I don't believe it,' Quintillus said softly. 'They're attacking us.'

Cato tore his gaze away from the enemy bearing down on them, and swept his eyes over the hillsides.

'There! There's your reason,' he said bitterly, thrusting an arm towards the trees on the hill to their left. Durotrigan warriors were pouring out from the shadows beyond the trees and forming up in a dense mass barely two hundred paces from where they were standing. Cato turned to the other hill. 'And there!'

For an instant the tribune's well-mannered façade crumbled as the deadly nature of the situation he had led the two cohorts into was thrust before his eyes. 'Oh, shit . . .'

'Wolves!' Cato quickly turned to his men, hand cupped to his mouth. 'Fourth, Fifth and Sixth Centuries! Refuse the left flank!'

As Macro sprinted off to join his men, the three centuries at the extreme left of the Atrebatan line folded back to face the Durotrigans massing on the slope above them. Unlike the natives in the two cohorts, the enemy were heavily armed, many with chain mail protecting their bodies. Already Cato could see that the Atrebatans were outnumbered; the tables had been completely turned on them and their Roman commanders. Cato spared their enemy an instant of grudging admiration before he turned to Tincommius and spoke to him in Latin.

'Get out of here! Get back to Calleva, as fast you can. We won't be able to hold them for long.'

'No,' Tincommius replied. 'I'll stay here. I'd never make it.'

'You'll go.'

Tincommius shook his head and Cato turned towards the tribune.

'Sir! Take him. Get him out of here!'

Quintillus quickly nodded and reached down for the hand of the Atrebatan prince, but Tincommius shook his head and, stepping back, he drew his sword.

'Quick, you fool!' shouted Quintillus. 'There's no time for heroics. You heard the centurion! Give me your hand!'

'No!'

For a moment the three men froze, each glancing anxiously at the others, then the tribune withdrew his hand and took a firm grasp of the reins.

'Very well. You had your chance. Centurion, carry on. I'm going for help.'

'Help?' Cato angrily turned on the tribune, but Quintillus ignored him. Savagely yanking the beast's head round, he kicked his heels and spurred the pony back towards Calleva, leaving Cato staring after him, lips pressed together in cold contempt and fury.

'Help?' Figulus snorted. 'How fucking thick does he think we are?'

Before Cato could reply there was a blast on a war horn to their left, immediately joined by another from the right. With a triumphant roar the Durotrigans poured down the slope towards the ordered lines of the Wolves and the Boars. Even as he glanced round his men Cato saw that some of them were already stepping back from their position in the line. He must keep them in hand, before the line started to crumble.

'Hold your position there!' he roared at the nearest unsteady

266

man, who guiltily jumped back into place. Cato cupped his hands. 'Cohort! Ready javelins!'

The second line took a pace back while the men in front changed their grip on the javelins and braced their feet apart, ready to throw the deadly missiles into the wildly charging ranks of the enemy. Cato glanced to the left and then straight down the vale. The small group they had seen initially, no more than thirty paces away, would reach them first.

'First, Second and Third Centuries . . . release!'

With a collective grunt of effort the men threw their arms forward and hurled their javelins. The volley was more ragged than that of fully trained legionaries, Cato noted, but it achieved nearly the same terrible effect. The dark shafts arced up into the sky and then dropped down on the Durotrigans, who tried to take cover from the volley. It was instinctive, but quite useless. Those who managed to raise shields to protect themselves were almost as effectively skewered as those who did not as the heavy iron heads punched through the shields and tore into the flesh beneath. There were nearly two javelins for each man in the small charge, and after the crash and clatter of the volley only half continued on towards the Wolves, leaving their comrades dead or screaming in the long grass. The survivors would be easily dealt with and Cato turned his attention to the much larger band of Durotrigans charging down the slope towards the other three centuries.

'Make ready!' Cato bellowed, his nervous voice rising in pitch. 'Release!'

The front ranks of the Durotrigans went down in a rippling wave of stumbling and stricken men. But at once, those behind rushed over their dead and injured comrades, and threw themselves towards the oval shields of the Wolves.

'Draw swords!' Cato called out, wrenching his own blade free of its scabbard. The ridged ivory handle fitted well into his tight grip and he pushed his way into the second rank of Figulus' century. 'Keep those shields up and hold the line!'

The volley of javelins had done its job and the enemy crashed singly into the shield wall rather than engulfing it in one wave. The first score of Durotrigans to reach the Wolves were cut down the moment they tried to burst into the shield wall, killed by swift thrusts of short swords from every side. But then the main weight of the charge crashed into the thin line of the Atrebatans, and the cohort reeled back from the impact. Cato fixed his eyes on the savage expression of a huge warrior making straight for him, sword swinging up for a killer blow. The centurion didn't give him the chance, and threw himself under the man's arm, ramming his blade into his foe's throat. A sheet of warm blood gushed over Cato's arm as the warrior dropped to his knees, clutching desperately at the huge wound in his neck. Cato ignored him, quickly finding another target: an older man with a spear. This veteran was not as strong as the first, but more experienced and more wary. He feinted at Cato and, as the centurion made to block the blow, the old warrior dipped the spearhead under Cato's blade and thrust towards his chest. Only a wild twist saved Cato from the full impact. Even so, the glancing blow spun him round, driving the breath from his lungs. The veteran quickly drew his spear back to deliver the fatal thrust, but a shield boss crashed into the side of his head and he crumpled down.

'Sir!' Figulus shouted, risking a swift glance at his centurion. 'You hurt?'

'No,' gasped Cato as he snatched up a shield from one of his men lying dead at his feet, helmet cleaved in two by an axe blow that had shattered the skull.

Keeping the shield high, Cato glanced round to see that the line of his cohort had disintegrated and the men were lost amid a general mêlée of stabbing spears and swinging swords and axes. His ears filled with the thud of blows landing on shields and shattering bodies, the metallic clash of desperate parries and the cries and screams of the dying. Cato stepped back and looked over his shoulder. Macro's men had also been driven in by the ferocious charge, and in between the two sides of the desperate skirmish the three centuries that had faced the first charge were breaking, dropping their weapons and streaming back towards Calleva, running for their lives.

'Oh, no . . .'

A sudden shout from Figulus saved Cato as he turned, saw the axe blade biting through the air towards his face, and ducked just in time. The axe hissed through the air above Cato's head, clipping off the metal bracket that held his crest. As the red horsehair dropped to the bloody ground beside him, Cato swung his sword into the warrior's kneecap, smashing the bone and severing muscles across the joint. That one would never be able to fight again, Cato noted as he struggled back on to his feet.

'Cato's down!' a voice cried out nearby. 'The centurion's dead!'

'No!' Cato cried out. But it was already too late. The cry was taken up on all sides, and the remains of the cohort broke. For a moment Cato stood side to side with Figulus, shield up and sword ready to thrust, but the Durotrigans left them alone as they went for the unprotected backs of those who had turned and were trying to escape the carnage. It was the worst thing the Atrebatans could do. A man armed and facing his enemy was far safer than any who dropped his sword and shield and ran for his life. But the first victim of panic is always reason, and those who ran were driven by an animal instinct to flee and survive that was senseless and quite foolish.

'Let's get out of here!' said Cato. 'Keep close.'

The two Romans pushed their way through the loose mass of figures spread across the floor of the vale. As long as they kept their guard up, they were ignored as the Durotrigans went in search of easier prey. But as the mass of struggling men gradually dispersed Cato knew that the Durotrigans would turn their attention on them.

'Figulus.'

'Sir.'

'We'll have to run for it. When I give the word, drop your shield and follow me. But whatever you do, keep hold of your sword.'

'Yes, sir.'

A moment later, the way ahead of them cleared, and in the distance Cato could see the sprawling mass of thatched roofs of Calleva. He took a last look round, then shouted. 'Now!'

The two Romans threw their shields down and ran after the figures streaming back towards the safety of Calleva. In among them ran the Durotrigans, screaming with exultation as they ran their foes down and stabbed and slashed at those too slow, or too panic-stricken to escape their pursuers. Cato led his comrade in a straight line, crouching low and running as fast as his legs could carry him. Only a few of the Durotrigans paid them any close attention, and of these only a handful tried to stop them escaping. But singly, they were no match for two legionaries and were quickly cut down.

They had run for just over a mile when Figulus suddenly pulled Cato's arm.

'Listen!'

'What?' Cato turned round, chest heaving as he gulped for breath. The effort of running such a distance in his chain mail had exhausted him. Spread out around them were the survivors of the two cohorts, still flooding back towards Calleva. The Durotrigans had dropped back, and were busy looting and mutilating the bodies of their Atrebatan enemies.

'Look!' Figulus gasped as he pointed back towards the smouldering remains of the decoy supply column. 'Over there!'

A line of horsemen was galloping over the crest of the hill that had earlier concealed the Durotrigan ambush. As soon as they reached the bottom of the vale they spread out, lowered the tips of their spears and urged their horses on towards the scattered remnants of the Wolves and the Boars, still struggling towards Calleva's ramparts.

'Shit!' Cato panted, unbuckling his belt. 'Run! Don't stop for anything.'

The dreadful screams of those being ridden down in the long grass began as Cato struggled out of his harness and desperately wrenched the heavy chain mail over his head. He dumped it on the ground, snatched up his sword and ran after Figulus, already some distance ahead of him. He was halfway back to Calleva when the wound to his side began to make itself felt once again. He had thought it quite healed, but now the extreme exertions of the fight and rout caused a stabbing throb down the entire side of his body, so that every breath was agony. His heart pounded so much that it filled his ears almost to the exclusion of every other noise, and drowned out the screams of the dying, the exultant cries of the Durotrigans and the thrumming of horses' hoofs as the enemy charged to and fro amidst the panic-stricken men fleeing for their lives.

Cato forced himself on, knowing that to stop would be to invite a merciless death. The sword weighed heavily in his hand, but he tightened his grip and ran on. A mile short of the gateway he came across a narrow stream meandering across the small plain in front of Calleva. Before he realised what was happening Cato stumbled on the loose earth hanging over the edge of the stream and splashed down into the shallow water. The sudden shock of the cold current jolted his senses. With a great effort of will he scrambled on to his knees and looked for his sword which had slipped from his grasp in the fall. The blade glimmered beneath the glassy surface several feet away.

Cato was about to reach for it when he heard a horse close by. A shadow wavered on the far side of the stream, and Cato lowered himself back into the water, pressing his body close to the bank just beneath the overhang of loose earth. An instant later there was the breathless champing of a hard-ridden horse immediately above him. A small avalanche of pebbles and loose earth cascaded into the water beside Cato. On the far bank was the faint shadow of the horse and rider, and Cato stilled his breathing. A fluke ripple in the surface of the stream refracted a strong shaft of light on to the blade of his sword and it gleamed brightly in the water for an instant.

But an instant was enough. The rider slid off the back of his horse and jumped down into the stream, right in front of Cato, sending spray into the centurion's face. The warrior waded a few paces downstream towards the sword and then Cato realised he would be seen the moment the man picked up the sword and turned round. There was not time to think. Cato rose and threw himself on the back of the rider as he bent over the sword. The impact drove both men splashing down. The centurion was on top, and he reached forward, searching for the rider's throat. He found it, clenched his fingers round the muscular neck and pressed as hard as he could. The rider thrust himself up, erupting from the water in a cascade of glittering spray, hands clawing behind his head, reaching for Cato's arms. He found them and tried to wrench Cato's grip free, failed and then reached further back, clawing for his attacker's face and eyes. Before he could succeed Cato rammed his knee into the small of the man's back and pulled him sideways into the stream, struggling to push the man's head beneath the surface.

The Briton was too strong for him, and in one convulsive heave he turned over on top of Cato, facing up to the morning sky and pressing back on the body trapped beneath him. The impact drove the breath out of Cato, and he just had the sense to clamp his lips shut before the water closed over his face. But he knew he had little time left. His burning lungs demanded air, and he would be forced to release his grip on the rider and try to force his way to the surface. Out of the corner of his eye something glimmered. The sword. Cato twisted his head and saw that it was within easy reach on the bed of the stream. He released his grip on the man's throat and snatched at his face with his left hand, fingers working towards the man's eyes. His right hand splashed back into the water, grabbed for the handle of the sword, brought the blade round, and then with the last of his fast-ebbing strength he thrust the blade up through the rider's back. The man jerked, in spasm, jerked again, frantically struggling to tear himself free of the blade, which Cato was working furiously up and down in his chest. The thrashing became weaker, and at last Cato heaved the body to one side and burst out of the stream, gasping for air. As he sat coughing and spluttering in the slowly spreading pool of crimson, Cato checked his enemy. The rider lay on his back. The tip of Cato's sword had burst through his heart and right through the front of his chest. Dark red billowed up round the edge of the blade and slowly dissipated in the gentle current. The man's head was tilted back beneath the surface of the water. His eyes stared sightlessly at the sky as his hair waved downstream, like the long tendrils of the weeds growing close to the bank.

As soon as Cato had caught his breath he heaved the man on to his side, placed a boot on his back beside the sword handle, and wrenched the blade free. It came out with a fresh gush of blood and Cato immediately pulled himself on to the bank and crept downstream, away from the enemy and roughly in the direction of Calleva. The Durotrigans would notice the riderless horse soon enough and come to investigate. He had briefly considered trying to mount the animal himself, but could not trust himself to do it well. Besides, he was a poor rider while the Durotrigans were experts, and they would run him down long before he got the beast anywhere near the gates of Calleva. So he moved downstream as swiftly and quietly as he could, ears straining for any sign that the body had been detected and the enemy were giving chase. A quarter of a mile later Cato realised he was trembling. He knew he was too tired to go on. He must hide and rest a while; recover some strength and then move on towards the safety of the town.

Safe? Calleva? He chided himself. The cohorts had been destroyed. The only thing standing between the Durotrigans and the Atrebatans were the handful of legionaries serving the depot and Verica's bodyguard. The moment the enemy realised that, Calleva would be at their mercy. He had to get back, gather the survivors up and try to save the town. Then he thought of Macro and Tincommius. Had either of them made it? Were they dead, somewhere out there in the long grass? Food for the carrion birds already spiralling overhead in the late morning sunshine.

Cautiously moving round a bend in the stream Cato came across a fallen tree, wrenched up from the ground years before by some wild storm. The soil round the base of the tree had been pulled up, and badgers had dug themselves a sett amongst the tangle of dead roots. Cato pressed himself into the narrow entrance and hurriedly used his sword to loosen the soil above him. Clods of earth tumbled over the hole, gradually filling it and burying the centurion under a shallow layer of soil. He would be revealed the moment anyone made a close inspection of the twisting roots, but it was the best he could do. He lay still, watching the stream through the small gap he had left, and waited for the long hot day to end.

Chapter Twenty-Seven

Cato woke with a start, dislodging the earth he had piled over his body. It was dark and something was snuffling through the dirt close to his face. As the centurion stirred the creature emitted a shrill squeak and scrambled away. An instant later Cato's mind focused with a sharp intensity as he remembered everything that had occurred earlier in the day. Furious with himself for falling asleep, he lay still, listening for any signs of movement, but the only sound he could hear was the stream chuckling over a shallow bed of pebbles. Overhead, through the tangle of dead roots, he could see a few stars behind scattered wreaths of silvery cloud. Cato groped for his sword, and then gently brushed the earth away from his body. He paused a moment to see if he had attracted any attention, and then eased himself out of the entrance of the badger sett. Staying close to the ground, he crawled up the bank and raised his head above the tufts of grass growing along the edge. The landscape was a dark almost featureless mass stretching out on all sides, broken only by the unmistakable silhouettes of trees.

But, there, barely a mile away, was Calleva. Sections of the ramparts were illuminated by blazing faggots that the defenders had hurled down on to the ground in front of the town in an attempt to reveal the presence of any enemies lurking nearby. Even as Cato watched a few more blazing bundles of kindling were raised above the ramparts by tiny figures wielding pitchforks. Then the faggots were thrown over in bright flaring arcs and burst on the ground in showers of sparks.

The position of some of the attackers was obvious from several small fires ringing the main gate. Every so often a fire arrow would rise up, curve gracefully over the ramparts and disappear amongst the huts beyond. Dull red smudges behind the ramparts showed where a number of small blazes had already been started.

The situation looked desperate, and Cato briefly considered what he must do. The Second Legion was at least two days' march away. Too far, perhaps, to arrive in time to save Calleva, and the legion's supply depot. There was an infantry cohort a day's march away in the opposite direction, guarding a river crossing, but they would be too few to make a difference. Besides, with the Durotrigans in the area, the centurion would have to make sure he stayed out of sight as much as possible, and that could double the length of time it would take to reach the nearest help.

There was no alternative, he realised. He must find a way back into Calleva and do what he could to help organise the defence of the Atrebatan capital. If Macro was dead then the command of the survivors of the two cohorts would fall to him. If Tincommius was dead then, with Verica barely alive, the Atrebatans would be leaderless. Cato had to get back as quickly as possible.

Crouching low, sword held tightly in his hand, he moved off in the direction of the main gate. A light breeze was blowing, rustling the tall grass and the leaves of the stunted trees that dotted the small plain. The strain of creeping forwards, muscles tensed for instant attack or flight, senses straining to detect any hint of movement or sound of the enemy, told on the young centurion, and after half a mile he stopped and rested a moment. Between him and the gate, their dark shapes rising above the grass, the Durotrigans extended in a loose screen, barring access to the town from any survivors of the two cohorts still lurking nearby. As Cato watched, one of the enemy moved closer to a comrade and the harsh laughter of their voices was clearly audible. Rising to his feet but keeping bent over, Cato quickly made for the gap in the screen and quietly slipped through, glancing both ways to make sure that he had not been spotted. No alarm was given and he pressed on. A short distance beyond was one of the small campfires lit by the Durotrigans. It was ringed by the dark forms of men sleeping under their cloaks, resting in preparation for the next day's assault on Calleva. One man stood guard, warming himself by the fire, the shaft of his spear resting against his shoulder.

The loom of the fire spread across a wide area and Cato realised that in skirting it he might well be seen by one of the men in the screen he had just passed through. Directly beyond the fire was the gate, barely a few hundred paces distant. With a last glance round to make sure he had not yet been seen, Cato rose up from the grass and started to run forward, picking up speed as he approached the fire. Then the first of the sleeping Durotrigans was at his feet. Cato leaped over him, and the next one, and sprinted straight for the man standing in front of the fire. The warrior glanced over his shoulder, his eyes instantly widening as he caught sight of the savage expression on the face of the Roman hurtling towards him. He fumbled for the shaft of his spear, but it was too late. Cato slammed into the man's back and thrust the enemy warrior, sprawling, right on top of the fire. As Cato rolled to one side, back on to his feet, and sprinted for the gate, a terrible shrieking from the warrior split the night. At once the men sleeping on the ground stirred and ran to help their comrade. Cato did not look back, but ran as fast as he could for the gate. Behind him there was a shout as he was seen, and more shouts as the alarm spread.

Cato had a good start, but already he was aware of dark shapes on either side, angling in towards him as they converged on the entrance to Calleva. Cato could see faces on the wall turning towards him. Someone drew an arrow to his bow and loosed a quick shot at the approaching figure. Cato sidestepped and there was a whirr close by in the darkness as he ran on.

'Don't shoot!' he cried out in Latin, before he remembered the most recent password. 'Boiled asparagus! Boiled asparagus! Don't shoot!'

Another arrow whipped close by, this time from behind, and Cato flinched as he forced every last effort out of his tired legs.

'Open the gate!' he shouted, as he raced up to the defence ditch surrounding the town.

'It's the centurion!' a voice shouted from the ramparts. 'Get the fucking gate open!'

Cato ran up to the thick timbers and desperately struck his sword against the unyielding wood.

'Open up! Open up!' he screamed.

There was a deep groan from the far side of the gate as the locking bar was slid out of its heavy bracket. Cato turned to look back at his pursuers. He was terrified to see several figures burst out of the darkness into the glow of the burning faggots thrown down in front of the gate. One of them stopped, only twenty paces away, and threw a spear. It was a good throw and would have skewered Cato had he not seen it coming. He threw himself to the ground. An instant later the iron head struck the gate with a splintering crack and shivered a moment. Cato scrambled back to his feet and hammered on the gate

'For fuck's sake, open up!'

With a deep grinding grumble the gate began to swing inwards. Cato desperately pushed against it, and then some sixth sense made him glance over his shoulder. Right behind him, no more than six feet away, a Durotrigan warrior was drawing back his spear arm, ready to make a killing thrust into Cato's back. A feral snarl of triumph twisted his features. Then, suddenly, there was a soft thud. The man froze, and Cato noticed the feathered shaft of an arrow protruding from the top of his head. As the man toppled back, Cato thrust himself through the narrow opening that had appeared at the edge of the gate, and collapsed on the ground inside. At once the defenders threw themselves against the back of the gate and heaved it into position, just as a few of the Durotrigans slammed into the far side. But they were too few to make a difference and moments later the locking bar was eased back into its bracket and the gate was secured again. Cato stayed on his hands and knees, head bent forward between his arms as he gasped for breath.

A dark shape leaned over him.

'You are in a sorry state, lad,' Macro chuckled. 'Where've you been all the bloody day?'

Cato drew a deep breath before he could reply. 'Glad to see you too . . . Tincommius?'

'No sign of him. Here, let me help you.'

Macro took a firm grip under Cato's shoulders and heaved him onto his feet. By the flickering light of a nearby torch Cato saw that Macro was as filthy as himself, and had a large blood-soaked dressing on his thigh.

'You all right?'

Macro was touched by the concern on his young companion's face. 'It's nothing. Some bugger thought he'd try and slow me down by having a swipe at my leg.'

'Bad?'

'You should see the other fellow.' Macro laughed. 'Won't be going very far without his head. Can't say that you've picked a particularly good time to join us.'

'How many have got back?'

'Most of the legionaries. Figulus was the first.'

'And the cohorts?'

Macro shook his head. 'Not good. So far, barely two hundred. There'll be some more, but not many now. They dumped most of the equipment when they ran. Except your standard bearer.'

'Mandrax?'

'That's the lad. Came in shortly before you did, still carrying the standard. Could do with a few more like him. Anyway, I've had Silva pull some more equipment out of the depot stores. He's over there, by that cart. You'd better get some replacement kit. Somehow, I think you'll need it. I'll be up on the palisade.'

As Macro strode off towards the ramp Cato glanced round and took in the situation. A number of houses had caught fire in the streets close to the gate and small clusters of townspeople were hurriedly trying to smother or douse the flames before they flared out of control. Silva, the veteran quartermaster, was distributing equipment to the most recently arrived survivors of the Wolves and the Boars. He waved a greeting as he saw Cato approaching.

'Centurion! Heard we'd lost you. Thought you were going for the record.'

'Record?'

'For the legion's shortest ever career in the centurionate.'

'Very funny. I need some equipment.'

'What do you want?'

'All of it. Except the sword.'

'Whatever happened to returning with your shield or on it?' Silva muttered.

'Sometimes living to fight another day takes precedence.' Cato peered into the cart and saw that it had been roughly loaded with helmets, swords, daggers, belts, javelins, shields and anything else that came to hand. 'You have any chain mail?'

'Sorry. All gone. Only thing left is this.' He tapped a set of the new segmented armour that was beginning to find favour in the legions. 'Take it, or leave it, sir.'

'All right then.' Cato took the armour and worked it over his tunic. Silva helped lace it up while the centurion tied a rag round his head to replace the felt liner he had lost.

'There.' Silva stepped back. 'Ever worn one of these before, sir?'

'No.'

'You'll find it comfortable enough. The only drawback is that it makes throwing a javelin a bit of a chore. Otherwise, it's fine, and cheaper too. I'll add it to your mess bill. Together with the other items.'

Cato looked at him closely. 'You are joking?'

'Of course not, sir. All this has got to be accounted for.'

'Right . . .' Cato fastened the buckle of his sword-belt and, pulling the standard issue sword from the scabbard, he tossed it into the cart and sheathed his own blade in its place.

'Make sure I only get charged for the scabbard.'

He grabbed a helmet and shield and turned away as Silva quickly noted on a large wax tablet the items the centurion had been issued.

Trotting up on to the parapet, Cato sought out Macro. The walkway over the gate was blocked by men preparing to heave over the next faggot. While four of them held the tight bundle of kindling wood up in the air on the end of pitchforks, a fifth man thrust a torch up into the bundle from beneath. The kindling caught fire quickly, cracking and sparking amid the licking flames. When it was well alight the order was given and the bundle was swung out over the rampart with as much force as possible. It thudded down beyond the rampart and rolled a short distance further, revealing a handful of the enemy bowmen.

'There they are!' one of the Atrebatans shouted, and a mixed volley of arrows, slingshots and javelins lashed down on the enemy, knocking several men to the ground, where they writhed and screamed in the orange glow of the burning faggot.

'Good work!' shouted Macro, reinforcing his praise to the natives with a thumbs-up. He caught sight of Cato and beckoned to him. 'You tell 'em next time! It'll sound better in Celtic.'

'I'm sure they got the message,' Cato smiled. 'What's our situation?'

'All right for now. I've got men posted all the way round in case they try to surprise us somewhere else, but they've not made any attempt to rush the ramparts. They've even stopped lobbing those fire arrows over the walls. Fuck knows why – they had us running around all over the place trying to put 'em out.'

'Has anyone seen the tribune?' asked Cato.

'Oh yes!' Macro laughed bitterly. 'He stopped by the gateway before he rode away. Stopped just long enough to shout something about going for help. Then he bolted. Silva told me.'

'Think he's really going to look for help?'

'Well, he's certainly going to look for somewhere safer than here.'

'Not difficult.'

'No.'

'Think we'll keep them out?' Cato asked quietly.

Macro thought about it for a moment, then shook his head. 'No. We have to count on them getting in at some point. There's not enough of us to hold the entire wall. And I don't think we can rely on any of the townsfolk coming to our aid – they're in no fit state to fight.'

'In that case . . .' Cato cast a map of Calleva into his mind's eye. 'In that case, we'll have to fall back on the depot when the time comes. The depot, or the royal enclosure.'

'Not the enclosure,' said Macro. 'Too close to the rest of the town. We'd never see them coming until the last instant. Besides, there's plenty of supplies we can draw on in the depot. It's our best chance.'

'I suppose.'

'Cato! Macro!' a voice called out from the darkness beyond the wall. The two centurions looked warily over the palisade.

'Cato! Macro!'

'Who the hell's that?' muttered Macro. He turned to a group of bowmen crouching nearby on the walkway, and mimed stringing an arrow. 'Get ready!'

The voice called out again, closer this time.

'I don't like this,' said Macro. 'It's bound to be some kind of a trick. Well, we'll be ready for the bastards!'

Cato peered into the night, straining his eyes towards the direction of the voice. Then, it came again, closer and clearer – and now he was certain.

'It's Tincommius.'

'Tincommius?' Macro shook his head. 'Bollocks! It's a trick.'

'It's Tincommius, I tell you . . . Look there!'

In the red wavering light from the dying flames of the last faggot to be hurled over the wall, a figure emerged from the darkness. He paused a moment, indistinct and shimmering beyond the heated night air.

'Cato! Macro!' he called again.

'Step into the light where we can see you,' Macro bellowed. 'Slowly now! Any tricks and you'll be dead before you can even turn round!'

'All right! No tricks!' the man called back. 'I'm coming closer.'

He picked his way round the faggot and slowly approached the gate, one arm raised to show that he carried no weapon. In the other hand he carried an auxiliary shield, one of those issued to the Wolves and the Boars. He stopped thirty paces from the gate.

'Macro . . . It's me, Tincommius.'

'Fuck me!' whispered Macro. 'So it is!'

Chapter Twenty-Eight

General Plautius was growing tired of the game being played by Caratacus. For some weeks now the legions had steadily advanced along the north bank of the Tamesis, trying to close with the Britons. But as soon as the Roman army moved forward, Caratacus simply withdrew, abandoning one defensive position after another and leaving the Romans nothing but the warm ashes of his campfires. And all the time the gap between Plautius' army and the smaller force commanded by Vespasian grew dangerously wider, almost inviting a sudden thrust by the enemy should he ever guess at the truth. Plautius had tried to force Caratacus to give battle by ordering his troops to burn every farm and settlement they came across. Every farm animal was to be likewise destroyed. Only a handful of the people would be spared so that their lamentations would ring in the ears of their chiefs, who in turn must beg Caratacus to put an end to Roman despoiling of their lands by turning round and falling upon the legions.

Finally it seemed to have worked.

Plautius stared across the shallow valley towards the fortifications Caratacus had prepared on the far ridge: a shallow ditch and, beyond, a small earth rampart with a crude wooden palisade. It would not present much of a challenge to the first wave of assault troops forming up on the slope in front of the

Roman camp. Behind them were arranged several small batteries of bolt-throwers, preparing to lay down a terrible barrage of heavy iron shafts that would smash the flimsy palisade and kill any man standing directly behind it.

'Should be over long before the day's finished!' grinned the weathered prefect of the Fourteenth Legion, the unit Plautius had chosen to lead the assault.

'I hope so, Praxus. Go in hard. I want them finished once and for all.'

'Don't worry about my lads, sir. They know the score. But there won't be many prisoners . . .'

There was no mistaking the disapproving tone and Plautius had to bite back on his irritation. There was far more at stake here than enhancing the retirement fund of a legionary prefect.

That bloody man Narcissus had announced to all and sundry in Rome that Britain was as good as conquered when the Emperor had returned from his sixteen-day visit at the end of the last campaigning season. A triumph had been held to celebrate the conquest of the island and Claudius had made an offering of spoils from his victories in the temple of peace.

Yet here the army was, nearly a year later, facing the same enemy. An enemy who was quite oblivious to the fact that they had already been defeated, according to the official history. And now the imperial general staff in Rome were getting a little uncomfortable about the discrepancy between the official account and conditions on the ground. Elsewhere in Rome, the families of young officers serving in Plautius's legions were increasingly perplexed by letters they received that recounted the endless raids of the enemy, the daily attrition of the army's strength and the failure to bring Caratacus to battle. Veterans and invalids returning from the distant front only confirmed the details in the letters, and the talk on the streets of Rome was starting to turn quite ugly. The dispatches General Plautius was receiving from Rome were getting increasingly impatient. Finally, Narcissus had written a terse and brutally frank note. Either Plautius finish the job by the end of the summer, or his career was over, and more besides.

The Fourteenth had finished assembling and the ten cohorts of heavy infantry stood in two lines, ready for the command to advance. Across the valley there was little sign of activity from Caratacus, no skirmishers or scouts out in front of the main body of his army, only the massed ranks of his warriors lining the palisade, waiting for the Roman attack. Here and there a standard waved slowly to and fro, and the shrill bray of war horns echoed across the valley to General Plautius, who smiled with satisfaction.

Very well, he decided, if Caratacus wants us to come and get him, then come and get him we shall. Plautius was further gratified by the knowledge that even now, two cohorts of auxiliary cavalry and the Twentieth Legion were completing their sweeping march round the flank of the enemy to seal off his line of retreat. A trusted local chief had offered to guide them through the wetlands that Caratacus had assumed was guarding his left flank. The guide had not volunteered to do this out of any loyalty to Rome, but for the promise of great reward, and the sparing of his family who were being held hostage in Plautius' camp. That, the general thought confidently, was enough to guarantee the man's good faith.

'Permission to start the bombardment, sir?' asked Praxus.

Plautius nodded, and the signalman raised a red banner. He paused, until the artillery signallers had raised their banners to show that they were ready to carry out the order. Then he dropped the banner. At once the air was filled with the sharp cracks of the torsion arms flying forward as they launched their heavy iron shafts over the heads of the Fourteenth Legion and into the Britons' defences. Holes suddenly appeared in the palisade as the barrage tore through, taking out files of soldiers behind.

'Damn! They're good!' Praxus shook his head. 'Just sitting there and soaking it up. Never seen discipline like it.'

'Maybe,' Plautius said grudgingly. 'But they'll still be no match for our lads. You'd better get in position. Your legate is going to need the benefit of your experience today.'

'Yes, sir.' Praxus gave him a wry smile. Not all legates were up to the job and those that weren't had to be carried by their senior professional officers until their tour of duty was complete. To be fair, Plautius reflected, the imperial general staff soon realised if a man did not measure up to the job and quickly reappointed him to a less vital government post back in Rome.

Praxus saluted and strode down the slope to join the colour party of the Fourteenth, casually tying the straps of his helmet as he went along. Plautius watched him go, then turned to see the standards of the Ninth Legion emerging from the camp as the second assault wave moved forward to its starting positions. The general bowed his head as the Emperor's image was carried by. A rather too flattering portrait of Claudius, he decided, and one whose noble features bore comparatively little resemblance to the twitching fool who had been catapulted on to the throne only three years before. The ranks of the First Cohort of the Ninth Legion filed by, and the general briefly acknowledged their salute before focusing his attention back on the enemy defences.

As soon as the palisade was badly torn up Plautius gave the order for the batteries to stop the barrage. After the last bolt-thrower discharged its missile, there was a brief pause and then the headquarters trumpets sounded the advance. The two lines of the Fourteenth Legion rippled forward, the sun glinting off the bronze and tin helmets of nearly five thousand men as they marched down the slope, crossed the narrow floor of the valley and started to ascend the far slope.

'Any moment now . . .' Plautius muttered to himself. But there was no response from the defenders. No volley of arrows, no rattle of slingshot. The enemy's discipline must have drastically improved, the general mused. In the earlier battles he had fought, the Britons had let loose their first volley the moment they thought the Romans were within range, thereby wasting a great quantity of their ranged munitions, as well as the devastating impact of a closely co-ordinated volley launched at short range.

The front ranks of the first wave of legionaries dipped down as they reached the defence ditch. On the far side, on the rampart, the Britons waited impassively for the Romans to reach them, and Plautius found himself tensing as he waited for the two sides to close in a deadly mêlée. Out of the ditch came the front rank of legionaries, struggling up the earth rampart and then hurling themselves on the enemy through the gaps in the shattered palisade. Such was the savagery of the final charge that the first five cohorts swept through the defences and into the enemy camp without stopping.

Then there was silence. No war cries. No enemy war horns. No din of battle. Nothing.

'My horse!' Plautius called out, the first dreadful doubt forming in his mind. What if Caratacus knew about the trap the Romans had prepared for him and refused to be taken captive? What if he persuaded his men that Rome would show them no mercy? After all, no mercy had been shown to those whose lands they had laid waste throughout the summer. Plautius felt sick. Had he gone too far? Had he convinced Caratacus that the only way left to defy Rome was suicide?

'Where's my bloody horse?'

A slave came running over, leading a beautifully groomed black stallion. The general snatched the reins and placed his boot on to the interlaced fingers of the slave. With a quick heave he swung his leg over and dropped on to his saddle. Plautius wheeled the horse towards the enemy fortifications and galloped down the slope. Some of the rear ranks of the men in the Ninth saw him coming and shouted a warning to their comrades. A path quickly opened up through the dense mass of legionaries and the general swept by, his sense of dread deepening with every beat of his heart. He urged his horse on, steering a path through the rear cohorts of the Fourteenth as he rode up the far slope. Plautius reined in at the ditch and swung himself down to the torn-up earth. He ran down the ditch and scrambled up the far side, then up on to the rampart.

'Out of my way!' he shouted at a group of his men standing quietly in a breach in the palisade. 'Move!'

They hurriedly stepped aside and revealed the Britons' camp beyond. Scores of dead campfires smouldered in the space behind the ram-part. But there was no sign of the enemy. Plautius looked along the ruined palisade and saw hundreds of crude straw figures knocked flat by the artillery barrage, or trampled down by the first assault wave.

'Where are they?' he asked out loud. But none of his men would meet his eye. They no more knew the answer than did their general.

There was a sudden commotion and Praxus emerged on to the ramparts dragging a Briton with him. The man, obviously roaring drunk, slumped down at the general's feet.

'This is the only one I could find, sir. When we got into the camp I saw a small band of them riding off towards the river, that direction.' Praxus nodded towards a serpent standard propped up against the palisade. 'They must have been the ones blowing the horns and waving the standards.'

'Yes,' Plautius replied quietly, 'that makes sense . . . That makes sense. Question is, where are they now? Where's Caratacus and his army?'

For a moment there was silence, as Plautius looked south towards the river. Then the drunken Briton started singing, and the spell was broken.

'Shall I send the scouts out, sir?' asked Praxus.

'Yes. Get back to headquarters and give the orders at once. I want every direction covered. I want them found as soon as possible.'

'Yes, sir. What about this one? Want him interrogated?'

General Plautius looked down at the man, and the Briton met his gaze with a glazed expression, and then wagged a mocking finger at the Roman. In that gesture Plautius felt struck by a wave of ridicule, and sensed in himself the first inkling of a deep self-loathing and rage. Caratacus had tricked him; made him look a fool in front of his own legions, and as soon as word got back to Rome they would laugh at him there as well.

'Him?' he replied coldly. 'We'll get nothing useful out of this scum. Impale him.'

As Praxus detailed some men to carry the prisoner away General Plautius gazed south again, this time across the river, to the grey haze of the horizon beyond. Somewhere over there, in the distance, was Vespasian and the Second Legion. If Caratacus had turned south then Vespasian would be completely unaware of the enemy army bearing down on him.

Chapter Twenty-Nine

'Open the gate!' Cato shouted.

'No!' Macro grabbed his arm, and leaned over the parapet to call down to the men below. 'Keep the gate closed!'

Cato shook off his friend's arm. 'What the hell are you doing, sir? You trying to get Tincommius killed?'

'No! Something's wrong. Cato, think about it! How'd he get through their lines?'

'I did.'

'And only just made it to the gate. Look at him! Full armour. Just walking up to us. They let him through.'

'Let him through?' Cato frowned. 'Why?'

'We'll know soon enough.' Macro peered over the palisade. 'I never really trusted that bastard . . .'

Tincommius was standing thirty paces away from the gate, apparently unperturbed by the presence of hundreds of the Durotrigans lurking in the surrounding darkness.

'Macro!' Tincommius called out in Latin. 'Open the gate. We need to talk.'

'So talk!'

The Atrebatan prince smiled. 'Some things are best discussed discreetly. Open the gate and come out.'

'Does he think we're mad?' Macro grunted. 'We'd be dead before we got halfway to him.'

'I guarantee your safety!' Tincommius shouted.

'Bollocks!' Macro replied. 'Step up to the gate! Alone!'

'Can you guarantee *my* safety?' Tincommius responded in a mocking tone. 'You'd better . . .'

'Come closer!' Cato pointed directly below the palisade. After a moment's hesitation Tincommius began to walk slowly towards them. The two centurions quickly made their way down the ramp and while Macro gave the order to open the gate, Cato gathered two sections of legionaries in case there was any attempt by the Durotrigans to rush the entrance to Calleva. As the gate creaked open, just wide enough to allow a man to squeeze through, Cato could see the Atrebatan prince waiting for them on the far side. He reached for a torch being held by one of the legionaries.

'Leave that!' Macro snapped. 'Want to make a fine target of yourself?'

Cato lowered his hand.

'Come on then, lad. Let's see what Tincommius is playing at.'

Macro led the way, easing himself through the gap and stepping aside for Cato, all the while keeping a close watch on the man waiting for them. With Cato at his side he slowly walked forward until they were two sword lengths away from Tincommius.

'What's going on?' Macro growled.

'What do you think?' Tincommius replied with a thin smile.

'I'm too tired, and too pissed off for games. Get on with it.'

'We want you to surrender.'

'We?'

'My allies out there.' Tincommius jabbed a thumb over his shoulder, then nodded at the Calleva gateway. 'And in there.'

'You've sold us out mighty quickly,' Cato said softly. 'How long did it take them to make you change sides, you coward?'

'Change sides?' Tincommius arched his eyebrows. 'I haven't changed sides, Centurion. I've always been on the same side. The side that hates Rome, and all that it stands for. I've been waiting a long time for this. Working hard for it. Now, you will surrender and let me take my rightful position on the throne.'

Macro stared at the young nobleman and then turned to Cato with a harsh laugh. 'He's joking!'

'No. No, he's not.' Cato felt sick inside; the hollow despairing ache of a man who has just realised how completely he has been fooled. By the light cast from the torches on the palisade above he looked Tincommius in the eye. 'All the time we've served together?'

'Longer. Much longer, Roman.'

'Why?'

'Why?' Macro snorted. 'Why do you think? The little lad here wants to be king. Problem is, your lot already have a king, traitor!'

Tincommius shrugged. 'For the moment, maybe. But Verica will be dead in a few days, one way or another. Then I'm king. I'll lead my people against the legions, at the side of Caratacus.'

'You're mad!' Macro shook his head. 'Once the general hears about this, the Atrebatans will be crushed like an egg under a millstone.'

'I think you seriously underestimate the gravity of your situation, Macro. Our lands lie right across the general's supply lines. In a matter of days we'll be able to hamstring your legions. I reckon you'll be lucky to escape from Britain with your lives. What do you think, Cato?'

Cato did not reply. He could see the strategic situation unfolding in his mind's eye and knew that the Atrebatan prince was right. Here in Calleva, feeling had been steadily turning against Verica, and the Romans he so closely associated himself with. There was a good chance that Tincommius would win enough support amongst his people to lead them in a rising against Rome. And Tincommius was right about the wider effects of such a revolt. The success or failure of the Roman bid to add these lands to the Empire rested on the edge of a blade.

A further terrible thought struck him.

'Verica . . . You attacked him?'

'Of course I did,' Tincommius replied quietly enough so that only the two centurions could hear him. 'He had to be got out of the way. It wasn't an easy thing to do. After all, he is my kinsman.'

'Spare us the self-pity.'

'Very well. He had to die for the sake of all the tribes of these lands. What is the blood of one old man, against the freedom of an entire race?'

'So it wasn't that difficult, then?' Cato asked quietly, a growing sense of horror swelling up inside him as he realised how totally he had misjudged Artax. 'And you might have killed him . . . if it wasn't for Artax.'

'Yes. Poor old Artax – and let's not forget poor Bedriacus . . . More principles than brains – a common failing in my people. I did try to make Artax see where his true interests lay, but he wouldn't have any of it. He came across me just as I was about to finish the old man off. Knocked me down. I didn't have a chance. He got the king away safely, and then you came on the scene.' Tincommius smiled. 'I could hardly believe my fortune when you went after Artax. Of course I had to make sure that he was killed before he could say anything that might incriminate me.' The Atrebatan prince laughed softly at Macro. 'If it wasn't for your unfortunate appearance, I might have killed the king and Cato here as well.'

'Why, you little bastard . . .' Macro's hand grasped his sword handle, but Cato clamped his hand on his friend's arm before Macro could draw the weapon.

'That's enough, Macro!' Cato said harshly, glaring into the other centurion's eyes. 'Hold still! We need to hear him out; hear his terms.'

'That's right, Centurion.' A smile flickered across Tincommius' face as he looked at Macro. 'Better rein in that temper of yours, if you want to live. You, and your men.'

For a brief while Cato feared that Macro would explode and not rest easy until he had ripped the Atrebatan prince limb from limb with his bare hands. Then Macro took a deep breath, his nostrils flared, and he nodded.

'All right . . . All right then, you bastard. Have your say.'

'Most gracious of you. I want you and your men to leave Calleva and rejoin the Second Legion. You may take your weapons with you, and I guarantee your safe passage . . . as far as the legion.'

Macro snorted contemptuously. 'And your word is worth . . . what? A pile of shit.'

'Quiet!' Cato cut in. 'Why should we leave?'

'You can't defend the walls, not with that handful of legionaries, and whatever's left of the two cohorts. If you try to resist then you will only die, and many of the people of Calleva will die with you. I'm giving you a chance to save all those lives. Life or death. That's what's on offer.'

'What happens after we leave?' Cato asked.

'Surely you can guess? I finish Verica off and tell the people of Calleva that Verica is dead. The council makes me king, and any man who is misguided enough to oppose an immediate alliance with Caratacus is disposed of. Then we tear your supply columns to pieces.'

'In that case, you know we can't surrender.'

'I was rather hoping you'd say that. Still, I'm in no hurry. I'll give you till dawn to make up your minds. By then there won't be many Atrebatans left who'll be willing to fight on your side. Not after I've told them that it was you who attacked their king.'

'What makes you think you'll live long enough to tell them?' Macro snarled.

Tincommius smiled nervously, and took a step back. This was too much for Macro, and he violently shook off Cato's restraining hand and whipped his sword out of its scabbard. 'You little prick! I've had my fill of you.'

Tincommius turned and sprinted away towards the ring of darkness surrounding Calleva. With an incoherent shout of rage Macro charged after him before Cato could react. The young centurion instinctively dived at his friend's legs and drove Macro to the ground. By the time both men were back on their feet Tincommius was no more than a shadow fading into the night. Enraged, Macro rounded on Cato.

'What the fuck are you doing?'

'Get inside the gate!' Cato ordered. 'Quick!'

Macro was having none of it, and raised the point of his sword threateningly. Suddenly, an arrow whacked into the gate close by, then more whirred out of the darkness, splintering the weathered surface of the timbers. Without another word Macro dived back through the narrow gap behind Cato, and the gate was hurriedly closed in the face of the invisible enemy.

'That was close!' Macro shook his head, then turned to look at his young friend. 'Thanks . . .'

Cato shrugged. 'Save it. We've got to get out of this mess first.'

Then, from out of the night, Tincommius' voice rose up, calling out in Celtic.

'What's he saying?' asked Macro.

'He's inviting the people of Calleva to join him . . . Telling them, the survivors of the Wolves and the Boars, to desert their Roman masters and become free men once again . . .'

'Oh! Nice touch. Boy should have been a lawyer. Come on, we have to put an end to this.'

Macro led the way back on to the rampart. They noticed several of the native troops eye them in a guilty, furtive manner and Cato feared that Tincommius was right: many of these men would be gone before the sun rose, silently slipping over the wall to run and pledge their allegiance to a new king. Some would stay; out of duty to Verica, out of duty to their comrades, maybe even out of duty to the officers they had come to respect with the grudging admiration of one warrior for another. Normally Cato disapproved of such sentimentality between men, but not tonight. Tonight he positively prayed for it with every superstitious fibre of his being. Tincommius continued to call out to the men on the wall, promising them a glorious victory over the Eagle soldiers, and a chance to win back the pride of place amongst all Celtic tribes that had once been the preserve of the warriors of the Atrebatans.

'Can you see him?' asked Macro, squinting into the darkness surrounding the ramparts.

'No. Sounds like he's somewhere over . . . there.' Cato pointed.

Macro nodded to the cluster of legionaries armed with bows and slings along the palisade. 'You there! Try a few shots. Aim for the voice.'

It was hopeless. The odds of hitting Tincommius were little better than trying to toss a pebble down the neck of an amphora at twenty paces, blindfolded. But it might put Tincommius off his stride and undermine his attempt to talk the native troops round. A steady flow of arrows and slingshot arced into the night, and still Tincommius called upon his people. Macro turned back into the town and shouted down towards the supply cart.

'Silva! Get me some trumpets up here, fast as you can!'

'Better hurry,' Cato muttered. 'He's telling them that it was you who attacked Verica.'

'Bastard!'

'. . . Now he's saying that we're holding the king prisoner, keeping him from his people. All because Verica has had a change of heart and could see Rome for what it really was . . . That's why we had to remove Verica.'

'Does he really expect them to swallow that load of bollocks?'

'Unless we start countering it, they might.'

Macro cupped his hands. 'Hurry up with those bloody trumpets!'

After a quick look round at the natives listening to the voice of their prince, Macro turned back to Cato. 'You'd better speak to them.'

'Me?'

'Yes, you. Talk 'em round.'

'What should I say?'

'I don't know. Use your head – you're not usually short of things to say. Just make sure whatever it is, you say it louder than Tincommius.'

Cato stood back from the palisade and, desperately trying to remember some of the stirring speeches he had read as a boy, he began to speak. It was not easy translating the high-flown rhetoric of Roman historians into idiomatic Celtic. He stumbled again and again as he tried to address the Atrebatans and persuade them to ignore the traitor Tincommius, and remain loyal to their king, whom the traitor himself had tried to murder. From the darkness, Tincommius called out more loudly, flatly contradicting everything that Cato said. The centurion smiled and renewed his appeal, abandoning any attempt at producing the classic speech style he had been taught by his Greek tutor. He said anything that came into his head, anything that might appeal to the Atrebatans, anything that might prevent them from hearing Tincommius, who was becoming increasingly shrill as he tried to override Cato. But the centurion was tired, and the well of inspiration was quickly drying up. He knew it, and the men on the rampart knew it, and had it not been for the arrival of Silva, carrying an armful of trumpets from the depot, Tincommius might yet have talked most men round.

'That was close,' Cato said hoarsely as Macro handed out the instruments to the confused legionaries.

'Not out of the woods yet, lad,' Macro replied, thrusting a trumpet into the hands of one of his men. The legionary looked aghast, as if someone had just thrust a venomous snake into his hands.

'Don't just bloody gawp at it!' Macro screamed into his face. 'Stick your laughing gear round that and blow for all you're worth. But you start slacking on me and I'll ram it so far down your throat you'll be farting tunes out of it! . . . Make myself clear?'

'Yes, sir!'

'Right, start playing then.'

The legionaries began to raise up a braying, nerve-rending cacophony into the night sky, and totally drowned out the cries of Tincommius.

'Good!' Macro nodded, hands on hips. 'Keep it up for a while, then have a rest. If the enemy starts his yacking up again, you start blowing. Understood? Carry on.'

He turned to Cato, leaning close to be heard over the din. 'Get the Atrebatans down from the wall. Tell 'em to rest. They'll need all their strength when the morning comes.'

Chapter Thirty

At first light Macro passed the order for every able-bodied man to stand to. Cato was to take all the remaining natives into the Wolf Cohort, and Macro gathered a scratch force of legionaries from the depot and assembled them immediately behind the gate as a reserve. Cato sent a man to bring the royal bodyguard down to the gate, and while Macro briefed his men Cato walked round the entire circuit of Calleva's ramparts. The appeals by Tincommius, made throughout the night, had had their effect, and by the time the centurion had returned to the main gate it was clear that upwards of fifty men had quietly slipped over the wall to join the enemy. A thin mist had aided their flight from Calleva, and even now the milky grey wreathed the ground lying beyond the defence ditch. Cato was gratified that few of those who had deserted had been men of the Wolf Cohort. His attempt to learn their tongue and to be more familiar with their ways had paid dividends. It was a shame, he briefly reflected, that Roman policy makers rarely, if ever, learned from such examples. So much bloodshed might be prevented, and the Empire would win a far larger pool of recruits for its far-flung cohorts.

'How many left?' Macro asked, as Cato joined him in the watchtower.

'Apart from the eighty effectives from the legionaries at the depot, there's a hundred and ten left from the Wolves and sixty-five from your cohort. Plus the king's bodyguard, that's another fifty or so.'

'Can we count on them?'

Cato nodded. 'Their loyalty is to Verica. They swore a blood oath to protect him.'

Macro's mouth moved in a wry smile. 'Tincommius' oath didn't seem to trouble him unduly. Can we trust Cadminius?'

'I think so.'

'Then where is he?'

'He won't leave the royal enclosure. Or let any of his men.'

'Why not?'

'He says they must guard the king.'

'Guard the king?' Macro slammed his fist down on the rail. 'They'd be far more fucking use guarding him out here!'

Cato waited a moment, before speaking quietly. 'I tried to explain that to Cadminius, but he wouldn't budge.'

Macro quickly glanced round the ramparts, surveying the solitary figures spread out along the palisade. 'Barely half a cohort all told . . . Not enough. Not nearly enough.'

Cato gazed round at the enemy preparations. 'Must be thousands of them out there. And some of our own lads.'

'And there's more to come. Some cavalry turned up while you were gone. Came in from the north-west.'

'We don't have a chance.'

'Thanks for that morale-boosting opinion.'

Cato bit back on the rush of anger that filled his head. Macro was right. He should keep such thoughts to himself. Centurions had no right to contemplate defeat openly. That's what Macro had told him nearly two years ago, when they first met. So the young centurion forced himself to breathe deeply and calm his raging doubts.

'I suppose we'll just have to hold on until some relief arrives.

Quintillus should reach the legion by the end of the day. Take them a little while to get here. We'll just have to hold them off until then.'

Macro turned and studied Cato's expression for a moment. 'That's more like it, lad. Never say die, eh? Goes with the job.'

'Some job.'

'Oh, come on! It's not so bad. Good pay, decent quarters, first dibs on the booty and a chance to shout all you like. Who could ask for more?'

Cato laughed despite himself, and was profoundly grateful that Macro was here at his side. Nothing ever seemed to shake him. Only women, Cato reminded himself with a faint grin.

'What's so bloody funny?'

'Nothing. Really, nothing.'

'Then wipe that stupid look off your face. Tincommius and his mates won't be coming for a while yet. Tell our lads to stand down. Then go and tell your native chums to do the same. And get some rest yourself. You look done in.'

Cato paused on the ladder at the back of the watchtower. 'What about you?'

'I'll rest when it's all over.'

'When do you think they'll attack?'

'How should I know?' Macro glanced round the enemy lines. 'But when they do, they'll rush us from several directions at once. Most of the attacks will be feints, trying to commit all our men before the real assault goes in. We'll have to watch for that.'

Macro stared across the plain towards the scene of the previous day's disaster. The two hills on either side of the vale rose clear of the mist, like islands on a pearly sea. It was fortunate that the mist covered the hundreds of Atrebatan bodies and concealed them from the men on the ramparts, whose spirits were low enough already. When the mist cleared they would see their fallen comrades scattered across the plain. They would also see the size of the force opposed to them, and Macro knew there would be even more desertions once the natives had had a chance to weigh the odds. There were few enough men as it was. He turned towards the rows of thatched roofs behind the town's defences. Not a soul had stirred from the huts.

'Shame we can't persuade a few more of the locals to fight for us.'

'Can you blame them?' Cato replied. 'They're not stupid. They know we don't have much hope.'

The young centurion realised that he was trembling in the cool dawn air and remembered that he had not eaten since the previous dawn, nor had he rested properly for days. He crossed his arms and rubbed his shoulders.

Macro eyed him curiously. 'Afraid?'

For a moment Cato thought about denying it, then realised he would not fool Macro, and simply nodded.

Macro smiled wearily. 'Me too.'

Once the mutual admission had been made there was an awkward silence before Cato spoke again.

'You know, it's possible that the tribune might get help to us in time.'

'Possible? Only if we can hold out for a few days yet.'

'We might.'

'No,' Macro replied, lowering his voice to make quite sure that he was not overheard by any of his men. 'Once they get over the wall – and they will – then we'll have to fall back on the depot. And once they break into the depot it's all over . . . Just hope I get a chance to take that bastard Tincommius with me before I'm finished . . .' Macro's vengeful train of thought was interrupted by a loud rumble from his stomach. '. . . Which reminds me, I'm hungry. I sent Silva to the depot to draw some rations. Should have been back long ago.'

'I don't think I can eat anything right now.'

'Course you can. You'd better,' Macro said seriously. 'Make sure the men see you eat. You let them know how nervous you really are and they'll lose what little heart they have left for this fight. You'll eat your full ration and like it. Understand?'

'What if I'm sick?' The mental image of himself, pale and puking in front of his men filled Cato with dread and shame.

Macro's eyes narrowed. 'The moment you throw up, I'll chuck you over the palisade. I mean it.'

For an instant Cato wondered if his friend was serious, and then the cold, hard expression told him Macro was in deadly earnest. Before Cato could respond, the groaning squeak of a poorly greased axle announced the arrival of Silva and the cart loaded with rations he had fetched from the depot. A pair of stocky mules was harnessed to his cart and Silva steered them towards the legionaries waiting by the gate. Macro licked his lips as he saw several jars of wine and haunches of cured meat in the back of the cart.

'Come on.' Macro nudged Cato. 'Let's eat.'

The two officers joined the legionaries gathering round the cart as Silva hoisted himself up beside the wine jars.

'Easy now, lads. There's plenty for everyone.'

'What about my men?' asked Cato.

'Them?' Silva replied with a trace of disapproval. 'They can take their turn after our boys have finished.'

'They'll have theirs now. Detail some of these men to see to it.'

An expression of distaste flitted across Silva's face before he nodded reluctantly. 'Yes, sir.'

While Silva carried out the order Macro pushed his way through to the cart, and used his dagger to hack off two chunks of cured pork. He tossed one to Cato, and the younger centurion nearly fumbled the catch. Macro laughed, tore off a strip of the meat with his teeth and began to chew.

'Come on, Centurion Cato,' he spluttered. 'Eat up! Might be the last meal you ever eat in this world!'

Cato's stomach still felt tight and twisted, and the prospect of eating the cold meat made the bile rise in his throat. He grimaced, but Macro shot him a warning glance and Cato raised the meat to his lips and bared his teeth.

A distant brass note sounded beyond the ramparts. At once it was taken up by several other war horns. Macro threw his meat down into the churned mud at the rear of the cart, and spat out the half-chewed pork.

'Get to your positions!' he roared. 'They're coming!'

Chapter Thirty-One

'Sir!' Figulus shouted from the watchtower as he saw Macro and Cato rushing up the ramp. 'Enemy's on the move!'

'Keep an eye on them!'

As they reached the palisade Cato put on his helmet and tied the straps. Macro glanced over the approaches to the main gate, straining to pick out the details in the rapidly thinning mist.

'Figulus! What are they up to?'

'Looks like a frontal attack on the gate, sir.'

Cato rubbed his tired eyes as the enemy began to appear. The Durotrigans were advancing behind a long line of crude wicker screens that rippled forward over the flattened grass. Looking round, Cato could not see any sign of movement towards any other section of the town wall.

'Shall I get some of the Wolves to reinforce the gate?'

Macro's gaze followed the route Cato's had just taken and he scratched the stubble on his chin, making a faint rasping noise under his dirty nails. He shook his head. 'We're too thinly spread as it is. I'll have to make do with our lads here. You get back to your standard.'

'Can't I fight here?'

'No.'

Cato thought about protesting, and then nodded. Macro

was right. One more Roman on the gate was not going to make much of a difference. He should stay with the natives and keep them ready for any new surprises the Durotrigans might have planned for them. But he couldn't help wanting to fight, and maybe die, alongside the men of his Second Legion. Cato smiled to himself as he realised that the legion was the nearest thing he had to a family in this world, and the thought of being separated from them when the end came was unbearable. Now, other men looked to him and he saw the Celtic warriors of the Wolf Cohort clustered around Mandrax and his standard, watching their centurion in the distance.

'See you later, Macro,' Cato muttered.

Macro nodded, without turning his gaze from the approaching enemy, and Cato strode back along the rampart towards his men. He had a headache and the throbbing in his head was so painful that he was sure that he would throw up, and worse, he realised he had a terrible thirst and cursed himself for not taking a canteen of water from Silva's supply wagon before heading up on to the rampart. His tongue felt thick and rough and the sensation made the nausea unbearable. Cato bit down on his lip and forced himself to try to think of something else. Anything.

'Macro!' a voice cried out, and Cato stopped to look back towards the gate. The Durotrigans had stopped just beyond javelin range, and a small gap had opened in the centre of the line. Tincommius stepped forward cautiously, both hands cupped to his mouth as he called on Macro again.

'What do you want?' the centurion shouted back. 'Come to surrender?'

Cato smiled at Macro's defiant tone. Tincommius lowered his head for a moment, and even at this distance Cato could read the disappointment in the man's posture.

The Atrebatan prince looked up and called out in Latin, 'You can't hold out much longer, and you know it. I'm afraid I have even more bad news for you. Caratacus is coming in person to seize Calleva. We've had word that he'll be here in two days, with his whole army. Then Calleva must fall.'

'So why the hurry to take us now? Scared you'll miss out on the glory? Or is it just that you need something to present to your new master?'

Tincommius shook his head. 'Don't be a fool, Centurion. You, your men and those of my people still foolish enough to stand by you are all going to die . . . unless you surrender the town to me.'

'You want the town? Come and get it, you wanker!' Macro cupped his hands and blew a loud raspberry to make sure the Durotrigans and the Atrebatan traitors got the point. The legionaries inside the gate cheered the centurion.

Tincommius listened a moment, then waved a hand dismissively as he stepped back behind the wicker screens. The gap closed, an order was shouted and the line moved forward towards the gate.

Cato turned away from the gate and hurried back to the Wolf standard.

'What did the traitor want, sir?' asked Mandrax.

'Told us to surrender. He'll let the Romans leave unharmed if we let him have Calleva.'

'What did Centurion Macro say?'

'You heard him.' Cato blew a loud raspberry and the men around him roared with laughter. One even went as far as slapping the young centurion on the back. Cato indulged their mood for a moment before he gave his orders. He took a quick glance at the small knots of men dispersed along the ramparts and made a quick calculation.

'I want one man every thirty paces. When the main gate

falls, everyone makes for the depot. Macro wants us all there. That's where we'll make a stand.'

'Our last stand?' asked one of the warriors, an older man. Cato noticed the wedding torc on the man's wrist and guessed that he must have family.

'I hope not. The tribune has gone for help. We may have to hold out a few days before a relief force arrives.' Cato nodded. 'We can do it.'

The man gave him an uncertain smile, then looked down and gently stroked his torc. Cato stared at him a moment, moved by the gesture.

'I don't recognise you. You must have been with the Boars. What's your name?'

'Veragus, sir.'

'You don't want to fight with us, Veragus?'

The man looked round at his comrades, searching their expressions for any sign of contempt, then he slowly nodded. Cato gently placed a hand on his shoulder. Although he needed every man who could hold a weapon to the enemy, he also needed to be sure that any man who fought at his side would stay there, and not run.

'All right then, go and join your family. There's no place here for any man whose heart is not in this. We may well be dead before the day is over, and I don't want any more blood on my hands than is necessary. Mandrax!'

'Sir?'

'Pass the message on. Volunteers only back at the depot. Any more like Veragus can drop their weapons and equipment and get back to their families. Tell them they have my permission and wish them luck. They'll need it soon enough if Tincommius seizes the throne.'

Mandrax trotted off along the rampart to pass Cato's orders on. There was an awkward silence as the remaining men and their centurion faced Veragus. The Briton fought back tears of shame and thrust his hand out towards Cato. The centurion took the man's hand and grasped it firmly.

'It's all right,' Cato said softly. 'I understand. Now go. Take what time is left to you.'

Veragus nodded, released his grip and laid his spear and shield down on the rampart. He fumbled with the strap of his auxiliary helmet and then placed that with the rest of the equipment he had been issued only weeks before. He stared at the gear briefly, nodded to Cato and then scrambled down the inside of the rampart and ran off into the maze of thatched huts. Cato looked round the remaining men.

'Anyone else?'

No one moved.

'Fine. Then pass the word to the rest of the cohort. Mandrax, you're with me.'

As the centurion watched his men spread out along the rampart he could hear Macro bellowing orders from the main gate. Cato glanced back and saw the legionaries hurling more javelins down on the enemy force renewing their assault on the entrance to Calleva. But this time there was the distinct thud of the battering ram striking home as the enemy tried to smash their way in, under the shelter of their wicker screens.

Chapter Thirty-Two

The palisade above the gate was suddenly deluged with slingshot and arrows; the slingshot striking the timbers with sharp smacks, punctuating the splintering thuds of arrow strikes. Above this din came the cries and screams as some of the missiles found their targets amongst Macro's small command. As he looked round there were already six men sprawled on the walkway. Still their comrades hurled javelins down on to the wicker screens below, desperately trying to pierce them and reach the enemy sheltering beneath, or at least make them unwieldy under the weight of the javelins embedded in the tight weave of willow. They were having little effect, Macro decided as yet another man fell back from the palisade, clutching at an arrow shaft that had pierced his throwing arm.

'Take cover!' Macro shouted. 'Get down!'

The legionaries heeded the order at once, crouching behind the palisade. Silva and his clerks scurried up the rampart and bent double as they carried away the injured. The fusillade of enemy missiles quickly subsided as the Durotrigans saw that there were no targets for them. But when Macro rose to take a quick look at the enemy, he drew an immediate response and ducked down as half a dozen arrows whirred over the palisade and arced down amongst the thatched roofs beyond. There was nothing for it but to keep down. He had seen a number of ladders in the enemy ranks, so some men would be needed on the palisade. The rest would have to defend the entrance the moment the gates gave way. Every so often the gateway shook with the impact of the ram, and the dust and earth shimmied amongst the timbers as small pieces of grit, shaken loose, pattered down under the walkway.

'First two sections, stay here! Rest of you, follow me!'

Macro, bent over, scurried to the ramp and, followed by the remainder of his force, made his way down to the open area behind the gate. As he reached the street another blow landed on the gates, and a small fissure opened between two timbers, letting a shaft of light filter through into the dust falling from the walkway.

'Silva!' Macro bellowed.

'Sir?'

'You and your men, off the wagon now!'

'But, sir, the wounded . . .' Silva gestured to the men lying on the wagon bed.

'Take 'em out. Carry them to the depot. Move it!

As soon as the injured had been unloaded Macro ordered his men to down shields and put their shoulders to the thick wooden wheels. Macro, with two other men grabbed the yoke and pulled it round towards the gate.

'Right then, heave! Heave, you bastards!'

The men strained at the dead weight of the big supply wagon, gasping for air through gritted teeth. Then, with a drawn-out groan from the axle, the wagon rumbled forward.

'Keep her moving!' Macro grunted as he pulled on the yoke, thrusting his feet down and dragging the smooth-worn yoke towards the gateway. 'Come on!'

Another blow landed on the gate, and the fissure widened into a gap through which the nearest of the enemy could be glimpsed, swinging the ram back ready for the next run at the gate. At the last moment Macro nodded to the other men on the yoke and they pulled it sharply to the side, knocking over a small brazier still smoldering from the night before. The wagon slewed round and rumbled across the entrance to the gate, blocking the way into Calleva.

'Clear the wagon. Get everything out, except the javelins. Then stuff the gap underneath with thatch. Move yourselves!'

The legionaries desperately prepared the makeshift defences, while the ram continued to batter away at the gates, the timbers splintering with every blow. As Macro watched, the very next strike shattered the locking bar, which sprang out of one of its holding brackets, and the end thudded down on the ground between the gates and the wagon.

'This is it!' Macro grabbed his shield and drew his sword, turning to his men. 'This section with me in the wagon. Figulus, your section behind the wagon. Anyone tries to squeeze under, or past the ends – kill 'em.'

'Yes, sir.'

'Rest of you – and you lot on the rampart! Get back to the depot and prepare for us. We'll hold here for a short while and then make a run for it. Go!'

As most of the legionaries ran in a loose pack up the street in the direction of the depot Macro and his rearguard readied themselves for the one-sided fight. The centurion hauled himself up into the wagon and snatched up a javelin. The surviving five men of the section took position either side of him, shields raised and javelins held ready to thrust into the faces of the enemy once they forced their way inside. The ram struck again and, with no locking bar to hold the gates in place, they burst open with a protesting groan, dragging the end of the bar across the packed earth in a short arc. At once the Durotrigans let out a roar of triumph. Dropping the ram, they unslung their shields, snatched up their weapons and thrust their way inside. The broken timbers lay at odd angles with splintered ends, which the first men through were forced on to by the press behind them. Two men howled in agony as they failed to struggle clear of the jagged ends and were impaled, then crushed down by their comrades, thirsting to get at the Romans.

As the front rank of the Durotrigans clambered over the warriors writhing on the bloody shafts of wood, Macro hefted his javelin and thrust it into the face of the nearest man. The warrior jerked to one side and rolled under the wagon. Macro ignored him and fixed his aim on the next enemy, stabbing him through the shoulder, wrenching the iron tip free of flesh and bone, and thrusting again into the sea of savage expressions heaving in front of him. On either side the legionaries were blocking the sword slashes and spear thrusts with their broad shields, then stabbing back at the enemy. Their faces were fixed in the grim desperation of those fighting overwhelming odds. A hand grabbed at the side of the wagon in front of Macro and the centurion quickly hurled his javelin into the solid mass pressing through the ruined gates. He snatched at his sword and hacked down on the hand, slicing off the fingers. The man crumpled down beside the wagon cradling the bloody knuckles to his chest. But on either side Macro could see more of the enemy scrambling in under the reach of the javelins and trying to heave themselves into the wagon.

'Draw swords! Draw swords!'

The men threw down their javelins and there was the rasping of blades hurriedly drawn from scabbards, then the small group of legionaries thrust and hacked at the enemy, who were now so close to them that the distinctive smell of the Celts filled every breath they snatched. Behind them Figulus and his section thrust their javelins at any man who tried to work his way round or under the wagon.

There was a cry of terror from one of the men close to Macro, and with a quick glance he saw a legionary pulled bodily over the side of the wagon. He crashed on to the ground and was quickly cut to pieces under a rain of frenzied blows from the Durotrigans. Macro leaned forward and thrust his blade into an exposed throat, then pulled back, shouting over his shoulder.

'Figulus!'

'Sir?'

'Set fire to the thatch! Then get your section out of here!'

Macro held his ground with increasing fury, stabbing and hacking at his enemies, face fixed in a snarl. He sensed a strange energy flowing through him, and an inner calmness. This was what he lived for. This was what he was best at, the one thing in life that was an unproblematic verity; he was born to fight. And even with violent death so close, he was content and happy.

'Come on, you wankers!' Macro, eyes wide with glee, shouted into the upraised faces of the Durotrigans. 'Is this the best you can fucking do? Tossers!'

The legionary next to him spared his centurion an anxious glance.

'What you looking at?' Macro snapped as he slashed his sword across an enemy's face, the skin splitting like an overripe watermelon. 'Get into the spirit of things!'

'Sir!' The legionary backed away from the enemy. 'Look! Fire!'

Thin tendrils of smoke were rising up from between the boards on the bottom of the wagon, where a hazy red glow was visible. More smoke curled up around the sides of the wagon, and one of the legionaries swung his leg over the rear of the wagon.

'Stay where you are!' Macro roared. 'Nobody jumps for it until I say!'

The guilty man turned back, hurriedly stabbing an enemy warrior, who tumbled over the side at his feet. Beneath them the dry thatch crackled as the flames quickly spread, and the smoke thickened around the wagon in a choking acrid cloud. Macro's eyes stung and watered so badly he could barely keep them open. And yet, incredibly, the Durotrigans still threw themselves forward, through the yellow flames licking up from under the wagon, then up the sides of the wagon, choking as they tried to shout their defiant war cries into the faces of their Roman enemies. The smoke was orange- and red-hued all about Macro, and his legionaries were no more than vague shapes, silhouetted against the flares raging up on all sides. His feet and legs were suddenly searing hot and Macro glanced down and saw that the flames were beginning to burn through the floor of the wagon.

'Get out! Out! Back to depot! Go!'

The legionaries turned, mounted the side of the wagon and leaped clear of the flames into the street on the far side. Macro shifted to a spot where the flames were not so intense and took a quick look round to make sure the enemy could not follow them through the fire. Then he turned, threw his shield and sword into the street and dived after them. He crashed on to the ground and rolled awkwardly to one side, the breath driven from his body. For a moment he could not breathe and when he did gasp at the air the smoke made his chest seize up. As Macro retched, someone grabbed his arm and pulled him to his feet. He blinked to clear the tears from his eyes and saw Figulus.

'Come on, sir!'

Macro's sword and shield were pressed back into his hands and then Figulus pulled him away from the blazing wagon.

'You're supposed . . . to be with . . . your men,' Macro wheezed.

'They're all right, sir. Sent them on ahead.'

'Wait!' Macro looked back towards the gate. The wagon was well ablaze and brilliant red torrents of flame crackled and roared upwards, firing the ramparts above. The centurion nodded his satisfaction. The gateway had been denied to the enemy, for now at least. But it would not take them long to scale the walls instead; Macro's actions had only bought the defenders a brief interval. 'Let's go.'

As soon as Cato heard the battering ram crash through the gates he gave the order to fall back. Mandrax hoisted the standard above his head and slowly swung it from side to side. All along the ramparts the men of the Wolf Cohort fell back from the palisade and ran through the streets towards the depot. Taking one last glance to ensure that every man had seen and understood the signal, Cato beckoned to Mandrax and clambered down the reverse slope of the rampart into the ten-pace gap that ran round the inside of Calleva's defences. They made for an opening between two clusters of native huts. A narrow winding street led them into the heart of the town. As they ran Cato noticed anxious faces peering at them from doorways as they pounded past. The people of Calleva would discover the worst soon enough, but there was nothing he could do for them now; nothing he could say that would be of the smallest comfort. And so he ignored them as he and Mandrax ran for the safety of the last line of defence against the Durotrigans. Once inside the depot, they would hold off the enemy for as long as possible and then die.

Cato was surprised at how calmly he accepted the prospect of his imminent death. He had thought there would be more to fear. He had been terrified that fear would paralyse him and unman him at the very end. But for now all that concerned Cato was defying Tincommius and the Durotrigans for as long as possible.

The narrow street suddenly opened out on to a wider thoroughfare that Cato recognised as the main route leading from the gate towards the royal enclosure. Several men from his cohort ran past and he and Mandrax joined them. A little further on a street branched off towards the depot and they turned into it and saw that the way ahead was filled with legionaries and native troops also streaming towards the depot. Nearly all still carried their shields and weapons, Cato noted with pride. Despite the appearance of a rout the men were falling back and once in their new position they would be armed and ready to turn on their enemy once more. Amongst them were the last few legionaries returning from the gates of Calleva.

'Anyone seen Macro?' Cato called out. One of the legionaries turned towards him, and Cato pointed at the man. 'You there! Where's Macro?'

'Dunno, sir. Last I saw, he was with a few lads defending the gate.'

'You left him there?'

'He told us to go!' the legionary replied angrily. 'Said he'd follow on, sir.'

'Right . . . Get inside and form up with the others.'

Cato looked down the street that led to the main gate. Two figures burst round the side of a native hut a hundred paces away. Figulus, taller and leaner, had a short lead over Macro, whose thick, muscular legs pumped hard as he struggled to keep up. Moments later they drew up beside Cato and bent over as they gasped for breath.

'You all right?' asked Cato.

Macro looked up, chest heaving. His face was blackened and the hairs on his arms and legs were singed. The sharp tang of burned hair still clung to him and Cato made a face.

'You should see the other man . . .' Macro chuckled and

then burst into a raucous cough. He doubled up for a moment, and then as the coughing fit ended he looked round at Figulus.

'Nearly forgot . . . You're on a charge, sunshine. Disobey an order again . . . and I'll have you flogged.'

'Yes, sir. I was only—'

A distant roar of voices sounded from beyond the depot gate.

Something was wrong. The entrance to the depot was filled with men trying to force their way out of the gate and up the street and the two opposed flows of humanity melded into a hopeless tangle. Cries of anger and desperation rose from the throng.

Cato pushed his way forwards. 'Silence! Silence there!' he roared out. Most tongues were stilled as faces turned towards him.

'What's going on? Somebody make a report!'

'They're in!' someone shouted. 'The bastards have got into the depot!'

Over the heads of the dense mass of men blocking the gate, Cato looked through the arch and beyond the administration block, towards the grain dump at the rear of the depot. Beyond that, swarming over the rampart, came the Durotrigans. Several bodies in red tunics lay by the palisade and a handful of others were being cut down as they tried to stem the onrush. Already, some of the fainter-hearted of the legion's noncombatants had thrown down their weapons and were fleeing back across the depot, desperate to escape the howling mass of enemy warriors, already spreading out across the parade ground, and racing towards the remaining defenders by the gate.

Chapter Thirty-Three

'If you know what's good for you, you'd better let me see the legate right now.' The stranger glared at the optio, who was standing between two legionaries. They looked like the kind of hardy veterans even the toughest criminals back in Rome would cross the street to avoid. Consequently the optio showed only the slightest concern in the face of the mud-stained individual in a filthy tunic who had presented himself at the camp gate as dusk closed in. The small measure of doubt was due to the stranger's patrician accent. Only a small fortune could have paid for enunciation like that, unless, of course, the man was an actor.

'Who do you think you are, mate?' asked the optio.

'All right then.' The man spoke with elaborate calm. 'I am Tribune Caius Quintillus.'

'Don't look much like a tribune to me.'

'That's because I've ridden through the night and today to get here.'

'Why?'

'There's something of an emergency back at Calleva.'

'Oh, yes?'

'Yes. The garrison is under attack and I'd rather like the legate to know, so that he can send help to Centurion Macro.'

'Macro? Oh, well, that's different. If Macro's in trouble you'd better come in.' The optio turned to one of his men. 'Take him to headquarters.'

Quintillus clamped his mouth shut as he followed the legionary through the gateway of the Second Legion's marching camp, and up the main thoroughfare towards the complex of tents where the legate had his headquarters. There would be time enough to humiliate that wretched optio later. Right now Quintillus needed to warn Vespasian of the danger to Calleva while there still might be a chance of saving the Atrebatans' capital. Then the tribune might yet salvage some political capital from the situation. After all, he had risked his life to get the message to Vespasian. Not that he had run into any of the enemy in his desperate ride for help, but he might have. Courage, he reminded himself, consists of action in the knowledge of the probability of peril. He had acted, and was therefore due his portion of admiration. That made him feel far better, and by the time they reached headquarters the tribune was bathing in the warm glow of high self-regard.

'Who the hell are you?' Vespasian snapped, once the man was admitted to his quarters. The legate was sitting behind his desk, preparing, by the faint light of the setting sun, the orders for the next phase of the campaign. In two days' time the Second Legion would be moving west once more, to destroy a string of hillforts along the northern frontier of the Durotrigans' lands. After that the legion would strike south, laying waste everything in its path until it reached the coast. By then, the Durotrigans must sue for peace, and there would be one less tribe allied to Caratacus.

Vespasian had just finished reading a report on the condition of the legion's catapults and had started on a light supper of cold chicken and wine before resuming his work. He continued chewing as the unwelcome visitor introduced himself.

'Tribune Caius Quintillus, sir. Attached to General Plautius' staff.'

'Never heard of you.'

'I only arrived in Britain a month ago, sir. Replacement.'

'Misplacement, more like.' Vespasian arched an eyebrow. 'Bit out of your way, Tribune. Don't tell me you went out hunting and got lost.'

'No, sir.'

'Well, then?'

'I was sent by the general to assess the situation in Calleva, sir.'

'I see.' Vespasian looked at him thoughtfully for a moment. He was uncomfortable about the idea of Aulus Plautius being concerned about a town within the Second Legion's operational area. Immediately Vespasian wondered if there was something he had overlooked. As far as he could recall, Centurion Macro had made no mention of trouble brewing up amongst the Atrebatans. Yet here was this man, claiming to be a tribune, stating that the general had deemed it necessary to send a senior officer to report back on the situation. Something was amiss, and Vespasian realised he must tread lightly until the precise nature of the general's anxiety became apparent. He smiled faintly at the tribune. 'And the situation will meet with the general's satisfaction, I trust.'

'Hardly.' Quintiullus looked drained. 'When I left the town the Durotrigans were about to attack it. Sir, if we don't act soon, Calleva must fall into enemy hands.'

Vespasian had been reaching for his wine, but now his hand froze halfway across the desk.

'What did you say?'

'Calleva's under attack, sir. Or at least it probably is, given what happened yesterday.'

Vespasian withdrew his hand and leaned back into his

campaign chair, forcing himself to remain composed. 'And what exactly happened yesterday?'

Tribune Quintillus briefly described the destruction of the two native cohorts, the flight back to Calleva, and his hurried orders for the town's defence. He went on, in as modest a tone as he could manage, to relate how he had volunteered himself to ride through enemy lines to find the Second Legion, and bring help to the remains of the garrison holding on back in Calleva. When he finished, Quintillus casually rubbed his eyes and stifled a yawn on the back of his hand.

'That's quite a tale,' Vespasian said evenly. 'You must be exhausted. I'll have some food brought for you. Then you can rest.'

'Yes, sir. But the garrison . . . we must help them at once.'

'Quite. Verica needs our support.'

'Verica? Verica's been wounded. Badly. Last time I saw him he looked pretty close to death.'

'You let the king ride into this ambush?' Vespasian said in an icy tone.

'No, sir,' Quintillus replied quickly. 'He was attacked by one of his noblemen.'

Vespasian bit back on his growing anger. Every time the young tribune opened his mouth the situation got worse. 'I hope there's nothing else to tell me.'

The tribune shook his head and then pointed to a chair beside Vespasian's table. 'May I sit down, sir?'

'What? Oh, yes. Yes, of course.'

While the tribune eased his saddle-sore body down into the campaign chair Vespasian's mind was racing as he reacted to the news of the disaster facing not only the men at Calleva, but his own legion as well. The campaign in the west would be stalled.

'How strong was the enemy force?'

'A thousand, maybe two thousand,' Quintillus guessed.

'But no more than that?'

'No, sir.'

Vespasian's mood lightened slightly. 'Right then, we can cope with that. It's a pain in the arse, and it'll delay my advance, but that can't be helped. We'll deal with the Durotrigans first.'

'Ah . . .' Quintillus looked up with an anxious expression. 'I'm afraid there's a little complication, sir.'

Vespasian's lips compressed into a thin, tight line for a moment as he resisted the impulse to give the tribune a stiff bollocking. Then he said quietly, 'What kind of a complication would that be, Tribune?'

'There's a small element amongst the Atrebatans that want to side with the enemy, and take the tribe with them. They're the ones behind the attack on Verica.'

'I see.' The situation was far worse then. Even if Calleva had fallen to the Durotrigans they would be swiftly ousted by Vespasian's legion, and the situation stabilised. But if the entire tribe could be persuaded to turn against Rome then not only would the Second Legion be in grave danger, but also General Plautius and the other three legions.

Vespasian silently cursed this tribune. Unless he acted at once, to defeat the Durotrigans and remove those Atrebatan noblemen conspiring against Rome, there was every chance that the Emperor would lose nearly twenty thousand legionaries, and as many auxiliary troops. Augustus had managed to survive the loss of General Varus and three legions. Just. But Augustus had firmly established his grip on the legions and the empire. Claudius enjoyed no such legitimacy, and would almost certainly be swept from power in the aftermath of such a terrible military defeat. What future could there be for Rome then? Vespasian felt himself in the cold grip of dark fears at such a prospect . . .

He suddenly realised that he had not heard the tribune's last words. 'Pardon?'

'I said, we'll need to deal with them as well, sir – the Atrebatan traitors.'

'No doubt.' Vespasian nodded. 'If Verica dies, who's to succeed him?'

'Well, there's another problem, sir.'

This time there was no concealing his frustration and Vespasian slammed his hand down on the desk. He glared at Quintillus, gently rapping his knuckles on the wood. With forced equanimity he nodded at the tribune. 'Go on.'

'The nobleman who attacked him – Artax – was Verica's heir.'

'This Artax, he's taken the throne?'

'No, sir. He was discovered in the act by Centurion Macro and Centurion Cato. He was killed on the spot.'

'So the succession to Verica is open, then?' said Vespasian. 'Who'd be best suited to succeed him from our point of view?'

The tribune answered directly. 'Verica's nephew seems the best bet; Tincommius. I persuaded the king's council to choose him to be Verica's heir after Artax was killed. '

'What's this Tincommius like?'

'Young, but smart. He knows we'll win. We can count on him, sure enough. He'll be loyal to Rome.'

'He'd better be, for his tribe's sake. If he can't keep control of his people once I've settled things, then I won't take any more chances with our supplies. The Atrebatan kingdom will have to come to an end. I'll annex it in the name of Rome, disarm the tribe and leave a permanent garrison in Calleva.'

Quintillus smiled; the legate was playing into his hands and unwittingly helping Quintillus into a position where he would have the chance to wield his procuratorial powers. 'That would seem to be the wisest course of action, sir.'

Vespasian leaned back in his seat and shouted for his chief clerk. Moments later the man hurried through the tent flap, wax notebook in hand.

'I want my senior officers in here now.'

'All of them, sir?'

'Every one. Wait there.' Vespasian quickly shuffled through his papers until he found the most recent strength returns. He read them quickly before continuing. 'I want the following cohorts assembled and ready to march: Labeo's, Genialis', Pedius', Pollio's, Veiento's and Hortensius'. Six cohorts should be enough. They're to carry arms and equipment, water bottles and light rations. Nothing else, understand? It'll be a forced march and the cohort commanders are to make sure that they leave behind any man they have doubts about. There will be no stragglers.'

The clerk could not hide his surprise or alarm at these instructions, but Vespasian refused to enlighten him. It would be most unseemly for a legion's commander to be seen to explain his orders to a lesser rank. He was determined to remain as detached from his men as possible. It had been hard work, often undone in the thoughtlessness of unguarded moments, which tormented him for many days afterwards.

'Anything else, sir?' the clerk asked.

'No. Get to it, man!'

A thin crescent moon rose even as the last rays of the dying sun shrank away beyond the horizon. There was a brief period of darkness before the eye grew used to the pale light of the moon, and then the landscape resolved into a monochrome patchwork of fields, forests and rolling hills. From the eastern gate of the marching camp a long column of men snaked down the track that led towards Calleva, some thirty miles away. Nearly three thousand legionaries tramped along the track in loose ranks, the chinking of their equipment all but drowned out by the thud of iron-studded boots on the dry earth. Vespasian rode behind the lead cohort, a few staff officers and Quintillus spread out behind him.

If he pushed the men hard, Vespasian calculated that they might reach Calleva by the end of the next day. There might be a hard fight after the march for his tired men, but they were legionaries, trained to a superb level of fitness. Tired or not, they would be more than a match for a few thousand Durotrigans.

Chapter Thirty-Four

'How the hell . . .?' Cato muttered.

'Doesn't matter,' Macro snapped back at him. 'We have to get out of here.'

'Get out of here?' Cato looked at him in astonishment. 'And go where?'

'Royal enclosure. It's all that's left now.'

'But what about our injured?' Cato waved at the hospital block. 'We can't leave them.'

'There's nothing we can do for those lads,' Macro said firmly. 'Nothing. Now get your cohort formed up. Close ranks and follow right behind my century.'

Macro steered Cato towards the survivors of the Wolf Cohort and then called his men to attention. 'Close ranks. Form column of fours in front of the gate. Move!'

As the legionaries ran forward and jostled into formation, Cato began to shout out his orders in Celtic. Driven on by the shouts of the section leaders the two units formed up on the track behind the gate, and closed ranks until they became a compact column, shield to shield along the front and left side. Macro looked round for Figulus.

'Optio! Since you're so bloody keen on hanging back, you've got command of the rearguard. Take two sections. Keep 'em tight and don't let one of the bastards get by you.'

'Yes, sir!' Figulus trotted back to take up position.

As soon as he saw that the formation was ready, Macro pushed his way through into the front rank.

'Column!' He called out the preparatory order, and waited until he heard Cato repeat it to his natives, then: 'Advance!'

The shields, helmets and javelin tips rippled forward, and the tramp of iron-shod boots echoed under the tower as the legionaries moved forward. Behind them came the Wolves, lighter-armoured, and not quite able to march in step with their legionary comrades. Cato had positioned himself near the rear of his men, and looked back at the Durotrigans, running at full tilt towards the legionary rearguard formed up across the inside of the depot gate. There was no need to issue an order to loose javelins: the men hurled the weapons as soon as the enemy were within close range, and several of them were struck down, pierced through by the heavy iron points. But the instant their bodies fell to the ground they disappeared from sight as the men behind surged on, desperate to hurl themselves upon the small column edging up the street in the direction of the royal enclosure.

'Form up across the street!' Macro bellowed from the front, waving his sword to hurry his men into position, so that a wall of shields extended across the gap between the huts on either side. Behind this barrier the head of the column trudged forward once again. Before the rearguard made it out of the depot the first of the Durotrigans slammed into them, slashing at the rectangular shields with their long swords. Both sides fought in silence; the Durotrigans, breathless from their run across the depot, the Romans from grim desperation. The clash of swords and thud of blades on shields sounded to Cato more like a weapons drill than the pitiless fury of battle. Only the cries of the wounded told of the deadly intent with which warrior and legionary fought. The rearguard knew their job well, and kept moving back, fending off blows and only striking when an enemy showed more recklessness than sense, and paid the price.

Ahead of Macro, the Durotrigans who had managed to climb the walls either side of the burning town gate spilled across the street, clashing their spears against their shields, and shouting out their war cries.

'Keep the formation tight!' Macro bellowed above the din, raising his shield so that he could just see above the rim. His sword rose to the horizontal, arm bent and braced to deliver the first thrust. The distance between the column and the howling mass of the Durotrigans narrowed at a measured pace. When there was no more than twenty feet between them, the nearest Durotrigan raised his spear and charged the shield wall. Immediately the rest roared out their battle cry and ran after their comrade.

'Don't stop!' Macro shouted as the man to his left faltered. 'Move forwards. Don't stop for anything.'

The column met the Durotrigans on a narrow front and there was no room for the enemy's weight of numbers to pin the legionaries down. Macro and the other men at the front slammed their shields forwards, thrust, recovered and advanced before repeating the sequence, an automatic rhythm they had practised hundreds of times. The Durotrigans attacked with ferocity and courage, but were no match for the Romans. They were forced back or cut down and then crushed by the column as it marched over them.

Here and there, a lucky spear thrust or sword blow found a gap in the shield wall and thudded home into the flesh of the man behind. Any legionary too badly wounded to continue marching fell to the ground and his place was quickly filled from the dwindling ranks of reserves to keep the shield wall intact. The wounded were left behind as the column passed on, and each man who marched by met the eyes of his wounded comrades and registered a last farewell. As the rearguard approached the injured covered their bodies with their shields and prepared to fight on as best they could before being killed. It was pitiless, thought Cato, quite pitiless. Yet he knew that if he fell he could not expect his men to risk their lives to save him, or any other injured man. That way all of them would die.

The rearguard steadily gave ground as the enemy pressed through the gateway and battered the end of the column, desperately trying to breach the line of shields and cut the small Roman force to pieces. Figulus, taller and broader than most legionaries, held his ground in the centre of the line and kept his men together with steady commands as he deflected blows off his shield and thrust his sword into the enemy massing behind the column.

Step by step the legionaries and the Wolves forced their way up the street towards the junction with the road that led from Calleva's main gate to the royal enclosure. The hard earth beneath their boots quickly became slick and muddy with the gore of the dead and injured, and the cloying smell of blood mixed with the sharper smell of disturbed soil. From his position in the middle of the column, detached from the intensity of the hand-to-hand fighting, Cato could see that they had reached the broad street that cut through the centre of Calleva.

'Cato! Cato!' Macro's voice rose above the din of battle.

'Sir?'

'Soon as we clear the junction take your men and clear the way towards the royal enclosure.'

'Yes, sir!'

The legionaries slowly fought their way across the junction until the column had passed into the route leading up to the gates of the royal enclosure, cutting off a small group of the enemy.

'Now, Cato!' Macro shouted.

'Follow me!' Cato called to his men, and charged up the street.

A few of the Durotigans, those with cool heads, tried to stand their ground. But they were quickly overwhelmed and cut down. The rest broke and ran down the street to the right, ducking into the shelter of any side alleys, casting terrified looks back at their pursuers as the Wolves chased after them.

Cato drew up and looked round, wide-eyed and breathing hard through clenched teeth. Mandrax was behind him, standard in one hand and blood-smeared sword in the other. The Atrebatan warrior grinned at the centurion, thrust his standard into the ground and snatched up the grey locks of a man Cato had knocked down. Mandrax yanked his head up and swept his sword back to cut the man's head off.

'No!' Cato shouted. 'Not now. Leave the heads till later. There's no time.'

With a look of disgust Mandrax released the man's hair and snatched up his standard. Then Cato saw that some of the rest of his cohort had already taken a few heads, and others were busy looking for more.

'Drop those!' Cato shouted in Celtic. 'Drop 'em, I said! Form up!'

Reluctantly, the men obeyed, hurriedly forming a solid block across the street that ran up to the gates of the royal enclosure. As soon as the Wolves were ready, Cato ordered them to move forward fifty paces, halt and wait for orders. Then he ran back to the junction. The legionaries were easily holding off the main body of the enemy that filled the street in the direction of Calleva's main gate for as far as Cato could see.

Macro suddenly appeared, shoving his way through the rear ranks of his men. He saw Cato and nodded grudgingly.

'Nice work . . . Take your men forward and make sure the route to the enclosure is kept open.'

'Right.'

'As my lot get close to the gate, you get yours inside. Be ready to close it the instant the last man passes through.'

Cato smiled faintly. 'That wouldn't be you, by any chance?'

'Get going.'

'Yes, sir.'

Cato trotted back to his men and ordered them forward. They met no further resistance from the Durotrigans who had been separated from the main body of the enemy, and the only ones they saw quickly ran off at the sight of Cato and his men. Then the street widened slightly as it turned a corner and there was the entrance to the royal enclosure. The gates were open and several of the king's bodyguard, fully armed, were standing along the palisade on either side. Cadminius stood in the entrance and beckoned to Cato and his men as they approached. Cato ran over to him.

'Macro and the last of our men are not far behind. We'll have to keep the gate open for them.'

'Keep it open?' Cadminius shook his head. 'Can't risk it. Get your men in and Macro'll have to take his chances.'

'No,' Cato said firmly. 'The gate stays open until I say.'

Cadminius opened his mouth to protest, but there was a ruthless gleam in Cato's eyes, and the Atrebatan looked away and nodded.

'All right . . . We'll need every man we can get to defend the enclosure.'

'That's right,' Cato replied quietly. He turned back to his men. 'Inside. Behind the gate, close formation.'

As the Wolves marched inside, Cato indicated the position for Mandrax, and the men formed up around their standard, facing back down the street towards the sounds of fighting. They did not have to wait long for the legionaries to appear. Macro's men came into sight, falling back at a steady pace, keeping a tight formation across the street as they fended off the Durotrigan mass desperately trying to force a way through the shields.

'Pass all the javelins to the front!' Cato called out to his men, and the few remaining javelins were thrust forward into the hands of the men of the front rank, who quickly sheathed their swords.

'You'll be using them as spears,' Cato said. 'No throwing. Front rank, close up, overlapping shields! Two paces forward. Thrust over the rims.'

There was a clatter as the men aligned their shields and readied their javelins in a tight overhead grip. This way they would have a longer strike range, and present a more unnerving danger to the Durotrigans as the iron tips stabbed towards their eyes. Then they waited silently, watching through the gateway as their Roman allies retreated towards them. Cato went forward to join Cadminius and a small group of warriors standing ready to close the gate the moment the order was given.

From the Roman ranks Macro shouted an order for the rear two lines to break formation and man the palisade. The men trotted past the sides of the Wolves and hurried up on to the narrow sentry walk either side of the gate. The Roman line, thinner now, gave way more easily under the pressure of the Durotrigan horde, and Cato feared it might cave in before Macro and his men reached them. The enemy saw the opportunity as well, and threw themselves forward in a renewed frenzy of hacking and slashing blades. As the legionaries reached the enclosure they were no longer able to maintain formation and stumbled back from the screaming mob. Then they were passing through the gate, exhausted and gasping for breath, but aware enough to keep clear of Cato's men. There was Macro, in a small knot of legionaries, cursing and shouting his defiance into the faces of his enemies as he thrust his blade at them, legs poised for balance as he carefully backed towards the safety of the enclosure.

With a quick rearward glance, Macro sized up the position and after a final savage roar at the Durotrigans he shouted to the last of his men, 'Run for it!'

They turned and sprinted through the gate as Cato ordered his spearmen forward. At the sight of the wicked iron javelin points protruding over the wall of oval auxiliary shields the Durotrigans instinctively shrank back.

'Close the gate!' Cato shouted, throwing his shoulder to the timbers as Cadminius and his warriors quickly heaved the gate into place. Suddenly the gate shivered and started to swing back as the Durotrigans recovered and charged forwards again.

'Help! Help here!' Cato cried out, and the Wolves surged forward, adding their weight to those desperately trying to seal the entrance. For a moment the gate was still, caught between the two straining forces, then Cato felt his boots sliding backwards.

'Heave! Come on, you bastards! Heave!'

More men joined them, Macro and his legionaries among them, and the gate was held still again, no more than a foot from the timber frame and locking bracket. Macro drew back and looked up to the men on the palisade.

'Use your daggers! Hit 'em with anything you've got. Throw your fucking swords at them, if you have to!'

As the men drew their daggers and hurled them down into the dense mass straining at the gate, the enemy's attention was distracted for a crucial moment, and with one last effort the defenders closed the gate and slammed the locking bar home.

While some of the men slumped to the ground or bent double as they struggled to catch their breath Cato forced himself to stand upright. He picked up his shield, pushed his way through the men and climbed the short ladder up to the palisade. Keeping his shield raised he looked down and saw that the

Durotrigans were already melting away from the enclosure, until only a small handful still hammered away at the timbers with their swords and spears.

'Keep hitting 'em,' Cato shouted to the men beside him, then leaned back to the men inside the entrance. 'Get every javelin up here, now!'

As soon as the iron-headed shafts began to strike down amongst them, even the most resolute of the Durotrigans recognised that their rage was useless, and they ran back from the gate, down the street and out of range. Cato nodded his satisfaction, and then dropped down into the enclosure to find Macro. His friend was sitting on the ground, bare-headed as he examined a dent on the top of his helmet. He ran his fingers tenderly across the scar on his scalp.

'You all right, Macro?'

The centurion nodded, and blinked his eyes. 'I'll be fine. Just a bit dizzy. Some bastard whacked me right above that injury . . . Give us a hand.'

Cato grasped his arm and heaved the other man to his feet. He looked round the exhausted faces inside the gate. 'Where's Figulus?'

'He was knocked over back there.'

'Dead?'

'I didn't see.'

Cato nodded once, then turned towards the gate. 'Our friends have gone, for the moment.'

Macro nodded, then looked up at the sky. It was near sunset, and a brilliant orange spread across the horizon.

'It'll be dark soon.' Macro looked at Cato. 'We'd better get some torches lit. Somehow I don't think Tincommius and his pals are going to give us an easy night.'

Chapter Thirty-Five

A strange silence settled over Calleva once night had fallen. In the royal enclosure Macro had ordered most of the men to rest. After the enemy had pulled back Macro had thrown his men into constructing an inner redoubt around the entrance of the great hall. All the spare wagons and carts had been heaved together to form a small semi-circle backing on to the stout stone walls of the hall. Wicker baskets were filled with soil and crammed beneath the wagons to reinforce them and hold them in position, and benches were brought from inside the hall to provide the defenders with a breastwork to fight behind. If the outer wall fell, which it must, thanks to its being little more than a glorified fence, then everyone would retreat to this last redoubt, and after that a last stand inside the great hall, guarding the king's bedchamber.

Once the work was complete Macro told his men to rest. They lay across the ground, dark shapes curled up by their weapons in the flickering glow of the torches that were ranged along the palisade. Verica's household slaves had been sent to bring the exhausted defenders food and drink from the royal kitchen, and the king's bodyguards were keeping watch for any signs of the enemy. Beyond the enclosure, the huddled mass of thatched roofs was silent, there were no cries for mercy, or the usual horrified shrieks that accompanied the fall of a town.

Macro sat with his head cocked towards the burned-out remains of the town's gate. The only noises that rose up in the distance were the periodic choruses of dogs barking, and once in a while a shouted order from the enemy.

After a while Macro gave up and nudged Cato, who had fallen asleep shortly before.

'You hear anything?'

Cato struggled up on one elbow, blinking away the ache in his eyes, fearful that Macro had detected the approach of the enemy.

'What? What is it?'

'Shhh! Listen . . .'

Cato sat up and strained his ears, but all was quiet. 'I can't hear anything.'

'That's what I mean,' said Macro. 'There should be more noise. They've taken the town; they should be enjoying the spoils.'

Cato shook his head. 'They're trying to win the Atrebatans over. I doubt Tincommius is going to permit them even the smallest amount of rape and pillage. Not if he's as bright as he needs to be.'

Macro looked at Cato, his features barely visible in the dark. 'You admire him?'

'No. No, I don't. He's a fool. If he succeeds in turning the Atrebatans, one way or another they'll be slaughtered. That's the kind of king people really don't need.'

'No . . .' Macro looked away. 'There's something else that worries me.'

'Oh?'

'Tincommius said that Caratacus was coming.'

'Yes. So?' Cato rubbed his eyes. 'I doubt it'll make much difference. We're not going to be around that long.'

'Maybe. But what if Quintillus has found the legion?'

'I doubt the tribune made it. They must have caught him.'

'What if they didn't? What if he reached the legion and Vespasian sends a relief force?'

Cato was silent for a moment before he replied, 'We can only hope he didn't make it. Best lose a few hundred of us than a few thousand.'

'True. We can see that, but Vespasian can't. Far as he knows the only opposition he'll face is the force that ambushed us. Even that coward Quintillus will find it hard to overestimate their strength enough to keep the legate away. If Vespasian comes, he'll bring most of the legion with him, right into the path of Caratacus.'

Cato paused as he contemplated this awful possibility. He looked at Macro. 'Then we've got to warn him, assuming Tincommius was telling the truth.'

'How?' Macro responded sourly. 'We're surrounded. The moment anyone tries to make a break for it they'll be bagged and killed on the spot, if they're lucky.'

'Somebody has to try,' Cato said quietly. 'If there's a chance that the legate might attempt to save us.'

'No. It's pointless. We need every man right here.'

'What difference does it make?' Cato persisted. 'We're all dead in the end. Let me go.'

'No. You stay. That's an order. I'll not send any man on a bloody stupid suicide mission. As I said, there won't be a relief force sent to us. All that's left is to hold on, and take as many of the buggers with us as we can.'

'Or surrender and take our chances.'

'Some chances!' Macro laughed harshly. 'Oh, they might spare our native lads, and they might even let Verica live long enough to die from his wounds. But not us. They'll have something special sorted out for us. You can count on it.'

'All right then,' Cato conceded, 'but they might spare the

Wolves, and Cadminius and his men. We could offer terms for their surrender and fight on ourselves.'

Macro stared at him, but in the dark Cato could not read his expression and he continued his line of argument. 'There's no point in more deaths than necessary. If the Wolves and the bodyguards are spared because we were seen to save them, it might count for something in the longer term. It might leave some sympathy for Rome.'

'It might. Then it might not. If they die with us, then their kin might blame the Durotrigans for their deaths. Better still, blame that bastard Tincommius.'

'I hadn't thought of that,' Cato replied quietly. He was silent for a moment. Then: 'Should we talk it over with Cadminius and the others?'

'No,' Macro said firmly. 'The moment we start giving in, the fight will go out of our lads. Think about it, Cato. Think about how you'd feel watching the natives marching out of here and leaving us to die. Not the best way of keeping your pecker up, is it? And what guarantee do we have that they'd let the native lads live? You'd trust their lives to Tincommius? He'd have their heads on the ends of stakes in a trice.'

'Which might well have a useful impact on the loyalty of the Atrebatans, from our point of view,' Cato replied coldly.

'Cynic!' Macro laughed, and slapped him on the shoulder.

Cato smiled. 'But you're right. We can't trust Tincommius with their lives. I guess they'll have to take their chances with us. I doubt they'll protest. The bodyguards aren't very fond of Tincommius – even the ones who think we might have had a hand in that attack on Verica.'

'They seriously believe that?'

Cato shrugged. 'Hard to say. I've heard some of them muttering about it, and I get the odd suspicious glance. Seems that Tincommius' words might have had some effect after all. The only one who can convince them of the truth is Verica.'

'Have you heard anything about him?'

'No. But I think we should find out. If there's a chance that he can recover enough to confirm that he was attacked by Tincommius, it might help.'

'All right then, you go and see. But don't be long. Our friends might try something.'

'Do you really think they will?'

'No . . . They must be as exhausted as we are. They'll want a rest. I doubt they'll be in any great hurry. We're bottled up in here with no way of escape, and they've got Caratacus and his whole bloody army on the way to help them out. I think they can wait until dawn before making the next move.'

'I hope so.' Cato yawned as he struggled back on to his feet. The short rest seemed to have made him feel more tired than ever. Every limb ached and felt stiff and heavy, and the night air seemed too cold for summer. His head ached and his eyes stung and for a moment he let his mind indulge itself in a vision of sleep in his warm comfortable bed back at the depot. The fantasy was so alluring that he felt a warm ripple flow through his body and he allowed himself to surrender to it.

'Oi! Watch it!' Macro called out, bracing Cato with his arm. 'You nearly fell on me.'

'Sorry.' Cato was now wide awake, ashamed of his weakness and afraid that it might happen again. He stretched his shoulders and walked over to a water trough, removed his helmet and swept the strands of hay covering the surface to one side before ducking his head in, rocking his face from side to side as the cool water quickened his senses. Then he stood up, not bothered by the drops of water cascading down his face and on to his segmented armour and tunic. With a last stretch, and rubbing his eyes Cato set off for the great hall. He climbed through the gap between two of the wagons and dropped down into the redoubt.

Cadminius and some of the bodyguards sat by the entrance to the hall, talking quietly and drinking from some wine jars in the glow of a small fire. They looked up as Cato strode across to them. The centurion was frowning. He beckoned to Cadminius and entered the hall. Cadminius took his time finishing off the wine in his cup, and then rose slowly and followed Cato inside.

'Drinking? Is that wise?' Cato asked with a look of contempt. 'You'll hardly be in a fit state to defend your king tomorrow.'

'Roman, drink is our way of life.'

'Fine, but it can ruin a good death. Is that how you want to die tomorrow? A drunken rabble so pissed you can hardly strike a straight blow.'

Cadminius raised his fist and for a moment Cato felt sure the warrior would hit him. But Cadminius slowly relaxed his expression and muttered, 'We'll be all right. I give you my word.'

'I'm counting on it. Now, I must see the king.'

'No point. He's just the same.'

'Nevertheless, I must see him. Macro has ordered me to report on his condition.' Cato did not give Cadminius any chance to protest further. He swung round and marched towards the door leading into the king's private quarters. A sole guard stood on duty, and he pushed his back away from the wall and reached for his spear, but Cadminius waved him aside.

The royal bedchamber was brightly lit by oil lamps and torches, and stank of smoke. A small crowd of nobles sat and stood about the king's table, talking in muted tones. Verica was almost impossible to see, swathed in fur covers up to his chin. Above them, his white hair flowed over a purple bolster. The king's skin was almost as white as his hair and the faint rasp of his breathing was audible even from the doorway. The surgeon from the depot hospital looked up as Cato entered and smiled.

'The king stirred briefly a few moments ago.'

'He regained consciousness?' asked Cato as he joined the surgeon at the bedside and looked down at the frail old man.

'Not exactly. He opened his eyes, muttered a few words and was unconscious again.'

'Words? What words? What'd he say?'

'Nothing I could make out, except Tincommius' name. The king seemed a bit agitated.'

'That's it? Nothing more?' The surgeon shook his head, and Cato's lips briefly tightened in frustration. 'If there's any change, either way, you send for me at once. Understand?'

'Yes, sir.'

Cato took a last look at the king and was turning to leave when the surgeon grasped his arm.

'Has anyone made it from the hospital?'

'No.'

'I see.' The surgeon looked Cato in the eye. 'What are our chances, sir?'

'Not good. Just do your duty, for as long as you can.'

'And when the end comes . . .?'

'Protect the king. That's all.'

Once he had reported back to Macro, Cato made a quick round of the palisade to make sure that the men were awake and watching for any sign of the enemy. With so few of the defenders left, even one unobservant sentry could lead to the death of them all. Then, satisfied that there was no more he could do, Cato found himself a place close to the gate, leaned back against a support post and almost at once fell into a deep sleep. He did not wake when the guard was changed, and it was only the urge to urinate that finally woke him, shortly before dawn. Consciousness returned quickly, and an instant fear that he had slept far too long. At once Cato tried to clamber up on to his feet. The stiffness of his muscles and the aching heaviness of total exhaustion almost denied him the ability to stand, and he groaned as he forced himself to straighten up.

Although it was still dark and gloomy overhead, away in the east the horizon was lit by the pearly grey of the coming dawn. The air was cool and the breath of the few men stirring around the royal enclosure came in faint wisps. There was a peculiar stillness in the air, and the sky was overcast, promising rain later on, or more likely the depressing drizzle that was so much a feature of this island's climate. It saddened Cato to think that the drama of his death would unfold against such a dour backdrop. A paltry skirmish in some dark corner of a crude collection of barbarian hovels that scarcely dignified its description as a town. That's where he, Macro, Silva and the others would find their graves – in obscure, uncivilised and backward Calleva. No place in the history books for them.

Stretching his back and shoulders Cato walked stiffly over to a small fire in the centre of the enclosure. Macro was supervising a small party of kitchen slaves as they cut a pig up into portions. The aroma of roast pork made Cato realise how hungry he was and this time he willingly helped himself to a hunk of meat with plenty of crackling on it. He nodded a greeting to Macro.

'You'll break your teeth on that,' Macro smiled.

'What good is life if we can't enjoy it?' Cato replied. 'Any bread going?'

'There, in that basket.'

Cato squatted down beside the fire and began to eat, chewing slowly and relishing the taste of every mouthful of pork and the king's finest bread. It felt strange to enjoy his food so much, and Cato realised that in ordinary circumstances he had had to bolt his meal down in order to get on with all the duties of the day. Today, by contrast, there was nothing to rush. Breakfast could go on for as long as he wanted, or at least for as long as the Durotrigans permitted.

Once the slaves had been sent round to rouse the defenders and hand them their food Macro sat down beside Cato and munched contentedly on a strip of roast loin as he warmed himself. Neither man spoke. Around them, as the pale light strengthened, the defenders awoke from deep sleep and huddled over the food brought to them. Most had enough appetite to tuck into the choice pickings of the royal foodstore, but some were too exhausted, or too preoccupied, and let the food grow cold at their sides as they sat and waited.

They were not kept long. A legionary sentry on the palisade above the gate called out to Macro, and the two centurions immediately threw down their food and ran across the enclosure. They climbed the ladder quickly, their earlier stiffness forgotten as they responded to the urgency of the sentry's tone.

'Report!' ordered Macro.

'Sir, down there!' The legionary pointed along the street. 'A couple of 'em just popped round the corner, had a quick look and ran back.'

'And you spoiled my breakfast for that?'

'Yes, sir. You said—'

'I know what I said, thank you. You did the right thing, son. We'll wait here a while and see if anything happens.'

'It's happening,' said Cato. 'Look.'

From round the corner, perhaps fifty paces away, strode a single figure, brash and bold. He stopped, at a safe range and cupped his hands to his mouth.

'So, you're both still alive!' Tincommius called out. 'I'm relieved.'

'He's relieved.' Macro raised an eyebrow as he exchanged a glance with Cato. 'I'm touched . . .'

'I've come to offer you one final chance to surrender, and save yourselves and those of my tribe who are misguided enough to serve the ends of Rome.'

'On what terms?' Macro called out.

'Same as before. Safe passage to your legion.'

'I don't think so!'

'I thought you'd say that!'

Cato was sure that he could see Tincommius smile for a moment. Then the Atrebatan prince turned round and shouted an order. There were sharp cries of pain and some shouting from beyond the bend in the street. Then a column of figures shambled into sight. Many wore bandages, some had streaks of dried blood on their faces and limbs. Some wore the red tunic of the Roman legions, and were tethered together by leather straps. Ranged alongside them were men armed with spears, prodding any of the prisoners who stumbled along too slowly. Cato recognised a few faces: men who had once served in the Wolf and Boar Cohorts and some of the Greek and Roman merchants who had hoped to make their fortune in Britain. Tincommius gave an order and the column halted. The first man was untied from the others and brought forward, hands still tightly bound. His escort kicked him behind the knees and the Roman fell down with a cry. He lay on his side, groaning, until Tincommius stepped over and kicked him in the head. The Roman tucked his head down, drew his knees up and fell silent.

Tincommius turned back to the gateway, pointing down at the man on the ground. 'You'll surrender to me now, or this man dies. And then the rest, one by one.'

Chapter Thirty-Six

'To prove I mean what I say, please observe . . .' Tincommius nodded to a man standing to one side of the column. Unlike the other natives he was carrying only a heavy wooden club. He strode forward, and stood over the Roman on the ground, bracing his feet apart. Then he swept the club up and smashed it down on the shin of the Roman's left leg. Cato and Macro clearly heard the bone crack from the gateway of the royal enclosure, fifty paces up the street. The scream from the Roman was audible from far further away. And it got worse when the warrior broke the prisoner's other leg – a shrill animal screech of pure agony that chilled the blood of all who heard it. The Roman writhed in the dirt of the street, his lower legs twisting obscenely below the knee, causing even more torment. His screams only ended when he finally passed out.

Tincommius allowed the silence to have its effect before continuing to address the defenders. 'That's the first. There'll be more, until you come to your senses and surrender. Those that survive can be taken with you when you quit Calleva. It's your decision, Macro. You can end this any time that you wish.'

Above the gate Cato noticed that Macro was gripping the pommel of his sword so tightly that his knuckles were white and the tendons leading back towards the wrist stood out like iron nails under the skin. Cato felt more sick than enraged. The spectacle had made him want to throw up, and the roast pork and fine bread he had been enjoying so much only moments earlier now churned in his stomach.

'Bastard,' Macro whispered through clenched teeth. 'Bastard . . . Bastard . . . BASTARD!'

His shout of rage carried down the street, and Tincommius smiled as Macro let his anger spill out.

'Fucking bastard! I'll kill you. I swear it! I'll kill you!'

'Centurion, you're welcome to come out here and try it. I dare you!'

'Sir,' Cato placed his hand on Macro's shoulder, 'You mustn't . . .'

Macro glanced round angrily. 'Of course not! Think I'm stupid?'

'No . . . just angry, sir. Angry and helpless.' Cato nodded at the other men who crowded the palisade, staring down the street with expressions of horror and rage. 'We all are.'

Macro turned to look in the direction Cato had indicated and saw that not only had all the remaining legionaries clambered up on to the palisade, but also the Wolves and some of Verica's bodyguards. He swept Cato's hand from his shoulder and roared at the men.

'What the bloody hell do you think this is? A fucking freak show? Get off the wall and get back to your positions! Want them to just bloody hop over the wall while you're gawping at that twat? The only men I want up here are the sentries. Move!'

The legionaries backed away from the palisade with guilty expressions and clambered back down into the enclosure, followed by the Wolves, who had no need of Cato's shouted translation. Macro glowered at them for a moment and then turned back towards Tincommius.

When he saw that he had the centurion's attention again Tincommius called out, 'Macro, will you surrender? Answer me!'

The centurion stood still and silent, lips compressed into a tight line on his weathered face. A terrible despair gnawed at his guts and a fathomless anger and hatred for Tincommius filled his soul as Macro watched helplessly.

'Very well. The next man, then.' Tincommius beckoned for the second prisoner to be brought forward.

The Atrebatan warrior selected a youth, scarcely more than a boy, whom Cato recognised as one of the mule herders from the depot. The boy shrank back, shaking his head, but his captor grabbed him roughly by the hair as he slipped the knot that bound the boy to the rest of the prisoners. With a savage wrench the warrior hauled the boy out of the column and dragged him, writhing and screaming for mercy, towards the prone form of the first victim. Macro stood still, but Cato could watch no more, and turned away. He hurried to the ladder and swung himself down into the enclosure. As he reached the ground he heard the sickening crunch of a blow being landed and the boy's scream cut through the morning air like a knife thrust deep into Cato's guts.

All morning it went on, and the broken bodies stretched across the street. There was no pause in the screams and cries of the Romans now that so many of them had been crippled and left to suffer the agony of their shattered limbs. Macro made himself stay on the gate, silent and unyielding in the face of Tincommius' regular demands for surrender. And each time, when Macro refused to reply, the next captive was dragged forward, in full view of the defenders on the gate, and beaten savagely on the legs until they broke. To add emphasis to the process Tincommius ordered the warrior with the club to begin breaking arms as well and once he had broken both shins he began on their elbow joints.

For Cato, even well away from the gateway, there was no

respite from the horror, as the screaming continued unabated. No one in the royal enclosure spoke. Most sat staring at the ground, visibly shaken every time a new victim added his cries to the shrill, nerve-shredding chorus. Some men spent the time sharpening their swords with vigorous rasping strokes of their whetstones that did little to drown out the hellish din from over the wall. Finally, Cato could stand it no more and climbed up to join Macro. The older officer had not moved, and stared down the street with a fixed, implacable expression. He spared himself only the briefest of glances at Cato.

'What is it?'

'I'm worried about how much more of this the men can take . . . sir.' Cato nodded discreetly towards the men in the enclosure. 'It's wearing 'em down.'

'Wearing you down, you mean,' Macro sneered. 'If you can't stomach this, then what are you doing in that uniform?'

'Sir!' Cato protested, shocked by Macro's vehemence. 'I . . . I . . .'

'You what? Go on, say it.'

Cato struggled for a response, but his mind was too tired to develop a line of reasoning to excuse himself. Instinctively he knew that Macro was right: he was thinking more about himself than the responses of the men, and he looked down guiltily. 'Nothing . . . I can't bear it.'

The veteran looked at him closely, a bitter expression on his face, the muscles of his cheeks tightening and twitching. For a moment Cato thought that Macro would explode and shout him down in front of all the men. The humiliating vision filled his mind to the exclusion of anything else, so profound was Cato's fear of shame and inadequacy. Then Macro looked past Cato, aware of the faces that had turned towards the two centurions. He breathed in deeply through his nose and forced himself to release the tension that gripped his body like a vice.

'Well, you have to bear it,' Macro said quietly. 'This is as bad as it gets, Cato. And you have to be calm, control yourself and not give way. Or at least, try to be as calm as you can.' Macro shook his head sadly as he recalled his initial wave of rage when the first prisoner had been broken.

'Is there nothing we can do about it?'

Macro shrugged. 'What did you have in mind?'

'I don't know. Perhaps we might try to rush them, and get our men back.'

'Cato, they're dead either way. If we rescue them, what then? They'll live a few more hours before the royal enclosure falls, that's all. And if our rescue attempt goes wrong, we all die a bit sooner.'

'So what difference does it make?'

'Not much,' admitted Macro. 'I just know it's our duty to guard the king, and hold out for as long as possible.'

'And we just let them carry on with that?' Cato pointed down the street.

'What else can we do?'

The younger man opened and closed his mouth. Despite the waves of revulsion, despair and a need to do something, there really was nothing to be done about the situation. He was a helpless member of the audience before the horror being staged.

'We *could* try to rush them,' he said in the end.

'No. I won't allow it. In any case, they'd try to kill those prisoners the moment we opened the gates. That's the end of it, Cato. The end, you hear?'

Cato nodded, and Macro patted him on the shoulder, before turning back towards the enemy. Sensitive to the need to divert Cato, he pointed towards the warriors standing round the remaining prisoners.

'Did you notice that the only men he's got with him are Atrebatans?'

Cato glanced round. 'Yes . . . Smart move.'

'Smart?'

'Keeping the Durotrigans out of sight while he calls for us to surrender. I imagine he thinks he can make this look like some kind of internal tribal squabble that can easily be settled.'

'Will our lads go for it?'

'It might have an effect on some,' Cato conceded, then his eyes widened as he saw the next prisoner being led forward, picking his way over the twisted bodies of the earlier victims. 'Oh, no . . .'

'What?' Macro strained his eyes. 'Who is it?'

'Figulus.'

'Figulus? Shit . . .'

As Tincommius beckoned to Figulus' escort, Cato looked round into the enclosure, calling out in Celtic. 'It's Figulus! They've got Figulus!'

There was a spontaneous groan from the Wolves, who had come to admire and like their Roman instructor. Cato called out to them, waving at them to come to the wall. 'They're going to kill him. See! See!'

'What the fuck are you doing?' asked Macro.

Cato flashed a quick smile at Macro. 'Time to play Tincommius at his own game.'

'What?'

'Just watch.'

As the Wolves reached the palisade they began to shout down the street, howling their protest and begging their former comrades to spare Figulus. The optio had dropped to his knees and the man with the club was standing to one side, looking from the prisoner, to Tincommius, to the other warriors guarding the Roman prisoners, up towards the enclosure and back to the prisoner again. Tincommius was shouting angrily at him and thrusting a finger towards the kneeling Roman.

Figulus just looked round, bewildered and terrified. Now, one of the warriors trotted forward and spoke with the Atrebatan prince, who shouted an order into his face. The man glanced at Figulus and shook his head.

'This looks promising!' Macro smiled.

Cato felt someone tugging the sleeve of his tunic and turned to see the surgeon with an excited expression on his face.

'Sir! It's the king!' The surgeon had to shout to be heard above the din. 'He's regained consciousness.'

'When?'

'Just now.'

'How is he?'

'Groggy, but lucid enough. Cadminius told him about our situation. He wants to see you. Both of you.'

Macro shook his head. 'Tell him we're a little busy.'

'No!' Cato interrupted, with an excited expression. 'Can Verica be moved?'

'I suppose so, if it's really necessary. Can't make his condition any worse, I'd say.'

'Good!' Cato slapped the surgeon on the arm. 'Then get him up here. Right away.'

The surgeon shook his head. 'I don't know about that.'

'All right, I'll make it simple.' Cato drew his sword and raised the tip under the surgeon's chin. 'I order you to bring him here immediately. That good enough?'

'Er, yes, sir.'

'Off you go then.'

As the surgeon ran off to fetch his patient Macro laughed. 'That was all centurion. You're coming on nicely, Cato.'

Cato was looking back down the street. Tincommius was surrounded by his men and he was arguing furiously, arms waving to emphasise his point. But they would not be moved by his pleas and shouted their protest back in an equally emphatic manner. To the side kneeled Figulus, silently watching the confrontation and not daring to move for fear of drawing attention to himself. Behind him stood the man with the club, waiting for a decision to be made.

'With any luck,' said Macro, 'they'll start laying into each other any moment now.'

'I doubt it,' Cato replied. He had seen Tincommius at work and knew that the prince was more than capable of turning things round. They had already underestimated him once. It would not pay to do so again. Cato looked behind him. 'Where's that bloody surgeon?'

As they waited for Verica to be fetched the smooth-talking Tincommius began to wear his men down. He was doing nearly all the talking while most of them hung their heads and listened to the haranguing and rhetorical appeals in silence.

'Here he comes,' said Macro, and Cato turned to see the surgeon emerging from the great hall, closely followed by a stretcher with a bodyguard at each corner. Walking beside the stretcher was Cadminius, anxiously looking down at the pale face resting on a soft cushion.

'Hurry!' Cato shouted. 'Up here! Quick as you can.'

The small party trotted across to the gate, trying hard not to jolt the king. When they reached the wall the burly bodyguards heaved the stretcher poles up to the hands of the men on the palisade. While Verica was carried carefully to the wider platform above the gate, Cato glanced back towards the confrontation between Tincommius and his men. The prince had had enough, and pushed his way through them, drawing his sword as he made for Figulus.

'Stop!' Cato cried out in Celtic. 'Stop him!'

Tincommius spared him a brief glance and continued towards the kneeling Roman. But before he could reach Figulus, the man with the club stepped forward and placed himself between the prince and Figulus, shaking his head.

'Out of my way!' Tincommius' cry of rage could be heard above the cheers of the defenders. Cadminius helped his king off the stretcher and gently supported him as Verica took two unsteady paces towards the palisade. As the king came into view the Atrebatan warriors in the street looked up in astonishment.

'Sire, Tincommius told them you were dead,' explained Cato. 'He told them that we had murdered you.'

The old man still looked a little dazed, and winced painfully as he turned his head towards Tincommius. The shouts of the men on the wall of the enclosure died away as they gazed at their king. Then the only sounds remaining were the sobbing and cries of the broken Romans lying in the street. Verica's body trembled.

'Sire?' Cadminius tightened his grip on the king's waist.

'I'm all right . . . all right.'

Cato leaned closer to him, talking quickly and quietly. 'Sire, you must tell them who attacked you. You must let them know that Tincommius is a traitor.'

'Traitor?' the king repeated with a hurt expression.

'Sire, please. That man's life depends on it.' Cato pointed towards Figulus.

Verica stared at the kneeling Roman, and his nephew for a moment, and then coughed – a terrible racking cough that left him breathless and clutching his head, wincing at the agony. Then he forced himself to stand as straight as possible and called out to his countrymen at the end of the street.

'It was Tincommius . . . Tincommius who attacked me.'

'It was Artax!' Tincommius screamed. 'It was Artax! I saved the king!'

Verica shook his head sadly.

'He lies!' Tincommius cried out in desperation. 'The king is being forced to lie by those Romans! See them beside him! Making him say this.'

'No!' Verica shouted, his voice cracking with the effort. 'It was you, my nephew! YOU!'

The warriors at the end of the street turned to look at the prince, and he was aware of the doubt and contempt in their faces.

'He lies, I tell you!'

Cato tore his gaze away from the drama and called out to his men. 'Mandrax!'

'Here, Centurion!'

'Pick twenty men, and get ready to fetch those prisoners when the gate opens.'

'What are you up to?' asked Macro. 'What did you say?'

'I'm going to try to get Tincommius if I can. Then return here as fast as possible.'

'You're quite mad,' said Macro, but made no attempt to stop him when Cato climbed down from the gate, snatched up his helmet and shield and turned to the legionaries positioned there. 'When I give the order I want the gate opened as fast as you can.'

His heart was beating fast with the anticipation of renewed action, and all the exhaustion of earlier had disappeared as Cato's senses quickened. As soon as Mandrax and his party were ready, Cato drew a breath and shouted, 'Open the gate!'

The legionaries slipped the restraining bar to one side and dragged the gate back.

'Follow me!' Cato called over his shoulder and ran out into the street. He made towards the men clustered around Tincommius, and resisted the impulse to draw his sword; it was vital that he did not look as if he was about to attack them. Tincommius turned towards the enclosure and thrust his arm out towards Cato.

'Get them!'

'Wolves! Boars!' Cato called out. 'Hold him. Hold Tincommius!'

For a horrible instant, Tincommius' men turned towards Cato and the centurion was sure they would fight, that he had badly misjudged their mood. But they simply stood their ground and watched as Cato and his men quickly covered the short distance from the gate. Tincommius looked round at his men with a terrified expression and then he turned and ran.

'Stop that traitor!' shouted Cato. But it was too late. Tincommius had burst through the ring of men and was sprinting towards the corner, and the safety of his Durotrigan allies. He might have made good his escape, but the man with the club hurled it after the prince and struck him on the back of the knee. The club was deflected between his legs and Tincommius tumbled headlong into the small huddle of the remaining Roman prisoners. With savage cries of rage they fell on him, beating him with their tethered hands. Cato stopped by the ring of men, who stared at him with uncertain expressions as they held their weapons ready. Cato immediately turned to the crippled men lying in the street and snapped out his orders.

'Get the live ones inside the enclosure! Move! The Durotrigans will be here any moment!'

Whatever authority and urgency there was in his tone, it had its effect. The men hurried towards the Romans on the ground, and began dragging them up the street, the need for speed making them ignore the renewed screams from their former prisoners.

Cato swung round to Mandrax. 'Get the rest of the prisoners up! Make sure you don't leave behind whatever's left of Tincommius!'

Mandrax grinned. 'Yes, Centurion.'

Leaving the men to carry out his orders, Cato trotted further down the street, round the corner that led towards Calleva's main gate. Then he stopped. Thirty paces away, and stretching all the way down the street were the Durotrigans, resting quietly between the huts that lined the streets. Hundreds of them. Almost at once there was a cry of alarm and one of the warriors jumped to his feet, pointing towards Cato. Others sprang up, reaching for their weapons.

'Whoops!' Cato muttered. He spun round and started sprinting back towards the royal enclosure, as the savage cries of his pursuers rang out. The centurion raced round the corner, and saw that most of his men, the prisoners and the surviving victims of the morning's horror had nearly reached the gate.

'Move yourselves!' he screamed. 'They're coming!'

The growing roar from down the street was all his men needed to hear, and they rushed the remaining distance up to the enclosure and through the gate, heedless of the added agony they caused the injured men they were dragging. Then it was just Cato left, running towards the safety of the gate, already being swung back into place by its defenders. Not again, he thought wryly. Cato glanced over his shoulder, just as the Durotrigans burst round the corner no more than twenty paces behind, shrieking for his blood. Weighed down by his armour Cato could not hope to outrun them, and threw down his shield as he pounded towards the narrowing gap. Above the gate Macro and the others leaned over, shouting desperate encouragement. Cato jumped over the prone forms of the prisoners who had died from their injuries, head ducked low, nailed boots pounding on the hard packed earth of the street. A dark shadow whipped past his head and a dozen feet ahead, a spear thudded into the ground.

'Come on, Cato!' bellowed Macro. 'They're right behind you!'

He looked up, saw the gate directly ahead of him, then

sensed danger at his shoulder and dodged to one side. A sword blade swished through the air and bit down into the earth as the man who wielded it hissed a curse. Cato threw himself forward through the gap left for him and rolled over inside the gate. Immediately the legionaries heaved it into place, but caught, between the gate and the stout timber of the support post, the shoulder and head of the man who had tried to cut Cato down with his sword. With a dull crack the man's skull was crushed, a legionary thrust the misshapen mass back through the gap and the gate was barred once more. The thud and clatter of the enemy on the far side testified to their rage and frustration as Cato strained to catch his breath on all fours.

'Cato!' Macro called down to him. 'You all right?'

Cato waved a hand.

'Good! Then you'd better get up here and deal with this bloody wasps' nest you've gone and stirred up!'

Chapter Thirty-Seven

'Get the wounded into the hall!' Cato ordered, heaving himself up the ladder to join Macro. Verica's bodyguards thrust themselves in front of the king as Cadminius eased the old man back on to his litter.

'What about him, sir?' asked Mandrax, nodding towards the bloody and bruised Atrebatan prince groaning on the ground at the foot of the Wolf standard.

Cato glanced over his shoulder. 'Take Tincommius into the hall. Make sure he's tied up. He's not to be harmed, understand?'

Mandrax, looking disappointed, prodded Tincommius with the end of the standard. 'On your feet, you.'

Cato spared the traitor no more thought as he pushed his way past the bodyguards to the palisade. On either side legionaries and natives from the Wolf Cohort were hurling anything to hand on to the Durotrigans packed into the street below. There were only a few missiles thrown in return as the heaving mass of warriors made it difficult for any man trying to cast a spear or stone back at the defenders, and far more men were being struck down before the gateway than on it.

'They never learn,' Macro shouted into his ear.

'Yes they do,' Cato replied breathlessly, still blown from his run back to the gate. He raised his arm and pointed. 'Look there!'

A short distance down the street were a number of small alleys leading off into the maze of huts clustered about the royal enclosure. The Durotrigans were streaming into the alleys and disappearing from view. Macro turned to Cato. 'I'll take care of things here. You find out where those alleys lead and make sure that you cover any approaches to the wall.'

'Yes, sir!' Cato turned round and grabbed the nearest native warrior. 'Do any alleys pass close to the walls of the enclosure?'

'Some might do, sir.'

'Might?' Cato eyed him coldly, biting back on his temper. 'All right, then, get some men, anyone who's not on the gate, and send them up on to the wall. I want them evenly spaced. There must be no blind spots. Understand?'

'I – I think so, sir.' The man was exhausted.

Cato grabbed him by the shoulders and shouted into his face. 'Do you understand?'

'Yes, sir.'

'Go!'

As the warrior ran off to carry out his orders, Cato turned and pushed his way along the narrow walkway until he was clear of the gate and began to run round the circumference of the enclosure. He had walked the perimeter a few hours earlier, as a diversion from Tincommius' display, to ensure that his sentries were alert to any dangers. An indirect approach to the walls of the enclosure was no mere possibility; it was a certainty. Now that Tincommius' final effort to achieve a quick surrender had failed the Durotrigans had no choice but to launch a bloody assault. Somewhere amongst the tangled outlines of thatched roofs the enemy was groping for a way through to the wall.

As Cato hurried along the walkway he saw that most of the huts did not back directly on to the royal enclosure and left a gap of perhaps five or six paces between their daubed walls and the line of timbers stretching round the great hall. But, as with all things Celtic, after a while the rule was gradually ignored and newer buildings and extensions to old ones had encroached on the wall. The defensive ditch had long ago been filled in with rubbish, and bones and shards of pottery poked through the foul-smelling topsoil. Many of the huts were attached to small enclosures of their own, fenced in wicker, with empty pens in which animals had been kept before food ran short. It would not take the enemy long to cut a path through to the wall, and wherever they emerged, the defenders would be hard-pressed to meet the threat in time to prevent the Durotrigans scaling the low walls. If they managed to attack in several places at once there would be no stopping them, Cato realised. The Durotrigans would stream over the wall and flood across the enclosure before the defenders could react. The Romans and the Wolves would be cut to pieces, unless they managed to reach the redoubt at the entrance to the great hall. After that there was no further retreat, and there they would fight to the end.

Cato stepped aside as Mandrax trotted past with a small party of warriors. The standard bearer quickly posted a man and the remainder ran on. The centurion glanced round and saw that they could muster only a pitiful screen to keep out the enemy. Over at the gate Macro and his legionaries were holding their own for now. The Durotrigans had brought up ladders, and as he watched, Cato saw the parallel shafts swing forward against the wall, only to be desperately shoved back by the defenders.

'Here they come!'

Cato turned and saw one of the Wolves close by, pointing over the palisade. Below him a mob of Durotrigans had burst through a pig sty and charged up to the wall. Already one man was being hoisted up by his comrades, and his hands were reaching for the top of the wall. Then, a short distance beyond, more of the enemy emerged from the huts and ran towards the wall.

'Wolves! To me!' Cato cried out, drawing his sword. 'To me!'

He sprinted along the walkway towards the sentry who had raised the alarm. Some of his men were hurrying from the other direction. The first of the Durotrigans had reached the top of the palisade and was straining to lift his body over the wall. Before he could swing his leg across, the sentry thrust a spear through his throat and the man toppled back, clutching at his neck with both hands as blood sprayed out in a crimson shower over his comrades. Revenge was almost instantaneous as several javelins flew up towards the sentry. He raised his shield to protect his face and warded off the first missile, but in doing so bared his midriff, and two javelins struck him in the stomach simultaneously, the impact driving him back off the walkway and down into the enclosure. Before any of the defenders could reach the spot another enemy warrior was climbing over the palisade and at once he was on his feet, shield up and sword raised to strike.

He glanced to both sides and, seeing that Cato was nearest, bellowed a war cry and threw himself at the centurion. As the man rushed towards him, time seemed to slow and Cato was able to register every mud-stained crease in the man's fearsome expression. He was young and built like a bull, but with too much fat on his frame. The timbers of the walkway thudded and creaked under his weight as he charged the Roman. Cato gritted his teeth and made himself run faster. The differences in their height and weight were firmly in the warrior's favour and his teeth bared in a savage grin as he braced himself for the impact. At the very last moment Cato threw himself against the palisade, angling his shield as the man thundered towards him.

Unable to shift his direction quickly enough, the man glanced heavily off Cato's shield and lost his footing on the edge of the walkway. For an instant he swayed, sword arm waving in an attempt to recover his balance. Cato thrust his blade into the man's back and, bracing his foot against the bare, sweating flesh, he kicked the warrior off the walkway. The collision had knocked the breath out of Cato and as he turned back, gasping for air, he saw two more men had clambered over the palisade, one facing Cato, the other running towards the small party of Wolves rushing at him. Beyond his men Cato glimpsed more of the defenders fighting off a second group of Durotrigans, thrusting their swords at any man foolhardy enough to try to haul himself up the wall.

Cato fixed his eyes on his new foe – a swarthy Celt, older and more wary than his blood-crazed companion. He approached the centurion with a measured stride and then lowered his lithe body into a crouch, poised on the balls of his feet, sword held up and to the side, ready for an overhead blow or a cut to the body. This man, Cato realised, was not going to fall for the same trick as his friend. When the centurion was no more than ten paces away he suddenly shouted with rage and charged home.

The warrior had been expecting a more subtle, calculated attack and the savage rush took the man by surprise. Cato's heavy legionary shield drove into his foe and knocked him off his feet. Cato stamped down on his face as he ran across his enemy and jabbed his sword into the man's chest. It was not a fatal blow, but one that might keep him out of the fight for a vital instant. The Durotrigan warrior grunted as the sword stuck in his ribs and winded him. Then he was gone, dropping behind Cato as the centurion turned on the next man to cross the wall. He was still stretching down for his spear when Cato attacked him and only had time to register a surprised expression before the tip of the short sword struck him in the eye and crunched through the skull into his brain. Cato whipped the blade back and, leaning forward, hacked at the next pair of arms reaching up for the top of the palisade. His sword bit deep into a shoulder and the man fell away. No one else moved forward to take his place and others further back raised javelins to throw at the centurion. Cato just managed to duck his head in time as the dark shafts arced over the wall.

Four of his men, bent double, came scuttling along the walkway behind Cato.

'Finish that one off.' Cato pointed to the older enemy, clutching at the wound in his chest. A sword flickered out and opened the man's throat. He died with a gulping choking sound, slowly slumping to the ground where he struggled feebly to rise for a moment before the dregs of life flowed from him. Cato watched him die, forced to stay down as the enemy continued to throw missiles over the wall.

'Sir!'

'What?' Cato started guiltily and looked up from the dead man. One of the native warriors was pointing over the centurion's shoulder.

'There, sir!'

Cato glanced round and saw a hand reach over the palisade twenty paces further along the wall. Having distracted Cato and his men with the barrage of missiles, the attackers had simply shifted their assault further along the wall.

'Come on!' said Cato, crouching low as he hurried to deal with the new threat. But it was already too late. Glancing ahead, Cato saw that a number of enemy warriors were already over the wall between himself and Mandrax's party. Three men were on the walkway, and then they dropped down into the enclosure, and more streamed over the palisade. Cato saw that three ladders were leaning against the wall, all the time disgorging more men.

The fight for the wall was over then. He stopped and turned back to his men, grabbing the shoulder of the nearest.

'You! Get back to Macro. Tell him . . . Just show him where they're crossing the wall. He'll know what to do then.'

'Yes, sir.' The warrior brushed past his comrades and scurried back along the wall towards the gate.

'Let's go,' Cato said to the others, and leaped down from the walkway. He ordered the Wolves to make for the redoubt, and as they dashed off across the enclosure towards the great hall Cato ran towards the Durotrigans gathering below the point where they crossed the wall. One of them saw the centurion and shouted a warning to his companions. Cato stopped and called out over their heads.

'Mandrax! Mandrax!'

Beyond the Durotrigans Mandrax glanced round, and saw the danger.

'Fall back!' Cato shouted, and thrust his sword towards the great hall.

The warning given, the centurion turned and ran. He had not got far when the Durotrigans raised a deafening war cry and charged into the enclosure. Cato snatched a look over his shoulder and took in the whole terrible scene in an instant. The enemy were starting to come over the wall in ever more places, and all the survivors of the Wolf Cohort were fleeing towards the redoubt. In their midst, rising above the tide of heads and the points of spears, was the standard with the gold-painted wolf's head. The Durotrigans had already run down some of the men slowed by their injuries, and now hacked at them as they fell to the ground. Away to the left, Macro had seen that the wall had fallen, even before Cato's message could reach him, and the legionaries were abandoning the gate and dropping down into the enclosure.

Cato faced forward again, and ran for his life, instinctively dipping his head between the shoulder bands of his armour as the howls of the Durotrigans rose up a short distance behind him. Ahead lay the hurriedly prepared breastwork of the redoubt; the opening set to one side where a heavily laden cart had been drawn back to allow access. Men were already crowding through it, casting terrified looks at the enemy charging towards them. As Cato closed the gap between himself and the final line of defence he shouted at the men desperately trying to shove their way into the redoubt.

'Wolves! Wolves! Turn and form by the standard! The standard!'

Some men heeded him and faced round, shields raised and short swords held ready. Others stared wide-eyed and too frightened to think of anything but flight from the enemy. Mandrax, long-limbed and fit, reached the redoubt well ahead of Cato and turned to face the enemy, planting his standard down defiantly. Men hurried into position on either side of the standard and closed ranks. By the time Cato reached them a small, solid line stood between the men pouring into the redoubt and the Durotrigans. Those who had not been able to reach safety before the Durotrigans overtook them either died as they tried to run away, or stopped and tried to defend themselves and were quickly cut down by the overwhelming odds. But they bought some time for their comrades and most of the defenders managed to reach the redoubt, rushing either side of Cato's small formation.

As the first Durotrigans came up against the unbroken line of shields they drew back, eyeing the Roman and his native troops warily, before turning aside in search of easier prey. Rising on his toes Cato craned his neck to try to see what had become of Macro and the legionaries. Then he saw them, a tight knot of men marching steadily towards the great hall with linked shields, Macro's crest bobbing and twisting at the front of the formation as he cut a path through the throng of Durotrigans, all the time shouting encouragement to his men and cursing the enemy. Suddenly, Cato was aware that the Durotrigans were massing in front of him, having dealt with all the Atrebatan stragglers. They stood twenty paces away, clattering their spears against the inside of their shields and chanting their war cries with faces distorted by the wild exultation of battle-rage. Cato sensed the men either side of him flinch back from the spectacle.

'Hold your ground!' Cato shouted, voice worn down to a grating croak by the strain of the last few days. 'Hold your ground!'

He glanced over towards the legionaries, cutting a path through the loose chaos that filled the enclosure. The Durotrigans were pouring in from all directions now, and some, with more presence of mind than most of their wild comrades, had thrown the locking bar to one side and opened the gate. Under the pressure of the massed warriors packed into the street on the far side the gate crashed inwards and, with a triumphant roar, the enemy swept inside. Unless Macro increased the pace they would catch the Romans before they could make the redoubt. Cato looked round at his men. 'Hold still! Just a little longer, lads.'

A spear flew out from the Durotrigans gathering on the ground in front of the great hall, and Cato jerked his shield up, just in time to block the iron tip. With a jarring crash the spearhead burst through the leather backing, just to the side of his helmet. A cheer went up from the Durotrigans for the warrior who had nearly speared himself a Roman centurion. At once the shield felt heavy and unwieldy and Cato cursed his luck. Once the enemy closed in, a shield was just as vital as a sword, but encumbered with the shaft of a javelin Cato would be at a serious disadvantage. He called out over his shoulder. 'Get me a shield!'

Those Durotrigans close enough to hear the order jeered him and those who fought with no armour brandished their bare chests in contempt. The incident had drawn together the spirit of the Durotrigans in that indefinable way that feeling flows through a mob, and it was clear that they would charge any moment now.

'Sir!' a voice called out behind him, and Cato looked over his shoulder. Mandrax held a shield out to him.

'Whose?'

'From one of our dead, sir.'

'All right, then . . .' Cato glanced quickly along the front of the enemy mob: they were all cheering, spears and swords thrusting up into the sky.

He threw his shield forward and turned and snatched the spare from Mandrax, quickly raising it in front of his body. Macro and his men still struggled towards the redoubt, hacked from all sides. A steady clatter and thud of blades and spear tips striking the legionary shields accompanied their progress. The men facing Cato turned towards the sound, and their shrill cries faded. Here was a chance, Cato decided, his heart racing.

'Make ready to charge,' he said, quietly enough for just the Wolves to hear. 'And make it loud!' He allowed a few breaths for the men to brace themselves up, then, 'Charge!'

Cato gave full voice to a wild animal roar, and the shrieks and cries of his men rang in his ears as the Wolves rushed forward. The Durotrigans turned back towards the small body of men they had been about to massacre, shock and surprise on their faces, and they had not moved when Cato and the Atrebatans slammed into them. Several were struck down before they could resist. Cato smashed his shield boss into the ribs of a thin man, who grunted explosively and collapsed to the ground, gasping for air. Cato kicked his boot down on the man's face for good measure and stepped over him, thrusting his sword at the next enemy who came within reach. His sword was parried at the last moment, but the desperate swipe at the centurion's blade left the man's side exposed to the Atrebatan warrior beside Cato and his guts were ripped open by a slashing blow.

The Wolves piled into the enemy, shouting and screaming as they thrust and stabbed with their short swords. They carved a wedge into the Durotrigans, and before the enemy could respond the Atrebatans had cut their way through to Macro and the legionaries.

'Close up!' Cato called out. 'Mandrax! To me!'

As the two units linked up Macro nodded a greeting to Cato, but the younger centurion knew there was too little time to waste.

'Sir, we have to get back to the redoubt before they recover.'

'Right.' Macro turned to look back towards the gate. A dense mass of Durotrigan warriors was surging towards them. Macro turned to his men. 'At the trot . . . advance!'

Cato relayed the order to his men and, with them at the front, the small column hurried towards the redoubt, making no attempt to stop and engage the shaken enemy, and only fending off the blows directed at them by the more intrepid spirits amongst the Durotrigans. But, behind them, the force that had torn through the gates was racing to catch up with the defenders. Their example was infectious and a renewed desire to close with and destroy the Romans and their allies rippled through the enemy warriors in the royal enclosure.

The men who had already reached the redoubt called out to their comrades from behind the makeshift breastwork, beckoning them on with desperate waves of their arms. Cato, at the front, was tempted to increase the pace, but knew that the moment they broke formation they would be cut to pieces as the enemy recovered their courage and set upon the defenders once again. Then the great hall was right in front of them and they made towards the narrow gap that led inside the redoubt.

'Wolves!' Cato called out, swerving to one side. 'To me!'

His men formed up on their centurion, and the legionaries ran past, panting for breath as their heavy armour jingled rhythmically. Immediately behind the Romans came the first of the Durotrigans from the gate, thirsting for a chance to get at the men who had caused them such grievous losses from the shelter of the palisade above the street. The rearmost of Macro's men had turned to face the threat and paced backwards as fast as they could, with no chance to check their footing as they warded off the enemies' blows with their large shields. As soon as his men were in line Cato looked round and saw that most of the legionaries had passed through the entrance to the redoubt. Only the small knot of the rearguard were left, fighting their way step by step towards safety.

Cato cleared his throat. 'Hold your ground! Wait until the last legionary has passed by.'

As soon as the rearguard came alongside him, Cato bellowed the order to fall back and the compact group of Romans and Atrebatans inched towards the entrance to the redoubt, all the while thrusting shields and swords into the faces of their enemies. The Durotrigans could scent victory now, and were desperate to obliterate the last of the defenders. So they closed on Cato and his men with a savage ferocity that knew no bounds, slashing, thrusting, kicking and even head-butting the shields of the defenders in their desperation to destroy. The last of the legionaries disappeared inside the redoubt and now Cato's men were falling back through the gap, until there was only Cato, Mandrax and a handful of others.

'Get the standard inside!'

Mandrax made a wild slash at the man facing him, who shrank back from the feint, and then the standard was gone, leaving Cato and one other man, facing the endless ranks of woad-painted faces beneath limed hair. Behind them, Macro appeared at the breastwork.

'Cato! Run, lad!'

As the young centurion thrust his shield forward he yelled at the man beside him to fall back. The native warrior, crazed by battle beyond all reason, did not heed the order and slashed at the nearest enemy, shattering the top of his foe's skull. The warrior's cry of triumph barely rasped from his throat before a spearthrust caught him in the mouth and passed right through his head, emerging in a bloody tangle of blood, bone and hair at the back of his head, and knocking his helmet off. Cato ducked behind the body as it slumped down, and ran through the gap.

'Close it up!' Macro shouted, and the men waiting behind the wagon heaved it forward. The axles groaned as the solid wheels rumbled towards the sturdy stone wall of the great hall. One of the Durotrigans made it into the gap and faltered as he sensed the wagon. He turned and was caught and crushed on the tailboard as the wagon crashed up against the masonry and the gap was sealed. As soon as the vehicle was stationary, wicker baskets packed with earth were heaved under the axles to stop the enemy trying to move the wagon or sneak underneath it.

Although most of the legionaries and the native warriors had gained the shelter of the redoubt the fight was far from over. The Durotrigans swarmed up to the breastworks, thrusting their spears and the points of their swords at the men above them. Macro had handpicked the defenders and, protected by the crude fortifications and their large shields, the legionaries kept the enemy at bay. Some of the Durotrigans tried to clamber up the sides of the wagons, but were quickly dealt with and, dead or dying, tumbled back down on to their comrades.

Inside the redoubt Macro cast a glance round the men

defending the half-circle protecting the entrance to the great hall and nodded his satisfaction. For the moment, at least, they could hold off the enemy and he could spare time to see to the men and consider the situation. Around him squatted the rest of his legionaries and Cato's men, exhausted and mostly injured; some with superficial cuts and a few with more serious injuries that would need attention. One of the men was beyond saving; he had been gutted by a spear and he sat, pale and sweating, with his hands clamped over the wound to keep his intestines from spilling out.

Macro went over to Cato, who was leaning against the back of the wagon as he caught his breath.

'That was close,' Macro said quietly.

Cato looked up and nodded.

'You're wounded.' Macro pointed to the young centurion's leg. Cato shifted it forwards and saw that his calf had been slashed below the knee. He had only been aware of a dull blow as he had turned and run through the gap. Now that he saw the blood flowing down the back of his leg and over his boot the wound began to burn.

'Get it bound up,' ordered Macro. 'Surgeon's just inside the hall. Once he's seen to you get him out here to deal with the others.'

'Yes.' Cato looked round the redoubt, watching the backs of the men who were keeping the Durotrigans out.

Macro smiled. 'It's all right, lad. I can spare you for a moment. Now go.'

Cato drew himself up and walked stiffly to the entrance of the great hall. He paused on the threshold to take a last look round the redoubt and Macro caught his eye and jabbed his finger at the hall. Cato went inside.

The contrast between the afternoon sunshine outside and the dim interior of the hall was stark, and at first Cato could make very little out; just shadows flitting across the rush-covered floor. Then, as his eyes grew used to the gloom, Cato saw that the floor was covered with injured men, being tended by the surgeon and Verica's household slaves. But they could do little more than bind wounds and make the dying as comfortable as possible. The surgeon looked up, and as soon as he saw Cato, he rose to his feet and hurried over.

'You hurt, sir?'

'My leg. Tie it up.'

The surgeon kneeled down and gently examined the wound. 'Nasty. Looks clean enough, though. Quite a lot of blood here. Do you feel faint?'

Looking round at some of the terrible injuries surrounding him Cato felt guilty and ashamed about the attention he was being given.

'Sir?' The surgeon was looking up at him. He had taken a roll of linen from his haversack and was winding it around Cato's calf.

'What?'

'How do you feel?'

'I'll be fine.' Cato smiled to himself. It hardly mattered what he felt like. He was as good as dead anyway. They all were, and yet here was the surgeon carrying on as if there were truly some chance that his patients would have the possibility of a full recovery. Cato felt an urge to laugh and had to fight the hysteria down. The surgeon had said something and seemed to be waiting for an answer. Cato shrugged and changed the subject.

'Where's the king?'

'In his quarters. I sent him there to rest.'

'How is he?'

'He's doing well enough, sir. But he could do without all the excitement.'

This time Cato could not help sniggering and the surgeon looked at him with a concerned expression. 'I think you'd better sit down, sir.'

'No. I need to see Cadminius.'

'Over there, sir.' The surgeon pointed to the far end of the hall where the captain of the king's bodyguard and several of his men were standing guard on the entrance to the training compound. The stout wooden door had been tightly wedged shut and timbers had been nailed across it. A steady series of thuds sounded from the far side. Cato stepped round the surgeon and picked his way over the wounded towards Cadminius.

'How are we doing?' Cato called out in Celtic, trying to sound calmer and more confident than he felt inside.

Cadminius turned his face sharply. 'They won't get in for a while. It'd take a battering ram to get through that door.'

'Doubtless they're sorting something out even as we speak.'

'Doubtless . . . Might just chuck them Tincommius' head to use meantime.'

'Tincommius? Where is he?'

'Safe enough,' Cadminius smiled. 'We've trussed him up nicely, hand and foot. He won't be doing any more harm. I've given orders for him to be killed the instant one of those Durotrigan bastards sets foot in the hall.'

'Good.'

'What's the situation out front?'

'We're holding them back, for now.'

'And later?'

Cato laughed and wagged his finger before he turned back towards the entrance of the hall. 'I'll see you later, Cadminius.'

Outside, the sunlight made Cato squint. The enemy were still shouting and chanting their war cries, but had drawn back from the redoubt, and the legionaries were looking warily over the breastwork. Someone had found a cache of hunting spears and almost all of the legionaries had one to hand.

'Cato! Over here!' Macro shouted from a wagon at the front of the redoubt. Cato picked his way over the men resting on the ground and hauled himself up beside Macro. From the slight elevation the view across the enclosure revealed a dense mass of Durotrigans no more than a javelin's throw away. Directly in front of the redoubt lay the piles of their dead and wounded from their first assault. Here and there a man moved feebly, some screaming in agony from terrible wounds, others moaning softly.

'How many did we lose?' Cato asked quietly.

'A few. But they took the worst of it and rather lost their appetite for the fight.'

Cato gazed wearily at the Durotrigans. Some of the warriors in the front rank were rushing forward, screaming defiance into the faces lining the breastwork and then running back. 'Looks like they're working another one up.'

'We'll be ready for them. How's the leg?'

'I'll live.'

'Oh, good. Better get ready. Looks like they're about to charge. I want you in the next-but-one wagon. Keep our lads on their toes. That's the last of the legionaries. Have your Wolves ready to fill any gaps.'

'Yes, sir.'

Cato dropped down into the enclosure, recovered his shield and called his men into formation. A quick head count gave him a strength of thirty-four. That was all. Thirty-four men from the original two cohorts he and Macro had trained and led into battle. The survivors stared straight ahead, red-eyed, filthy and many stained with their own blood and that of their enemies. They looked like beggars, reminding Cato of the human flotsam he had seen as a boy, drifting around the mean backstreets of Rome. As a boy? That was just over two years ago, he reminded himself. The two years he had served with the Eagles seemed like more of a life than all the years before.

Yet these men were no beggars, and pulled themselves erect as they stood behind Mandrax and his Wolf standard. Cato made no attempt at stirring them on to yet greater valour, as the generals in all the history books did. He simply told them to take the place of every man who fell defending the breastwork. Then he saluted and took his position in a cart to the left of Macro. A short distance to Macro's right he saw Figulus and returned the wave that the optio made to him.

'Here they come!' shouted Macro.

The enemy rippled forward, then all at once a roar swept through their ranks, and they charged towards the redoubt.

'Hold steady!' Macro bellowed above the din. 'Just keep them out!'

Cato tightened his grip on the shield handle and braced it against the inside of the breastwork. Over the rim he watched the enemy rushing towards him, a sea of woad-patterned flesh and spiky lime-washed hair. They closed on the redoubt, clambering over the bodies of their comrades who had fallen in the first assault. Then they reached the hastily erected defences and tried to get at the warriors thrusting at them from above. The advantage of height and reach was with the Romans, and scores of Durotrigans fell to quick thrusts of the spears. Cato had only his sword and watched for his opportunity. Then directly below him a man threw himself forward and braced his arms against the side of the wagon Cato was standing on. Immediately the warrior behind scrambled on to the man's back and launched himself towards Cato. The centurion slammed his shield boss into the man's shoulder and the warrior toppled to one side. As he fell he grasped the shaft of the spear being wielded by the legionary fighting beside Cato, wrenching the weapon from the Roman's grasp.

'Shit!' The legionary snatched at his sword, but was too late to spot the spear thrown from one side. The tip caught him under the chin and passed straight through his neck, the impact hurling him back so that he crumpled over the rear of the wagon.

'Get a man up here!' Cato shouted over his shoulder. 'Now!'

As soon as the gap opened in the defenders' line a group of the enemy swarmed forward to press home the advantage, and Cato found himself facing three men, armed with swords, hacking and thrusting at him. He pressed himself inside the curve of the shield and slashed and hacked back at them in a desperate frenzy that bore little resemblance to the rigorous sword training that had been harshly drilled into him by the legion's instructors. There was a lucky strike as his blade caught one of his opponents across the knuckles, shattering the bones of his sword hand. The man screamed and fell back into the swirling mass of the warriors thrusting their way towards the redoubt. But his two comrades were more wily, and while one feinted at Cato the other waited for a chance to strike round the edge of the centurion's shield, and only the curved surface of his segmented armour saved him from injury as a blow glanced off the side of his chest. Then the gap was plugged as an Atrebatan took his place at the breastwork and thrust his sword down towards one of the men trying to kill Cato.

How long the fight raged around the redoubt, Cato could never be sure. There was no time for thought; only the instinct to fight and survive. As he stabbed and parried with his sword, and blocked savage blows with his shield, Cato shouted out encouragement to the men around him, and called for replacements whenever he was aware that one of them had fallen out of line. Even though five or six Durotrigans must have perished for every one of the defenders struck down from the breastwork, they could afford to take the punishment. Indeed, the very number of their losses seemed to provoke an ever-greater desire to close with the Romans and their Atrebatan allies, and they pressed forward tighter than ever, heaving against the defences so forcefully that Cato could feel the wagon shifting beneath him.

As the sun began to dip behind the bulk of the hall the redoubt fell into shadow and the slanting light illuminated the enemy with an intense contrast of light with dark that made them seem all the more vivid and fierce. Cato's arms felt drained of strength, and desperation was no longer enough. Only iron will forced his shield arm to stay up and his sword arm to thrust with enough punch to strike a lethal blow. But for every man he sent reeling back into the mob, another took his place with the same implacable urge to obliterate the defenders.

Then, strangely, Cato found himself waiting for his next opponent. But as he readied his shield and steeled his trembling sword arm, the sea of hostile faces before him thinned, and ebbed away from the redoubt. A glance to either side was enough to reveal that the Durotrigans were all falling back. Their war cries faded away with them and, looking across the enclosure, Cato could see them running through the gate. Soon, only a few stragglers were in view, making best speed to catch up with their comrades, and the full extent of the battlefield was revealed to Cato's eyes. Hundreds of the enemy lay strewn on the ground before the hall, many still living so that the tangle of bodies glistening with sweat and blood seemed to shimmer in the fading heat and light of the late summer afternoon. Cato looked across to Macro and the older centurion pursed his lips and shrugged.

'Now, where the hell are they off to?' Figulus said loudly.

The men on the breastwork stayed in position, watching for

the enemy's next move, not yet daring to believe that they might not come back. The clink and clatter of the Durotrigans' armour and weapons faded into silence and then there was just the sound of the injured.

'Cato!'

'Yes, sir!'

'Strength return, right now.'

Cato nodded, and slipped down on to the ground. He staggered a moment on his tired legs and then began to count off the survivors at the breastwork, and the handful of men still standing in reserve.

'They're coming back!' shouted a legionary, and Cato ran to take up his position. In the fading light dim figures could be seen making their way through the gateway into the enclosure.

'One last effort, boys!' Macro called out, even his voice cracking under the strain.

Each defender tightened his grip on shield and spear and steeled himself for a final struggle. Then Cato laughed – a high-pitched nervous sound – and he lowered his spear and leaned forward to rest his elbows on the breastwork.

Striding through the gate was a broad man with a red cloak. The sun gleamed on his highly polished helmet, and above the helmet curved a brilliant red crest. The man barked an order and a screen of troops fanned out on either side of the gate, and cautiously picked their way across the enclosure towards the hall. As they approached Cato's keen eyes recognised the officer.

'It's Centurion Hortensius!' Cato laughed with nervous relief.

Hortensius marched up towards them, smacking his vine cane into the palm of his spare hand.

'Macro and Cato,' he called. 'I might have guessed. Only you two could have ended up in a fucking mess like this!'

Chapter Thirty-Eight

Once Vespasian had sent off the scouts to make sure that the Durotrigans were keeping clear of Calleva, he led the relief column in through the blackened frame of the town's main gate. The legate immediately made for the depot, and the charred ruin of the headquarters block and the grisly remains of the hospital. Although the Durotrigans had razed the Roman buildings to the ground they had at least left the supplies largely untouched. No doubt they had intended to gorge themselves and carry off what they could, but the sudden arrival of the legate and his six cohorts had caused the Durotrigans to panic and flee the Atrebatan capital empty-handed.

Vespasian gave orders to begin repairs to the depot's defences and then, with tribune Quintillus at his side, they rode off to join Hortensius' cohort, which had been sent on ahead to secure the royal enclosure. As soon as he caught sight of Macro and Cato the legate had demanded to know the full story.

'No,' Vespasian decided, as he glanced round the shadows lengthening across the scattered bodies in the royal enclosure. 'It's out of the question. There's too much to be done here. We're staying.'

Cato exchanged an anxious look with Macro. Surely the legate would see the danger?

'Sir, we can't stay,' said Cato.

'Can't stay?' Quintillus, at his commander's shoulder, repeated with a slight smile. 'Centurion Cato, the truth is we can't afford to leave. Even you must be aware of the strategic situation? Verica will die soon. His warriors are nearly all dead. This kingdom will fall to the first enemy that passes through the gate you two saw fit to burn down. Only Rome can guarantee order here now.'

Cato placed his hand behind his back and clenched his fist, pressing his nails into the flesh of his palm. He was exhausted and angry, and needed his wits to be sharp.

'Sir, if we lose these six cohorts and a legate, there won't be a strategic situation to worry about, only a rout.'

'Really!' The tribune laughed and turned to Vespasian. 'I think this young man has become physically and mentally exhausted over the last few days, sir. It's only natural he might have an inflated fear of the enemy.'

This was too much for Macro. His bull neck swung forward. 'Afraid? Cato afraid? It wasn't Cato who ran off when they gave us that first pasting—'

Vespasian stepped between them and raised his hand, speaking in an urgent undertone. 'That's quite enough, gentlemen! I'll not have my officers arguing in front of the men.'

'Nevertheless,' Quintillus continued quietly, 'I will not stand for a common centurion inferring that I'm a coward. I was the one that rode for help.'

'Quite,' Macro smiled sweetly. 'And I wasn't *inferring* that you're a coward . . . sir.'

'Enough!' said Vespasian. 'Centurion Cato, given how things have turned out, I think we can discount anything Tincommius may have said. It wouldn't be the first time he's managed to fool a Roman officer.'

Quintillus tightened his lips.

Had he not been so weary Cato might have been a bit more circumspect in his approach to the commander of the Second Legion, but he had to press upon the legate the seriousness of their situation. 'Sir, he said that Caratacus and his army would be arriving tomorrow. If we're not well clear of Calleva by then—'

'I've made my decision, Centurion. We stay. I'll have the scouts out at first light. They can warn us of any approaching danger.'

'It might be too late by then, sir.'

'Look here, this Tincommius is a liar. He deceived you.'

'He deceived all of us, sir.'

'Quite. So why should we believe him now? How can you be sure he's speaking the truth? Let's accept that Tincommius wasn't lying. I doubt Caratacus would have given General Plautius the slip. He'd be fighting a rearguard action all the way. He'd have more reason to worry about us than we about him. Look, it was probably no more than a simple ploy by Tincommius to get you to surrender. Surely you can see through that?'

Macro glanced down to hide his anger at the accusation they could have been so easily gulled.

'But what if he was telling the truth, sir?' Cato persisted. 'We'd be caught here in Calleva and cut to pieces. Verica would be killed, Tincommius placed on the throne and the Atrebatans would change sides.'

Vespasian gave him a stony look. 'A commander of a legion does not let himself be ruled by hysterical hypotheses. I want proof.'

He looked closely at the two centurions. 'You two need rest more than anyone else – you and your men. I order you to get some sleep right away.'

It was a cheap and crude way to end the discussion, but

Vespasian had made his decision and would no longer brook any questioning of it. But still Cato made one last effort as Macro saluted and turned to quit his commander's presence.

'Sir, the price of sleep now may be defeat and death tomorrow.'

Vespasian, who had not slept for over two days himself, was fractious, and snapped irritably back at his subordinate, 'Centurion! It is not for you to question my orders!' He raised his finger threateningly. 'One more word from you, and I'll have you reduced to the ranks. Now get out of here.'

Cato saluted, turned away and marched stiffly to catch up with Macro as they headed back to where their men were resting outside the redoubt. Most were asleep, curled up on their sides, heads pillowed on their bent arms.

'Not very bright of you,' Macro said quietly.

'You heard Tincommius – why didn't you back me up?'

Macro drew a deep breath to stave off his irritation with the younger officer. 'When a legate makes a decision, you don't question it.'

'Why not?'

'Because you don't fucking do it. All right?'

'I'll let you know this time tomorrow.'

Cato slumped down beside Mandrax, who was snoring loudly, propped up against a wheel with the standard planted firmly in the ground beside him. Macro remained silent as he carried on walking towards the pitifully small cluster of sleeping men that were all that remained of his first independent command.

Just before he turned on to his side and promptly fell asleep Macro remembered Tincommius' shouted warning that Caratacus was bearing down on Calleva. The Atrebatan prince might have been telling the truth . . . Well, they would know soon enough. Right now, sleep was the thing. A moment later, a deep rumbling snore added to the chorus of other sounds of slumber.

'On your feet, you!' Cadminius swung his boot into the prone figure lying in the dim corner of the hall, furthest from the guarded entrance of the royal quarters. Night had fallen and a few torches hissed in the wall brackets. Tincommius shuffled away from him before Cadminius could land another blow, and the captain of the royal bodyguard quickly grabbed the length of rope tied around the prisoner's neck and gave it a jerk.

'Shit!' Tincommius choked, raising his bound hands to his throat. 'That hurt.'

'Shame you won't live to get used to it,' grinned Cadminius. 'Now, on your feet. King wants a word with you. Perhaps your last word, eh?'

The Atrebatan prince was led by the rope like a dog, cringing before the hatred in the eyes of everyone he passed down the centre of the hall. A wounded man with a ragged dressing covering most of his head propped himself up on an elbow and tried to spit at him as Tincommius went by, but he was too weak and the spittle ended up on his breast. Tincommius stopped and sneered.

'You're pathetic! Have the Romans made you so weak that that's the best you can do?'

Cadminius stopped as the prince started speaking, but now he gave the rope a harsh tug. 'Come on, my beauty, let's not get spiteful.'

As Tincommius gasped at the rope snapping tight around his neck, the men in the hall gave a ragged cheer and shouted insults at the traitor. He swallowed nervously and coughed to clear his throat, but his voice came out only as a croak.

'Laugh now . . . while you still can . . . you slaves!'

When Cadminius reached the entrance to Verica's quarters

he hauled the prisoner inside. Verica was propped up in his bed, but his skin still looked drained of colour and he gestured feebly to the captain of his bodyguard to have Tincommius brought closer. Beside the bed, on stools, sat Vespasian and Tribune Quintillus. A stocky centurion stood close by, powerfully built, with a hard and cruel expression on his face. Verica tried to lift his head, but couldn't find the strength, and rolled it to the side, looking down his cheeks at his treacherous kinsman as the latter was forced to his knees at the foot of the bed.

'Bring him nearer,' Verica said softly, and Cadminius nudged his captive along with his knee.

For a moment no one spoke, and the only sound was the faint wheezing of the king, and the occasional cries of the wounded in the hall.

'Why, Tincommius?' Verica shook his head. 'Why betray us?'

Tincommius was ready with his answer and snapped straight back. 'I betrayed you, Uncle, because you betrayed our people.'

'No, young man . . . I saved them. Saved them from slaughter.'

'So they could be the slaves of your friends here?' Tincommius chuckled bitterly. 'That's some salvation. I'd rather die on my feet than—'

'Quiet!' Verica snapped. 'The times I've heard young hotheads utter that rubbish!'

'Rubbish? I call it an ideal.'

'What are ideals?' Verica asked mockingly. 'They just blind men to the horrors they set in motion. How many thousands of our people are you willing to see die for your ideal, Tincommius?'

'*My* ideal? Old man, do you not realise that they share my vision?'

'They? Who, exactly?'

'My people. You don't believe me? Then ask them. I

challenge you to let us both address them and see what they think.'

'No.' Verica made a thin smile. 'You know that's not possible. In any case . . . an old man . . . would lack the persuasiveness of an impassioned youth. People do not like the odour of mortality. They want to hear their dreams fashioned by unblemished lips. Your voice would sound strident and clear. You would make the world simple for them. Too simple. How could I compete with that, burdened as I am by my knowledge of the way the world really is? Tincommius, you would sell them a dangerous dream. I can only peddle painful truths . . .'

'Coward! What is the point of all this? Why not just murder me now?' Tincommius suddenly looked hopeful. 'Unless . . .'

'Tincommius, you will die,' Verica said sadly. 'I just needed you to understand why you were wrong . . . You were like a son to me. I wanted you to know . . . to know I would give anything not to have you executed.'

'Then don't execute me!' Tincommius cried.

'You leave me no choice.' Verica turned his face away and mumbled, 'I'm sorry . . . I'm sorry. Cadminius, let the Romans have him now.'

Tincommius glanced over at the legate and the tribune, then beyond to the hardened face of the centurion. He turned and threw himself on to the bed.

'Uncle! Please!'

'Get up!' Cadminius shouted, grabbing the prince by his shoulders, and tearing him away from the old man. Tincommius writhed in his grip, pleading to his uncle, but the captain of the bodyguard pulled him back, got his head in an armlock and dragged him over to Vespasian.

'The king says he's your now. To dispose of as you please.'

Vespasian nodded sternly, and beckoned to Centurion Hortensius. 'Take him into the redoubt, and soften him up a little,' Vespasian said quietly, so that Tincommius would not hear his words. 'Don't hurt him too badly, Hortensius. He'll need to talk.'

The centurion stepped forward and pinioned the struggling prince before lifting him off the ground and dragging him from the chamber.

'Now then, sir, do be a nice quiet gent, or I'll have to get rough with you straight away.'

When Tincommius kept begging for his uncle's mercy the centurion threw him against the stone wall. Tincommius howled with agony, bleeding from a gash on his forehead. The centurion calmly picked him up and placed him back on his feet. 'No more nonsense then, there's a good gentleman.'

After they had eaten a quick meal in the royal kitchens Vespasian and Quintillus made their way to the redoubt. The semi-circle inside was lit by a small fire into which the point of a javelin had been thrust. The iron tip rested in the wavering heart of the fire and glowed orange. To one side Tincommmius was bound to a wagon, and leaned limply against the rough planks. On his bare back were scores of bruises and raw scorch marks. The air was thick with the pungent smell of burned flesh.

'Hope you haven't killed him,' said Vespasian, the back of his hand pressing against his nostrils.

'No, sir.' Hortensius was affronted by the legate's lack of faith in his expertise. There was more to being a torturer than merely inflicting a painful death. Far more. That's why the legions trained men so carefully in this most arcane of military skills. There was a fine line between hurting men enough to guarantee they would speak the truth, and overdoing it and killing them before they were ready to crack. As any half-decent torturer knew, the trick was to inflict more pain than the victim could bear, and keep it at that level of intensity for as long as possible. After that, the victim would tell the truth all right. The terror of not being believed and thereby inviting further agony saw to that. Hortensius nodded towards the fire. 'He's just a little cooked.'

'Has he said anything useful?' asked Quintillus.

'Just some native gibberish for the most part.'

'Does he still maintain that Caratacus is coming to his rescue?'

'Yes, sir.'

Vespasian looked at the mutilated flesh on the prince's back with a horrified fascination. 'In your judgement, do you think he's telling the truth?'

Hortensius scratched his neck, and nodded. 'Yes, unless he's got more balls than a herd of billy goats.'

'Interesting expression,' Quintillus remarked. 'Haven't heard that one before. Regional speciality of yours?'

'That's right, sir,' Hortensius replied drily. 'We made it up for the benefit of tourists. Now, shall I get on, sir?' The last remark was directed at the legate, and Vespasian tore his gaze away from Tincommius.

'What? Oh yes, carry on. But if he doesn't change his story soon, you can finish up here and get some rest.'

'Finish up, sir?' Hortensius bent down and pulled the tip of the javelin out of the fire. Against the darkness it glowed more intensely than ever: a fiery yellow on which pinpricks of even brighter light sparkled. The air wavered beside it. 'Do you mean finish off?'

'Yes.'

'Very good, sir.' Centurion Hortensius nodded, and turned back to the Atrebatan prince, lowering the tip of the spear towards Tincommius' buttocks. The legate strode out of the redoubt, making a great effort not to walk too fast in case the centurion and the tribune guessed that he was acutely discomforted by the scene. As soon as Vespasian and Quintillus were outside the redoubt they heard a hiss followed by an inhuman shriek that split the air like a knife. Vespasian strode off towards one of the king's store sheds, which he had made his temporary headquarters, forcing Quintillus to quicken his step to keep up.

'Well sir, what do you think?'

'I'm wondering if Centurion Cato wasn't right to be so cautious after all.'

Quintillus looked at him anxiously. 'You can't be serious, sir. Caratacus coming here? It's not possible. The general's got him pegged to the other side of the river.'

Another scream pursued them, and Vespasian jerked his thumb over his shoulder. 'Well, he believes it sure enough.'

'It's like you said earlier, sir, he's just trying to put the frighteners on us.'

'Not much point in that now, if it's not true.'

'Maybe,' Quintillus conceded reluctantly. 'Then perhaps he was lied to in turn.'

Vespasian stopped, and turned towards the tribune. 'Just why are you so keen to keep us here? Nothing to do with you wanting to be the first Roman governor of the Atrebatans, I suppose?'

The tribune did not reply.

'Thought so,' Vespasian sneered. 'There's a little more than your career at stake, Quintillus. Bear that in mind.'

The tribune shrugged, but stayed silent. Vespasian sighed with bitter frustration at the man's inability to acknowledge the potential peril of their situation.

'Tribune, if anything happens to me, you will be the senior officer here, understand?'

'Yes, sir.'

'And your duty will be to carry out my last orders. In which case you must see to the safety of the men under your command. You will take no risks with their lives. If that means abandoning Calleva you will do it.'

'As you wish, sir.'

'As I command.'

'Yes, sir.'

Vespasian stared at the tribune to reinforce the gravity of the order, before he continued, 'I want you to tell the cohort commanders to have their men ready to move first thing tomorrow. Go.'

The tribune saluted and strode off into the darkness, and Vespasian watched until even the last dim outline of the man had disappeared. If anything did happen to him, and Quintillus took command, Vespasian dreaded the consequences for his men. Perhaps he should put his instructions to the tribune in writing and ask one of the cohort commanders to witness the document. Almost as soon as the idea jumped into his head Vespasian dismissed it with contempt. Much as he disliked the tribune, it would never do to treat him so dishonourably. Quintillus had his orders and was honour-bound to obey them.

His thoughts returned at once to the spectre of Caratacus and his army manoeuvring towards Calleva. It was hard to believe that the British commander had managed to give General Plautius the slip. Yet Tincommius held to his story. In which case, the legate mused, there were a number of possibilities. The prince might be hoping that the Romans, fearing for their lives, would quit Calleva, and then the Durotrigans would return and complete what they had started. Conversely, if Caratacus *was* coming, surely Tincommius would lie and hope that his ally might catch Vespasian and his six cohorts in Calleva, and thereby destroy the best part of a legion? That would deal a lethal blow to General Plautius' campaign. There was nothing that could be done, he decided, until he had more information.

Back in the storeroom, he undid the ties of his breastplate and stretched his shoulders. Then he sent for the decurion in charge of the small squadron of scouts and ordered the man to assemble his riders. They were to leave the fort at once and begin reconnoitring to the north and west for any signs of a native army. Once the order was given, Vespasian gladly laid himself down on a pile of cured animal skins and fell fast asleep.

Cato woke with a start. The young centurion struggled into a sitting position, bleary-eyed and his mind still fogged with sleep. As he looked around numbly, Cato saw that the royal enclosure was still shrouded in darkness, and away to the east glimmered the faint glow of a false dawn. All about him shadows moved in the gloom as the Roman officers moved down the lines of slumbering soldiers, shaking their men awake. Macro approached him.

'What's happening?' asked Cato.

'Get up. We're moving.'

'Moving?'

'Getting out of Calleva and back to the legion.'

'Why?'

'Legate's orders. Get your men ready. Now move yourself!'

Cato stretched his stiff limbs and rose to his feet with a groan. The enclosure was alive with the low grumbling of men roused from sleep, and the harsh shouts of the centurions aimed at those who were slow to rise. Torches flared by the storehouse being used by the legate and the small staff he had brought with him. Cato saw Vespasian hurriedly briefing the cohort commanders by the glow of spluttering flames.

Bending down to retrieve his segmented armour, Cato wriggled his body inside and fumbled with the leather ties. Some of the men from the Wolf Cohort were already awake and gazing around anxiously.

'Centurion!' Mandrax approached him, and Cato realised that it was the first time for some days that he had seen the man without the standard to hand. 'Sir, what's going on?'

'We're leaving.'

'Leaving?' Mandrax looked surprised, then frowned. 'Why, sir? We won. The enemy have gone. Why abandon Calleva now?'

'Orders. Now help me get our men formed up.'

For a brief moment Mandrax stood quite still, staring at his centurion with an expression that Cato read as suspicion. Then he nodded slowly and turned away to see to his duties. Cato felt guilty about the order. These men he had fought alongside looked to Rome as their ally, and this order to quit Calleva would smack of betrayal, even though it made sense. Vespasian must have changed his mind. Or worse, Tincommius had proved to be telling the truth after all. Cato fastened his sword belt, tucked his helmet underneath his arm and strode over to the two lines of his men.

The Wolf Cohort existed in name only: Cato counted thirty shadowy figures standing behind Mandrax and the standard. Many bore dressings on their arms, but each still carried the oval shield, javelin and bronze helmet they had been issued months before. A surge of pride welled up inside Cato as he quickly inspected them. These men had proved themselves the equal of the legionaries in valour and steadfastness, and with more drill they would match their Roman comrades in skill at arms. The bond he shared with them through training and battle was as tight as any he had shared with his comrades in the Second Legion.

But now they were ordered to quit Calleva, and their kin, and the centurion feared how they might react when they looked back over their shoulders and saw Calleva lying defenceless, a ripe fruit waiting to fall into the eager hands of Caratacus and his allies. That would be the true test of their loyalty to him and their standard.

'All officers to the legate!' a voice bellowed across the enclosure. 'All officers to the legate!'

Cato turned to his men. 'Wait here!'

A small group of centurions clustered around Vespasian and the legate wasted no time on the usual formalities as he addressed them.

'The scouts report a large force camped a few miles to the west of here. Too many campfires to be the same band having a go at Calleva yesterday. Looks as if Caratacus might have stolen a march on the general after all. Thing is, the scouts also saw the loom of another army's fires in the distance, far beyond Caratacus' lot. It might be Plautius; it might not. I've ordered some scouts to find out who they are. It is possible that Caratacus is moving in two columns, and that the general is still chasing his tail north of the Tamesis. In which case, we're well and truly buggered.'

A few of the officers chuckled nervously before their legate continued, 'If we sit here and try to hold what's left of Calleva's defences we might last a day or two before we're overwhelmed. Then the enemy will turn on the rest of the legion and destroy it in detail. Our best chance is to get out of here as soon as possible, head south and try to swing round the enemy's flank and join up with the other cohorts at the legion's camp. That we can defend, for as long as the food lasts, or Plautius reaches us. We're taking Verica with us, and what's left of his men. They can return to Calleva once the crisis is over. We'll march in a tight column. We'll take as few wagons as possible; just enough for the wounded. The men are to carry nothing but their weapons and armour and food for two days, nothing else. Any questions, gentlemen?'

'Yes, sir.' Heads turned towards Tribune Quintillus. 'What happens if the enemy catches up with us before we link up with the other cohorts?'

Vespasian answered curtly, 'If that happens, Tribune, you'll have to continue your career in another life . . . Gentlemen! Let's make sure it doesn't happen. Anyone else? . . . Good. Back to your units. We march as soon as I give the signal . . . Centurion Macro! A moment, please.'

Macro, a man who favoured the back row of any gathering – a hangover from a very brief period of formal education as a child – waited until the other officers had dispersed before approaching the legate.

'Sir?'

'You know Centurion Gaius Silanus?'

'Yes, sir. Second Cohort.'

'That's him. Or was. He was killed in a skirmish yesterday. I want you to replace him. Take what's left of your garrison with you.'

'Yes, sir. What about Centurion Cato, sir?'

'What about him?'

'Are his men to march with us?'

Vespasian nodded. 'We need every man who can hold a weapon. Cato's cohort – what is it you call them?'

'The Wolves, sir.'

'Wolves? Good name. Anyway, they'll guard the carts.'

'They won't like that, sir,' Macro replied quietly. 'They'll want to fight.'

'Really?' said Vespasian with a trace of irritation. 'Well, they'll do as I tell them.'

'Yes, sir. I'll let Cato know.'
'You do that.'

As the first rays of the sun washed the sky, the dense column of heavy infantry, and the remaining handful of their native allies, emerged from the ruin of Calleva's main gate. A pale blue light hung across the landscape and, looking up, Cato could see that it would be a cloudless day. A hot march lay ahead with the sun beating down on them. As soon as the First Cohort cleared the gate it turned south, towards the legion's camp. The wagons carrying the wounded and King Verica were positioned in the middle of the column and on either side marched Cato's men, and the royal bodyguard under Cadminius. Vespasian had made it quite clear that all the native troops were placed under the command of Centurion Cato, without exception, to the obvious chagrin of Verica and the captain of his personal guard.

As the tail of the column emerged from Calleva, Cato looked back and saw a line of faces along the palisade, watching them depart in silence. The bitter expressions well told of the betrayal and despair felt by the Atrebatans. To one side, where the watchtower had once stood, a tall pole rose up from the charred timbers. Impaled on the top was the head of Tincommius, his features so bruised and swollen that it was barely possible to recognise the once handsome prince.

A small column of refugees hurried from the gate, heading in the opposite direction in a bid to escape the inevitable bloodshed when Caratacus and his army arrived before Calleva. Away to the west the tiny figures of a screen of cavalry appeared on a distant hillside and moved towards Calleva with painstaking slowness. Behind them, crossing the brow of the hill, crawled a thick black column of infantry. The Durotrigans who had withdrawn from Calleva the previous night now marched with their allies. Caratacus, it seemed, had made an early start as well. Nearly five miles separated the two sides, by Cato's estimate. Not much of a margin, but one that the hard-marching legionaries should be able to maintain until they reached the Second Legion's fortified encampment.

Before long the enemy column changed course, moving obliquely away from Calleva and straight towards the Romans. Vespasian's small force crested a low ridge and marched out of sight of the Atrebatan capital. The sun rose and climbed steadily into a clear sky, and not a breath of wind disturbed the air so that the deafening crunch of army boots and the squeaking creak of the wagons' wheels filled the men's ears. Dust was thrown up by the leading cohort and it left grit in the mouths of the men further down the column. By late morning the sun was shining brightly and sweat poured off the men marching without respite, since any stop would close the gap between them and their pursuers.

So it was that at noon, the head of the column was approaching a narrow vale that curved round a small bare hillock. At the head of the column rode Vespasian and Tribune Quintillus, eschewing the normal practice of riding behind the vanguard. The legate was keen to reunite his forces as speedily as possible and did not want to waste any time having the lay of the land ahead relayed to him.

'We're making good time,' Quintillus was saying conversationally.

'Yes . . . good time,' the legate replied, then he straightened his back and stared ahead.

'What is it, sir?'

Vespasian did not answer, but urged his mount into a trot along the track as he craned his neck to see more. A few moments later he had a clear view round the hillock. Half a mile ahead of the column a dense mass of chariots and cavalry lay across their path.

Chapter Thirty-Nine

Caratacus had sent his light forces on ahead, even though he knew that they could not defeat the Romans by themselves. But then again they didn't have to, Vespasian smiled bitterly. They just had to delay the legionaries long enough for Caratacus and his heavy infantry to arrive and pile into the rear of the Roman column. If the legate moved quickly, he could form his men into a dense wedge and force his way through the enemy blocking the way ahead. But such formations had never been designed for speed and the natives would simply fall back before the wedge and harry the Romans until their comrades could catch up and throw their weight decisively into the fight.

'Sir?' Quintillus was looking at him expectantly. 'Shall I give the order to turn the column round?'

'No. Caratacus will have moved between us and Calleva by now.'

'Well . . . what shall we do?' Quintillus stared at the enemy waiting ahead of them. 'Sir?'

Vespasian ignored the tribune as he wheeled his horse round and raised his arm. 'Halt!'

The vanguard cohort pulled up and the order was swiftly conveyed down the column. Each century stopped marching and the wagons grumbled to a standstill, then nothing moved on the track. The legate was already assessing the surrounding landscape, and fixed his gaze on the small hillock to their right. He had already decided that the column's best chance of survival was a static defence. If they tried to continue they would be worn down and cut to pieces long before they came in sight of the rest of the legion. If they could inflict enough damage on their enemies they might just demoralise them enough to withdraw so that the column might still reach the legion's fortified camp . . . Fat chance of that happening, he mused.

Vespasian drew a breath before he gave the order that would commit him and his men to action.

'Column . . . deploy to the right!'

'Sir?' Quintillus urged his horse alongside Vespasian's. 'What are you doing?'

'We're making a stand, Tribune. What else can we do?'

'Making a stand?' Quintillus raised his finely plucked brows. 'That's madness. They'll kill us all.'

'Very likely.'

'But, sir! There must be something else we can do . . . Anything?'

'What do you suggest? You can't ride for help this time, Quintillus. Not unless you want to chance your arm with that lot ahead of us and make a break for it.'

The tribune blushed at the barely concealed charge of cowardice, and shook his head slowly. 'I'm staying.'

'Good man. Now make yourself useful. Ride to the top of that hill and keep watch for Caratacus. Also . . .' Vespasian wondered how far he should trust to luck after the fates had led him into this trap. 'Also, keep an eye out for that other force the scouts reported. They might be ours.'

'Yes, sir!' Quintillus turned his horse up the slope and galloped towards the brow of the hill.

The First Cohort, twice the size of the legion's other cohorts, was marching past Vespasian, following the colour party up the grassy slope. Behind them the rest of the column rippled forward. Century by century they moved along the track until they reached the legate's position, and then turned abruptly to their right. Vespasian was watching Caratacus's blocking force for any sign of movement, but the enemy was content simply to deny the Romans passage along the vale, and sat on their chariots and horses watching the Romans climb up the hill. A more enterprising commander, Vespasian reflected, would have tried to occupy the hill ahead of the Romans, but the Britons' lack of self-control was a defining feature of the way they waged war, and the British commander was probably wise to have his men stand their ground.

As the wagons turned up the slope their drivers urged their lumbering oxen on with shouts and sharp blows from their canes. The legate watched for a moment, conscious of the slow progress of the vehicles, then he shouted an order.

'Centurion Cato!'

'Sir?'

'Set your men to those wagons. I want them on top of the hill as quickly as possible.'

Cato saluted and ordered his men to load their weapons into the wagons. Then with a handful of warriors assigned to the rear of each of the eight wagons, the big Celts heaved and strained to move the wagons up the hill. Cadminius and his men took charge of the wagon provided for Verica and did their best to ensure that their king was not jolted. All the while the legionaries marched past them, until only the rearguard remained, tasked with protecting the wagons until they reached the position the legate had chosen. It was back-breaking work that required as much nerve as strength. Every so often the forward momentum would slacken and the big chocks of wood carried in the back of each wagon would have to be quickly dropped into place behind the wheels to ensure that the wagons did not begin to roll back down the slope. Once that started it was almost impossible to stop, and men might be crushed, vehicles might collide and the oxen, harnessed to the wagons would be sent sprawling with a very real chance of breaking their legs. And all under the merciless glare of the midday sun. By the time the incline of the slope began to even out Cato and his men were running with sweat and slumped down beside the vehicles, chests heaving as they struggled to catch their breath.

'What the hell are you doing? On your feet!' Vespasian shouted at them as he rode up to the wagons. 'Centurion, get your men formed up! I want these wagons drawn up in the centre. Make sure that the king is well protected. I'm holding you responsible for his safety.'

'Yes, sir.'

Cato drew himself up and licked his lips, dry – like his throat – from all his exertions. Then, using a combination of orders and harsh curses he ordered his men to manoeuvre the wagons into a dense mass, before the chocks were pounded tightly against the wheels. The sharp smell of the oxen was made worse by the baking heat, but only when the work was finished did the centurion allow his men a small measure from their waterskins. Around them curved the lines of the cohorts, drawn up in a tight circle about the crest of the hill. Down in the vale the Britons had not moved and sat watching the Romans, as still and silent as before. Away along the track towards Calleva, a dark column of infantry was marching towards the hill, throwing up a thin haze of dust that obscured the full extent of their numbers. Still further in the distance was a smudge on the horizon that might be a thin band of cloud, or another force of men on the move.

Vespasian passed the order for the men to rest and eat their rations. The coming fight might well be their last, but men fought best on full stomachs and the legate was determined to wring every advantage that was available to him out of the situation. They had the high ground, clear lines of visibility and the best training and equipment of any army in the known world. In all this, Vespasian was content. But three and half thousand men, no matter what their quality, would not prevail against many times that number, and every moment that passed revealed more and more of the enemy's strength as their column crept over a distant ridge and headed relentlessly towards the tight ring of legionaries defending the top of the hillock. There seemed to be no end to the enemy forces spilling across the landscape, and the Romans viewed it all with quiet resignation as they chewed on strips of salted pork drawn from their haversacks.

Macro came over to see Cato, and pulled himself up on to the driver's bench beside his friend.

Macro nodded towards Verica's wagon. 'How's the king doing?'

'Well enough. I looked in on him a while back. He's sitting up and complaining about being bumped about.'

'Think he'll recover?'

'Does it matter?' Cato nodded towards the approaching enemy column.

'No,' Macro conceded. 'Not now.'

'After all that fighting back in Calleva, we end up here,' Cato grumbled.

'That's the army for you,' replied Macro, straining his tired eyes as he stared in the same direction as Cato. 'Any idea who that second lot are yet?'

'No. Too far. Moving quickly, though. Few more hours and they'll be up with us.'

'Knowing our luck, they'll just be more of those bastards.' Macro pointed towards the enemy column approaching the hill. 'Don't know where they all come from. Thought we'd destroyed their army last summer. Caratacus must have found himself some new allies.'

'With people like Tribune Quintillus handling the diplomatic side of things, it's a wonder the entire island isn't against us.'

'Right.' Both centurions turned their heads to look down the slope a short distance to where Vespasian and his senior officers were conferring. The tribune was talking in an animated fashion and pointed back in the direction of Calleva.

'I expect he's trying to persuade the legate to make a break for it.'

Cato shook his head. 'Isn't going to happen. Premature suicide isn't the legate's style. The tribune's wasting his breath.'

'He's proved to be a real asset for our cause all right,' said Macro. 'Things dropped in the shit the moment he arrived.'

'Yes . . . yes, they did.'

'It's almost as if the twat was trying to make a mess of the situation in Calleva.'

'Well, why not?' Cato replied quietly. 'There was a lot at stake for him. If Verica managed to keep on top of events the tribune would just have had to go back to the general and make a report. I imagine he's been stirring things up as much as he can behind the scenes. Anything to upset the situation, and give him an excuse to use his procurator's powers. Not that he was very successful there. I think he must have assumed that Celtic aristocrats played to the same bent rules as Roman aristocrats. Didn't account for their sense of honour.'

'Honour?' Macro raised his eyebrows. 'Tincommius didn't seem to know much about honour.'

'Oh, he did, in his own way. The man wanted his tribe to remain free, almost as much as he wanted to rule it. And he must have been an eager enough student of Roman political techniques while he was in exile.'

'You've got to hand it to us,' Macro smiled, 'there's not much we can't teach these barbarians.'

'True. Very true . . . As it is, the Atrebatans are finished. Plautius will have to annex their kingdom and turn it into a military province.'

Macro looked at him. 'You think so?'

'What else can he do? Assuming the general can recover from this balls-up. The loss of a legion is going to stall the campaign for quite a while. And it won't play well in Rome.'

'No . . .'

'But look on the bright side,' Cato smiled bleakly, 'at least Quintillus is going to have to live, or die, with the consequences of his actions.' He waved his hand towards the enemy.

'I suppose.'

As they watched, the column started to split in two as Caratacus' forces moved to surround the hillock. The chariots and cavalry in the vale advanced to complete the encirclement and with a last glance towards the distant haze above the still unidentified column closing in from north-west of Calleva, Macro jumped down from the wagon.

'I'll see you afterwards,' he nodded to Cato.

'Yes, sir. Until then.'

Chapter Forty

As Macro strode off to his century the headquarters trumpeters blasted out the signal to stand to. All across the crest of the hillock men rose wearily to their feet and shuffled into the tight defensive formation that Vespasian hoped would hold off the Britons' assault when it came. The legionaries closed ranks and grounded their javelins and shields in an unbroken ring four ranks deep. Centurions paced along their men, bawling out insults and threats to any man who had committed even the smallest infraction of the rules. An untied helmet or bootstrap, poorly slung sword or dagger – all provided the centurions with an excuse to charge in and give the miscreant the fright of his life. Which was very much to the point. With an enemy massing for the attack, any diversion from thoughts of the coming battle would help steady the legionaries.

Shortly after noon the enemy made their move. Dense blocks of native warriors surrounded the hill, and worked themselves up into a frenzy of excitement around their gaudy serpent banners as they waited for the order to attack the hated Romans. The deafening war cries and braying of long war horns carried up the slope and assaulted the ears of the legionaries waiting silently on the crest. Then, without a discernible word of command, the Britons rippled forward, walking fast, then breaking into a slow trot as they reached the foot of the slope.

Vespasian gauged the distance between his men and the enemy carefully, to judge the best moment to issue his first order. As the gradient increased the Britons slowed down, bunching together as they struggled up the hill to close with the legionaries. When they were no more than a hundred paces away, and some of the men began to look round anxiously at their legate, Vespasian cupped a hand to his mouth and filled his lungs with air.

'Shields up!' bellowed the legate, and all round the hilltop the red shields with their ornately painted surfaces rose up; metal trims and polished bronze shield bosses glittering in the sunlight. For a brief moment the shields shimmered as each man aligned himself with his neighbour and then the defensive wall was complete and the Romans peered over the rims with grim expressions.

'Prepare javelins!'

The men in the front rank took a pace forward and braced themselves, right arm drawn back along the length of their javelin shafts.

'Ready! . . .' Vespasian raised his arm in case the order could not be heard above the din of the enemy.

'Ready!' The centurions relayed the order to their men, and turned back to watch for the legate's next order. Below them, the Britons, howling their war cries and straining every muscle to make sure they smashed into the Roman shields at full pelt, surged forward in a writhing mass of helmets, spiked hair, tattooed bodies and flashing and glinting blades.

'Release!' roared Vespasian, sweeping his arm down. At once the centurions repeated the order and the men hurled their right arms forward; their effort filling the air with a chorus of strained grunts. The dark shafts of the javelins rose up and out like a thin curtain of water thrown up from a rock cast into a pond. Already the centurions were bellowing out orders for the second rank to pass their weapons forward to replenish the front rank. The iron tips of the first volley passed the apex of their trajectory and dipped down towards the Britons. The foremost ranks of the enemy charge faltered as they beheld the peril. Some sprinted forward, hoping to run in under the volley, others covered themselves with their shields and prepared for the impact. The rest – light spearmen and swordsmen with no armour – either went to ground, or gazed upwards, hoping to duck, or dodge any javelin that fell towards them.

The volley crashed down in a rolling clatter and thudding that turned to grunts and screams as the javelins found their targets. Then, as if an invisible hand of some giant god had swept through the front ranks of the Britons, scores of them were bowled over and fell to the ground. Other men tumbled over their fallen comrades and sprawled amid the tangle of limbs, shields and the long shafts of the javelins. Then the men behind them forced a way through and charged on up the hill.

'Javelins! . . . Ready! . . . Release!'

Again, a wave of the Britons was taken down, adding to the confusion of those already lying stricken on the slope. Then the third and the fourth volleys swept into the enemy massing about the crest of the hill and added to the ruin of the Britons' first attack. No longer were they screaming out their war cries. Instead, a deep murmur of shock rippled back down the slope, and at that moment the legate decided to press home his temporary advantage. 'Swords out!'

'Swords out!' the centurions shouted, and a sharp metallic rasping echoed round the hilltop.

'Advance!' Vespasian called out, clearly audible in the sudden expectant hush. As the centurions relayed the order the cohorts marched down the slope, shields to the front and swords held at the hip, ready to thrust forward. Before the Britons could recover the legionaries fell upon them, finishing off the enemy injured and then battering their way into the mass of troops milling beyond the carnage caused by the javelins. At first some of the Britons tried to resist, but they were too disorganised to stop the Roman advance. And as soon as they were cut down, or fell back, any spirit to carry the charge up the hill crumbled. The initiative had passed wholly to the defenders, and now it was their turn to attack. The legate ordered his trumpeter to sound the charge. Urged on by the curses and cries of encouragement from the centurions the legionaries threw themselves at their foes, using their broad shields to smash the tribesmen down, and thrusting their short swords into the packed ranks before them.

The enemy broke, turning down the slope in their desperation to get away from Romans and running back into their own lines, adding to the confusion and panic until the entire force was fleeing down the slope. From his vantage point, Vespasian saw in the vale at the base of the hill a small group of richly adorned nobles. As the attack disintegrated, the largest of the nobles, a tall man with fair hair, immediately began to send his companions forward to rally their troops. That, Vespasian decided, must be Caratacus himself, and the legate was surprised that the king of the Catuvellaunians had been foolhardy enough to risk such a frontal assault. It was not his usual carefully considered style of waging war. But there was no time to dwell on the enemy's mistakes, lest the legate should start to make mistakes of his own. The Roman counterattack had done its job and now there was the danger that the legionaries might get carried away.

'Sound the recall!' Vespasian ordered, and shrill brass notes blared down the slopes. Regular battle drills proved their worth as the men pulled up, reformed into their units and began to climb back to their initial positions. The legate glanced round at the bodies littering the crushed grass of the hillside and was relieved to see only a few red tunics amongst them. As the legionaries picked their way back through the tidemark of destruction wrought by their javelins they leaned down to recover any undamaged weapons that might be reused when the enemy dared to attack again. Most of the iron javelin heads had bent on impact, or the wooden pegs that bound them to the rest of the shaft had been shattered. But some were still intact and had to be retrieved to deny them to the enemy. As soon as the six cohorts had returned to their starting points their centurions hurriedly turned them about and reformed the units into an unbroken ring around the wagons on the top of the hill.

Cato had watched the charge with glee, and had, for a mad instant, even dared to hope that the Britons had been beaten. Now he felt like a fool, a raw recruit who had let his excitement overrule his reason. He looked anxiously for any sign of Macro and was relieved to see his friend emerge through the rear rank of his temporary command and shout an order for the legionaries to dress their ranks. Macro glanced round and gave him a quick thumbs-up before hurling a stream of curses at a hapless legionary who had not heard the order. To the front of the unit, Figulus stalked along the line of grounded shields and saw to it that any spare javelins were passed forward to the men closest to the enemy.

Down at the foot of the hill the Britons were already herding their scattered men back into formation around the brightly coloured serpent banners. With no breeze to lift the long tails in the stifling heat, their bearers had to wave the banners in loops to make them visible above the heads of the Britons. The heat wavering in the air made the banners shimmer and writhe like live things.

'Well done, men!' Vespasian called out. 'We taught them a hard lesson that time. But the javelins are spent. It's down to our swords. The fight'll be hand-to-hand from now on. As long as we keep our formation we'll survive this. I swear it!'

'And if you break your vow?' a voice called out, and the men laughed. For a moment Cato saw Vespasian frown. Then the legate saw the morale-boosting effect of the insubordinate remark and made himself play along.

'If I break my vow, then there's an extra issue of wine for every man!'

Even the most laboured of jokes is a welcome distraction in desperate circumstances and the men roared with laughter. Vespasian made himself smile benignly even as he watched the enemy begin to advance up the hill again. In the distance the second column crawled closer, and was now no more than three or four miles away – but still too far for the legate to identify the tiny black figures at the front. A thin screen of cavalry trotted ahead of the column. Down below, Caratacus was watching the approaching column and pointing it out to his nobles but whether from anxiety or jubilation it was impossible for the legate to tell. He turned back to his men and called out an order.

'Shields up!'

The last of the laughter and light-hearted chatter died away as the legionaries braced themselves for the second assault. This time the enemy came on in a more determined manner. There was no wild charge, but a steady approach in tight columns. When the Britons were halfway up the slope, the war horns began to sound, and slowly the enemy found their voice, shouts and war cries swelling up in their throats as they closed in on the Romans. As they reached the point where their first attack had been broken the last few javelins were hurled down from above, but this time they were simply swallowed up in the mass of the enemy and made no perceptible impact on the Britons. When they had advanced a short distance inside javelin range, the war horns gave a shrill blaring chorus to signal the charge and a roar of rage and excitement blasted the ears of the Romans as the warriors hurtled up the slope.

All around Cato there was the thud and crack of weapons striking the broad surfaces of Roman shields, and the sharper clang and clatter of blade on blade. The tight formation of the cohorts, and the advantage of being uphill of their attackers allowed the Romans to hold their ground. Where both sides were most tightly packed together there was little chance to fight, and Briton and Roman alike rammed their boots into the churned earth and heaved their weight behind their shields. In other places there was enough freedom of movement for intense duels to take place between individual legionaries and warriors; feinting and thrusting as each sought for the chance to deliver a lethal blow.

For half an hour the two sides struggled against each other, the Britons aiming for a breakthrough that would shatter the Roman line and turn the fight into an open mêlée where numbers counted for more than battle-drill and discipline. At length, under such relentless pressure, the Roman line began to buckle and bulge, and the ring of defenders turned into an ellipse, and then gradually into the shapelessness of a casually discarded belt lying on the floor.

When the enemy breakthrough came it was sudden and shocking.

'Centurion!' Mandrax called out, and Cato spun round towards the standard-bearer. Mandrax was jabbing his sword towards a section of the line behind the wagons. As Cato watched, the rearmost men were pushed bodily aside and the Britons burst through the Roman line. These were heavily armed warriors, bearing shields and helmets and many wore chain mail. As they found themselves opposite the wagons they gave a savage roar of triumph and surged forwards.

'Wolves!' Cato cried, snatching up his shield. He drew his sword and ran over to Mandrax, standing in front of the king's wagon with Cadminius at his side. 'On me!'

His men just had time to brace themselves for the impact before the enemy slammed into them. Cato was knocked back against the side of the wagon, the breath driven from him in an explosive gasp. A muscular warrior with a gallic helmet snarled at the centurion, spraying Cato's face with spittle. His arm rose high above and he slashed down at Cato's head. Cato cringed, waiting for his skull to be shattered, but there was only a deep thud as the end of the blade bit deep into the side of the wagon above him. The warrior looked at his sword and then glanced down at Cato, and both broke out in hysterical laughter. Cato recovered first, and kicked his boot into the man's groin. The mad laughter abruptly turned into a groan, and the warrior doubled up and vomited on to the grass. Cato punched the pommel of his sword on to the back of the man's neck and he went out like a lamp. On either side the Wolves were locked in a desperate struggle with the enemy, and a quick glance towards the legate revealed that Vespasian had seen the danger and was anxiously rounding up a small party of officers and men pulled from the rear of one of the cohorts to plug the gap. Cato knew he and his men must hold the enemy back for a few moments yet, if the battle was not to be lost.

Stepping over the body of the man he had knocked out Cato saw an exposed armpit and instinctively drove the tip of his short sword into the man's chest, yanked it back and looked for the next target. Mandrax had lost his sword and was using the Wolf standard like a cross-staff, thrusting with the ends and knocking men down with vicious swipes from the side. Cato kept his distance and turned just in time to see a man rushing at him with a levelled spear. The Centurion threw his shield up and the blade struck the curved surface of the boss and glanced off to the side. Without any warning the warrior let go of the spear and grabbed the rim of Cato's shield, wrenching it from the Roman's grip. Before Cato could react the man's hands were at his throat and the impetus of the warrior's attack drove Cato on to the ground. He felt rough hands tightening their grip, thumbs pressing hard on his windpipe. Cato's right arm was pinned down under his back, the left was too weak to shift the man on its own, and Cato could only flail at his back, grabbing the man's hair and trying to yank his head back.

Suddenly the man lunged forward, teeth bared, as though he were trying to bite Cato on the nose. The centurion yanked his head to one side and caught the man with the edge of his cheek guard. For an instant the grip on his throat relaxed and Cato smashed his helmet up, crushing his enemy's nose with the solid metal brim. The warrior howled, and instinctively reached for his face. As soon as he was free of the stranglehold Cato grabbed the handle of his dagger and ripped the short broad blade from his scabbard. Raising it behind the man's back he thrust the tip into the base of the Briton's skull.

The man stiffened, muscles suddenly rigid, then he started trembling. Cato let go of the dagger handle and heaved the body to one side as he scrambled back to his feet.

He snatched up his sword and saw that several of the enemy were surrounding the end of Verica's wagon. The royal body-guard had died defending their king and now only Cadminius remained on his feet, his kite shield held out in front of him as he dared his foes to attack, sword held to the side ready to swing at the first man foolhardy enough to challenge him. Even as Cato watched, an enemy warrior howled and threw himself forward. But the captain of the king's bodyguard had won his position because he could best any other fighter in the Atrebatan nation, and the sword blade flickered round to meet the attack faster than Cato would have believed possible. The point went right through the stomach of the enemy warrior and burst out of his back. At once Cadminius jerked the blade free and with a snarl of contempt shouted a challenge to the rest of the men ringed about him.

But the odds facing him were just too great, and as one man feinted, Cadminius turned to meet the threat before he realised it was a trick. The blade of a spear thudded into his shoulder, causing him to drop his shield as his fingers spasmed. Then they rushed him. With a howl of rage Cadminius slashed his sword through the air and the blade struck off a man's head, the blow sending it leaping into the air. Then Cadminius was thrown back against Verica's wagon, swords and spears plunged deep into his chest and stomach. He made one last wild effort to wrench himself free, but he was pinned to the timbers behind and screamed in frustration, blood and spittle spraying from his lips.

He half turned his head and cried out, 'My lord! Flee!' Then slid to the ground, his head lolling on to his broad chest.

All this Cato saw in the briefest of moments, as the centurion grabbed his shield and raced the short distance to the rear of Verica's wagon. A tangle of white hair rose up from the wagon, and Verica peered down at his attackers with alarm. Then he recovered his poise and his expression fixed in contempt for his enemies. The first of the warriors reached a hand up and began to pull himself towards the Atrebatan king.

'Wolves!' Cato screamed out as he charged home. 'On me! On me!'

The four remaining enemies turned towards Cato, but it was already too late for the first to react. The centurion's blade caught him high in the back and ripped through muscle and ribs to pierce his heart. Cato slammed his shield into the face of the next man as he tried to wrench the blade free, but it was jammed, and as the body slumped down the sword handle was ripped from Cato's grasp. He stepped astride Cadminius' body with his back to the wagon, unarmed, with only his shield to save him now.

'Wolves!' he called again. 'For fuck's sake! On me!'

The last two warriors took a moment to realise that the centurion was not armed and with triumph gleaming in their eyes they closed in on Cato. One grasped the edge of the shield and wrenched it aside, as his companion drew back his spear and thrust it at the Roman. There was nowhere to go and Cato watched in horror as the spear tip came towards him, time slowing as he stared wide-eyed at his death. Suddenly he was knocked to the side as a figure flew over his shoulder and the spearman tumbled back on to the ground.

Mandrax and the surviving members of the Atrebatan cohort came running up, and the last of the attackers was impaled on the end of the wolf standard. As the men formed a small screen around the wagon Cato crawled over towards Verica. The king was lying on top of the spearman he had felled, his bony hand clasped round the handle of an ornate dagger whose blade was buried in the eye socket of his enemy.

'My lord!' Cato gently lifted the king off the dead man. Verica's eyes flickered open and he seemed to struggle to focus as his gaze fixed on Cato.

Verica smiled feebly. 'You're all right?'

'Yes, my lord . . . You saved my life.'

Verica's lips parted in a pained smile. 'Yes, I did, didn't I? . . . Where's Cadminius?'

Cato looked round and saw that the captain of the bodyguard was struggling to sit up. The big man coughed, splattering blood down his chest.

'Mandrax!' Cato called out. 'Look after the king.'

Once the standard bearer had the king cradled against his chest, Cato squatted down beside Cadminius, reaching around the man's shoulders to keep him propped up. He was breathing in shallow gasps that rattled in his throat as he looked up at Cato.

'The king?'

'He's safe,' said Cato.

Cadminius smiled faintly, satisfied that he had done his duty. 'I'm finished . . .'

For an instant Cato thought of saying something reassuring, some lie to comfort the dying man, but then he simply nodded. 'Yes.'

'Cadminius!' Verica stretched a hand towards the best of his warriors, then snapped at Mandrax. 'Help me over to him!'

Cadminius' life was draining away fast and his mouth gaped as he struggled to draw breath. 'My lord!'

In the last moment, the warrior's fingers groped for Cato's hand, found it and clamped tight, as a sudden final reservoir of strength was spent. Then the pained expression round his eyes eased and his fingers lay limply across Cato's palm. Cato watched him a moment, to be sure there was nothing more to be done, no last vestige of life to be eased into oblivion, then he rose to his feet and looked round.

The survivors of the Wolf Cohort stood about the body, silent and strained. Then Verica slowly dropped to his knees beside Cadminius. He reached out a hand to Cadminius' face and tenderly brushed away a strand of hair. Cato quietly backed away; this was a moment for the Atrebatans. Whatever the bond that existed between him and these men, there was a deeper one of race and blood that the centurion would never share.

Leaving them to mourn Cato turned back to the battle, but the enemy was gone. Vespasian's hurriedly gathered reserve had driven them back and closed the gap. Beyond the front rank of the Romans the enemy were flowing away, like a wave rushing back from the shore, leaving a flotsam of bodies and discarded weapons on the crimson-stained grass. Cato stared at them in surprise. Why withdraw now, when they must know that one last effort must surely carry the day?

'Cato! Cato!'

He turned and saw Macro trotting up to him, his craggy face split in a smile of delight. His friend slapped him on the shoulder and when Cato stared at him blankly Macro quickly glanced over him.

'You wounded, lad?'

'No.'

'Verica?'

Cato pointed to where the Atrebatans were gathered round the end of Verica's wagon. 'He's still alive. Cadminius is dead. Him, and the rest of the royal guards.'

Macro rubbed his chin. 'That's too bad . . . too bad. But look there.'

He took hold of Cato's arm and pulled the youngster round, towards Calleva. The approaching column was clearly visible now and the eagle standard rising up above the foremost ranks was unmistakable.

'You see?' Macro was smiling again. 'See there? It's the bloody general himself!'

Chapter Forty-One

Work on the new procurator's quarters in the fortified depot began almost at once. Engineers from all four legions laboured to clear the ruins of the hospital and headquarters block as quickly as possible and then the foundations were dug into the fire-blackened soil. Beside the extensive foundations of the administration buildings several pairs of long barrack blocks had already been constructed to house the permanent garrison of two large cohorts of Batavian auxiliaries. The Batavians were an arrogant lot; blond giants from the borders of Germania who looked down on the people of Calleva as they swaggered through the town's narrow streets and made crude advances to the native women. They drank heavily as well, and were constantly spoiling for a fight.

The worse they behaved, the more guilty Cato came to feel about the fate of the Atrebatans. This was poor reward for all those who had given so much to fight alongside Rome, but were no longer permitted to bear arms. For the Atrebatans would be warriors no more. Plautius had been horrified when he had discovered how close the tribe had been drawn towards an alliance with Caratacus and had acted swiftly to ensure that the Atrebatans never again posed a threat to his supply lines. Verica remained a king in name only; all the real power over the lives of his people now rested in the hands of the Roman procurator and his officials. Since his return Verica had hardly moved from his bed, still recovering from the injury to his head. Outside, in the great hall, his advisors were bitterly arguing about who to choose as the king's heir, for the third time in less than a month.

Caratacus had retreated back over the Tamesis and once more the legions and the auxiliary cohorts were containing the enemy, pushing him back towards the rugged uplands of the Silurians. Even so, the security of the Roman supply lines could not be trusted to any native ruler, however much they might profess their loyalty to Rome. So the kingdom of the Atrebatans was annexed as soon as Vespasian and his legion set up camp outside Calleva.

Centurion Cato was ordered to report to army headquarters a few days after their return to the town. It was a hot, humid day and, wearing only his tunic, Cato made his way from the Second Legion's encampment through Calleva to the depot. Passing through the gates he was surprised to see that the timber framework for the procurator's house and headquarters was complete and sprawled over much of the parade ground, as well as the land on which the original depot buildings had once stood. Clearly Tribune Quintillus . . .

Cato smiled. Quintillus' army days were over. Now he was an imperial procurator, one of the Emperor's élite on the first rung of a career that would see him rise to the highest offices of state. Quintillus would even have his own small army to command in the two Batavian cohorts garrisoned in Calleva.

To one side of the parade ground stood an array of tents where the legate had erected a temporary headquarters for himself and the new procurator. The area was heavily guarded by Vespasian's praetorian unit and, despite his rank, Cato was told to wait beyond the roped-off area surrounding the tents. While five guards stood by, watching him closely, the sixth trotted off for instructions regarding the centurion. Although there looked to be at least a hundred men under arms within the area allotted to senior officers and their staff, the Second Legion itself was camped outside Calleva, in a huge fortification that was almost as big as the adjacent capital of the Atrebatans. It provided a salutary reminder to those who still harboured any rebellious impulse of the monolithic nature of the force they would have to overcome.

A clerk approached from the long, low tent that fronted the headquarters area. He caught the attention of one of the guards. 'Let the centurion pass.'

The praetorians moved aside to let Cato by, but he stiffened his back and glared at them.

'It's customary to salute a superior officer,' Cato said in a quiet, icy voice, 'even for members of the legate's personal guard.'

The veteran optio commanding the praetorians couldn't help showing his surprise. Not so much that the officer standing in front of him was nearly young enough to be his son, but because he was carrying no badges of rank and only a stickler for military etiquette would have insisted on a salute whilst wearing only a tunic. But Cato refused to move. He was in a sour mood over the high-handed treatment of his men since they had returned to Calleva.

The Wolves had been denied access to the army camp. Instead they were given some of the least damaged tents from the depot and told to pitch them in the royal enclosure. Cato had spent the first night with them, but when Vespasian heard of this he immediately ordered the centurion to return to his legion and remain in the camp until he received further orders. He and Macro were told that the legate would reassign them as soon as circumstances permitted. With no duties to do Macro took every chance to sleep, while Cato had wandered through the ranks of goatskin tents for hours on end, trying to make himself tired so that he could get some rest. But even when the summer sunlight finally failed and he curled up on his bedding, Cato's mind turned the recent events over and over, and his concerns about his men denied him the rest his exhausted body needed.

So now, as he faced the praetorian optio, he would be more than happy to give the man a good bollocking; and the optio knew it. With a look of disdain the optio raised his arm in salute and slowly stepped aside. Cato nodded back as he strode past. He followed the clerk through the large opening of the nearest tent. Inside the air was hot and sticky and the legate's clerks were stripped down to their loincloths as they worked over the orders and records needed for the establishment of the new province.

'This way, please sir.' The clerk held a flap back at the rear of the tent. On the far side was a bare compound on to which six large tents opened. Inside tribunes and their staff worked on long trestle tables. Orderlies sat on the worn grass, ready to carry messages, passing the time with a game of bone dice. The clerk led Cato across the open space, which seemed to be almost as hot as the inside of the tents, due to the complete lack of the slightest breeze. Sweat trickled down the back of Cato's tunic as he followed the clerk towards the largest of the tents on the opposite side of the square. The flaps were tied back and Cato could see wooden flooring with a circle of iron-framed stools. Beyond that was a large table at which two men were sitting, sharing a flask of wine. The clerk ducked under the flap and, with a discreet wave of the hand, indicated that Cato should follow him.

'Centurion Cato, sir.'

Vespasian, and Quintillus, wearing a freshly minted gold chain and pendant, looked round. The legate beckoned. 'Please join us, Centurion . . . That'll be all, Parvenus.'

'Yes, sir.' The clerk bowed his head and backed out of the tent, as Cato marched forward to the table and stood to attention. Vespasian smiled at Cato, and the latter got the distinct impression that his commander would have something unpleasant to say.

'Centurion, I've got some good news. I've found a command for you. Sixth Century of the Third Cohort. Centurion Macro will be appointed to the same unit. You work well together so you might as well continue to serve in the same cohort. The general and I have a lot to thank you for. If the enemy had taken Calleva, and disposed of Verica I have no doubt that we'd have been in full retreat by now. You and Macro have performed in accordance with the highest traditions of the legions and I've recommended that you both be decorated. It's the least that can be done by way of reward.'

'We were only doing our duty, sir,' Cato replied in a flat tone.

'Quite. And you excelled in that, as you always have before. It was well done, Centurion, and I offer you my personal gratitude.' The legate smiled warmly. 'I look forward to seeing you handle your own legionary command, and I dare say Centurion Macro will be keen to get back into the campaign. Both appointments are effective immediately. The cohort suffered rather badly in that last action – lost some good men.'

That was putting it mildly, Cato reflected. To lose two or more centurions in a single, swift skirmish was proof of how desperate the fight had been. At once his heart thrilled to the prospect of being given his own century. Better still, he would serve in the same cohort as Macro. Then it occurred to Cato that this was the kind of information that Vespasian would have preferred to give to both men in person. So why was he here alone?

'Well, Centurion?' Quintillus raised his eyebrows. 'Are you not grateful?'

'He does not need to be grateful,' Vespasian interrupted quietly. 'He's earned it. They both have. Many times over. So please, Quintillus, keep your peace and let me deal with this.'

Here it comes, thought Cato, as Vespasian looked at him with a sympathetic expression.

'I'd be delighted to have someone of your potential serving as one of my line officers. That does mean, of course, that you will have to relinquish command of your native unit. You understand?'

'Yes, sir.'

'In addition,' said Quintillus, 'the legate and I have decided that, in view of recent events, the Atrebatans must be disarmed.'

'Disarmed, sir? My men?'

'All of them,' Quintillus confirmed. 'Especially your men. Can't have a gang of disgruntled locals armed with swords wandering around, can we?'

'No, sir,' Cato said coldly. To call the Wolves a gang was almost as much as he could take. 'I suppose not. Not after all they've done to save our necks.'

Quintillus laughed. 'Careful, Centurion. You mustn't allow yourself to get too close to these barbarians. And I'd appreciate it if you would show my office the deference it demands in future.'

'Your office. Yes, sir.' Cato turned to his legate. 'Sir, if I may?'

Vespasian nodded.

'Why not retain the Wolves as an auxiliary unit? They've proved themselves in battle. I know there aren't many left, but they could act as a training cadre for others.'

'No,' Vespasian said firmly. 'I'm sorry, Centurion. But those are the general's orders. We can't afford to have any doubts about the loyalty of the men serving alongside the legions. The stakes are too high. It's over. They're to be disbanded and disarmed at once.'

The emphasis on the last two words struck Cato forcibly. 'What do you mean, sir?'

'They're outside, behind the tents. I had them sent for before you were summoned. I want you to give them the news.'

'Why, sir?' asked Cato, the sick taste of betrayal in his throat. 'Why me?'

'You speak their language. You're their commander. It would be best coming from you.'

Cato shook his head. 'I can't do it, sir . . .'

Quintillus quickly leaned forward, glaring at the young centurion. 'You will do it! That's an order, and this is the last time I will brook any insubordination from you!'

Vespasian laid his hand on the procurator's shoulder. 'There's no need to concern yourself with this, Quintillus. The centurion will obey my orders. He knows what will happen if his men are told to disarm by someone else. We don't want them to cause us any trouble. Trouble they might regret.'

So that was it then, Cato realised. The Wolves were finished, and if they protested too much they would face summary punishment of one kind or another. And he would do the dirty work for the new governor. Worse still, there was no choice in the matter. For the sake of his men, Cato must be the one to tell them how little value Rome placed on the blood the Atrebatans had shed on behalf of the empire.

'Very well, sir. I'll do it.'

'I'm most grateful, to be sure,' said Quintillus.

'Thank you, Centurion.' Vespasian nodded. 'I knew you'd understand. Best get on with it straight away then.'

Cato turned and saluted his legate, and before the procurator could react to the slight, he marched out of the tent and back into the brilliant sunshine. The heat closed round him like a blanket, but the prickly discomfort of his tunic no longer bothered Cato as he made his way out of the administration tent and walked slowly round the side of the headquarters area. He felt sick. Sick from the cold-hearted betrayal of his men. Sick at the fact that the Wolves would regard him with hatred and contempt. The bond of comradeship they had once shared would twist in their guts like a knife, and it would be his hand behind the blade. All thought and pleasure he might have had of his new command was banished from his mind as Cato turned the corner of the tent complex and walked stiffly towards the double line of the surviving men of the Wolf Cohort. To one side of the Atrebatan warriors a few sections of legionaries were being drilled in full armour. Just in case, Cato smiled bitterly to himself.

As soon as he caught sight of the centurion, Mandrax called the men to attention. They stopped chatting and straightened up, spear and shield neatly grounded by every man. Shoulders back, chests out and chins up, as Macro had showed them on their first day of training. Their bronze helmets gleamed in the sunlight as Cato walked up and stood in front of them.

'At ease!' he called out in Celtic, and his men relaxed. For a moment he stared over their heads into the distance, fighting off the urge to glance down and admit to his shame. Someone coughed and Cato decided this was a deed best done quickly.

'Comrades,' he began awkwardly – since he had never used the term before, even though that's what they had become in the desperate days of their last fight – 'I have been transferred to another unit.'

A few of the men frowned, but most continued to stare ahead without any expression on their faces.

'The procurator has asked me to thank you for your fine performance in recent months. Few men have fought more bravely against such great odds. Now, it is time for you to return to your families. Time for you to enjoy the peace you so richly deserve. Time to lay down the burden of your arms and . . .' Cato couldn't continue any further with the charade. He swallowed and looked down, angrily blinking back the first dangerous tears. He knew that once he released his true emotions there would be no stopping the outpour. And that he would rather die than weep before his men, whatever the injustice, hurt and shame of the situation. He swallowed again, clenched his jaw and looked up.

'The Wolves have been ordered to disband. You're to leave all your arms and equipment here and quit the depot . . . I'm sorry.'

The men looked at him in silence for a moment, confused and unbelieving. Mandrax spoke first. 'Sir, there must be some mistake. Surely there's—'

'There's no mistake,' Cato replied harshly, not trusting himself to offer any sympathy, or even an explanation. 'Lay down your arms and equipment now. That's an order.'

'Sir—'

'Obey my order!' Cato shouted, as he noticed the legionaries were no longer drilling, but were being formed up a short distance from the Wolves. 'Disarm! Now!'

Mandrax opened his mouth to protest, then clamped it shut and shook his head. Cato stepped up to him and spoke in a whisper.

'Mandrax, there's no choice. We must do it before they make us.' Cato indicated the legionaries. 'You must lead the way.'

'Must I?' Mandrax replied softly.

'Yes!' Cato hissed. 'I will not have your blood on my hands. Nor theirs. For pity's sake, do it, man!'

'No.'

'If you don't, none of them will.'

Mandrax looked at Cato with great hurt in his eyes, then he glanced at the legionaries watching them closely. He

428

thought for a moment and then nodded. Cato breathed deeply. Then Mandrax drew his sword and thrust it into the earth at Cato's feet. There was a short pause before the next man moved, laying down his spear and shield before unfastening his helmet. Then the rest followed suit, until they stood before Cato in their tunics and the ground was littered with their equipment. Cato stiffened his back and called out one last order to his men.

'Cohort . . . dismissed!'

The men turned towards the gateway that led back into Calleva. A few of them glanced back once or twice at Cato, then turned away, and walked silently along with their comrades. Mandrax remained, still holding the Wolf standard. He stared at Cato, still as a statue, neither man knowing what to say. What could they say now? There was a bond between men who had fought side by side, and yet there was no bond between them now, and could be no bond in the future. Then Cato slowly raised his arm and extended his hand towards Mandrax. The standard bearer looked down and then nodded slowly. He reached forward and grasped Cato's forearm.

'It was a good time, Roman. It was a fine thing to be a warrior one last time.'

'It was a fine thing.' Cato nodded faintly. 'I'll not forget the Wolf Cohort.'

'No. Don't.' Mandrax relaxed his grip and his arm fell back to his side. Then he looked up at the gilded wolf's head at the top of the standard. 'Can I keep this?'

The request took Cato by surprise. 'Yes. Of course.'

Mandrax smiled. 'Farewell then, Centurion.'

'Farewell, Mandrax.'

The standard bearer turned away, lowered the shaft over his shoulder and walked slowly towards the distant gateway.

Cato watched him go, feeling hollow and ashamed, and

despicable. As Mandrax passed through the gate and out of sight Cato was aware of the sound of footsteps closing on him from behind.

'Cato! Cato, lad . . .' Macro panted, and drew up beside his friend. 'I've just heard the news . . . Legate just told me . . . Said you were round here . . . We're going to be back in the thick of it! Just think. With us serving in the same cohort those Britons won't know what's hitting them!'

'No . . .' Cato said quietly. 'They won't.'

'Come on, lad!' Macro punched him on the shoulder. 'It's great news! Two months ago that quack in the hospital was saying you might never serve with the Eagles again. Now look at you!'

Cato finally turned round to face Macro, and forced himself to smile. 'Yes. It's good news.'

'Better still,' Macro's eyes were wide and shining with excitement as he leaned closer, 'I was talking to a clerk at headquarters, and it looks like we're on the move again. In the next few days.'

'On the move?'

'Yes. The legate has to link up with the other legions and finish off that bastard Caratacus. Then it'll be over. All but a nice session of dividing up the booty. So cheer up, lad! We're centurions in the finest legion of the finest army in the bloody world, and you can't ask for better than that!' Macro tugged his arm. 'Come on, let's go and find some drink and celebrate.'

'No, let's not drink,' said Cato, and Macro frowned. Then Cato smiled slowly before he continued. 'Let's get drunk. Really, really drunk . . .'

Historical Note

It is, perhaps, ironic that the difficulties facing General Plautius in the second summer of campaigning were forced on him by his success of the previous year. The Britons, and their commander, Caratacus, had taken a beating in a series of bloody set-piece battles that had ended in the fall of Camulodunum – the capital of the most powerful tribe on the island – and the capitulation of a number of tribes. With dwindling resources of men to make good his losses it is likely that Caratacus adopted a different approach in AD 44. The Romans had shown what they could do on the battlefield and Caratacus would have been most reluctant to risk his forces against the massed might of the legions again.

Retreat was the most prudent strategy for the Britons' commander, and not just because it kept a native army in being. General Plautius and the legions would be drawn after him, intent on destroying the core of native resistance in a final decisive battle. The further they advanced, the more extended their communications became, and the more forces they had to leave in their wake to guard their supply lines. Nor could the legions disperse in order to push forward on a broad front; there were too few of them and they would have been picked off piecemeal. Which makes it all the more surprising to see Vespasian sent off with a small battle group to campaign in the south-west.

Such a division of Roman forces in the face of an enemy that still outnumbered them looks like a very rash command decision. Of course, General Plautius may have had good reason to believe that the risk was slight, but we shall never know. With hindsight historians always comment on the string of successes Vespasian enjoyed, but one wonders what would have happened if the Britons had been able to concentrate sufficient forces against the Second Legion. If Caratacus had managed to give the Second a nasty surprise, and defeat them, then the way would have been open for him to sweep across the rear of the rest of General Plautius' army, destroying his lines of supply. That would have spelled disaster for the legions and may well have led to another defeat on the scale of the Varian débâcle in the German forests, where three legions had been massacred.

Such a hypothesis once again reminds us of the delicate balance of all military campaigns – a facet of history that is almost always lost in the neat narratives that subsequent historians weave around events. But for the men on the ground – the likes of Macro and Cato – the reality is always confusion, doubt and a bloody struggle for survival. A world far distant from the tidy maps and plans of generals and policy makers.

Caratacus is still at large. Defiant and increasingly desperate, he is looking for one last chance to reverse the misfortunes of the Britons. In the coming months Centurions Macro and Cato, and their comrades in the four legions of the Roman army, cannot afford to make one mistake as they seek to end the deadly duel with their increasingly desperate and fanatic enemy.

Don't miss Simon Scarrow's latest novel in the Eagles of the Empire series . . .

DAY OF THE CAESARS

Eagles of the Empire XVI

Rome, AD55. The Emperor Claudius is dead. Nero rules. His half-brother Britannicus has also laid claim to the throne.

A bloody power struggle is underway and the future of the Empire is in Cato and Macro's hands . . .

Available now to buy and download in eBook.

www.headline.co.uk

www.simonscarrow.co.uk

SIMON SCARROW

THE EAGLES OF THE EMPIRE SERIES

Under the Eagle	£8.99
The Eagle's Conquest	£8.99
When the Eagle Hunts	£8.99
The Eagle and the Wolves	£8.99
The Eagle's Prey	£8.99
The Eagle's Prophecy	£8.99
The Eagle in the Sand	£8.99
Centurion	£8.99
The Gladiator	£8.99
The Legion	£8.99
Praetorian	£8.99
The Blood Crows	£8.99
Brothers in Blood	£8.99
Britannia	£8.99
Invictus	£7.99
Day of the Caesars	£20.00

THE WELLINGTON AND NAPOLEON QUARTET

Young Bloods	£8.99
The Generals	£8.99
Fire and Sword	£8.99
The Fields of Death	£8.99
Sword & Scimitar	£8.99
Hearts of Stone	£7.99

WRITING WITH T. J. ANDREWS

Arena	£8.99
Invader	£7.99

Simply call 01235 827 702 or visit our
website **www.headline.co.uk** to order

Prices and availability subject to change without notice.